W9-BSH-759

SILVER SEDUCTION

"You're shivering, Silver," he said gently. "Let me warm you." He lay down on the bed, still fully dressed, pulled her against his chest, and held her close.

"If you . . . if you want me, I'll let you."

He sighed, and she felt the tension in his big frame. "If that's the way it'll be, thanks but no thanks."

"You're saying no?" She was shocked.

"I'm saying I expect a little passion from a woman."

She flushed with embarrassment. "I don't know about that." Almost shyly, she reached to kiss his lips. "Teach me," she whispered . . .

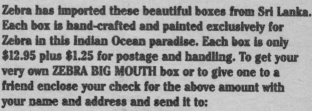

GET YOUR VERY OWN
ZEBRA
BIG MOUTH BOX
...PERFECT FOR THE LITTLE THINGS YOU LOVE!

The Zebra Big Mouth Box is the perfect little place you need to keep all the things that always seem to disappear. Loose buttons, needle and thread, pins and snaps, jewelry, odds and ends...all need a place for you to get them when you want them.

Just put them in the Big Mouth!

Zebra has imported these beautiful boxes from Sri Lanka. Each box is hand-crafted and painted exclusively for Zebra in this Indian Ocean paradise. Each box is only $12.95 plus $1.25 for postage and handling. To get your very own ZEBRA BIG MOUTH box or to give one to a friend enclose your check for the above amount with your name and address and send it to:

ZEBRA BIG MOUTH BOX
Dept. 101
475 Park Avenue South
New York, New York 10016

New York residents add applicable sales tax.
Allow 4-6 weeks for delivery!

QUICKSILVER PASSION

GEORGINA GENTRY

ZEBRA BOOKS
KENSINGTON PUBLISHING CORP.

ZEBRA BOOKS

are published by

Kensington Publishing Corp.
475 Park Avenue South
New York, NY 10016

First printing: September, 1990

Printed in the United States of America

Dedicated with warm thanks
to my friend and former teacher,

Dwight V. Swain

whose book, The Technique of the Selling Writer,
helped me get where I am today;

and

to the people of the great state of Colorado,
who care enough to help keep the legend alive . . .

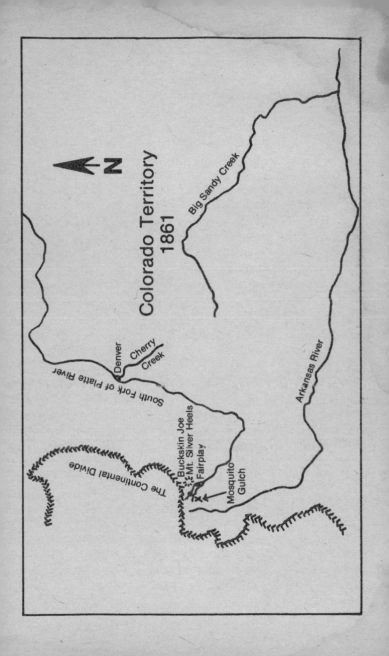

Prologue

In the state of Colorado today, there is a beautiful, snow-capped mountain with an unusual name. It is probably the only mountain in the world named for a saloon girl.

How this came about is the most beloved and enduring legend of the Rockies. The girl, if she ever lived, is gone these hundred years. But the tale endures, like the mountain itself, because of those who are idealistic enough to believe that true love sees with the heart and is meant to last forever. . . .

Chapter One

The boom town of Buckskin Joe,
Colorado Territory,
March 1861

There were only two kinds of women in the West: the kind men married and the other kind. Not that it mattered because Silver hated men . . . and she had good reason.

Just like that big bruiser standing in the street below, gawking up at her in the growing twilight. Men. She leaned against the windowsill, toying with her expensive jewelry, and listened to the laughter and music drifting up the stairs. *Now that she owned this big saloon, she was safe and would never again be at any man's mercy.*

She watched the wide-shouldered hombre while readjusting the scarlet plume in her pale blond hair. Dark and too rugged to be handsome; a 'breed, maybe, because he wore his hair cut like a white man. There he stood with his pack burro in the hustle and bustle of the muddy street. Another poor fool looking to get rich in the Rockies.

11

Come in and spend that gold dust at my bar, fella, she thought with cold contempt, *but you can't buy me. I recognize that hunger in your eyes. No man will ever hurt me or put his hands on me again.*

It was almost time for her act and it pleased her to do it. Silver went to her dressing table to dab on a light scent of wild flowers, then turned toward a mirror to admire the tight, revealing scarlet dress and all the glittering gold and gems she wore.

Her ornate room sparkled with mirrors. The walls were covered with them. She checked the heavy eye makeup around her pale aqua eyes and her lip rouge again. *A flawless face,* Ma had said. *Your face will make your fortune, but your beauty won't last forever.*

The thought troubled her and she looked twice to make sure there were no wrinkles, no lines. But then she was not yet twenty and already rich. She still had her beauty and owned the biggest saloon in town. What else could a woman want?

Cherokee paused with a weary sigh in the middle of the muddy street, unsure where to find the livery stable to leave his burro. After the trip from Mosquito Gulch, he felt much older than his thirty years tonight. Cherokee felt someone watching him and looked up. The most beautiful girl he had ever seen stood looking down at him. The light behind her silhouetted the ripe body and the hair pale as newly minted silver dollars.

By damn! He wanted her. Without thinking, he ran his tongue over his lower lip, watching her full breasts swell in the top of the low-cut red dress when she breathed. Yep, he wanted her. But the pleasure of a woman would have to wait until he saw to the comfort of his animal, even though Cherokee ached with weariness himself.

12

After months up on the claim, snowed in with his two partners, Cherokee needed a woman bad. Tomorrow he'd get the burro shod, buy his supplies, and get back to work. But tonight he'd buy that girl . . . if she'd take a 'breed. If she turned him down, he'd offer a little extra. All white women were whores, even the ones who pretended to be high-class ladies. The memory made him wince.

He looked down the street, saw the livery stable sign, and glanced back up. The girl had disappeared from the window. Had he only imagined her? What was a beauty like that doing out here in the wilderness anyhow?

Many saloons and bordellos lined the bustling streets of this boom town. He made a mental note of this place so he could find it again; Silver's Nugget Saloon. With his mind still on the mysterious pale blonde, Cherokee Evans hurried toward the livery stable.

Fifteen minutes later, he pushed through the swinging doors, elbowing his way through the noisy crowd of men. The place swirled with music and laughter. Cherokee took a deep breath of smoke and cheap perfume, then made his way to the ornate bar. "Coffee. With cream, if you've got any."

The short bartender had a face like five miles of bad road and gorilla-like shoulders and arms, unusual for a man with gray in his hair. He paused in wiping a glass and stared back at Cherokee. "I must not have heard you right, sport. This ain't no café. And cream? You must have been eatin' loco weed."

He owed the man no explanation of why he no longer drank. "Coffee," Cherokee drawled in a louder voice. "I know you got some; I smell it."

The men on each side of him turned and looked him up and down. The bartender hesitated. "I keep a pot on all the time for the boss, who don't drink neither."

"Then I'll have some out of the owner's pot."

The bartender looked as if he might argue, then shrugged and got out a dainty china cup and saucer, set it before Cherokee, and poured the coffee. "There you go, sport. No cream, though. Never let it be said that Silver wouldn't give a customer what he wanted."

"Does that include women?" Cherokee sipped the drink, ignoring the curious looks and nudgings up and down the bar as other men noticed. He must not let himself get pulled into a fight. That wasn't his top priority tonight.

"Sure, we got women," the bartender nodded, "even though the boss would just as soon not deal in that. Pick you out one from what's available."

"I already know which one I want," Cherokee drawled, but the bartender had moved on down the line to serve the rowdy crowd.

Cherokee reached for his tobacco, ignoring the grinning, whiskered man next to him. "Looky here, boys, coffee in a bar! Next thing you know, Al'll be servin' lemonade and sugar cookies!"

The men up and down the bar laughed and nudged each other.

He must not lose his temper. A brawl would interfere with his primary purpose—bedding that blonde. Besides, his Cherokee grandmother had taught him restraint. With the saloon full of white men who might relish any excuse to gang up on him, he'd be a fool to start a fight. He should have listened to Grandmother's warning about

14

whiskey before it caused him to betray a friend.

"Might not be a bad idea." Cherokee finished rolling a cigarette and grinned. "Most of us like sugar cookies."

The burly man looked disappointed. "You'd let a man say something like that without sluggin' him?"

He must not be baited into a fight. The fact that he could kill the man who taunted him would prove nothing. Cherokee took a deep breath to restrain himself and stuck the cigarette between his lips. "No offense meant, none taken."

One of the others, obviously made bold by Cherokee's lack of temper, sneered at him. "In a saloon, grown men drink whiskey, cracker!"

Georgia cracker. By damn! How many times had he been called that? He could never get the drawl out of his deep voice, no matter how hard he tried. Well, it was better than "Injun," or "'breed."

Cherokee forced himself to grin back. "Don't I look big enough to be a grown man?"

The others looked him up and down, seeming to be suddenly aware of his size, and drew back.

"First time I been in here," Cherokee drawled, hoping to distract his tormentors. "I've been snowed in all winter and was out in Nevada before that."

"The Nugget's the best there is, stranger," a rumpled, mustached man at his elbow said, "purtiest girls and honest card tables. Silver won't allow it no other way. I'm Doc Johnson, the town sawbones." He held out his hand, genuine friendliness in his old face.

They shook hands. Here was a *yu-ne-ga,* a white man who seemed open and friendly. Cherokee said, "Honest card games?"

There was a murmur of assent up and down the bar.

15

Whoever this Silver fella was, the miners in the area really thought a lot of him, Cherokee realized.

Cherokee blew smoke and looked around. "I been a long time up on the claim. I want a pretty girl tonight, but I don't see one I fancy."

He watched the painted, laughing girls moving through the crowd and thought of the blonde in the upstairs window.

"Then you must be blind," his original tormentor said, laughing. "Blind as a bat!"

He ignored the insult. Getting into a brawl would deter him from his purpose of finding and bedding that girl. "The girl I want has hair the color of a silver dollar and the most beautiful face a man could dream of."

The bearded one stared back at him a long moment, mouth open. Then he nudged the other man. "Didja hear him, Doc? Didja hear who he's talkin' about?"

"Oh, hush, Zeke, before you start something you can't finish." Doc pulled at his mustache thoughtfully. "Stranger, you can put that one out of your mind. That one—"

"Is the best in bed you could want," the tormentor interrupted, digging the other in the ribs with his elbow. "Isn't that right, Doc? All he's got to do is ask her when she comes downstairs to sing. Yep, cracker, you just offer that girl money and she'll rush you right up the stairs. Ain't that right, boys?"

Doc frowned but the others grinned. Some of them nodded. "Yeah, that's right."

Somehow, Cherokee had a feeling there was a joke here and he'd been left out of it. But then he'd been raised up in the hills by his grandmother and he'd never understood white people very well. He ought to go to the Indian

16

Territory and get himself a virtuous Cherokee wife. But in his heart, he had a weakness for the white ones with light hair. That made him think of his friend's wife. There was no way to make amends for what he'd done. Guilt haunted him.

Now he smoked his cigarette and sipped his coffee, watching the stairs. Cherokee had a real hunger burning his groin and that blonde had sparked a fire like he had never felt before. He thought of her breasts, imagined burying his face between them. Her nipples would be pale pink, her skin the color of cream beneath his bronze body. He imagined her silky long hair tangled in his callused hands, her small body writhing beneath him. No matter what she charged, he had to have her tonight.

A hush fell across the crowd suddenly, even though the off-key piano over by the small stage still banged away. Cherokee looked up from his erotic thoughts and glanced around at the faces turning now toward the stairs. He had never seen such longing and awe in men's eyes before.

Slowly he, too, turned toward the stairs. The girl he had seen in the upstairs window stood halfway down, looking around at the crowd. She was even more beautiful and desirable than he remembered, the dress hiding yet revealing her curves, expensive jewelry on her body, the light playing on the fine features. What a perfect face!

Cherokee tossed the cigarette into the spittoon and pushed his cup away. He must ask her before some other man got to her first.

But before he could move, she came down the stairs, moving gracefully through the crowd toward the stage while the burly miners applauded and shouted, lifting their glasses in a toast: "Silver! Silver! Silver!"

She acknowledged their homage with a slight nod as she went up the steps and the bald piano player paused, waiting. A hush fell over the crowd and every man seemed to hold his breath as she moved gracefully to the center of the stage.

Silver. U-ne-ga. He translated it automatically into his native language. Good name for a blond dance hall girl. Was she related to the owner? Cherokee realized that he, too, was holding his breath. He felt suddenly very possessive of her, and resented the other men even looking at her, much less paying money to share her bed. He realized that he'd clenched his fists in anger.

The piano began to play softly and she leaned against it, looking around the room with pale, aquamarine eyes. Eyes the color of cold Arctic glaciers, Cherokee thought, hard eyes; eyes that had seen too much of life. But her mouth looked full and soft beneath the heavy lip rouge.

Cherokee watched the light reflect on her pale hair, wanting her more than he had ever wanted a woman before. Even more than he had wanted his white friend's wife . . .

For a long moment, the piano played softly and then Silver began to sing:

"I dream of Jeannie with the light brown hair, borne like a vapor on the summer air . . ."

Cherokee felt the men around him sigh with sadness and nostalgia, perhaps remembering an old love, maybe thinking of a new one. But Cherokee had eyes only for the singer. Her voice came light and high as a brook tinkling down through the mountains:

". . . I see her tripping where the bright breezes play . . ."

Her gaze moved from man to man as she sang, and the hardness seemed to melt from her features, revealing a soft, defenseless vulnerability. Her gaze moved to Cherokee's face.

He sent her a silent message with his eyes. *Sweet darlin', I want you. I intend to possess your body tonight.*

For a split second, her voice faltered as she stared at him, then looked quickly away. She had gotten his message. Why was she so shaken? Didn't she take money for letting men have her every night? The image the thought brought him made him grind his teeth with a fury that surprised him. What did it matter if other men had her tomorrow night as long as he could relieve this ache in his groin tonight?

"... *Many were the blithe notes her merry voice would pour, many were the song birds that warbled them o'er. O, I dream of Jeannie with the light brown hair* ..."

Her voice reminded him of a mountain breeze whispering through the blue spruce and the aspen trees. Yes, she was special, all right; a girl with hard eyes and a soft lips; a whore with a fragile beauty. She finished her song and took a bow. Though her painted mouth smiled as she acknowledged the thunderous applause, her hard eyes looked sad and haunted.

She left the stage and came toward the bar. Men made way for her, backing up as if careful not to touch the beauty.

He would ask her now. Cherokee took a deep breath, hesitating, his stoic shyness making him hold back.

The other men had returned to their cards and roulette, the piano broke into a loud rendition of "Oh! Susanna," and the whores moved once again among the crowds of men.

A girl with dyed blond hair and a gaudy green dress looked up at Cherokee and smiled. "Hello, sugar, buy me a drink?"

"Hell, Nellie," boomed his tormentor, "the cracker don't even drink his own self! He drinks coffee and wants cream in it yet. For what you got in mind, you need a real man!"

The crowd laughed and Cherokee forced himself to smile good-naturedly, loath to tear his gaze away from the flawless beauty coming toward the bar. He must not take offense and get into a fight. Nothing must interfere with him getting that silver-haired girl tonight.

But Silver had paused to talk to some drunken old geezer on her way over. "Hank, you had anything to eat?"

The old drunk shook his head, weaving slightly. "What I need, Miss Silver, is another drink. Now if you'll just extend my credit . . ."

"You've had too much already, Hank." She smiled gently. "I'll have Al get you some food and then you go home."

She came over to the bar, the men clearing a space for her. But Cherokee didn't move. She leaned on the bar next to him. "Al?"

The bartender put down the bottle of medicine he'd been swigging. His ugly face betrayed his adoration as he set a cup of coffee before her.

"See that Hank gets some food and goes home."

Al made a gesture of protest. "Miss Silver, you can't keep feeding every old bum in the Rockies—"

"Drat it! Just do it, Al." Her voice left no room for argument.

Al shrugged his gorilla-like shoulders, threw up his hands in a helpless gesture, and moved to do her bidding.

The girl sighed as she sipped her coffee, ignoring the

men around her.

Cherokee watched her, not daring to breathe. Now that she stood there, his courage deserted him. She stood so close, he could almost reach out and touch her, but he didn't. The slight scent of wild flowers drifted from her warm skin. Cherokee had to fight himself to keep from reaching out and stroking her hair. It looked like spun moonbeams reflecting the light.

His tormentor grinned at him across the top of the girl's head. "Miss Silver, this big half-breed has something he wants to ask you."

She paused in sipping her coffee and staring at her own reflection in the big mirror behind the bar. Turning, she looked directly up at Cherokee. "Oh?"

She wasn't more than chest high on him and the light played on that flawless face. Cherokee had a sudden urge to pick her up, throw her across his wide shoulder, and carry her kicking and screaming back to his isolated cabin at Mosquito Gulch so he would have her all to himself.

He had never felt so shy, so unsure of himself as he did now with this blond whore. "Can I—can I buy you a drink?"

"I don't drink, stranger. All the boys hereabouts know that." She looked up at him, sure of herself, slightly amused at his hesitancy.

He had a feeling all the men along the bar were watching and listening. Behind her, his tormentor mouthed the silent words: *Ask her. Go on and ask her.*

"That was a nice thing you did for the old man," Cherokee stammered, "but you girls probably can't afford to do things like that."

"Let me worry about that." She grinned and sipped her coffee.

"You should smile more often," Cherokee blurted without thinking. "That's the first time I've seen you smile."

A murmur ran through the crowd at his words. The girl's expression went as cold as her eyes. "That's hardly your concern, now is it?"

"I reckon not," he drawled, feeling the flush rise up past his collar.

She seemed to sense his embarrassed discomfort and looked almost sympathetic. "Where you from, plow-boy?"

"Georgia, but I've spent some time in Tennessee." She was a Yankee, most likely, although he couldn't place the accent.

"I thought Southern men drank bourbon."

He felt big and awkward and foolish. "Used to. But . . ." He didn't finish. The night he had awakened in Savannah's bed, he'd sworn he'd never touch another drop. Cherokee Evans was a man of his word.

All the other men were waiting, listening. If he didn't ask her soon, some other man would. And if another man tried to take Silver up those stairs, Cherokee wouldn't be able to stop himself; he'd kill him with his bare hands.

The girl finished her coffee and started to turn away.

If he didn't ask her now, the moment would be lost. It didn't matter that the others were listening. "I'd—I'd like to be your customer tonight," he blurted.

"What? What did you say?" She whirled on him, her pale aqua eyes blazing.

He heard a titter of laughter down the bar as men nudged each other and repeated what he'd said. Out of the corner of his eye, he saw Al moving toward him behind the bar. "You know what I mean. I'll pay what-

22

ever you usually charge and then some—"

Her hand shot out and she slapped him so hard, he felt his head snap back. The sound might have been heard all over the saloon.

Automatically, Cherokee's hand felt his stinging cheek while laughter rang up and down the bar.

"My Gawd, did you hear what he asked Miss Silver? Must be a greenhorn!"

The girl herself stood with small feet apart, hands on her hips. "Fella, the boys have made you the butt of a joke tonight. Don't you realize I own this place?"

She whirled to leave while the laughter echoed around them. He felt rage sweep over him; he would kill all these white men for their joke. He would . . .

Silver was walking away and that fact overrode his anger. Without thinking, Cherokee reached out and caught her arm. "Wait! Don't go!"

Abruptly, he felt the distinctive outline of the barrel of a double-barreled shotgun against his back and heard Al's low growl. "Get your hands off her! No man alive puts his hands on Miss Silver!"

Cherokee loosened his grip and turned slowly. The gorilla-like man with the face like five miles of bad road had the shotgun cocked and ready to blow Cherokee in half. There was no mistaking the look in his eyes. Al adored the blonde more than enough to kill for her.

Cherokee kept his hands where the other man could see them. "I never meant no harm," he drawled softly. "I didn't know—"

"If you want a girl, mister, there's plenty here who'd take you upstairs. Every man in the Rockies knows Silver don't allow no man to touch her!"

She made a soothing gesture. "It's all right, Al. I

23

suspect the boys played a trick on him." She gave Cherokee one last, searching look, then turned and went back to the stage. Cherokee couldn't keep his gaze off her undulating hips moving in the tight red satin. Al put down the shotgun, reached for his bottle of tonic, took a big drink, and moved farther down the bar.

Zeke scratched his beard. "Sorry, hombre, we play that joke on a lot of greenhorns. Hope you don't mind."

Mind? By damn! He'd like to kill the man for humiliating him like that. But his major emotion was sadness and loss that she wouldn't be sleeping in his arms tonight. To Doc, he said, "Does she really own this saloon?"

"Yep. Silver and that bartender got off a stage a year ago and she bought the place. Paid cold, hard cash, I hear."

Cherokee watched her talk to the bald piano player. "Where'd they come from?"

"Nobody knows. In the mining camps, it ain't polite to ask too many questions."

Cherokee rolled a cigarette and lit it. He never took his gaze off the girl as he slowly shook out the match. "Does any man . . . well, does she ever . . ."

Cherokee looked around at the men at the bar and knew the answer from the longing and regret on their weathered faces even before they shook their heads. Obviously Silver affected other men the same way she affected him.

Cherokee watched her. She was a fire in Cherokee's blood now—as desirable and unattainable as any queen. The fact that he hadn't lain between a woman's thighs in months only added to the fire in his veins, making his groin ache with pent-up seed.

With a sinking heart, he looked around at the elegant

24

saloon. The whore had more wealth than he did. Add to that the fact that he knew he was a rough, backwoods half-breed without a white man's polished manners, and he realized that even if he'd had plenty of gold, she wouldn't be interested in him anyway.

The pretty, yellow-haired whore sidled up to him again. "Buy me a drink now, sugar?"

Cherokee tore his gaze away from Silver. His body ached for the release of a woman's body. He grabbed the whore's arm, propelling her ahead of him. "Sweet darlin', let's the two of us go upstairs."

"A man who knows what he wants. I like that!" She pressed against him and smiled. "I can take care of what ails you in a few minutes!"

"A few minutes, hell! Darlin', you better figure on me stayin' all night! What's your name again?"

"Nellie."

"Come on, Nellie, you got your work cut out for you."

She giggled, looking back at him over her shoulder as they pushed through the crowd. "With you, sugar, it's not gonna be work, it'll be pure pleasure!"

They had to pass the piano to reach the stairs. As he passed Silver, he slapped Nellie on the rear and laughed loudly. "Sweet darlin', you ever take a man a dozen times in one night?"

The girl giggled again, reached out, and took his hand possessively. "No, but you look like the man who could do it and make a girl die happy!"

"Damned right!" he said, sneaking a look at Silver as he started up the stairs. Then he paused, and their eyes locked for a long moment, though her expression betrayed nothing. He knew she had to have heard what he'd just said. He'd meant for her to. What had he expected her to do? How ironic—going upstairs with one girl and loco to have the one standing by the piano. Cherokee hesitated, wishing he could back down. He'd rather stand here and watch Silver than go upstairs with Nellie.

"Hey, sugar," Nellie yelled from the top of the stairs, "where are you? I thought you were in a hurry?"

"Yeah. Here I come." He tore his gaze away from the other girl reluctantly and went up the stairs.

He watched Nellie's hips sway in the tight green dress ahead of him. Cherokee followed her into her room and kicked the door shut with his boot. "If the boss lady is an iceberg, why does she allow you girls to work here?"

"Would you believe she don't take a cent of our money, except for room and board? Says we work too hard for it." Nellie quickly undid her tight dress with experienced fingers and stepped out of it. She wore a lace chemise underneath, but she didn't have the body Silver had. At least her hair was somewhat the right color.

Cherokee concentrated on the strawlike hair. Maybe he could pretend she was Silver. His manhood ached with need. "She doesn't take a cut of your money?"

"Silver'd just as soon we didn't work here. Doesn't really approve. But the girls need the jobs and we'd just work somewhere else if she didn't allow it."

She came over, put her arms around his neck, and rubbed up against him. "You feel hard as stone, sugar. I'm gonna make you real happy!"

He closed his eyes, pulled the girl against him, and saw Silver's face in his mind. His manhood *was* hard as stone . . . if stone could swell and throb and ache.

He didn't open his eyes as he pushed the lace straps off her shoulders so he could cup her breasts and pull her

26

body closer to his pulsating hardness. Her breasts felt small, and when he buried his face in her coarse hair, the strong, cheap perfume she wore almost gagged him. He longed for the fragrance of wild flowers.

"Oh, sugar," she cooed, wiggling her hips against his hardness, "you really do want me bad, don't you?"

A woman; he needed a woman bad. A vessel to spew his hot seed into; that was all he needed now.

He felt her fumbling with the buttons of his pants. "Oh, sugar, I ought to charge you by the inch!" She giggled with delight as she went to her knees and kissed his manhood.

He looked down at her through half-closed eyes, pretending that it was Silver on her knees before him in a lace chemise. He tangled his fingers in the girl's hair and pulled her mouth against him again, throbbing at the wet hotness of her lips on him. "You know what I want," he gasped. "Beg me for it. Beg me to take you."

Yes, that was what he wanted. He wanted the frigid Silver on her knees in submission, her lips caressing him, begging him to take her.

"I'll beg if you like, sugar, but let's get on the bed where we'll be more comfortable." She took his hand and led him to the bed.

Cherokee sat down on the edge and reached to remove his boots.

And then the music began again and Silver's high, sweet voice floated up the stairs and under the door. It was almost as if she sang directly to him. With horror, he felt his desire ebb, his manhood begin to soften.

By damn! He wouldn't let her do this to him. He'd mount Nellie and satisfy his pent-up desire before Silver's voice could affect him further. Without even taking off his boots, he grabbed Nellie and pushed her onto her back. "I'm in a hurry," he gasped. "There's no reason to pull anything off!"

"If you want me that bad . . ." The silly girl had her chemise off and obediently lay on her back with her legs spread.

Silver's voice floated faintly into the room. Damn her anyway! Even as he took the girl in his arms, he felt his body soften in protest. It didn't want Nellie, it hungered for the other girl. He was both frustrated and angry as he sat up suddenly. "I've changed my mind."

"Changed your mind? As hot as you were?"

He didn't want to explain or argue with the girl. "Here's your money and then some."

He tossed two silver dollars on her bare belly, rolled over to sit up on the edge of the bed, and took a deep, shuddering breath.

He had already lost the rigidity he needed to complete the act. Even though he had been without a woman for months, all he wanted was the girl downstairs—a woman as unattainable as the stars to a half-breed prospector like himself.

"Sugar, you ain't leavin'?"

"Just watch me!" He stood up, looking down at the girl lying naked in a tangle of sheets and lace. "Sorry about that, Nellie."

"But why?"

"Never mind why. It isn't your fault. I—I just changed my mind." He started buttoning his pants.

The song floated faintly through the door and Nellie sat up, glaring at him. "It's her, ain't it? You want her? Well, Silver don't sleep with no one, 'specially not some lowdown 'breed! You can eat your heart out, 'breed, but

28

you won't ever get in her bed! You should have been happy to get me."

Her words stung like gravel thrown against his face, but he resisted the urge to fling insults back. Cherokee could never hurt a woman, not even a whore. *And didn't he know that all white women were whores?* "Sorry, Nellie," he drawled softly and strode out the door.

Maybe he could sneak out without Silver seeing him. With all the fuss he'd made about spending the whole night with Nellie, he'd just as soon Silver didn't know he was leaving early.

He started down the stairs as the piano changed to another tune and the men began to applaud and cheer. Through the haze of smoke and smell of whiskey, he saw Silver taking the steps to the small stage.

The piano banged loudly and the men sang along:

"De Camptown ladies sing dis song, doo-dah, doo-dah! De Camptown race track, five miles long—Oh! Doo-dah day!"

Silver danced across the stage, her small feet flying to the melody. She had such a natural grace and rhythm that Cherokee forgot he was trying to sneak out unnoticed; that he was furious with the girl for denying him what he wanted.

He had never seen anyone dance so well, graceful feet moving to the music while the men cheered her on. If the flawless beauty sang well, she was an even better dancer. And when she whirled, her skirts flew up, revealing long, beautiful legs.

Halfway down the stairs, Cherokee leaned against the rail, and watched her dance, unwilling, no, unable to tear himself away. He had a sudden vision of his own dark, naked body lying between those thighs, her shapely legs

29

locked around his hard-driving hips, pulling him deeper into her wet warmth. He would put his hands under her small hips, tilting her up for his deep thrusting. His mouth would find her pink nipples and she would arch her back to encourage him to suck harder, while she made soft, vulnerable noises of surrender in her throat.

And his mouth on hers, he urged her on. *Come with me, sweet darlin', oh come . . . come with me, sweet Silver. . . .*

The music stopped, pulling him out of his fantasy. Here he stood, his manhood hard and aching again with a ready girl upstairs. Oh hell, what a fool he was!

Silver took a bow to thunderous applause and then she turned and looked directly at him. Her pale, aquamarine eyes expressed no surprise at seeing him. In fact, it was almost as if she realized he would be standing there, her worshipful subject as were all the other men in this place. No wonder she didn't have a man, she had a hundred male slaves eager to do her bidding—willing to throw themselves over a cliff or lay riches at her tiny feet for just one smile, one gesture.

Cherokee had the most insane urge to run down the stairs and up to the stage, grab her, throw her over his wide shoulders, and carry her off. But he knew these men would lynch him for trying. Cherokee both hated and desired her at the same time, as men always want that which they cannot have.

With an oath, he stumbled down the stairs, through the swinging doors, and out into the chill spring night. He'd go to another bawdy house, find another girl with hair as pale as moonbeams.

But he didn't. He went to a hotel and lay sleepless on his bed, staring up at the stained ceiling. It must be his imagination that the sound of her high, sweet voice seemed to drift faintly on the night air, accompanied by the rhythmic tap of her dancing feet.

Tomorrow he'd buy his supplies, get his burro shod, and head back to the claim. By the next time he got to town, the girl would probably have moved on. Pretty whores didn't stay too long in one spot. They ended up in places like San Francisco, got married, or found a rich man to keep them in luxury as long as their looks lasted.

Silver. Whore. The two didn't seem to go together. He remembered her hard eyes that looked as if the owner had seen too much, experienced too much. And yet her full, soft mouth betrayed a vulnerability and sensitivity rare in a saloon girl. No wonder the men of Buckskin Joe loved her.

It was a long time before he dropped off into a troubled sleep. In his dreams, he heard her singing and saw her dancing only for him in some remote place where no other man could enjoy her beauty or lust after her.

Then she came into his arms, soft and giving, opening up her thighs like some exotic flower so he could mesh with her, become one in an ecstasy of love. Her flawless face smiled at him as she reached for him and he saw his reflection in her pale eyes. She was special to him at that moment, not because of her beauty, but because he saw his reflection in her eyes, and knew she loved him, too.

Cherokee came to her, gently taking her, murmuring sweet words, whispering that he loved her, wanted her with him for all time. Even when her looks were gone, when she was wrinkled and old, she would always be beautiful to him as long as he saw that love for him in those aqua eyes.

"Silver, oh, sweet darlin' . . ." In his dreams he crushed her to him, poured his seed deep into her. At that moment, he awakened, sweating and thrashing in his bed. Her hair spread over the pillow. Cherokee blinked sleepily, reached to stroke those silken locks. But it was only moonlight spilling through the window and across the pillow.

Cherokee sat up in bed with a curse. It couldn't be long until morning. He'd get his business taken care of and get out of town before thoughts of the woman drove him loco. The only other alternative was to kidnap her and take her up to his cabin, where she would be at his mercy while he sated his lust on her small, ripe body.

Chapter Two

Silver paused in the doorway of the shoemaker's shop before picking her way along the wooden sidewalk in the early morning chill. The shop had promised the new dancing slippers delivered just before tonight's show.

Drat! The street looked muddy in front of Haw Tabor's general store and that was where she wanted to go. Maybe if she was careful . . .

Gingerly, Silver lifted her full, aqua skirt and eyed the mud. These new, fashionable hoops didn't help matters any. She looked up and down at the busy street. All she had to do was indicate her need and some miner or cowboy would rush over eagerly and carry her across.

The thought of a man's touch made her shudder all over. After all that men had done to her, she never intended that another one even touch her hand.

Her mind went to the dark half-breed from last night. His hands were as big as he was, and probably as hard and tough as the man himself. She had a sudden vision of those callused hands stroking her breasts and felt her nipples harden into pink points at the thought.

The feeling shocked her. Never had any man made her feel desire. Revulsion and fear—those were the emotions men aroused in her. But her mind was still occupied with him as she began picking her way across the wet street.

The mud was deeper than she had thought. The slippery ooze pulled at her shoes. Silver paused halfway out, still struggling to keep her skirts above the mire. What a sight she would make if she tripped and fell! Worse than that, it would ruin the fine new dress that had just arrived on the Denver stage last week.

She took another step and felt the cold mud ooze over her shoe tops. Drat! Why hadn't she had Haw deliver what she needed? There was no real reason to be out this morning. Certainly, she told herself, it wasn't because she thought the big 'breed might be on the street or in the stores where she might see him.

She paused again. The half-breed came out of the hotel coffee shop on the other side of the street, then stopped, stood looking at her.

"Ma'am," he yelled in that thick Georgia drawl, "if I may be of service to a lady—"

"No, thank you," she snapped back, taking another tentative step. She didn't appreciate such sarcasm, although he didn't look as if he meant anything by it. She knew the "respectable" people of this area would not consider her a "lady." Besides, she didn't want his big hands on her body.

Silver managed to take two more precarious steps and was beginning to hope she might make it to the sidewalk with no more than soiled shoes. Then she stepped into a hole.

The man leaned against the general store's sign, smoking a cigarette and watching her. Others had stopped to watch, too. But the local men knew her well enough not to offer. They knew how Silver felt about a man's touch.

Silver struggled to raise her foot out of the mire and lost her shoe. She stood there like a crane on one leg, struggling to maintain her balance. What the hell did she do now?

He tossed away his cigarette. "Still don't need any help?"

"No, thank you." In an agony of decision, she looked around, trying to decide what to do.

But at that moment, he strode out through the mud, swung her up in his arms, and carried her to the sidewalk.

Silver kept her body rigid as a dressmaker's dummy, quaking inside with the horrible memories the feel of a man's body against hers brought back. The heat and the strength of the rugged man seemed to burn through both their clothing.

She was actually trembling as he slowly stood her on her feet. He looked down at her a long moment, evidently puzzled by her fear.

"I'll get your other shoe, ma'am." He spoke in a soft, reassuring drawl as if speaking to a frightened child.

Silver didn't say anything. She stood there with nails digging into her palms, watching the giant of a man stride out to retrieve her shoe. He was one of the biggest men she had ever met, she thought, watching him walk. A big man like that could hurt her worse than that one in Chicago or even her stepfather. . . .

"Here it is, Miss Silver, but it needs a lot of cleaning." He doffed his Western hat and almost bowed, holding the shoe out. "Maybe I should accompany you back to the Nugget—"

"No, I'll be fine." She jerked the slipper out of his hand and put it on, very aware of men stopping to stare curiously at the pair. This must be the only man in the Rockies who didn't know how Silver Jones reacted to being touched. "Thank you for your help, Mister . . ."

"Evans. Cherokee Evans." He bowed again with that gallantry that seemed to come natural to any Southern male—even a half-breed. "I'm always happy to help a lady."

No, he wasn't being sarcastic. His dark eyes were honest, friendly. Too friendly. She must not encourage him. Next thing she knew, he'd want to share her bed and Silver had never done that with a man—willingly.

She gave him a nod of dismissal and turned toward Tabor's store.

But Cherokee Evans rushed to open the door for her. "I allow as how I was going in here for supplies, too."

What could she do? There was no law against a man going into a store. Silver decided to ignore him. Maybe he'd take the hint. She walked to the back counter.

Immediately, Haw's sour-faced wife, Augusta, looked up, saw her, frowned, and suddenly discovered something in the back of the building that needed immediate attention, probably so she wouldn't have to wait on Silver. It had happened before.

Such treatment from "respectable" women no longer hurt Silver; she'd grown used to it. The only satisfaction she got was knowing that often the "respectable" women's husbands were frequenting the Nugget Saloon at night while their wives thought the men were at a town meeting or working late.

Cherokee followed her. Either he didn't realize Silver was ignoring him, or he refused to take the hint. She

36

knew what he wanted from her—what all men wanted from women. Silver never intended to be put through that humiliation and pain again. And as big as he was, there'd be a lot of pain, besides the sheer weight of his big body pinning her against the bed.

Genial Haw rushed over to wait on her. Silver made her purchases, gave a curt nod to both men, and sailed out of the store, her shoes squeaking wetly. She walked as fast as she could back to the Nugget, ran up the stairs, slammed her door and shot the bolt, and leaned against the locked door, trembling. Now she was safe. Not that the 'breed had made any threatening moves. It was just that he kept looking at her with that dark, intense gaze that let her know if he decided to take her, locked doors and dozens of witnesses couldn't stop him. Maybe in a day or two, he'd get discouraged and go away.

Cherokee stared after her with both longing and regret. In truth, he had seen her come out of the shoe shop from the hotel coffee shop and had bolted his breakfast so he could be standing outside when she crossed the street.

What had he expected? He watched her walk on down the sidewalk while he remembered every detail about the few seconds she had been in his arms. The feel of her body against his, the warm softness of her, the scent of her wild flower fragrance had made him almost dizzy with desire as he had carried her to the sidewalk. She seemed to fit into his embrace almost perfectly, her small body light in his arms.

But the girl had been rigid, trying to keep from touching him. And she'd actually been trembling when he had stood her on her feet. There had been no mistaking the fear in her eyes as she looked up at him. He had had the most insane impulse to take that flawless face between his two big hands and gently brush his lips across hers. "I won't hurt you, Silver," he had almost whispered. "I'd never hurt you or let anyone else. You're safe with me, you'll always be safe and protected while I'm around."

Who was he kidding? Himself? He looked out the front window at the slight blonde in pale aqua as she hurried down the wooden sidewalk. All his body could think of was getting that expensive aqua velvet and fine jewelry off that slim body so he could run his hands over her white, naked skin.

"She's a pretty one, ain't she?" the shopkeeper's voice broke into his thoughts and Cherokee looked around, realizing he had been staring after the girl like a hungry hound after a tender morsel.

"Oh, I reckon. Maybe a little too small for my taste." Cherokee shrugged and reached to add a bag of salt to his supplies.

"Then you're the only man in the Rockies who thinks so!" The jovial Tabor jotted the purchase on a pad on the counter before him.

"What's her story?" Cherokee asked a little too carelessly, damning himself because he wanted to know everything about her.

Tabor stuck a pencil behind one ear and shrugged. "No one knows really. About a year ago, she got off the stage here, accompanied by that ugly bartender of hers, Al. Nobody knows where they came from or anything else about them except the stage driver thought from their tickets that they had started out from Chicago."

She did have a Northern accent, Cherokee thought, but somehow, Silver had struck him as a country girl, not someone from a big place like Chicago. "Does she really own that saloon?"

"Lock, stock, and barrel!" Tabor hooked his thumbs in his white apron. "She had two thousand dollars in cold cash, gossip says, and promptly bought the place. That's a lot of money by anyone's standards."

He was even more intrigued. "And there's no other man?"

"Who? Silver? Perish the thought!" Tabor made a gesture of dismissal. "Not her! Folks say she wouldn't even allow whores there, but they begged for the jobs. Her card tables are honest, which is rare, and the Nugget don't water the whiskey. Silver's always treating some old bum or hungry passerby to a meal."

Hard-eyed whore with a heart of gold. It was the stuff novels were made of. But if she wasn't a whore, just what was she? Whatever she was, Cherokee didn't want to leave town until he unraveled the mystery, even though his partners needed him back at the claim.

"You been here long, stranger?" the other interrupted his thoughts.

Cherokee shook his head. "First time in town, though I've been up on the claim for months. How'd it get a name like Buckskin Joe?"

"Oh, some call it Laurette now, sounds fancier, I reckon, but it won't stick." The storekeeper stuck his pencil behind his ear. "Most of us think it should stay named for the old mountain man who founded it."

Cherokee grunted, his mind still on the girl.

"We'll be a state someday, sure you're born," the shopkeeper said. "Why, us becomin' an official Territory last month is just the beginnin', and I intend to be part of her future!"

39

"Oh?" Cherokee smiled politely as he reached for his money. "I got business at the blacksmith and then I'll be moving on."

Tabor snorted. "Sorry, fella, you'll have to wait 'til tomorrow for the blacksmith. He's out of town at a funeral."

"Is there another one?"

"Nope. What's your all-fired hurry, anyhow? He'll be back tomorrow. You probably ain't findin' much gold nohow."

Cherokee felt both guilty and elated. He sighed and reached for his parcels. "Prospectin' is just something that gets in your blood, I reckon. My papa spent his whole life chasing after the pot of gold at the end of the rainbow that was always just over the next hill."

Tabor scratched his head. "He ever find it?"

"No." The Welshman had gone off with a white saloon whore named Lulu, chasing yet another rainbow while his deserted Indian wife and son made out the best they could in the Georgia hills.

An empty ache came to his heart. He had still been only a child when the government decided to move the Cherokees thousands of miles away to Indian Territory in the wintertime. The Removal. *Tsi-ge-gv-wo-o-ta-ne-i,* his people called it. His mother was forced to go and died along with thousands of others. Cherokee's grandmother had taken him deep into the woods and they had hidden out for years. It had earned its other name—the Trail of Tears.

Tabor pushed his parcels to him. "Take my advice, fella, find another way to make money besides digging for gold. Now myself, I've grubstaked a few prospectors. If any of them ever hits pay dirt, I'll be a rich man without ever touching a shovel."

Cherokee only half listened. Already he was thinking how glad he was that he had an excuse to stay in town at least another night. Immediately he felt guilty. Those two old prospectors he had taken in as partners needed help back at the claim.

He whistled jauntily as he picked up his packages and went out. Cherokee had brought a small poke full of silver, intending to spend it on a good time. But now he had a sudden desire to buy the beautiful girl a present. Maybe then she might look at him with favor. *What could he buy that would please her?*

She wore expensive jewelry, but he knew he couldn't afford that. Besides he had no experience at choosing pretties for women. Probably wasn't much to buy in this town anyway. He half turned back toward Tabor's store, then decided the sour-faced wife wouldn't have ordered really fine fabrics or anything that Silver hadn't already bought if she wanted it.

Muddy shoes. Hers had been ruined this morning. Sho'd been coming out of the shoe shop when Cherokee had first seen her this morning. Would she accept a gift anyway? Probably not.

Undaunted, he stroke over to the shop and went inside. The dim interior smelled of leather and polish. A slight man with his hair parted down the middle and a cobbler's hammer in his hand looked up. "Can I help you, mister?"

Cherokee lost his nerve. "Uh, I was thinkin' of havin' me some new boots made."

"I can do her! Never did hold with these factory-made jobs; don't even come to fit your foot, no left and right."

Cherokee only nodded, looking around, wondering

41

what kind of shoes Silver would order. And then he realized that the shoemaker was working on the smallest shoe Cherokee had ever seen. Only one woman had feet that small. "Are those for Miss Silver?"

The shoemaker held the slipper up, evidently proud of his workmanship. "I always do my very best work for her. She's one of those women every man would like to call his own, but I doubt anyone ever will."

Cherokee held out his hand and the man put the shoe in it. He could close his big fist around it. Cherokee had seen bigger children's shoes. The workmanship was good, but the shoe was not quite finished. "I owe Miss Silver a favor," he said.

"Half the town does," the man said, leaning against his workbench. "The womenfolk don't cotton to her, but she's kind to even the most down-and-out old drunk. And that face! You ever see such a perfect face?"

Cherokee agreed, turning the small dancing shoe over and over in his hand, thinking. "When these got to be finished?"

"She wants them for tonight's show. I told her I'd bring them over myself right before the performance." He winked broadly. "Gives me a perfect excuse to stay a few minutes, if you know what I mean."

"If she owns the place, why does she sing and dance there?"

"Because it draws a crowd and she likes to do it, I suppose."

That made sense. Somehow, when she sang, the small blonde had a way of making a man think she sang and danced only for him. Cherokee handed the slipper back and reached for his poke. "I want you to do something to these shoes—something she'll like but she wouldn't

42

accept from me."

"I don't know about this." The cobbler scratched his thin hair doubtfully.

"Tell her you did it as a way of saying 'much obliged' for her business. That way, she can't turn it down." Cherokee opened his poke. He had an idea that pleased him and he thought it would please her . . . as long as Silver didn't have to feel obligated. He explained his idea.

The cobbler smiled. "She'll like that! I'd do it myself, but I don't have the silver. There's nothing I wouldn't do for her!"

Every man in town felt the same way, Cherokee discovered as he wandered about that day. Nearly all had a tale to tell of her kindness and generosity. A dozen told him they'd begged to marry her, but Silver's nunlike life was as well known as her flawless face.

If he could, Cherokee intended to put an end to that. He had never wanted a woman as much as he wanted this one, but he was a little unsure how to go about it. He'd had little experience with women except for paid whores—with one exception. He frowned at the memory. No, they were all whores—even the ones who pretended to be respectable.

It seemed a long day, but finally the sun set and Cherokee leaned against the Nugget's ornate bar, impatient to see the girl again.

Al looked up, reached for a cup of coffee, and slammed it down by Cherokee's hand. "You're wasting your time, sport."

"Let me be the judge of that."

The ugly little man glowered at him. "She don't sleep with nobody. That's the way she wants it and my shotgun sees that Miss Silver gets what she wants."

Cherokee sipped the coffee and watched the bartender take a gulp of patent medicine then wipe his mouth. "You known her a long time, Al?"

"Long enough."

"You related to her?"

"Nope."

"You don't say much, do you?" Cherokee said in exasperation.

Al grinned then put the medicine bottle in his hip pocket. "You ever hear about the man who got rich mindin' his own business?"

"No."

"Then maybe that's why you ain't rich."

Cherokee stared past him into the big mirror behind the bar. He wasn't going to learn anything about Silver from this gorilla.

The saloon grew crowded and smoky as darkness fell and men drifted in. The piano banged out off-key songs, the roulette wheel whirled, glasses clinked, and women laughed.

More than one girl sidled up to him, took his arm, and brushed her ripe body against him, trying to take him to her room. Even Nellie made another try at it, but Cherokee kept his attention on the stairs. If he could kiss Silver or make love to her even one time, the fever in his blood might cool. After all, she was just a girl like many others, although she had the most flawless beauty he'd ever seen.

The shoemaker came in with a package under his arm, walked upstairs, and came back down. Cherokee watched him go to the roulette wheel but wouldn't let himself question the man. How Cherokee wished he could have seen her face as she opened the box. Would she like his gift? Would she accept it? But of course she didn't know he was the one responsible.

The noise abated suddenly, and heads turned. Cherokee knew even as he looked toward the stairs that Silver must be coming down.

She wore a sparkling silver dress that accented her light hair and diamond jewelry. It was tight on her small body, emphasizing her slim waist. Her full breasts swelled from the top of the low-cut bodice. On her feet, she wore the dancing slippers with real silver heels. The shoes glittered in the light as she crossed over to the piano and leaned against it.

The rough crowd quieted then began to applaud. Cherokee found himself clapping, too, caught up in the moment, in the love that flowed from this crowd toward the girl and her almost angelic beauty.

Silver motioned for silence and signaled the piano player. Cherokee found himself holding his breath as she sang:

"Listen to the mockingbird, listen to the mockingbird, the mockingbird still singing o'er her grave . . ."

Once as she looked around the crowded, smoky saloon, her gaze found Cherokee's face and they looked directly into each other's eyes.

I love you, he said silently with his eyes, *I need you, Silver, and you need me, too.*

Her voice faltered a split second and she looked away.

Thereafter, she seemed careful not to look his direction as she finished her song.

He didn't care. He was certain she had gotten his silent message and he was satisfied.

She sang several songs while the place remained quiet as a lover's sigh. Every man there seemed to hold his breath so as not to miss a single note of her high, sweet voice. Finally she finished to thunderous applause and the piano broke into a fast, rhythmic beat even as Silver ran lightly up the steps to the stage.

As she began to dance, the silver heels of the shoes caught the light and sparkled with her movement. Men began to nudge each other, pointing them out and nodding in approval.

Cherokee leaned back on the bar with both elbows and smiled. It didn't matter that she would never know he had provided the silver for the shoes; she wouldn't have accepted them if she'd known that. It was enough that the silver he had dug from his own claim decorated her tiny feet.

As she finished and took a bow, the men began to shout: "Silver! Silver Heels! Silver Heels!"

She blushed prettily, took another bow, and the roar from the rowdy miners grew. "Silver! Yes, Silver Heels!"

She came down from the stage and motioned to the piano player to play another number. As she ambled through the crowd, the men gave her one last, wistful look and returned to their cards and drinking.

She was coming toward him. Cherokee felt awkward and a little unsure of himself. He pretended nonchalance.

She stepped in front of him. "I think we need to talk."

"Us?" He touched his chest in mock surprise. Good!

She was going to be grateful. At least that was a start.

Silver gestured to the bartender. "Al, bring us some coffee, and the cash box."

Al appeared to be grumbling under his breath, but he moved to do her bidding. Silver marched away from the bar. Cherokee, not knowing what else to do, trailed after her, feeling very much like a lost hound pup.

She walked to a private cubicle that was curtained off from the saloon, where she could sit and watch the customers through a gap in the red velvet curtains. Cherokee followed her there. She sat down at the table.

He almost got up the nerve to sit next to her, then took a look at her face and decided against it. He sat down across from her. Her eyes were almost a clear, deep green now. She looked angry.

Al brought the coffee and the cash box, put them on the table, and hesitated. "I'm as near as a shout, Silver."

She smiled at him. "I know that, Al. Close the curtains as you leave, will you?"

The barrel-chested little man looked as if he might protest, then shrugged and did as she ordered. The heavy velvet curtains blocked out much of the noise and music.

Cherokee decided to make light of it. "Al seems to think I'm a threat of some kind."

"Are you?" She looked directly at him and he realized abruptly that this was an honest person. This was no coy, game-playing female.

"To you?" He looked directly into her eyes. "Not to you. Not ever to you." He tried to appear nonchalant by rolling a cigarette, but his hand shook and he spilled some of the tobacco.

"I seem to have forgotten your name, Mister—"

47

"Evans. Cherokee Evans."

"That's a nickname. Don't you have a *real* name like John or Jim?"

He looked steadily back at her. "Do you?"

He had flustered her with his probing question. He wondered for a long minute if she was Scandinavian. She looked it.

"Is Cherokee all you've ever gone by?"

"My grandmother named me Tsu-no-yv-gi. It means 'rattler.' It's a deadly snake."

She glared back at him. "I know what it is. Sounds appropriate. What is it you want from me?"

"Me?" He raised his eyebrows innocently, deciding he could be as blunt and straightforward as she had been. "I think you know already. Why do you bother to ask?" He lit the cigarette and shook out the match.

"At least you're honest about it. But surely you know by now you'll never get it." She leaned back in her chair, studying him.

Cherokee shrugged his wide shoulders and blew smoke in the air. "Man lives by hope, I reckon."

"There's a dozen girls in the Nugget, and any one of them would fall on her back for free just to have a man like you take her in his arms."

"But not you?" He watched her closely. She was actually trembling. Was she really afraid or was it an act? And if it was real, what was it in her past that haunted her so? "I won't hurt you, Silver." He blurted it out without thinking.

"That's what the others said!" She seemed to blurt her words out, too, without thinking.

Then it was almost as if she'd revealed too much. Her

48

face became remote as if to keep her soul private. Her eyes were cold but her mouth trembled as she looked back at him. "Why'd you do it?"

"Do what?"

"Don't play innocent with me—the silver heels on the slippers. I'm not stupid enough to think a shoemaker can afford something like that."

"You know, those shoes were just perfect tonight," Cherokee said, smoking his cigarette and watching her small hands clasped around her coffeecup. They clasped and unclasped, tense and nervous. He stifled the urge to reach out and cover her two small hands with one of his big ones. "I think from now on, you'll have a new nickname. I think the men will call you Silver Heels."

She opened the cash box. "What do I owe you?"

He was taken aback. "Owe me? They were a gift!"

She smiled without mirth. "It's my experience with men that they never give a pretty girl anything without expecting something in return. I'm obligated to no man. What do I owe you?"

He threw away the cigarette in disgust. "By damn! Just keep the shoes and forget it, all right?"

"If you aren't going to tell me, I'll just have to guess." Her tone was cold and hard as her eyes. She reached into the cash box and began counting out money onto the scarred table.

"I won't take it."

Without a word she leaned over, took off the shoes, and put them on the table. "Then you'll take the shoes."

He was both exasperated and embarrassed at her stubbornness. "What the hell am I supposed to do with a pair of slightly used dancing shoes?"

49

She shrugged. "Give them to Nellie; but I'll bet her feet are too big for them."

"Nellie doesn't mean anything to me. I know you won't believe it, but nothing happened up in her room last night."

She didn't believe it, he could see it in her eyes. "It doesn't matter. After all, that's what she's here for."

"Besides," he said, "I bought them just for you. There's not another woman in the Territory with feet that small."

"Then you've made a bad investment on which you'll get no return."

He felt the flush creep up his neck. "I'm not ready to write it off yet."

"Then you're a fool."

"Just let me give you the damned shoes. I have no use for them." He shoved back his chair and stood up.

"I'll buy them from you." She pushed the pile of money toward him.

"That's more than they're worth." Cherokee made a gesture of refusal. "If you won't take them as a gift, at least don't pay more than they'd cost you back East."

She hesitated, then took back a few dollars. "Is that about right?"

He nodded, both embarrassed and angry. "I—I reckon it was a clumsy gesture on my part. I wanted to do something special for you." There was a long pause. In the background, the music and noise drifted faintly through the heavy drapes. "You're special, Silver."

She looked up at him. "You wouldn't say that if I weren't pretty. When a woman's looks are gone, her admirers are, too."

50

"You don't think very highly of men, do you?"

She seemed to be weighing her words. "My past experience is all I've got to go on. You must not think much of women if you think you can buy your way into my bed with a gift."

He thought of elegant, high-born Savannah. "It's been my experience that all white women will bed any man, given the right circumstances."

"Not this one." She, too, stood up.

The scent of wildflower perfume drifted from the deep cleft between her full breasts. He had the most insane urge to sweep her into his arms and crush those soft breasts against his massive chest. He was overwhelmed with the need to kiss her until she, too, was breathless and shaking with desire as he was now.

"Don't try it," she said and stepped backward. "I might not be able to keep Al from killing you if he heard me scream."

He looked at her long and hard, wanting her so badly, he felt on fire. "Would you scream?"

She hesitated and he saw confusion in her face. She stepped backward again. "You know I would."

The confusion had been replaced by fear. He had to fight himself to keep from sweeping her into his arms and covering her lips with his own. It would be like capturing some small, wild thing in his embrace. He imagined holding her very close against him, feeling her heart beating violently through her breast. He would kiss her so thoroughly that she would be unable to scream—not that she'd want to, not really. For a moment, he even thought of throwing her down across the table and taking her then and there.

51

"Silver," he whispered, "I would never hurt you. I only want to make love to you."

"Same thing, damn it! Same thing!" The girl began to shake uncontrollably and a tear made a hot, crooked trail down her cheek. Fear like that couldn't be faked. Deep shame swept over him.

He felt a deep urge to reassure her, to protect her from whatever ghosts were mirrored in those hard eyes. Cherokee looked down at her. "I—I'm sorry. I didn't mean to make you cry."

He reached up and she shied away, but he wiped the tear from her cheek with one big finger. For a moment, he thought she would scream. Instead, she took a deep, shuddering breath and turned away from him. "Don't touch me. Don't even think about it!"

He would never get the beauty on her back beneath him—at least, not on this trip. "I'm going back up Mosquito Gulch in the morning as soon as I get my burro shod. You won't be bothered by the likes of me anymore."

"Good!" Silver glared at him. She brushed her hand across her mouth slowly. He couldn't be sure if she was regretting her decision or making sure he hadn't kissed her. *What had crossed her mind just then?*

There was so much more he wanted to say. But when he started to speak, she made a contemptuous gesture of dismissal. "Whatever it is, I don't want to hear it. All you men only want one thing from a woman!"

She grabbed her cash box and stalked from the cubicle, leaving him to gather up the money off the table with a sigh. Cherokee suddenly wanted to possess more than her body; he wanted her heart and soul. Whatever it was in her past that haunted her made her unable—or unwilling—to ever let a man caress her, or make love to her.

He left the Nugget and trudged back to his hotel. To break down that frigid reserve, he'd need time and an opportunity to get her away from her ugly bartender watchdog. He couldn't see how he could do either one . . . not unless he kidnapped Silver and held her prisoner up at his lonely, isolated mountain cabin.

Chapter Three

Silver lay in bed, staring at the ceiling. It must be sometime in the wee hours of the morning, but she couldn't sleep, even though the town had finally quieted down.

She was afraid of the dark. Had been ever since . . . no, she would not think of that tonight. She would think good thoughts. After all, she was still pretty and her face was her fortune. Wasn't that what Ma had said? But she wouldn't always be pretty.

Silver got out of bed and went over to study herself in one of the many mirrors in her room. Even in the dim moonlight, she could see well enough to reassure herself that her face still reflected her flawless beauty. Without that, Ma had said she was worthless. In fact, the plain, dumpy Norwegian had seemed to resent her only child's looks.

You're just like your father, Sylvia, Ma would whine resentfully, *good-looking and worthless. Lars Hanssen drank hisself to death, he did, and left me with his brat and nothing else but a few poor acres and a couple of cows.*

They both labored from sunup to sunset to sell enough milk and eggs in the nearby town to survive. But as the years passed, Ma begin to think of Sylvia's blond beauty as an asset when men started to comment favorably on her child.

You may be worth something yet, Ma opined. *Use that beauty to marry some rich man who'll take care of your old Ma in style.*

Sylvia didn't say anything. Secretly she wanted to be a teacher and help those who were even worse off than she was. Then Ma had married one of their customers, Elmer Neeley. *She would not think of her stepfather tonight.*

Silver returned to her bed, pulled the covers up to her neck, and shivered a little in the chill air. She had only been sixteen when Ma married Neeley and they moved into his big house in town.

The young girl was uncomfortable with the way the man looked at her all the time he was courting her widowed mother. And when he kissed Sylvia after the wedding, he forced his tongue between her lips.

Afterward, he never missed an opportunity to kiss or hug Sylvia, or brush against her in a hallway. The girl didn't know what to do or whom to tell. She was too innocent to know whether all stepfathers acted this way or not.

Ma seemed to be blind to it all. She prattled on and on about how Sylvia would now have a chance to meet rich, eligible young men because of Neeley's social connections. Elmer Neeley himself said Sylvia was too young to be courted yet and wouldn't allow boys to call on her. After all, he said, she was a mere schoolgirl.

He began to spy on her when she changed clothes or took a bath. In spite of everything she could do, she never

55

knew when she would look up suddenly and find her step-father staring at her half-dressed or even naked state.

Finally one night, she awakened to find him in her bed, his hand tightly clasped over her mouth. *I've waited a long time for this, you sweet blond bitch! I only married your mother to get you!*

Elmer Neeley was a big man and she was small. She fought him in vain. If he hadn't had his hand over her mouth, she would have screamed from the pain and terror of his brutal assault, of his wet mouth all over her breasts and body.

She told no one. Who would believe her anyway? Probably not even Ma, who was deliriously happy with her new role as a respected member of small town society. Sylvia ran through all the possible people who might help her. There were none. As a shy, country-raised girl, she had no friends to confide in.

Elmer Neeley was a wealthy, respected pillar of virtue in the small Illinois community. She thought about the schoolmaster, the preacher, the police. She had a sinking feeling that no one would believe her and she would be ostracized, and hated, even by her own mother. Sylvia locked her door after that night. Elmer Neeley had a key made. She pulled furniture against the door before she went to bed. He was big enough to push it open anyway.

She hated and feared the darkness because she knew that often, while her mother snored loudly down the hall, her stepfather would come to her room. He told her again and again that it was her fault for luring him with her ripe young body. He laughed that if she told, no one would believe her and that he would see that she was sent to one of those terrible places for wayward girls or an insane asylum. He was a rich, respected businessman and no one would believe a stupid little schoolgirl.

Weeks turned into months while she tried to think of what to do. In desperation, she decided there was no alternative but to run away. She had no money and no destination in mind—she only wanted to escape from her stepfather's lust. There were no friends or family anywhere she could turn to.

Meanwhile she came to fear the darkness—the endless nights of terror and pain. Sylvia often prayed that her mother would awaken suddenly, come in, and discover her husband in her daughter's bed. Not that it would do any good. She had a feeling Neeley would say the beautiful Jezebel of a daughter had seduced him in spite of his noble, fatherly intentions. Rather than face the terrible truth, Ma would turn on her child in a jealous rage and drive her out of the house.

And that's exactly how it finally happened. Sylvia fled into the night with nothing more than the clothes she grabbed off a chair. She hitched a ride on a hay wagon into Chicago and found herself out of the frying pan and into the fire. Little Sylvia Hanssen soon discovered that Chicago was no place for a pretty blond girl with no money and no friends. It was Sodom and Gomorrah all over again. If it hadn't been for Al . . .

She would not think about those horrible Chicago years now. Silver pulled the blankets up and curled into a ball. She would think about something that made her happy. She searched her memory. There wasn't much. But at least she was financially secure. Her violated beauty had bought this prosperous saloon and a bureau drawer full of expensive jewelry. Her beauty kept the men coming in just to look at her. When she danced and sang, she didn't feel worthless anymore—not with all those adoring faces staring at her. Let them look in vain. Never again would she have to submit to the lust of a man. And when her looks were gone, she would still have the security of the money the Nugget earned.

Cherokee Evans. She thought about the rugged half-breed who had come in two nights now. She knew what he wanted from her. She could see it in his eyes. And he was big—bigger than Neeley or Bart Brett at the Velvet Kitten. It would be sheer agony and humiliation if he forced her.

He wouldn't even offer her the security of marriage. She knew men didn't really want girls like herself. They all wanted innocent virgins. Oh, a man might marry her to get her body for his private use. But someday when she was no longer pretty or he tired of her, she'd be at the world's mercy again.

It was almost dawn. The first gray light touched the elegant bedroom. Cherokee. She saw his face before her suddenly, remembered the heat of his hard muscles as he lifted her and carried her to the sidewalk. And last night . . . She had struggled between terror and an unfamiliar emotion when he had stepped toward her and she had stumbled backward, knowing he wanted to cover her mouth with his hot kisses. She wished she could believe that he might really feel something besides lust. How often in the night, when the nightmares came, did she awaken shaking and covered with perspiration, aching for the warm strength of someone who would hold her and reassure her that everything would be all right?

Silver got up, blew out the lamp, and reached for a peignoir. She heard the slow beginnings of the hustle bustle of the boomtown activities on the muddy street out front. As she went to the window, she stopped at the

58

nearest mirror to assure herself that, yes, she was as beautiful as the day before. *Or was that a new, tiny wrinkle?*

At the window, she stared out. The half-breed came down the street, leading his burro. Possibly he felt her gaze, because he stopped in the middle of the street and looked up into her eyes. Very slowly, his hand went to his lips as if he was wishing. *Or was he taunting her?*

With an arrogant sneer and jerk of her head, she turned and moved away. It seemed an eternity that she fought with herself to keep from returning to look out. When she finally did, all she saw was the outline of his broad back in the distance as he and the burro headed toward Mosquito Gulch. Somehow she was a little disappointed. She didn't know what she had expected— maybe to find him still standing in the middle of the road staring up at her.

Drat him! She didn't need the kind of trouble the big bruiser would bring her. Silver watched him until he disappeared in the distance. Then she went over and picked up the silver-heeled shoes. Like it or not, the half-breed had given her a new nickname. Silver Heels. *What difference would it make a hundred years from now?*

She'd be dead and forgotten a hundred years from now. If she could have done something worthwhile with her life, someone might have remembered her. Thinking of passing time made her think of aging. Silver turned and stared at her reflection.

Your face is your fortune, but otherwise, you're as worthless as your drunken father. Her mother had said it so many times. It must be true.

Cherokee resisted an urge to turn around and look

back over his shoulder at the settlement. If he saw her one more time, he might not be able to resist this overpowering urge to run up the stairs and carry her off kicking and screaming. If he could just have her in his power for a few hours until he got his fill of her beauty and her body, surely he could forget about her. Unsatisfied male lust—that's all it was.

As far as kidnapping her—no doubt the sheriff and a lynch mob of prospectors would come to the rescue. Best he put her out of his mind and get on with his life. Next time it was his turn to come in for supplies, he'd go to another saloon and avoid the Nugget. He'd find some blond whore and take her to bed for a week. With his body satisfied, he could forget the frigid beauty who haunted him now. To hell with Miss Silver Heels!

But despite himself, he couldn't get her off his mind as he led the animal back toward the claim in Mosquito Gulch. Hours passed before he came to the little gully that lay below their crude camp.

Cherokee paused, drinking in the beauty around him. The air felt crisp and cold, the mountains shone with snow. The scent of blue spruce trees drifted on the clean air. He glanced off in the distance. Always a chance for one last blizzard in the early spring. He didn't like the looks of the horizon. Clouds hanging over the silhouetted peaks loomed a threatening gray. What did it matter? He was safely back from his trip. He hoped everything was all right here.

"Bill?" He put his hand to his mouth and shouted again, "Bill?"

Cherokee's elderly partners must be up on the claim.

He hoped nothing had happened to the two old men. Bill was deaf as a rock and limped on a bad leg. Willie had a twisted left hand from an old mining accident. The three of them should put their small store of nuggets in a bank instead of piling it under the woodpile. Even a stupid thief would think to check that favorite hiding spot. But Bill and Willie didn't trust banks.

He saw the reflection of the rifle barrel in the rocks even as he threw up his hand to protest. The bullet took his hat off. Cherokee hit the dirt. *Not only deaf, but half blind, too!* "Bill? For God's sake, don't shoot! Don't you know your own partner?" He lay there in the bottom of the gully, his face pressed into the gravel. "Bill?"

"Cherokee, is that you?" The whiskered face peeked over the ridge.

"Who the hell you think it was?" Cherokee scrambled to his feet, brushing the dirt off his clothes. "If you can't see well enough to recognize me, you should at least be able to see something as big as the burro!"

The old man limped toward him, a sheepish smile on his face. "Sorry about that. I always think it's better to get in the first shot, ask questions later."

Cherokee leaned over, picked up his hat, and examined the bullet hole with a frown. "You better watch out! You accidentally shoot some innocent man, there'll be a lynch party lookin' for you."

Bill spat tobacco juice to one side and leaned on his rifle. "If'fen they ain't got a claim up here, they ain't got no business up here! Now that we've hit some promisin' pay dirt, we'll have claim jumpers nosin' around."

There was no point arguing with the stubborn old coot. Cherokee sighed and slapped him on the back. Both the prospectors had been friends of his father's. It had been

Cherokee's claim, but he needed their expertise and experience to keep things running last autumn while he was off searching for his papa. He'd found him, or at least his grave over in the Nevada diggings. He never did know what became of Lulu, the plump and pretty white whore Papa had run off with. "Let's get on back to the cabin," he said. "I brought you two a few treats."

Bill's face lit up. "I want to hear about everything you saw. Did you blow your whole poke on women like you planned?"

Cherokee hesitated, chagrined. He didn't want to admit he'd used part of it to decorate a pair of dancing slippers for a girl who wouldn't let him touch her. He wasn't even sure how much he would tell the two of the platinum-haired girl. He didn't want to look foolish. "Let's just say I invested it in a bad deal."

The other laughed and slapped his leg. "Lost it in a card game, huh? I swear, Cherokee, that don't sound like you!"

"You just be careful with that rifle." He put his big arm around the stooped shoulders. "You're liable to shoot some innocent hombre."

"Phash! I kin recognize every man jack who has a claim up here from a distance. The others don't have any business nosin' around."

Cherokee started to point out again that Bill had almost shot his own partner, then shrugged and started toward the cabin. He'd have to watch the trigger-happy old man.

The day seemed long to Silver. She looked forward to sundown. There was less time to think when the Nugget

62

held a noisy crowd. But when she put on the silver-heeled slippers, she couldn't keep her mind off the half-breed. That night she danced as she had never danced before and the men shouted in unison: "Silver Heels! Silver Heels! Silver Heels!"

If nothing else, Cherokee Evans had given her a new nickname. She had a feeling the name would stick for a long time.

But later, it was another troubled night for Silver, although she kept her lamp burning brightly. Every time she dozed off, she dreamed of the rugged half-breed. In her dream, she looked into his face and saw her own reflection in his adoring eyes. Then he reached for her, pulling her into his embrace. She woke up shaking. Why had she dreamed of him? Why couldn't she forget him? She hated men. She need never let one hurt and humiliate her ever again.

It was her insecurity, that was all. She was so afraid of losing both her beauty and her money. What would happen to her then? Maybe she needed to buy into something besides a saloon. That way if the Nugget caught fire or business went down, she'd still have something for her old age. Maybe she ought to invest in a claim of her own.

That morning Silver had coffee in the empty saloon with Al and brought it up as casually as she could. "I been thinking, maybe putting all my eggs in one basket isn't such a good idea. Everyone says there's bound to be a civil war. Maybe all the men will go off to fight and no one will come in the Nugget anymore."

Al looked at her a long moment, then poured a big slug of his medicine into his coffee. He stirred it and sipped, not saying anything.

"Al, you oughta lay off that stuff, it'll kill you."

He laughed and winked at her. "I promised my mama I wouldn't touch liquor, Silver, I told you that before. But these bitters have enough alcohol to suit me. Mama didn't say nothin' about taking medicine."

There was no point in pressing the matter further. She never drank anything but coffee herself, wanting to be cold sober at all times—completely in control. At the Velvet Kitten, Brett had forced whiskey down her throat every night before he took her, so she'd be easier to handle.

Al must have read her thoughts. "Forget Chicago. Don't think anything but good thoughts, Silver. You look like you haven't slept a wink."

Silver started to comment that Al didn't look so good either. His face seemed a little gray this morning, then she decided it might be her imagination. "I don't know what I'd do without you, Al."

"Oh, maybe some nice man will come along and take over for me sometime." He said it a little too brightly.

She shook her head, revolted at the thought. "The others aren't like you, Al. You know what a husband would want, don't you?"

"Don't think about it, Silver. I'm here for you as long as you need me. I just keep thinking about the future . . ."

That was something she didn't want to think about. The future meant time passing. Time passing meant aging. Maybe even Al wouldn't love her when she was a wrinkled old lady. That brought her back to her original thought. "I've been considering making some investments so I wouldn't have all my eggs in one basket."

He shrugged. "Nugget seems to be doing fine to me.

What'd you have in mind?"

She tried to look casual. "Maybe a gold claim."

"A gold claim?" His mouth dropped open and he slammed his cup down so that coffee sloshed into the saucer. "Silver, if you want to invest in gold, do it the way Haw Tabor's doin'. He grubstakes miners for a share of their profits. Mark my word, he'll be a rich man someday."

Drat! She might have to do a lot of explaining and she wasn't sure herself why the idea had come to her. "I—I thought I might just buy a claim, you know, hold it for an investment." She sipped her coffee.

"This doesn't sound like you, Silver. You've always been a shrewd businesswoman. Drop this wild idea!" He reached out and patted the back of her hand.

Automatically she jerked away from the touch.

"Sorry, Silver, sometimes I forget and let my feelings for you—"

"I know, Al," she whispered, "it's all right." She owed him everything, but all he wanted was to have her love him as men and women loved each other, and that she was unable to do. She could never love a man like that. She owed Al more than she could ever repay. He had killed a man to rescue her from the Velvet Kitten.

"Where is this claim you want?"

"Oh, I don't know of any in particular." Silver tried to sound casual. "I heard there might be some good diggings up in Mosquito Gulch. Thought I might ride out and take a look."

Al shrugged. "It's the most loco idea I ever heard, Silver, but if you insist, I'll hire a rig and we'll drive up there and—"

"The trail's too rough for a buggy," she interrupted. "I thought I might just hire a horse and ride out there—"

"Alone?" The ugly little man looked thunderstruck. "Do you mean alone?"

Al was right. She must be loco. If she thought about it very long, she'd realize just how crazy the notion was. "Oh, quit acting like the Mother Superior at a nunnery, Al. No one would bother me. All the boys in the area know me."

He only stared at her a long moment. "This ain't like you, Silver. In fact, you ain't been the same in the last couple of days. Take my advice—if you want to invest in mining, do it the way Tabor's doing."

"No, I think I'll ride out there, have a look around—"

"Then I'll go with you."

"You don't know how to ride." She stood up. "Remember I was raised on a farm. I'll be okay."

He sighed heavily. "Is there nothing I can say to stop you, Silver?"

"You know me better than that."

"You're liable to get raped! Think about some filthy animal crawling all over you!"

The thought brought back her past with a shudder. "I can take care of myself. Tell you what, I'll borrow some of your clothes and put my hair up under a hat."

Al stood up, too. "You think with that body you'd fool anyone?"

She was determined to go. Silver stuck her chin out stubbornly. "So I'll wear that oversized jacket of yours."

She saw the anger and frustration in his homely face. "I don't know what's gotten into you, Silver. If you're determined to do this, at least take my shotgun."

66

She started to point out the fact that she was a poor shot, then realized it would start the fuss all over again. "Okay, if it'll make you feel any better, I'll carry the shotgun. Now see if you can find me some clothes to wear."

Later out in front of the livery stable as she swung up on the bay gelding, she began to doubt her own sanity, too. But maybe it wasn't such a loco idea. Men did it all the time—found a sparkle of gold in an outcrop of rock, filed a claim. If it was promising, she wouldn't even have to work it; she could sell it at a profit.

Al looked up at her, then off at the horizon. "Is there nothing I can do to talk you out of this? You see those clouds building over the mountains?" He pointed. "Looks to me like we might get a late snow."

"Oh, you're as worrisome as an old woman. It's early. I'll be back in time for tonight's show."

He handed her his shotgun with evident reluctance. "Somebody might take you for a claim jumper and shoot you."

"Drat it, stop mothering me. I'm just going to ride around a little, I won't be gone but a few hours."

Al reached for his bottle of tonic and took a gulp. "I still think I should go with you."

"Too bad you never learned to ride." She smiled. "You just finish tallying up last night's receipts. I'll be back before dark, and it's barely after breakfast."

"If you aren't back, I'll have the biggest posse in the world out scouring those hills for you."

"You do that." She balanced the shotgun across her

saddle, touched the brim of her hat with two fingers, and rode out.

Cherokee looked at the late afternoon sky and straightened up. His back ached from digging. With warm weather, they'd get more done. The claim was beginning to look a little more promising. "By damn, Willie, where's Bill? I didn't realize he'd quit early."

Willie scratched his long beard with his crippled left hand. "Up at the cabin starting dinner, I hope. Or he might be on lookout. He's worried some claim jumper might come along, find our stash."

Cherokee shook his head in exasperation. "No better than he sees or hears, he's gonna kill some poor devil yet." He looked up at the sky and shivered. "You know, the temperature's dropped considerably in the last few minutes."

A random flake fell on his jacket and he brushed it off. "*Gu-ti-ha.*" And then he remembered that his old friend didn't speak the Cherokee language. "It is snowing."

"I been sayin' it looks like snow," Willie said.

"Hope it's the last one of the season." Cherokee studied the leaden sky. Fat snow clouds piled in layers on the far rim of the mountains. A few more flakes swirled out of the sky.

"Maybe we better quit for the day," Willie said. "Make sure the burro's got plenty of feed and we got enough firewood in case this does turn into something more than a light dusting."

The snow fell faster. "We're in for more than a dusting," Cherokee grumbled, rolling a cigarette. "Looks to me like we might even be gettin' a blizzard."

"It ain't likely, but anything's possible during spring in the Rockies." The old man hefted his pick onto his shoulder.

They started toward the distant cabin, snow swirling more thickly now.

Cherokee puffed his cigarette. "With any luck, Bill's in there makin' stew and coffee for us, not looking for claim jumpers."

Willie guffawed. "Any claim jumper would take one look at that sky and head back to town! I gave Bill that rabbit I shot this morning. Maybe he's made biscuits and some tasty vittles!"

Silver reined her horse in at the bottom of the gully, unsure which way to go. The snowflakes had begun falling on her a few minutes ago and she'd paused, hoping the snow would stop. Instead they were coming thick and fast.

Drat! She brushed at the ones clinging to her over-sized jacket and pulled her hat lower over her eyes for warmth. Al was right. What was she doing out here any-way? She'd better turn around and head back to town in case this turned into a real storm.

Silver reined in the bay uncertainly. On the other hand, it was a long way back to town and she hadn't realized how late the hour was. She'd been too lost in her own thoughts. If she was a little late, there were several girls who could sing and dance a little.

She nudged the gelding forward. Prospectors were always abandoning worthless claims. Maybe she could find a deserted cabin and hole up in it until the weather decided what it was going to do. Al would be frantic, of course, but she'd be better off to find shelter than to try to ride back if this became a hard snow. He'd come looking for her at first light, and while she might be miserable, she had matches in her pockets, and a little food in her saddlebags. She could manage until the storm ended.

Why hadn't she listened to Al? What kind of a fool's errand was she on anyway? It had nothing to do with gold claims, she realized that now. Silver had lied even to herself. She had come looking for that big 'breed. To what purpose? She knew what he wanted to do to her. *Was she crazy?*

She must not panic even though the wind now blew cold against her face. Silver rode across the gully. The lead-colored clouds had blocked out the sun. Fading light reflected off something shiny in the rocks on the other side of the ridge.

"Hallo!" she shouted. "Is anyone around?" But the wind blew her words back into her throat. The sudden temperature plunge frightened her, set her to shivering. *Had she seen a movement behind those trees?*

Silver turned her coat collar up around her ears and hunched down in the saddle. She was not only cold, but more than a little scared. Maybe there was a cave or at least a windbreak up in those rocks ahead. She had to find shelter for her and her mount. The snowflakes drifted so thick and fast, it was difficult to see more than a few feet. She urged the horse forward.

For a moment, she thought she heard a man shout, then dismissed it as the wind. She rode across the gully.

Silver felt the pain cut like fire through the shoulder of

her jacket and slam her backward. She tried to hang on, but the world was spinning around her. *Thunder*, she thought dimly as the horse whinnied and reared. *But why would there be thunder with a snowstorm?*

That was Silver's last conscious thought as the horse threw her and the ground rushed up to meet her.

Chapter Four

Cherokee jerked up, listening to the sound echoing and reechoing through the hills. "What the hell was that?"

Willie looked back at him, mouth half-open. "You don't reckon—?"

"By damn! Do you suppose Bill—" Without finishing his sentence, Cherokee took off at a dead run toward the sound, although the cold wind whipping the snow flurries about him made it hard to pinpoint the source. His heart felt heavy with dread as he ran toward the gully.

It had never seemed so far before. Cherokee's lungs felt on fire as he sucked in the cold air and raced through the underbrush. Behind him, Willie protested that he couldn't keep up and to slow down, but Cherokee didn't slow his pace. It was more likely Bill had shot an innocent passerby rather than a claim jumper. Cherokee had a sudden vision of all the miners in the South Park area taking justice into their own hands and lynching the three of them.

Crazy old coot! Cherokee should have taken the rifle away from him when he had the chance. He topped the rise and stopped, gasping for breath as he took in the scene below. The falling snow made it difficult to see, even if it hadn't been late afternoon. A figure lay sprawled like a dark blotch on the white ground while Bill bent over it, rifle in one hand. On the trail, a bay horse snorted and backed away. A bright splash of blood smeared its withers where the rider must have slid from the saddle.

Behind him, Cherokee heard Willie limping through the brush, protesting that he couldn't keep up. But Cherokee didn't take his gaze off the fallen figure in the snow. Maybe it was a claim jumper; otherwise, why would the man be out here? Still Bill shouldn't have shot him without making sure the stranger was actually doing something wrong.

Cherokee took off down the slope at a run. "Bill, catch that horse! We'll need it to get him into town to a doctor!"

Bill looked up, his face pale as the snow around him. It seemed to be a moment before the words registered. "Honest, Cherokee, I yelled at him to stop and he just kept coming! I thought I'd scare him—"

"Catch the horse!" Cherokee thundered, going to one knee by the slight figure sprawled on its face. He hesitated to turn him over, dreading the fact that the man was almost certainly dead.

Bill stumbled after the horse. But the bay was evidently spooked by the blowing snow and the smell of fresh blood. It snorted nervously and backed away. Cherokee turned his attention to the trespasser who lay sprawled on his face, blood smeared from his jacket to the white snow.

Such a slight build, probably a boy, Cherokee thought

with a mixture of pity and dread. He took one of the limp wrists in his hand, felt for a pulse, then heaved a sigh of relief. "At least he's not dead . . . yet."

He glanced over at Bill edging toward the skitterish horse. "Be careful, Bill! If we're to get him back to town or ride in for a doctor, we need that horse."

Willie arrived just then and the horse reared again, gave one final neigh, and took off back down the trail.

Cherokee jumped up, but it was too late. The three of them watched the horse gallop away.

"By damn! Now what?" Cherokee sighed and knelt by the sprawled body. "He's still alive! We'll take him up to the cabin and see what we can do. Maybe if the horse goes back to town, someone will trail it out here."

"Not likely," Willie grumbled. "I'd say we're in for a full blizzard. In an hour or so, probably won't have any tracks left to follow."

That was true. Cherokee didn't answer as he reached and carefully turned the wounded man over. "Why, it's just a boy! Bill, you've half killed some kid who was maybe just looking for his mama's lost milk cow."

"What's that?" Bill cupped his hand to his ear.

"I said he might have been looking for a lost cow!" Cherokee shouted at the deaf old coot.

"Way out here?" Bill said. "I still think he was hopin' to catch us away from the cabin, steal our poke!"

Willie scratched his beard with his crippled hand. "Maybe he's right, Cherokee. Look, there's a shotgun under him. No kid lookin' for a lost milk cow would be packin' a shotgun." ˙

What was it about that shotgun that looked so familiar to him? He'd probably seen one like it in a store window someplace. "We can't just go around shootin' folks because they get lost near our claim and pack iron—especially a boy. I'll carry him back up to the cabin. We got to at least get him out of the cold!''

Cherokee was amazed at the boy's light weight as he lifted him. But the movement dislodged the boy's hat and it blew away. A cascade of hair almost as light as the snow itself fell free.

''Oh, my God!'' Willie gasped. ''It's Miss Silver! Bill's killed Miss Silver!''

No, it couldn't be. Cherokee stared down into the beautiful face, now pale as death. There was not another so lovely in all the territory, even with the discolored bruise swelling on her temple. *If she died . . .*

The horror of the thought galvanized him into action. With a curse, Cherokee turned his back to the storm, shielding her from the cold wind with his wide frame. He started toward the cabin with long strides.

Behind him, he heard Bill blubber. ''I didn't mean to! She had her hair up under that hat! How was I to know it was a woman?''

Cherokee was too disgusted and horrified to answer. He protected the unconscious girl against his warm chest and kept walking. If she died, the miners wouldn't have to take revenge on the old man. Cherokee would be tempted to do it himself!

God, it was cold! The chill wind took his breath away as Cherokee strode toward the cabin. Snow already blew almost ankle deep around his boots. No, there wouldn't be any tracks left to follow . . . if the horse did head back to town. What was more likely was that the bay would find a windbreak in some brush or fallen trees until the weather let up.

She was warm and soft in his arms—so different from

75

the stiff, prim body she had been when he had carried her across the street. It couldn't be more than another hundred yards to the cabin, but it seemed like miles through the cold. The long blond hair whipped around them both. *If she died . . .*

No, he couldn't even face that possibility. Cherokee felt he had looked for this girl his whole life, and now that he had found her, Fate might conspire to take her from him. He'd never been much on prayer, but he said a few as he struggled through the storm back to the cabin.

Finally it loomed on the horizon with its welcoming warmth, the smoke barely visible from its stone chimney. Cherokee staggered inside with his precious burden. His partners came in behind him and closed the door. Cherokee paused in the middle of the room, grateful for the sudden heat of the blazing fire, the scent of a rabbit stew bubbling in the big iron pot of the fireplace.

Bill's bunk was the nearest one to the fire, so Cherokee carried Silver over to it, gently lay her down, and checked her pulse. Thank God she was still alive!

Behind him, Willie cleared his throat. "Bill, I swear you do the craziest things! How could you shoot Miss Silver?"

"How was I to know it was her?" Bill blubbered. "What was she doin' clear out here anyhow?"

The same question had occurred to Cherokee, but he didn't have time to ponder that now. His anger flared and he had to struggle to keep from getting up and knocking both their heads together. "None of that matters! We've got to have some help, I'm no doctor!"

"Neither are we!" Willie shrugged helplessly. "Didn't you used to help the vet on that plantation you was on?"

"But that was animals," Cherokee snapped over his

shoulder. "I don't know anything about humans and bullet wounds!"

"What?" Bill asked.

Willie shouted Cherokee's words at him.

"Cherokee, you know more than we do." Bill took out his bandana and blew his nose loudly. "Maybe if we could get some of this hot stew in her—"

"With her unconscious?" Cherokee sighed. "You two go ahead and eat. I'll see just how bad it is."

In truth, he didn't want to undress her in front of the two men. It seemed shameful somehow, with her helpless and unconscious. She's just a whore, he told himself, probably hundreds of men have seen her naked body. But he didn't like that thought and it still seemed a rotten thing to do. Maybe he wouldn't have to undress her at all.

"Cherokee, we don't feel none like eatin'," Bill protested.

"Eat anyhow!" he drawled. "You both got chilled out there and I don't need three sick people to look after!"

While the two men got themselves a bowl of stew, Cherokee carried a kettle of hot water over to the cot and reached for his knife. With the oversized, blood-soaked jacket, there was no way of telling whether it was a shoulder wound or close to the heart. In that case . . .

His hands trembled at the thought. His pards were right—whatever help she got until a doctor could get here, Cherokee would have to give her. Gently as he could, he cut the blood-soaked fabric at the shoulder, baring the wound while being careful not to expose her breast. It was a shoulder wound, but with all the blood, he couldn't be sure how bad it was.

Willie brought his bowl over and stood looking down at her. "Will she be all right, Cherokee?"

77

"How should I know? I'll do what I can, but it looks like it's bleeding pretty bad." A sense of dread and impending doom closed over him. Oh, God, if she died right here in his arms . . .

How many times had he wished he had her at his mercy in this cabin? *Be careful what you wish for, you might get it.* No, this wasn't what he had dreamed of at all.

He tore a piece from one of his own clean shirts and tried to wash the blood away, but the wound kept bleeding. At least it looked as if the slug might have gone through. He wouldn't have to deal with the complication of digging a bullet out. Not that he could bring himself to hurt her, even to save her life.

Gently, Cherokee folded the piece of soft cloth and applied light pressure to the wound. "If I can get the bleeding stopped, she'll have a better chance."

Bill stared down at his stew. "Honest, pard, I didn't mean to shoot her. I thought she was some dry-gulcher nosin' around to rob us. Reckon what she's doin' out here?"

"That's the least of my worries right now," Cherokee sighed. "I just wish we'd caught that horse so we could get her into the doctor."

"We got the burro," Willie offered.

Cherokee shook his head. "Not big enough to carry even someone as small as she is. And besides, in the shape she's in, she might die while we were trying to get her to town. By damn! Why don't we even have a wagon?"

He held the cloth against the wound, absently stroking her hair and staring down into the pale face. She moaned softly, deep in her throat, and shrank back against the bed. He remembered then that she didn't like to be touched.

78

Willie cleared his throat. "I got some whiskey, Cherokee. Maybe that will help."

"Right now, I'm open to suggestions," Cherokee said. "Get it!"

Bill sat with his head in his hands. "I reckon the snow will wipe out the tracks so Al and the others can't bring help."

Al. He had forgotten about the short-tempered bartender. Of course that was his shotgun Silver had been carrying. He couldn't imagine why Al had let the girl ride off alone like that. But maybe Al didn't know where she was. What in the hell was she doing way out here alone? If she belonged to Cherokee, he'd never let her out of his sight! What the hell was he thinking of? She was a whore; she belonged to any man who paid for her time.

They needed a doctor. Cherokee stood up, went to the window, and looked out. "It's getting worse."

As if to taunt him, a blast of cold air rattled the windows. At least there was plenty of food here inside, and they could melt snow for water. Firewood lay stacked in the corner near the fireplace. Even the burro was cozy in its shed on the backside of the cabin. Yes, the three men and the burro could manage to ride out the storm, but the girl needed help now.

Cherokee made his decision as he turned away from the window. "I have to make it into town and bring the doctor."

Willie and Bill both made sounds of dismay. "You mean, leave us to try to look after Miss Silver?"

Cherokee shrugged. "Someone's got to."

Willie wrung his hands. "But we don't know nothin' about no doctorin'!"

"Phash! He's right!" Bill protested, "That's something

we don't know nothin' about. Why don't you take care of her and Willie and me'll go for help?''

"You'd never make it," Cherokee sighed, leaning over to check the girl's color with a critical eye. Her fair skin looked starkly white against the scarlet blood that smeared her shoulder. It was bleeding again and she began to shiver.

Cherokee felt her clothing. It was not only dirty, but damp in spots because of the small trickle of water in the gully and the snow that had melted beneath her body before Cherokee picked her up.

Both old-timers stood staring down at the unconscious girl. Bill wiped his eyes again. "I swear I never meant to hurt Miss Silver! Every man in the territory worships her."

Including me, Cherokee thought with sudden realization, but he didn't say that. "I know, Bill," he said, and patted his partner's shoulder. "Everyone'll know you didn't go to do it; you didn't do it apurpose."

"That don't make me feel any better," Bill said. He went over to the window and looked out. "It's gettin' dark out there and the storm's not letting up. It's my fault she's hurt; I'll go for the doctor."

"No," Willie protested, "I'm younger than you, you old coot, and in better shape, too! I'll be the one to go."

"Neither of you have as good a chance as I do of making it," Cherokee argued.

"But she needs someone who knows what he's doing," they said almost in unison.

"Cherokee," Willie said, scratching his straggly beard with his misshapen hand, "why don't you doctor the girl and we'll both go for help."

"No, I can't let you do that. You might not even make

it to town. I couldn't live with myself if anything happened to you two!"

"And can you live with yourself if we stay here where it's warm and safe, and Miss Silver dies?" Bill asked.

What a decision to make. Cherokee looked at him helplessly, unable to deny the logic of his partner's words. What good would it do if Cherokee left her in their clumsy, inept care, and she died while he was bringing back Doc? In that case, Cherokee didn't even think he'd care if that short-tempered watchdog of hers came looking for him with a shotgun.

Al went to the window at the Nugget, stared out a long moment, then checked his watch. The streets of Buckskin Joe were deserted in the bluster of a cold late afternoon. He shouldn't worry so much. Any moment now, Silver would come riding up, and he would scold her for her wild, reckless impulse. He never should have let her go in the first place.

As if he could stop her. No one stopped Silver from doing what she wanted to do. His belly began to hurt again and he took a big swallow of the tonic. The laudanum and the alcohol helped dull the pain that was almost constant now. *Two years at the outside,* the sawbones in Chicago had said. How old was he? Forty-one. He wouldn't live to reach the half-century mark.

It was the day the doctor told him the news that Al made the decision to betray his boss and help Silver. A man ought to do at least one good thing in his life and Al had never regretted his decision. That day had been a little more than a year ago.

Right now, Al didn't feel like he'd make it the full two

years. He felt sweat bead on his forehead at the agony and he almost doubled over as he stumbled to a chair and took another big drink of the tonic.

He'd never told Silver he was dying. His every waking thought these days was occupied by hiding his pain while he tried to make plans to protect her. She would be so alone when he was gone. If only he could find the right man who, like Al, would be content to adore her from a distance, protect and cherish her.

The problem was, every man who saw her wanted to get between her legs, not understanding her terror at a man's touch. Like that big half-breed who had drifted in the other night. Al snorted and wiped his brow. He'd never seen such lust and hunger in a man's eyes. That Cherokee was big enough to protect her, all right, but he was a horse of a man. If he ever got the chance, that Cherokee would ride her like a stallion topping a mare, not caring about anything but satisfying his animal instincts.

Al saw a sudden image in his mind of the two naked together, the big dark body pinning her fragile pale one against a bed. Cherokee would be built big all over, and she was no match for him. With dismay, Al imagined the half-breed covering Silver, meshing his body with hers, ramming deep inside, impaling her against a bed while she beat on his chest and scratched helplessly at his face. Then he would bend his head and put his mouth on Silver's full, ripe breasts. . . .

The image upset him so, he shook his head to clear it, then stared out the window at the snow flurries.

Snow. It had been snowing the first time Al had ever seen Silver, that winter afternoon in Chicago. . . .

*   *   *

Jake Dallinger, the army scout, had found her wandering the streets and brought her to the elegant Victorian mansion. It looked so respectable, but the business inside wasn't.

Brett. Bart Brett. The handsome, black sheep son of a wealthy family owned this place. Al remembered standing in the background in Brett's office, watching the scene.

Jake was the kind of guy who'd steal milk from an orphan's cup, a big, bearded redneck who carried a bull whip coiled on his belt. He kept his hat pulled low to hide the fact that he was half-scalped from a run-in with Indians in his past.

Jake said, "Brett, this here little lady doesn't seem to have anyplace to go, and I knew you was looking for a cleaning girl."

Brett stood up, amusement on his handsome face. "A cleaning girl? Oh, of course, Miss—?"

The slight blonde looked from one to the other. "Uh, Jones. Sylvia Jones," she said.

"Funny," Brett said, "you look Swedish or Norwegian."

"Does it matter?" She seemed nervous and scared.

Al studied her, and decided she was just a kid, not more than seventeen, maybe. If he'd ever found a woman he cared about, who cared about him, Al might have had a daughter this girl's age. When he looked at her, he saw the young, innocent sweetheart every half-grown boy dreams of and usually never gets.

Brett bowed with smooth charm. "Forgive my rudeness, Miss Jones. It just seems that with that dazzling hair, 'Silver' would be more appropriate."

The girl blushed, then smiled, looking at Al with obvious curiosity.

"Oh, forgive me, Miss Jones," Brett said, "this is my right-hand man, Mr. Al Trovato."

The girl curtsied prettily and Al nodded, curious as to how she would react when she realized too late what she had gotten herself into. The elegant mansion was known as the Velvet Kitten, a high-class brothel that catered to an elite, upper-class clientele.

Al had grown hard over the years because of his own past. He'd done time in jail, and had a job unloading crates in a warehouse when Brett first hired him as a bouncer. Gradually, Al had become more than Brett's employee. He was Brett's most trusted confidant. Now behind the girl's back, Brett winked knowingly at him, then at Dallinger.

The scout would get a fat fee for bringing the girl in. An innocent-looking, fragile beauty like this one would put money in Brett's pockets when wealthy businessmen and politicians came in for an evening's amusement.

Brett said, "Miss Jones, did you say you have relatives in Chicago?"

"No. I—I'm an orphan."

Her wide, innocent eyes betrayed that she lied. *A runaway*, Al thought, *that was even better.* In a big city like Chicago, girls disappeared into whorehouses without a trace.

Dallinger pushed his hat back and scratched the bald spot where he'd been scalped. "Like I said, Mr. Brett, I found her on the street, hungry and cold. I told her I knew someone who needed a servant girl and she said she was used to hard work."

"That's true," the girl broke in eagerly. "Oh, Mr. Brett, I can cook and clean. I'd be ever so grateful for the chance!"

Al almost protested, then fell silent. He must be getting soft in his middle age. What did it matter to him what happened to the girl? After all, no one had ever looked out for him much since he'd been left on the orphanage steps in a basket. Whoever left him there didn't even care enough to write a note or give him a name, so the nuns gave him one. *Trovato.* Like the word *trove* as in treasure trove or something found. *A foundling.* It was a name nuns sometimes hung on an illegitimate baby. If it hadn't been for Brett, Al would still be a street tough struggling to survive.

"Then it's settled." Brett stuck his thumbs in his silk vest and beamed at the girl. "I have several other young lady employees. But first, I'll take you to the kitchen and get you something to eat and maybe one of the other girls will give you some clean clothes. Al, will you, ah, take care of Mr. Dallinger and see him out?"

The blonde heaved a sigh of relief, looking out the window at the blowing snow. Al realized she hadn't had any place to go tonight and was certainly hungry. Those wide, innocent eyes betrayed that. When she found out what she was into, she would wish she'd stayed on the street and taken her chances, but after tonight, it would be too late.

Brett escorted the girl out of the room and down the hall of the elegant Victorian mansion.

Al sat on the corner of Brett's desk. "I always thought you were a rat, Dallinger, but I think this is a new low, even for you. God, you stink! Don't you ever take off that smelly fur vest or take a bath?"

The scout laughed and poured himself a drink from the crystal decanter on the polished walnut desk. "Gawd Almighty! You don't hurt my feelings none! If I hadn't found her, she might have ended up in a worse place than this! At least she won't be workin' some cheap crib near the stockyards. Maybe one of the fancy gentlemen will even buy her off Brett!"

"She must be either innocent as some country lamb or desperate to trust the likes of you!" Al got up and went to open the safe.

"Said she hadn't et for two days and was lookin' for work." Dallinger grinned, helping himself to the expensive cigars in the humidor on the desk. "I knew Brett had just the kind of work a beauty like that could do and get me a nice piece of change for bringing her in."

Al didn't say anything as he worked the combination. Why was he objecting? Hell, it was no skin off his nose and his allegiance was to Brett. Because of him, Al had a comfortable room here at the house, plenty of pocket money, and a life of virtual ease, except for an occasional bit of action with his fists. He could even take his choice of the girls when he felt the urge and they wouldn't dare turn him down just because he was ugly. As Brett's right-hand man, Al Trovato was a man of influence and importance. He counted out the money and closed the safe.

"Trovato," Jake drawled, "Brett must sure trust you. You got the combination to his safe and the run of the place?"

Al handed him the money. "He trusts me because I've proved to him I won't let him down. And I'm grateful for everything he's done for me."

Jake Dallinger grunted as he accepted the money and counted it. "Plumb touching! Being a trusted fool and looking out for others is what gets a man in trouble. Do you even get your choice of the women? Now I'd like that!"

86

"Sure," Al said. He was already thinking about the small, innocent blonde. After all, what difference did it make? Women were born to satisfy men's appetites. Here she'd at least get fine clothes, jewelry, and a life of ease. If she'd stayed out on the farm where she so obviously belonged, she'd be spreading her thighs for some oaf of a husband who'd work her into an early grave and put a baby in her belly every year. She'd be better off here.

Jake turned toward the door. "She does look innocent, and trusting, don't she? What do you suppose happened that would cause a beauty like that to run away to the city?"

Al shook his head. "What does it matter? After a few months, she'll be just like the other girls here who have learned to use their bodies to get what they want. We had a pretty brunette last year that some senator went crazy over and paid Brett to let her go. Now she's got a fine house, the best of everything, and even her own carriage."

Jake guffawed. "That purty little blonde ain't gonna feel so lucky for a while." His eyes grew thoughtful. "Reminds me of a gal I was loco over once a long time ago, but she spurned me for some Cheyenne buck named War Bonnet."

Al started to ask more, but the man's expression warned him off. He shrugged. "They're all just alike. Hell, you can't tell one from another in the dark and that's all they're good for anyway."

Dallinger nodded agreement and tucked the money in his smelly fur vest. "I'm just passin' through, had to escort another wagon train out West. I may not see you again soon. But if'fen I'm in the area, I'll be on the lookout for tender, innocent gals for Brett." He looked back over his shoulder longingly. "I don't suppose as slow as things is on a late, cold afternoon, that Brett would let me use one of the gals—"

"Not likely," Al said smoothly, taking him by the elbow and leading him to the ornate front door. "These girls are top of the line, Jake, reserved for the richest, most important men in the city. In the next few weeks, little Silver will end up under a bunch of wealthy businessmen or politicians, who'll pay Brett well for the pleasure."

Jake laughed and went out. Al stood shivering in the doorway, watching the rough, dirty frontiersman as he hunched his shoulders against the blowing snow and went off down the street.

Blowing snow. Al stared out the window of the Nugget and wondered again what had ever happened to the scout. Certainly Al had not seen him again before he and Silver fled many months later.

Silver. Where in God's name was she? Al got up and went to look out the window. The wind whimpered and cried around the corners of the settlement's buildings like a heartbroken woman.

Just as Silver had done when she discovered where she actually was that long ago night. Brett had invited the girl to his private quarters to discuss her "duties." He had told Al in advance to bring a bottle of his best wine and two glasses to his room. Business was slow that evening with the weather so bad.

Hell, she was better off, Al thought as he climbed the stairs, carrying the tray back to the end of the hall and Brett's fancy private quarters. She could be out in the cold on Chicago's streets tonight, freezing and hungry. At least she was warm and fed. And she'd be sleeping on satin sheets in the finest of silk nightgowns. Brett always sampled a new girl's charms first before he put her out for customers' use. Sometimes he took a shine to a girl and kept her for his private pleasure for a week or so before he allowed wealthy men to pay to use her.

Al came into the room and set the bottle and glasses next to Brett's chair. The small blonde sat across from him, twisting her hands together nervously. "Really, Mr. Brett, you're being awfully nice to a hired girl."

Brett laughed and poured two drinks. "Oh, I'm very democratic. After all, Miss Jones, you're going to be like a member of the family the way all my employes are!"

Al sneaked a look at her face. He saw the loneliness there, the eagerness to be loved and accepted. The way Brett looked at her betrayed the fact that he was smitten by her charms. Al had seen it happen before. In a week or two, the boss would tire of her, and she'd be available to any wealthy man who felt his manhood harden when he looked over the merchandise. "Is that all, boss?"

"Sure, Al. You can go. Miss Jones and I are going to have a drink and discuss her duties. See that we're not disturbed."

The girl held up a hand in protest as Brett offered the goblet. "Oh, but I've never—"

"Then you should try it," Brett said smoothly and smiled as he put the glass in her hand. "It's a vintage year. I'd be insulted if you don't join me."

She hesitated, but she took it, looking up at Al uncertainly. He ignored her look and busied himself around the room.

"Al, I said you could go," Brett said a little more pointedly.

Al shrugged and went out. He paused in the hall and heard Brett get up, come to the door, and lock it. Then he heard the girl's voice, slightly nervous and protesting. Brett told her to finish her drink and he didn't sound polite this time.

Al went down to the grandiose parlor where a few gentlemen were beginning to arrive. As always, he looked after all the details, saw to it that the gentlemen had cigars, and took their money. Brett trusted Al with every detail.

"Where's Brett?" one of the girls asked.

"Busy," Al said, "like you should be, making a little money for him."

A gorgeous redhead laughed. "Good old loyal Al! I wonder if Brett knows what a treasure you are."

"I owe him," Al snapped, but his mind was imagining what must be happening upstairs. Brett was a big man—a lusty man—and the girl was small and probably as innocent as she looked. For a long moment, he had a terrible urge to save the girl—to run back up those stairs, bang on the door, and stop Brett.

Al went about his duties mechanically for the rest of the evening. Pity was a new emotion to him. Ugly as he was, even the sisters at the orphanage had not given him the love and warmth he needed. From the age of twelve, he was on his own on the mean streets, doing whatever it took to survive. If Brett hadn't given him a job . . .

To take his mind off the girl, when the place closed down and he'd put the money in the safe and locked up, Al chose a girl at random. Maybe it was only a coincidence that she was blond.

"Aw, Al," the whore complained, "you know how many guys I already had tonight?"

"So what's one more?" He took her by the arm, led her to her room, and used her. She didn't dare complain—not with him being Brett's right-hand man. But he didn't get any pleasure out of it. All he could think of was the young innocent being raped repeatedly tonight.

On the way back to his own room, Al stopped to listen at Brett's door. He heard Brett's snoring and the girl's soft weeping.

Hell, in a few days, she'd get used to the idea and the soft life. There were thousands of overworked factory and farm girls who'd jump at this chance if they had the looks for it.

The next morning, Brett looked up at him thoughtfully from his coffeecup when Al came into the office. There were scratches down his handsome face. Brett was probably madder than hell at the little spitfire.

Al said, "With the holiday season, boss, we have a big convention of cattle brokers in town. One of them specifically asked for a big-breasted blonde if we have one. Should I set him up with that new girl?"

"No," Brett said, reaching up to touch the marks on his face. "She's different, Al."

Al made a noise of derision. "How different can any of them be? You told me yourself not to get emotionally attached to any woman. She's just one of your business assets, that's all. After you've made a nice profit off her, somewhere down the line, some wealthy old codger will decide he can't live without her, and you'll charge him a fortune to take her out of here."

Brett stared into space. "You're right, Al. I know I should listen to you; you always look after my best interests. But for a while anyway, she's not to be touched by any customer—not at any price."

Al shrugged. "Okay. It's your financial loss until you come to your senses."

"Take some coffee up to my room for her. She ought to be up by now."

"Can't one of the maids do it?" Somehow he didn't want to see the girl this morning. He had a feeling he couldn't look her in the eye. Shame and pity were new experiences for Al.

Brett ignored him, staring into space like a lovesick, half-grown boy. "And Al, call some of the better stores, have them bring over some things for her to chose from, you know, furs, jewels, the works."

Al whistled softly. "Boss, remember, she's just merchandise. How special can she be?"

Brett just stared down at his desk. "There's something different about her. I don't know. Maybe in a few weeks, this feeling will wear off. I never felt this way about a girl before."

There wasn't any point in discussing it, Al thought with a shrug of his wide shoulders. Brett would get over it. Al took the tray upstairs.

She sat wrapped in one of Brett's expensive velvet smoking jackets, staring out the window. Al put the tray on the table next to her chair. Her cheap dress, torn down the front, lay thrown across the foot of the bed.

Al said, "You're lucky, you know. First time I've seen him so smitten by a girl. You can have anything in the world you want if you play your cards right."

She looked up at him, still spunky, but wounded, her tear-filled eyes as haunted as her soul. "What I want is to leave."

"Don't be a fool! He's not going to let you go. That flawless face just bought you a chance most farm girls would never get."

"Then why don't I feel lucky?" She got up, went to the mirror over the bureau, and stared at her reflection. "Ma always said I was worthless except for my looks."

Al went to the door. "Your looks can't last forever. Take advantage of this situation. Brett is the black sheep son of a fine family. He's rich, handsome, a man of power. You could do worse."

"Stop telling me how lucky I am!" She whirled on him, eyes blazing. "If I hadn't been pretty, that Dallinger wouldn't have brought me here!"

"No, you'd be freezing to death on the streets. You'll learn to trust no one."

"Brett trusts you."

Al shrugged. "It's in my best interests to be reliable. Besides I owe Brett for taking me off the streets, giving me the good life. It'll only last as long as he can trust me to look out for his interests." He went to the door. "Oh, by the way, there'll be messengers here later with all sorts of jewels and clothes for you to choose from. Your beauty has bought all this for you—remember that. And it won't last forever."

"My beauty—that's all I've got. That's all any man wants from me." She stared at her reflection in the mirrow and her eyes were hard, expressionless. "My face is my fortune—that's what Ma said. Then why don't I feel rich and lucky?"

She picked up a gold-handled hair brush and crashed the mirror into a thousand silvers of glass, then collapsed in a chair and wept.

Why did he feel like such a rotten skunk? Brett was right;

this girl was different. With a sigh, Al left the room, closing the door softly behind him.

As the weeks passed, Al watched her, waiting for Brett to tire of her and put her to entertaining customers. A number of wealthy men had seen her, had asked about when Silver would be available.

"When the boss gets tired of her, just like the last one," Al answered mechanically.

What he hadn't counted on was that Bart Brett would fall madly in love with Silver and ask her to marry him. Or that he himself would finally care so much about the fragile blonde that he would be driven to betrayal, robbery, and murder to rescue Silver from the Velvet Kitten.

Chapter Five

Cherokee looked from the girl's ashen face to the snow falling outside the cabin window. *U-nu-tsi.* Snow. It was damned if you do, damned if you don't, he thought. They didn't have a wagon, and he could hardly walk into Buckskin Joe carrying her all the way. The weather was getting worse. He had to make a decision now. Reluctantly he turned to the two old men. "Do you two think you can make it to town and bring back the doctor?"

"By cracky, shore!" Willie said. "Bill, get your coat and a knapsack of food, and let's get out of here before the afternoon gets any older."

Cherokee helped them get their gear together. "You think you can find your way?"

Bill leaned closer to catch the words. "Phash! Ain't we been to town a couple of dozen times? We got a compass, and besides, once we get within a mile, we'll be able to see the lights of the town."

He sounded more confident than he looked, Cherokee thought. Colorado Territory was the kind of country where a man got lost in a storm and his remains weren't found until the spring thaw.

Silver moaned a little and Cherokee knelt beside her bunk. "It's all right, Silver. You're okay now." Without thinking, he stroked her hair back from her face and she seemed to shrink against the pillow. He remembered again that she didn't like to be touched.

Bill shook his head. "Our talk is disturbin' her. I never meant to hurt her. Every man in the Rockies would die for Miss Silver."

"She must know that," Cherokee said gently, standing up. "Neither one of you would hurt a flea."

Bill wiped his face on his sleeve. "There's just been so much claim jumping and gold stealin' around these parts."

"You two could put yours in the bank in town like I did," Cherokee said.

"Nope." Willie combed his beard with his crippled hand. "I had my money in a bank once. It went broke and took everybody's money with it. I'll take my chances hidin' it in the woodpile and outsmartin' robbers, thank you."

"We're wasting time," Bill said and opened the door. Cold wind blew in. "It may be morning before we can get back with help, pard."

Cherokee looked at the swirling snow outside. "If this keeps up, no one will be able to get back through the drifts. This country's so unpredictable in the early spring."

By damn, he hated to send them out in this weather! "Maybe her horse will go back to the stable and a search party will start out."

Bill leaned forward, his hand behind his ear to catch the words. "Phash! You can't count on that. The horse may find shelter out of the wind and not go home for days. There ain't no other answer, Cherokee, face it—someone's got to go for help and it's got to be us! Now shut the door behind us, you're wastin' precious heat!"

The two went out and Cherokee closed the door, walked to the window, and watched. The pair trudged down the trail and out of sight.

The girl whimpered and he went over to her, realizing the room was chilly now. He got more wood and built the fire up. Still she shivered. He got extra blankets off the other beds, covered her, and checked the wound. It looked like it was still bleeding. He held her wrist and her pulse seemed weak to him. *Suppose she was dying? Was her heart still beating?*

He slid his hand under the cover and put it on her breast. Her breasts were large and firm and warm. Immediately, she seemed to pull away from him. "No," she whispered, "please no . . ."

"Silver, you're all right." He took his hand away. "I won't hurt you. I would never hurt you."

He felt guilty as hell. When he had his hand cupping her breast, all he could think of was sucking that nipple until she arched up under him and opened her thighs wide to accept him. He wanted to make love to her, he thought, but he would never hurt her. There was something not quite right about a saloon whore afraid of a man's touch. Surely she was used to men pawing her breasts when they used her for their pleasure.

Yet she looked so small and defenseless lying here. He brushed her hair away from her bruised forehead. "You'll be fine, sweet darlin', sweet Silver," he murmured. "No one's going to hurt you. They'd answer to me if they do."

She shivered again and he remembered that her clothes were damp. He'd never get her warm unless he got those wet things off her. Very gently, he pulled back the covers and got a knife. He wasn't going to disturb her trying to lift her out of those clothes. He took the knife, cut the shirt and pants away, and bared her body to the firelight.

What a beauty! She was small for a woman, narrow enough in the waist to span with his two big hands, but big breasted and wide-hipped. She was meant to mother a brood of children—or pleasure men.

He felt himself throb with desire just looking at her creamy body, then he chided himself. What kind of man was he that he could look at an injured, unconscious woman and all he could think about was how he would like to make love to her? Her full breasts moved with the effort of breathing and the hollow of her belly looked so inviting, he had to force himself not to lean over and kiss her there.

Silver moaned and thrashed about. Immediately he put out a restraining hand and she jerked away. "Silver, I won't hurt you; I won't let anyone hurt you. You're safe with me. You've got my word on that."

And then he cursed himself for his slip of the tongue. When he gave his word, he kept it. Well, she was safe until she consented and later, when she was well, he'd work on that. He bandaged her shoulder, pulled the damp clothes out from under her, and spread the blankets over her. What else should he do? He was no doctor, but he had helped the vet a little when he'd doctored Shawn O'Bannion's fancy Tennessee Walking horses on the Shannon Place plantation.

He got a bottle of whiskey out and trickled a spoonful

between her lips. "No," she whispered, "no, Bart."

Who the hell was Bart? Cherokee shrugged and trickled a little more between her lips. She became even more agitated, mumbling and thrashing about in fear. Whatever good the spirits might do her was being canceled by the frightening memory the taste of liquor brought to her delirious mind. He gave up and looked at the bottle a long moment. Whiskey had never looked so good to him as it did at this moment. But he had sworn never to touch it again after what had happened that night when another blond beauty had gotten him drunk at Shawn's country place.

Silver didn't seem so completely unconscious now. Maybe he could get a little broth in her. His big fear was that he would cause her to choke. Gently, he turned her head to one side, put a few drops of broth between her lips, and watched her. It seemed to trickle down her throat and she swallowed. Good. Anything would help to raise her strength and get her warm. He spent over an hour putting broth in her mouth, a few drops at a time. Then finally, he ate a plate of stew himself.

It was dusk now and the storm seemed fiercer than before. The wind rattled the windows as if it were a monster trying to get inside. Cherokee went over and looked out. It was snowing hard and blowing in drifts through the trees outside the cabin. He cursed, feeling both helpless and guilty. Two old men were out in this trying to make it into town and here he was inside safe and warm.

The room was almost dark. Silver roused and murmured, obviously disturbed about something. He'd better check that wound again and make sure it had stopped bleeding. When he brought the lamp over by her bunk, she seemed to relax immediately and he put the lamp down on the crate by her bed. Was she afraid of the dark? And if so, why? There were a lot of things about this girl that mystified and intrigued him. He pulled the blanket back to check the bandage. Her creamy breasts moved as she breathed. Cherokee had to fight the urge to reach out and cup that fullness with his hand, stroke that rosebud pink nipple. He had just given her his word. Did it count if she didn't hear it said?

I heard it said, he chided himself without thinking. Of course he wouldn't touch a wounded, helpless girl, but when her shoulder healed, he'd pay her whatever it took to let him lie on that smooth belly and kiss those breasts. Surely her reluctance was an act to lure men into paying more for her favors.

"Okay, sweet Silver," he said softly, "you win. Whatever money I got, you can have. Just once—that's all I ask—and then maybe I'll see you're just a female after all, just like all the rest."

Only she wasn't like all the rest. He'd never met anyone like her before—soft, vulnerable mouth, eyes hard as ice. He wondered again where she'd come from, what her past was, and how that bartender figured into the picture. A girl as beautiful as this one didn't have to sleep with an ugly ape like Al; she could have her choice of men.

He sat down on the floor by her bed, watching her face in the glow of the lamp light. After his father had deserted his mother for that saloon girl, his Indian grandmother had said all white women were whores. Cherokee had believed everything the old woman told him because she had looked after him, and was the only one in the world who cared about him. *E-li-si.* My grandmother, he

100

thought in his language. Most of the others of their tribe had been taken away by force to walk the Trail of Tears to Indian Territory.

But Silver didn't look like a whore. Asleep with her pale hair spread out on the pillow around her, she looked like a little girl or a wounded angel. His body was tired and cramped from sitting here, but he was afraid to go to bed. Suppose she took a turn for the worse or needed something in the middle of the night?

He reached out and took a strand of hair between his fingers. Fine as silk and the color of silver. He had a sudden vision of himself tangling his fingers in that hair as he took her. Then he was ashamed that he could think such thoughts about a defenseless girl. He had been a long time without a woman and his groin ached with need. But he had promised to look out for her and he had given his word.

By damn! What a stupid fool he had been to promise that when she was in his power and he could do anything he wanted to her. But if the boys were lucky, there'd be a rescue team on its way here tomorrow and she'd be safe back under Al's shotgun tomorrow night while she recuperated in her room at the Nugget.

He got up and went to the window. Had the boys made it okay? For an instant, he was tempted to go looking for them, but he couldn't leave her alone. His partners had been in this country awhile and were seasoned frontiersmen. If the weather got too bad, they might find shelter in the lee of a hill or brush pile and wait the storm out. There wasn't any way for Cherokee to know what was going on out there. And if it kept snowing like it was doing now, a rescue team couldn't get back up here through the drifts even if the boys made it into town.

101

He went back and stood looking down at her. The two of them might end up isolated here for days as her wound healed. *How could he handle her naked body, look at her beauty, and not break his word?*

With a loud sigh, he sat back down on the floor by her bed. He wanted very much to take her hand, to comfort her. But he didn't. She must be in pain and he wished he could bear it for her. Somehow, he wanted to put himself between everything and anyone who threatened her security or made her unhappy.

You must be loco, Cherokee, he thought. Why are you getting so protective and possessive about a saloon whore just because she's small and hurt and helpless? She's not yours to worry about. He wanted to take her in his arms and hold her against his chest, assure her that whatever it was in her past that scared her, made her afraid of the dark and being touched, he wouldn't let it get her.

"You're safe, Silver," he whispered. "No one or nothing is ever going to hurt you again, not as long as I have the strength to raise a hand to stop it!"

She didn't move, and without thinking, he reached out and took her small hand in his. Immediately, the unconscious girl began to thrash and pull away.

By damn! He'd forgotten. Cherokee tucked her hand under the covers. He must remember not to touch her. She was afraid of being handled. Her soft, full lips looked so inviting, but he must resist the urge. He was going to be her protector, not her rapist. A frown crossed her face and she mumbled something, obviously disturbed. *What was she thinking? What kind of thoughts did she have?* Maybe she was imagining that she was shot and falling again. There was nothing he could do but sit here on the floor by her bed and watch her, and hope his partners

102

were even now walking into the Nugget and organizing a rescue mission.

That Al would be fit to be tied, Cherokee thought, but after all, it hadn't been Cherokee's doing. The whole thing had been an accident.

She whimpered again in her sleep and Cherokee moved the lamp closer to comfort her. He wondered if she was in much pain and wished he could do something about it. Even if she didn't drink, a little liquor would numb her pain. He got the bottle again and spooned a little between her lips.

Silver shook her head. "No, Bart. Please don't . . . I won't fight you tonight . . . no whiskey . . ."

She was afraid, and pleading. Cherokee put the bottle down and clenched his big fists. Whoever this Bart bastard was, Cherokee wished he could get his hands on him. Rage flowed through his veins at the thought of anyone making Silver beg that way. She sounded so alone, so afraid.

And he was no better than the bastard who had hurt her, Cherokee thought with shame. All he'd thought of since the first moment he'd seen her was how he could get her under him, if he had to kidnap her to do it. He'd fantasized about what it would be like to carry her off to this isolated cabin and have her at his mercy, and now he felt like the world's worst heel.

In her dreams, Bart Brett handed her a goblet. "Here, drink up."

She took it, her hand trembling. "Does this mean I have to get in your bed again?"

His handsome face turned dark with anger. "A lot of

103

women would like to change places with you, baby! You've been here a couple of months now and I've been patient, and good to you."

She looked up at him from her chair by the fire in his bedroom. "You've bought me fancy clothes and jewels. And almost every night, you expect me to get in your bed, spread my thighs, and let you—"

"If you were married, you'd have to let some other man do that to you. Some women even like it, Silver. What happened in your past before Dallinger brought you to me?"

She thought about her stepfather and shivered. "I don't want to talk about it. If you'd use a little tenderness, and be patient—"

"Be patient!" he stormed. "Ain't I been? Look, Silver, you're mine; you might as well get used to the idea. I'm rich and powerful. I pay off a lot of people. No Prince Charming on a white horse is gonna ride in here and rescue you, so you might as well make the best of the situation. All I'm asking is a little response." He pulled her negligee open and put his hand on her breast.

Silver closed her eyes and trembled.

"Damn it!" he swore, and stood up. "I hate it when you pull away from me like that," he growled, lighting a cigar. "You've made a fool of me, Silver. I never let a woman do that to me before."

She looked at her hands in her lap. "I don't mean to make a fool of you, Bart. All I want is out of here."

"And away from me?" He crossed the room, leaned on the fireplace with both hands, and stared into the flames.

She didn't answer, knowing the truth would infuriate him.

"You know why Jake brought you here? You know

104

what you would be doing tonight if I hadn't taken a fancy to you? There's fifty rich, fat men in this town who keep asking when I'm putting you up for my clientele's use. How would you like to have to let dozens of strangers ram into you every night? I'm tempted to do that; it would serve you right."

"Do you want me in your bed now?" she sighed. The sooner she did it, the sooner it would be over with.

Burt cursed. "Okay, if that's the way it's got to be." He threw the cigar into the fireplace, came over, caught her arm, and dragged her to her feet. "I got no pride where you're concerned, Silver, or I'd deny myself the use of that ripe body and let my customers have at you!"

He dragged her over to the bed and ripped the night-gown down the front. "God, you have the most flawless face, the most beautiful body I ever saw!" He pushed her down on the bed.

At that moment, she longed for a man who would really love her, even if she weren't pretty—a man who would take her in his arms and talk softly, kiss her gently. A man who would protect her against the darkness and all the terror it brought. A man who would love her without insisting on making her take his hard manhood inside her. She was always so dry and rigid with fear because the act hurt so much.

Bart knew she didn't like being touched, so he ran his hands over her roughly every chance he got. And then he would spread her out, hold on to her breasts, and use her until he was sated.

She lived in a satin and jeweled hell.

Al had seemed sympathetic to her when he'd found her weeping one day. "Silver, I'm warning you, you can't keep this up. Bart Brett is a proud man and you could do worse. At least pretend to care about him. Pretend some passion."

She looked up at him through her tears. "I'm not a very good liar."

"How are you as a whore?" he said. "When Bart finally loses interest in you, you'll be servicing a couple of dozen men a night, not just Brett. Think about that."

"You seem like such a nice guy to be working for him," she said.

Al colored. "Brett's the nearest thing I got to a friend and he pays me well."

But Bart Brett didn't lose interest in Silver. Maybe it was the challenge of having a woman who didn't want him when every girl in the house hinted they would gladly take Silver's place. Months passed. Brett continued to make use of her body whenever he felt the need. After a while, she didn't fight him anymore. She didn't respond at all.

"Damn it, Silver!" he would shout. "Fight me, love me back, just react in some way! I feel like I'm making love to a beautiful dead woman!"

"I am dead in spirit," she said, and responded even less because her soul felt so crushed and because it was the only way she knew to fight back. Silver couldn't escape and she had too much pride to let him conquer her. Her revenge was engendering the rage he felt at not being able to reach her soul or make her respond to him.

Brett took her driving in his fine carriage, even dressed her up and escorted her to the theater. Men commented on her beauty and Brett displayed her like some lovely rare pet. He was at his zenith during these times, preening like a peacock while other men lusted after the beauty he owned.

Early on, Silver thought about running away on these outings or simply screaming for help. But she had a feeling no one would help her. Bart Brett was a powerful man with much influence and she couldn't escape the silken prison he had made for her. She felt like a pet in a golden cage or a slave girl in a harem. The rest of the time, she never left Brett's rooms at the big Victorian house. She made no friends with the girls of the establishment. Most seemed coarse and vulgar to the little farm girl, and they were all jealous of her place in Brett's affections, making envious comments to her.

Bart Brett even tried forcing Silver to drink liquor before he took her to bed. If she wouldn't drink it, he pried her mouth open and forced it down. Then she either swallowed or choked.

"This'll lessen your inhibitions," he snarled, "maybe you'll respond to me instead of acting like a lovely corpse."

What might have made her respond was gentleness, tenderness, a feeling of sincere caring rather than lust for her voluptuous body, but of course she didn't say that because she wasn't sure he was capable of dealing with that kind of response. Half the time when he dragged her to bed, she was half drunk as well as wet with the spilled liquor. It made her feel degraded, but at least the pain wasn't so bad.

The more frustration he displayed, the more determined she was that he would never get the response he wanted from her. He could use her body, but he could never break her spirit.

Months passed. She saw the leaves turn brown then

107

blow away with winter's coming. Silver knew everyone in the house whispered that she had become his obsession and that the master now was the slave. It didn't matter to her. Nothing mattered except escaping this place and Bart Brett's bed. He began to drink heavily.

And one night, he got drunk and wept. "What does it take to get through to you, Silver? What does it take to make you come into my arms the way I want you to?"

She toyed with a button on her negligee, not knowing what answer he wanted to hear. Maybe someday she could love a man if he was kind and gentle with her and loved her for some other reason besides her beauty. But Bart Brett was not that man.

"Look," he said, kneeling before her chair, "look, I'll marry you. Is that what you want? You want the ring and the whole thing? Is that what you're holding out for?"

"Marriage?" She looked at him blankly. The thought had never occurred to her.

"I've never told you this, but I'm from a very rich and prominent family." He took her hand between both of his. "My brother Lon and I are the black sheep, but the rest of the family is highly respectable."

She simply stared at him, feeling nothing, registering nothing.

He must have taken her silence for interest. "Look"— he squeezed her hand—"I'll sell this place. We'll close the door on all this and go back East where I come from. No one need know anything. You could be part of the best society there, Silver. I'll invent a past for you. With your beauty, you could be the most talked about, admired wife of the social set."

Her beauty. Always her beauty.

"Bart, you know someday my beauty will fade. I wonder if you will care for me when I am wrinkled and old."

The idea must never have occurred to him. "Let's not even think about that," he said eagerly. "That's a long time away. I can't even imagine you not being the flawless beauty you are, Silver. That's what I love the most about you, you know."

She knew. It was what Elmer Neeley had loved and lusted after, too. Ma had been right; she was worthless without her pretty face. Was there no man anywhere who would love her for any other reason? Who would love her when her beauty faded?

The only other person Silver ever saw and talked to was the ugly Italian whom Brett trusted more than anyone in the world. She sensed that Al pitied her, admired her spunkiness, was maybe even drawn to her. But he was loyal as a watch dog to Bart Brett. The one time she did manage to slip out the door and make it as far as the train station before Al caught up with her and returned her to the mansion, she sensed almost a shame on his part as they got inside the elegant carriage and she wept all the way back.

Al began to look a little gray, a little drawn.

"You ought to see a doctor," she said. "What would Brett do if something happened to you and there wasn't anyone around to lick his boots, run his errands, and count his money for him?"

The ugly Italian colored. "You got no right to talk to me like that. If you were mine, I wouldn't let you go either."

It was then she realized that Al was in love with her;

109

she saw it in his eyes and he saw at that moment that she had guessed his secret.

"You love me, don't you," she said quietly.

"What does it matter?" he snapped defensively. "Every man who sees you loves you."

"Not loves me, *wants* me," Silver sighed. "There's a difference. If you love me, Al, doesn't it bother you that he pours liquor down my throat and forces himself on me a couple of times a night?"

He stood there, his powerful shoulders shaking, his fists clenched. "So much that I could kill him for it," he whispered through clenched teeth. "A beauty like you should be put up on a pedestal, and adored and worshiped. If you were mine, I wouldn't expect you to let me make love to you—not an ugly bastard like me."

"Thanks for the kind thought, Al." Without thinking, Silver reached out and patted his arm. He pulled away as if she had touched him with a hot poker.

"I am Bart Brett's right-hand man," he said "and that's where my loyalty lies. I'll forget we had this conversation."

"Drat it all! I didn't really expect any help," she said. "You just seemed nicer than most men I've met, Al. I thought you might want to do one noble thing in your whole life."

Al looked a little grayer, his features more pinched with each day. He took to carrying a bottle of bitters and sipped on it often.

"What's with you?" she asked him one afternoon.

"I just remembered lately that I promised my old mother I wouldn't drink whiskey, but this has a high alcohol content."

110

"I thought you were an orphan and since when don't you drink?"

There was something about his veiled expression that made her suspect he was hiding something from her. Maybe not. What difference did it make?

Al had come up to ask if she would like to see some fine jewels that an elegant store wanted to send out on approval. She shook her head. In all this time, Silver had become a connoisseur of fine jewelry, but she cared little about it. Brett used gems to display her, to make other men envy him his beautiful pet.

Al started to leave the room, then hesitated. "Silver, do you—do you believe in God?"

She was taken aback. "Of course I do. That's a strange comment from you. What brought this on?"

He took the bitters bottle from his pocket and took a big swig. "Oh, I don't know." He sounded a little bit too careless. "Something that's come up lately made me think about it. It's occurred to me I never did anything noble in my whole life—you know, where there wasn't something in it for me."

Silver shrugged. "That's the way the world works."

"It shouldn't. We might be held accountable."

She looked at him, puzzled. "I don't understand what you're driving at."

He seemed to be carrying on some inner struggle. "I'm going to help you get out of here."

She didn't dare to hope and she couldn't be dishonest with him. "Al, I won't be your mistress either."

He laughed. "An ugly guy like me and a beauty like you? I wouldn't expect that. It would be enough just to be close to you, to look at you."

111

She had been through too much despair to hope. Maybe she even thought it was a trick. "What are you planning?"

"Don't ask," he said softly. "The less you know, the better off you'll be."

"Al, you've got a good place with Brett. You'd be throwing it all away to help me. Why?"

He paused, his hand on the doorknob. "Let's just say I never done nothing noble in my whole life and I might not get another chance. And my life . . . well, it's not worth much. If anything happened to me, I wouldn't want to think I left you a prisoner in this place. You matter to me, Silver, you matter a lot."

Things were much the same as the days passed and she said nothing to Al about it. Maybe he had only been tormenting her; maybe he had thought it over and realized how much he had to lose and how little he had to gain.

When it finally happened, Silver was not expecting it, but evidently Al had planned it down to the last detail. It was late at night, all the customers had gone, and the house was quiet and asleep—except for her and Brett. He was very drunk and using her brutally. Silver lay across the bed while he raped her, his back to the door.

She saw the door open and was too frightened to do anything but watch Al come in. Brett was deep in the throes of passion, his mouth all over her breasts as he rode her body.

Al came up behind him, anger and disgust etched on his homely face. In that split second, one of his hands went over Brett's mouth and Al jerked him back with a snap of his powerful arms. She thought she heard Brett's neck break as he went limp in Al's hands.

For a moment, they could only both stare with disbelief at the still form and then Al let it fall on the bed.

"Oh my God, Al, I think you've killed him!"

"I meant to! When I saw what he was doing to you— never mind, get dressed, we've got a train to catch."

She clutched her gown to her heaving breasts, staring at the limp body. "You broke his neck! I didn't know you were going to kill him." She began to weep.

"Silver, I'd do it again to get you out of here." He grabbed her arm, his hands trembling. "Get dressed. I've got everything planned."

She felt so numb, it was all she could do to get up and get dressed while Al threw a few of her things, including her jewels, in a bag.

"Silver, you may not care about these, but remember jewels can give you as much security as money." He took her arm and led her out of the house into the night.

It was a blur from then until she found herself on a train headed away from Chicago. "Where—where are we going?"

"We'll catch a stagecoach later. There's boomtowns aplenty out West and I know a little about running a saloon; Brett taught me."

"Brett had power and influence; they'll be looking for us."

"Let them look." His face was pale and grim with determination.

"We can't run very far with no money," she argued.

"We got money; a whole valise full. Did you forget I have the combination to Brett's safe?"

Silver was horrified. "You robbed him?"

He smiled without mirth. "It was dirty money—illegal

113

money from prostitutes and gambling."

"Oh, Al, how could you have done this? He was your friend. Brett trusted you."

Al looked out the window at the passing scene. "Judas betrayed his friend, too. This is something I have to live with, Silver, it's not on your conscience. To help you, I'd do it all over again."

She leaned back in the seat, totally drained and exhausted. "I never dreamed you intended murder and robbery."

"That's why I didn't tell you. At heart, you're a good person, Silver. You would have tried to stop me."

She closed her eyes and wept softly.

"Don't, Silver," Al whispered, "it's all right now. You don't ever have to let a man put his hands on you again. If I get to see you every day, that'll be enough for me."

Days later, they stepped off a stagecoach in the town Al had chosen—a raw boomtown in the Rockies. Al bought a saloon and put it in her name. At first she expected to see the law turn up on the doorstep. But months passed and nothing happened. She was safe finally—Al's shotgun saw to that.

She opened her eyes slowly. Her shoulder felt as if it were on fire. *Where was she?* This wasn't her room at the Nugget, it was a log cabin. *What was she doing here?* The last thing she remembered was riding across that gully and the sound of thunder before pain flashed through her body and she fell from her saddle.

"Silver, are you awake?"

She looked up into the dark, rugged face of Cherokee

114

Evans. "What . . . what happened? Where is every-one?"

His big fingers touched her face ever so gently. "You've been shot. My pards have gone for help."

Panic welled up in her. "We're—we're here alone?"

"Alone," he nodded.

She had not been so afraid since the night Al had killed Brett. She saw that look in Cherokee's eyes. He wanted her body as Bart Brett had wanted it. She wasn't safe any-more!

Chapter Six

Silver stared up at him, a little delirious. She had never felt so hot before. Maybe she was having a nightmare. Or maybe she'd died and ended up in hell. She would close her eyes and wish it all away. When she opened them again, she would be safe in her bed at the Nugget with the door double-locked and the light burning by her bedside.

She was afraid of that big half-breed; that was why he had come into her nightmare. The way he had looked at her in the Nugget let her know what he wanted from her—as all men did. Only he looked bigger and more virile than the others, so he would hurt her more. Somewhere, she heard the wind howling. It sounded lonely and cold. *Then why was she so hot?*

She managed to run the tip of her tongue along her dry lips. "Hot . . ." she murmured. "So very hot."

A man's voice said, "Would snow taste good?"

Snow. So many memories about snow. She was a little girl laughing and playing in the snow with her daddy— her *real* daddy. They made snow ice cream, all frosty and sweet on the tongue while Ma complained about them

116

wasting the precious sugar. He pulled her on a sled and they laughed and made angels by lying on their backs and moving their arms up and down.

"Snow," she whispered, "yes, snow."

And miracle of miracles, there it was on her lips and tongue, so cold and good, melting and trickling into her mouth. But her body was still hot. She squirmed in misery, remembering the hard work in the broiling heat of the farm. "Hot," she said again.

She must be in bed; someone was pulling back the covers. Then there was cool water on her feverish skin and she smiled in her sleep.

"Feel good?" a man asked.

She didn't open her eyes; she was afraid of what she would see. She dreamed she was swimming naked in the cool creek that ran through the farm. It felt so good and it was so naughty. Ma told her it was. When she caught her at it, Ma whipped her and whipped her with a peach tree switch, leaving little red welts all over her small bottom.

She would not think about that now. She would enjoy swimming in the cool water that felt so good on her feverish skin until Ma came to scold her.

Cherokee paused in sponging the girl's feverish body. She was smiling in her unconscious state. Her fever had risen and he didn't know what to do except put bits of snow between her lips and sponge her naked body down with cool water.

Be careful what you wish for, you might get it. He smiled ruefully, remembering something his friend Shawn had said one time. Cherokee had the girl in his power, all right, just like he had dreamed of. That was as far as it

117

went. He wasn't enough of a monster to rape an unconscious girl, and more than that, he was worried about the fever that made her skin shine with perspiration.

What a beauty she was! He studied her closely as he sponged her skin all over, feeling a little guilty that she was helpless to escape his eyes—but not guilty enough not to look at her as he wrung the cloth out and began at her breasts and worked his way down her body to her toes all over again.

He'd bet she didn't weigh more than a hundred pounds. Maybe not even that. He had the most uncontrollable urge to kiss her belly, her mound, and the deep cleft between her breasts, but he didn't. She might wake up and she'd be terrified. *Why was he feeling so protective of her?* A white woman had stolen his father and made his Indian mother weep. An elegant pale-skinned beauty with yellow hair had caused Cherokee to betray the best friend a man ever had. They were all alike, these white women. No matter what they appeared to be, they were all whores at heart.

It was a long night and he never left Silver's side. Cherokee's back ached from leaning over her, sponging her endlessly. At last the fever seemed to fade and she slept peacefully. He'd had no sleep at all and his head hurt.

One of her small hands was out from under the covers. He took it in his and kissed the palm, the way his Cherokee grandmother used to when he was a frightened little boy after the soldiers had taken his mother away. "Here's a treasure to keep," he whispered and folded her fingers over her palm. "Take it out when you need it

118

and know I love you."

She slept all morning, but he never closed his eyes. Cherokee stayed by her bed, afraid she might wake up and need something, or be frightened and he wanted to reassure her that everything was all right. Finally he couldn't help sitting on the floor by her bed, laying his head against the blanket and dozing off.

Silver came awake with a start. *Where was she?* Who was that with his face next to her hand? She felt so weak, she wasn't sure she could move. "What . . . happened?"

Cherokee Evans jerked awake. "That fever down?"

"What happened?"

"You came riding across the gully and my deaf old partner thought you were a dry-gulcher. He shot you."

She craned her neck to look around the cabin. "How long have I been—"

"Here?" He brushed her hair out of her eyes and she pulled away from his touch. "Sorry, Silver. I want to touch you so bad, I keep forgetting how much you hate it. This all happened yesterday afternoon. It's morning now."

He looked tired and she wondered if he had had any sleep at all.

"Want to go back to town . . ."

He shook his head. "Sorry, there's a terrible snow storm that started yesterday. Don't you remember?"

Did she? She had a vague memory of trying to find shelter as the wind rose, and then the thunder and the pain.

"Who else is here?" Surely some woman had been looking after her most intimate needs. Silver wasn't sure,

119

but she felt naked under the blankets.

"Just us. Willie and Bill started into town to bring back Doc. I hope they made it." The big half-breed's rugged face furrowed into a frown and he went to the window and stared out.

The obvious horrified her. "Are we—are we here alone?"

He turned from the window and grinned at her. "Not quite. The burro's in the shed out back."

"That's not what I meant." She was afraid now, but too weak to do more than raise her head off the pillow.

"I know what you meant, damn it!" He came over and squatted by her bedside. "If you're asking did I 'have my way with you' while you were unconscious, I'm not that big a bastard, no matter what you think!"

But she was conscious now. The way he kept looking down at her made her shrink back against the bed.

"You bet I want you," he muttered almost in answer to her thoughts, "but I don't have any use for a man who'd force himself on a woman; I couldn't do it. Maybe you're lucky; otherwise, when I had you stripped naked last night, you were sure tempting—"

"You took my clothes off? Handled me?"

"It was a tough job, but someone had to do it and the burro didn't volunteer." He grinned.

Silver felt as if she were blushing all down her body to her toes. "Al would kill you for it."

"Better I should have left you in those damp, bloody clothes?"

She didn't have any answer for that. "How long—how long do you think before help gets here?"

He went back to the window and stared out. Past his shoulder, she saw snowflakes falling thick and fast.

"It depends on whether my partners made it into town. For all I know, they're dead in a drift out there somewhere, trying to bring back Doc." His voice betrayed that he cared more about the old men than he would admit.

"I'm sorry," she whispered. "If I hadn't gotten myself shot—"

"No, it's not really your fault." He turned around to face her. "Bill's a little deaf and they both think claim jumpers or dry-gulchers are hiding behind every bush and rock. Crazy old coots."

She lay there, watching him, very aware that if he decided to make use of her body, there was no one to stop him. If she could keep him occupied and talking about something else . . .

"Cherokee, those two—are they relatives?"

"Nope. Friends of my old man's. Just three old geezers always off looking for a pot of gold at the end of the rainbow. All my old man found was six feet of dirt near a mine in Nevada, after the white whore he left my mother for deserted him."

She didn't say anything else, afraid now that he would ask about her own past.

"May I have some water?" She licked her dry lips.

"I'll have to help you hold your head up," he said uncertainly, bringing over a dipper. "I don't think you've got the strength to do it alone."

She tried to make a liar out of him, but as she struggled, his big arm went under her head and she felt the strength of him lifting her. "Take it easy, Silver, I'll help you."

She couldn't do anything but let him although the heat of his body, the sound of his heart beating against her ear, frightened her. She closed her eyes so she wouldn't have to look up into his and drank deeply of the cold water. It tasted good, like melted snow. "Did you ever eat snow ice cream?" she asked without thinking.

He didn't lay her back down, just kept his arm under her shoulders. "Snow ice cream? What brought that up?"

It was more than the cold taste, it was the security of his big arm around her. And yet his face told her his feelings toward her were anything but fatherly. "Nothing."

"Who's Elmer Neeley and Bart Brett?" he asked.

Her eyes blinked open and she stared up at him. "I—I don't have any idea what you're talking about." She managed to pull away from him and sank back down on her pillow.

His face grew serious. "Silver, you're safe. Whoever these bastards are, I won't let them hurt you. No one's going to hurt you when I'm around."

"Except you?" she blurted.

"Not me." He shook his head.

She closed her eyes but she could feel his curious gaze on her. She could never tell what had happened to her that made her fear men; it was too terrible, too humiliating.

"Never mind. Your expression tells me more than words ever could. I suppose I never thought about whores . . ."

She felt the blood rush to her face. They were all the same, thinking of her that way, thinking of the pleasure her beauty could give them. "Leave me alone."

"If I've offended you—"

"Offended? Drat it all! Why should I be offended? That's what I am, right?" She glared up at him.

"That's the way I've grown to think of all white

122

women." He looked uncertain, defensive.

"I don't need you; I've got Al. I want to go back to the Nugget." She managed to pull up on one elbow and the covers fell away. Silver grabbed the blanket and pulled it around her bare breasts.

"Silver, I've seen everything you've got. I spent a large part of the night sponging you off with cold water to bring your fever down." He rolled a cigarette. "Don't look at me that way; it had to be done. I wouldn't rape an unconscious woman."

She saw the desire in his eyes. "But you thought about it?"

"Shall I lie and say no? Of course I thought about it. In fact, I haven't thought about much else but taking you since the first moment I laid eyes on you."

She lay back down on the bed, and he leaned over and helped her pull the blanket up around her ears. His hand brushed her cheek and she sensed that he pulled away very reluctantly.

"Al will be up here to get me. If you try anything, he'll kill you when he gets here."

The big 'breed looked amused. "I don't have to worry about that for a while. With that blizzard blowing, no one will be going or coming for a couple of days."

As if to reinforce his words, the wind rattled the windows.

Panic began to build in her. "You mean we're trapped here . . . together?"

"That's right. Does it scare you?" He smoked his cigarette and watched her. "It needn't."

He was toying with her, watching her reaction. "I'm not scared. You wouldn't dare touch me. Al would—"

"By damn! If I decided to take you, Silver, fear of your

123

watchdog wouldn't hold me back!" His voice was almost a threat. "I'm not sure I'd even pay to sleep with you. I'll bet you're wooden and cold; I like response in my women."

"I'll bet you do! I bet the kind of women you like would leave claw marks all over your back."

"Have you ever left claw marks on a man's back, Silver . . . or only on his face?"

In her mind, she saw Brett's face that first time as he ripped her clothes away, the bloody marks on his face where she'd fought to protect herself. It took all her control to keep her voice steady. "You try anything, you'll find out!"

With that, she turned her face to the wall and listened to him breathe, smelled the scent of the tobacco he smoked. She felt so tired and so weak, but she must stay awake until help arrived. She didn't trust the big 'breed not to climb into bed with her first chance he got.

"I've got some coffee and some bacon and bread," he said.

She was too hungry to refuse. "If it wouldn't be too much bother, I'll see that you're rewarded for all you've done for me when we get back to town."

"I didn't do it for a reward," he snapped, busying himself at the fireplace.

"I'll reward you anyway. I can afford it."

"You are a stubborn little wench, aren't you? People always tell me I'm stubborn, but I think I've met my match."

"I don't like to be obligated to anyone." She turned her head and watched him fry bacon.

"You shouldn't be so scared of people, Silver. They're not all after something from you."

124

"Couldn't prove it by me."

He fried bacon in silence, fixed her a plate, and brought it over. "What we haven't answered with all this talk is what you were doing out here in Mosquito Gulch."

She stared out the window at the blowing snow. "I'd been thinking about buying a claim; I wanted to look at some."

"You could have done that in town, sight unseen."

"I don't buy a pig in a poke." She didn't meet his eyes as he poured coffee and came over to the bed. "I like to see if what I'm getting is what I thought it was."

"I feel the same way," he said. "I had wondered what you were really like under those gaudy costumes."

She was too vain not to ask. "And?"

"You'll do." He put the food on the chest next to her bed and sat down on a box.

"Is that all?"

"Okay. If you must hear it: I never looked on a woman's body and wanted her so bad as I wanted you last night. I've admitted it. Does that make you happy?"

She couldn't hold back the tears that welled up. "I'm afraid and I'm hurt and I want to go back to the Nugget."

"Silver, don't you understand? No one's going anywhere for a while—not until a rescue team from town makes it through that snow. That is, if the boys made it into town. Otherwise, no one's even looking for us—"

"Al'll be looking and if you've done anything—"

"Silver, stop it!" He tilted her chin up with his big hand. "You're safe; but it's not because I'm afraid of Al. I gave my word to you. I won't break it."

She didn't believe him, but she didn't say so. No point in annoying him any further.

Her shoulder hurt when she tried to reach for the cup.

He picked it up and slid his arm behind her shoulders. "Here, let me help."

The heat of his sinewy arm seemed to be burning into her skin and his hand was hot on her shoulder as he steadied her. Silver started to protest, not wanting him to touch her, but she was too weak to sit up. "You could put pillows behind me," she said, sipping the coffee.

"I could," he agreed, "but I like having you in the curve of my arm. You fit there so well."

The blanket had slipped a little and she realized the swell of her breasts was visible as he looked down at her. Self-consciously, she reached to pull it back up. She knew from the feel of his arm that he was one of the most powerful men she had ever met. If he decided he wanted her, fighting him would be a futile gesture.

With a resigned sigh, she let him hold her like a helpless baby, spooning food and sips of coffee between her lips. He was close enough that she could hear his heart beat, smell the scent of tobacco and leather and soap on him.

"Now," he said when she'd finished, "I probably need to change that bandage."

She glanced down, realizing he would have to uncover her right breast to do that. "I'm sure it's fine and doesn't need a new bandage."

He acted as if he didn't even hear her. He lay her down slowly, went over and got fresh rags and a pocket knife, and came back to her bedside.

She pulled the cover even tighter around her chin.

"Silver, I've already seen your breasts. Don't be foolish."

She remembered then that she was his prisoner and that he was big enough to force her to do anything he

126

wanted. With a resigned sigh, she pulled the blanket away from her right breast.

She felt her face burn with shame, but he didn't say anything, just cut the old bandage away from the wound.

"It looks better than I expected," he said. "At least it's a clean wound; the slug seems to have gone through."

Impulsively, she put her other hand over the exposed breast. "I wish you wouldn't look at me."

"Look at you?" he said softly, his voice intense with emotion. "I'd like to do more than look at you, sweet. I'd like to spread my two big hands over those, feel the nipples go hard with wanting against my palms."

She shrank back against the pillow, avoiding his eyes. "Just change the bandage and get your hands off me!"

"Teasing men into paying to touch you, that's how you live, isn't it? You've got me ready to pay whatever you want."

He finished the bandage and she slid as far away from him as she could get on the bed. The feel of his big, calloused hands on her skin made her very aware of him as a man. Her muscles in her back hurt.

"What's the matter?" he asked. "You're frowning."

"I must have pulled some muscles when I fell from the horse," she muttered without thinking.

"I'll rub your back."

"No, don't touch me."

But he was already reaching under her, lifting her. She had underestimated the strength of the man. She knew that as he turned her gently onto her face and began to rub her back through the sheet. "Where does it hurt?"

"Please don't touch me!" She couldn't stop herself from sobbing, "Oh, please . . ."

"You are indeed a puzzle, sweet darlin'," he said

127

softly. "Do you want me to turn you over?"

"No, I can manage." She turned over clumsily, not wanting him to touch her again. His hands were big and hot and strong—and they aroused a yearning in her that she had never felt in her whole life. It was like playing with fire—exciting, yet dangerous.

She saw the hard bulge in his pants as he stood looking down at her. "I'm not sure who the prisoner is," he said, "you or me."

She cowered against the bed, avoiding his stare. She had no doubt who the helpless captive was. It wouldn't take much to have him jerk the covers off her and throw himself across her naked, defenseless body. Silver had a sudden vision of herself lying spread-eagled, his dark, powerful body pinning her small, white one to the bunk.

"Yeah, that's what I'm thinking, all right," he drawled, taking a deep, shuddering breath. "I'd like to make love to you right now until you begged me not to stop!"

"Not a chance! No woman really wants to be hurt like that. If there's any pleasure, it's for men only." She was trembling, but she wasn't sure if it was because he terrified her or aroused her. No, not that. No man had ever made her want to spread out under him, all defenseless and vulnerable while he dominated her and made her submit to his will.

He stood looking down at her for a long moment, his face full of barely controlled fury. "If I could get my hands on the sonovabitch who hurt you, Silver, I swear to God I'd kill him!"

"You're not any better! You'll be all over me, first chance you get!"

"By damn! I gave you my word!" He looked as if he was

128

mad about it.

"And am I to really believe that means I won't wake up with you on top of me tonight?"

"Don't tempt me, Silver, don't tempt me." His big hand reached out and caught one blond curl in his fingers. "I haven't had a woman for months."

"I thought you had Nellie at the Nugget."

He shook his head. "She was willing enough, but my body wanted you; it still does."

She felt helpless in her nakedness. "You could at least give me some clothes."

"Why?" He shrugged. "You aren't going anywhere."

"So I won't have to worry about you seeing me naked."

"I've seen you naked."

"So you told me. Don't humiliate me by reminding me."

"I didn't strip your clothes off to humiliate you."

That was what Bart Brett had said. *I did it to hold you prisoner.* She remembered Brett grinning at her, proud of his cleverness. *Yes, my dear Silver, you will be naked and defenseless in my quarters so that I may gaze on you any time I wish like I would a work of art or any one of my other possessions. This way, you can't escape. When I take you for a drive or to the theater, I'll give you your fine gowns and jewels so I can show my pet off to other envious men.*

"Silver? Are you all right?"

She jerked alert, and she realized he was staring at her. "Please, I'd feel better if I had some clothes on."

His hard face softened. "When I come back from feeding the burro, I'll dig out some of Willie's clothes for you and help you into them. Willie's small. His clothes will still be too big for you, but they'll have to do. Your boots aren't hurt, but then you aren't going to be allowed out of bed anyhow." As he watched, he went out the door.

Silver thought about it a minute. She wasn't all that weak and she didn't want him handling her under the lame excuse of helping her dress. She would find the clothes and have them on by the time he came back in. She sat up and swung her legs over the side of the bed. The rough pine boards felt cold under her bare feet, and she was a bit dizzy. She'd better sit here a moment to make sure she wouldn't faint when she stood up.

Taking a deep breath, she wrapped the blanket around her body and stood up slowly. So far, so good. If she didn't hurry, he'd be back inside and she wouldn't be able to dress without him watching her. Silver took about three wavering steps and grabbed the back of a chair. If she could just sit down again for a moment . . .

"What the hell do you think you're doing?" He stood there in the doorway, big as a mountain.

"Just getting some clothes and I don't need any help." But as she took another step, she realized she might not make it. She forgot to hang on to the blanket as she grabbed for the edge of the table.

The blanket fell to the floor even as Cherokee crossed the room and caught her as her legs gave out. "You little fool, I told you to wait and I'd help you!"

She struggled with him, but she was no match for his strength. His hands were warm and hard on her bare skin as he swung her up against his rough, woolen shirt and reached down to grab the blanket.

She couldn't do anything but press her face against him as he held her. His heart pounded strongly in her ear.

"You're cold," he said softly, and he carried her back to her bed. She kept waiting for him to put her down but he only stood there, holding her, his hands burning into her bare flesh.

"Drat it all! Then get me some clothes and get your damned hands off me!" she snarled at him and struggled, but it was futile.

He lay her down gently and paused, his gaze sweeping up and down her body before he threw the blanket down over her, walked to a trunk, and dug out a pair of pants and a worn but soft plaid shirt.

"Here!" He threw the clothes on the bed. "You can slip these on under the covers if you're so damned afraid I'll see you."

It was awkward and the movement made her shoulder hurt, but she managed to slip the clothes on under the blanket. That made her feel a little more secure.

It was a long afternoon. Silver pretended to sleep while she schemed. She'd have to wait for darkness before she could do anything. The storm seemed to be letting up outside; the snow had slowed to a few flurries. It couldn't be all that bad outside—he'd said that to make her think she couldn't escape.

She looked around, noting that her boots lay by her bed and an old jacket hung on a nail in the wall.

She had already made her plans. Yes, it would be dangerous, but not any more so than remaining trapped at close quarters with that eager stud of a man who got hard just looking at her. She didn't have any faith in all that nonsense about "his word." She knew men. Cherokee Evans was only waiting until he was rested and she was asleep. Then she'd wake up suddenly to find him on top of her, ripping the shirt down the front, forcing her

131

thighs apart.

He looked exhausted from staying by her bed all night. No doubt he'd sleep like a rock once he dozed off. Better to take her chances outside in alluding him. That was better than waiting to get raped. As soon as he dropped off to sleep, she'd make her move. By the time he woke up in the morning, she intended to be heading down the trail, walking to meet Al and the rescue team that must surely be on its way!

Chapter Seven

By the middle of the afternoon on the day Silver rode out, Al was frantic. It had begun to snow heavily. At first he hesitated, thinking that any moment, he would see her riding up the street toward the livery stable.

But every time he pressed his face against the glass and looked out, hoping to see her riding in, he saw only snow flurries. His stomach began to hurt so badly, it was all he could do to keep from doubling over with cramps. Sweat beaded on his homely face and he went through two bottles of bitters before he gave up, grabbed a coat, and headed for the stables.

"Miss Silver come in yet?"

The paunchy owner paused in pitching hay into a stall. "Not yet. We been wondering where she was. Mighty bad weather for a lady to be out alone."

Al felt a sense of impending doom. "I tried to talk her out of it, but she's headstrong. Wouldn't listen to me."

The other man scratched his head. "Just where was she so dead set on going?"

Al's belly began to hurt again. "Something about a

gold claim she wanted to see before she bought it." He looked around the stable. "Saddle me up a horse, I'm going out to find her."

The owner leaned on his pitchfork. "I don't think I'd do that if I was you. As I recall, you don't even know how to ride."

"Someone's got to do something." Al sighed and considered the alternatives. "It's late afternoon. No telling where she is."

"Now, now." The other man made a soothing gesture. "Could be you're getting upset for nothing. The horse hasn't come back without her, so maybe she's stopped to take shelter with a friend someplace. You have any idea where she went?"

"Said something about Mosquito Gulch."

The owner shook his head doubtfully. "That's pretty lonely country. Does she know anyone out that way?"

"How should I know?" Al snapped. "When Miss Silver gets something in her mind, hell and a team of horses can't hold her back!"

The other nodded in agreement. "The men should be gathering in for a drink about now," he suggested. "Why don't you get a search party organized?"

"That's the best idea I've heard all day," Al agreed and took off, shoulders hunched against the cold.

By the time he got enough men organized, it was almost dark and the weather had worsened. At first, as the men stood around at the Nugget and talked about it, everyone was enthused. Then the wind picked up, the snow blew thicker, and the crowd was more and more

134

reluctant to leave the warm stove and the good whiskey.

"I'll go," old Hank volunteered.

Al shook his head. "Thanks, Hank, she'd appreciate it, but you're too old and we may have to go a long ways."

The prospector glared at him. "You don't look so chipper yourself!"

"Look," Zeke began, motioning for silence. "We ain't sure anything bad's befallen the lady yet. Her horse ain't come back without her, has it?"

There was a murmur of agreement among the miners.

Al frowned in exasperation. "That don't prove nothing. The horse could have fallen and broke a leg."

One of the others leaned back against the ornate bar on both elbows. "We all care about her, Al, but with the wind blowing the way it is, there's no trail to follow. Mosquito Gulch is a big place to search."

"Damn it!" Al slammed his fist on the bar. "Enough of this talk, I'll go alone if no one else will go—"

"You mean well," old Hank said, "but we all know you can't even ride, Al."

Zeke nodded. "It's going to be dark soon. We can't do nothing in the dark. Why don't we get organized and start out at first light?"

Al slammed his fist on the bar again and swore. "She could be froze to death by morning if she's layin' out there in the snow somewheres."

Doc pulled at his mustache. "That's a possibility, Al, but if we go stumbling around in the dark, some of us may get lost and freeze to death without doing her much good anyways."

All Al could think of was Silver out there helpless in the snow. "You damned cowards can stand here and jaw all night if you want to, but I'm going looking for Silver!"

He started for the door, almost doubled up with pain from his stomach. He heard a movement behind him, half turned, and threw up an arm, but he barely felt the blow on the back of his head. The floor came up to meet him. Al knew he needed to get up, but his limbs wouldn't work.

From what seemed like a long ways off, he heard Doc say, "Zeke, you shouldn't have hit him."

"I couldn't help it, Doc, he was fixin' to get hisself lost out there in the weather and that'd be a waste. We'll make plans, and when the weather clears at first light, we'll start out."

The weather didn't clear. When Al gradually came to in the early morning hours with his head aching, the storm blew even harder and the snow swirled down the streets and piled in big drifts. He got up and stumbled to the window, looked out, and began to curse. "We should have started last night."

Doc sighed. "We'd hoped it would clear, but now we'll just have to do the best we can. Everyone get their gear together and we'll meet at the livery stable."

Enough men cared about Silver to gather there, but they hadn't gotten a mile out of town when even Al began to realize how hopeless it was. The snow was deep enough in spots to lose a horse and the men on foot bogged down helplessly. The wind whipped ice like sharp needles into their faces.

Zeke yelled above the howling wind. "Al, we'll have to go back, we ain't gonna be able to make it clear out to Mosquito Gulch!"

136

"No!" Al shouted. "Hell, no! We can't leave her out here to freeze to death!"

"Maybe she found shelter," Doc suggested over the wind. "If not, we won't find her alive anyway, Al."

The thought almost stopped his heart. He couldn't imagine Silver dead. He only lived to look at her every day. "If you cowardly bastards want to quit, go on, but I'm going up to Mosquito Gulch!"

Then a man came out of the storm, walking toward them and leading a horse.

"Hey, ain't that Tom who lives near the Gulch? Ain't that the horse Silver rode?"

Al's heart beat harder but he hardly dared to hope. That was the horse, all right, with two riders slumped on its back and Tom leading it. "He's found her! He's found Miss Silver!"

A cheer went up as the man led the bay through the white blizzard toward them, the gelding's black mane and tail blowing wildly.

Then the cheers died as he got close enough to see that neither of the two slumped on the horse was Silver.

Al crunched through the drifts to meet him, stared up at the two old men on the bay's back, and yelled at Tom, "Where'd you find it? Where'd you get Bill and Willie?"

Tom yelled back, "Long story. They say she's all right! Let's get out of this wind and I'll tell you what I know!"

"Where is she?" Al demanded again, but the other man gestured toward the stable. There was nothing Al could do but join the others wading through the snow back to town.

He and Zeke helped the two old men slide off the horse. They looked half-frozen.

Doc frowned. "We better get them into warm beds and get some whiskey in them."

"Never mind." Al leaned over Willie. "Where is she? Is Miss Silver all right?"

Willie opened his eyes. "Made it to our place. . . . She's okay, plenty of food and firewood, but . . ."

Doc looked down at him. "These two are in pretty bad shape. We need to get them in where it's warm. Tom, where'd you find them?"

The prospector rubbed his hands together. "They said they was about give out when they found the horse in a windbreak and struggled through the drifts all night long. They did tell me Miss Silver's at their cabin. Something about needing a doctor."

Al wiped his forehead on his sleeve. In spite of the cold, the pain in his gut made perspiration run down his face. "For who? Who needs the doctor?"

Tom shook his head. "I told you all I know."

Al couldn't decide whether to be elated or freshly fearful. But at least he knew Silver had found shelter where there was food and fuel. All he had to do was go out and bring her in. He said as much.

Doc looked askance. "Are you loco, man? If she's all right, there's no use risking men's lives. She can stay in their cabin and do just fine until this storm lets up!"

There was a murmur of agreement and Doc motioned again for some help in placing Bill and Willie on boards and carrying them to the saloon.

Nellie and the girls volunteered beds and Al offered drinks on the house to every man who had gone along. While he would still feel better when Silver was back at the Nugget, at least she wasn't in any danger of freezing to death. When the old men came to, Doc would get some details from them.

It was late afternoon before Doc finally came downstairs again.

Al stepped from behind the bar and went to the foot of the stairs to meet him. "Well?"

"They're both still half-froze and dazed, but they'll be all right. Wonder they made it all that way without freezing to death."

"Get to the point, Doc," Al said.

"Can't a man get a drink first?" Doc elbowed everyone out of the way and headed for the ornate bar.

Al went behind it and poured for him. "Well?"

"She's all right, near's I can make out." Doc sipped his whiskey with a tired sigh. "She was lucky enough to find their claim just after the storm moved in. It seems Willie and Bill actually came in to get me."

Al's heart almost seemed to stop. "Why? She hurt?"

"I don't know." Doc looked out the window at the swirling snow. "That's a moot question right now, I reckon. We'll have to wait 'til the weather lets up before we can get out there."

Al frowned. "But if she's there alone, she'll be afraid—"

"She's not alone," Doc said. "The third partner is there with her."

Al took a sip of his bitters. "Partner? Who's that?"

"You met him," Doc said, lighting a cigar, "you know, that big half-breed who was in here the other night— Cherokee Evans."

139

The images that came to Al's mind were even more horrible than Silver being lost in the snow. "You mean to tell me Miss Silver's trapped in a cabin with that big 'breed . . . alone? No one else there?"

Doc looked at him, then looked away. "That's about the size of it, Al."

Silver thought it was the longest afternoon she'd ever spent. Most of the time, she kept her face to the wall and pretended to be asleep when the big half-breed bent over her. But she felt him pull the blankets up gently around her shoulders, tuck them in, and brush her hair from her eyes. Each time, her mouth went so dry from fear, it was all she could do to keep from protesting. She was certain that he meant to crawl into bed with her, but he didn't. When she sneaked a look at him, he sat before the fire, staring into the flames, a lonely and solitary figure.

At dark, he brought her some broth he'd made, apologizing that it wasn't too good. Then as he prepared to go to bed, he paused at the window. "Looks like it's quit snowing, but the drifts are bad. We may be here alone for several days before a rescue team can make it this far."

"You don't need to sound so damned happy about it," she snapped at him.

"Look, lady, my old partners are out in that somewhere, maybe even frozen to death because you were foolish enough to be up here trespassing on our claim."

"That gave them the right to shoot me?"

"Okay, so it didn't," he conceded, "but you might give some thought to poor old Willie and Bill."

He had a heart after all. She softened a little toward

140

him. "I like the pair, too. I'm really sorry. If anyone had asked me, I'd have told them not to go; I'm not worth the risk of two lives."

He looked at her a long moment. "We all thought you were." He went to the window again. "I've half a mind to go looking for them, but then I'd have to leave you alone and you're in no shape to take care of yourself or drag wood in for the fire."

Her cheeks burned at the knowledge that he had been doing the most intimate things for her. She felt helpless and vulnerable. It was not a good feeling—to depend on a man when she didn't trust any of them but Al.

As she watched, Cherokee gathered up a rifle, Al's old shotgun, a couple of knives, and an axe, and laid them next to his bed.

She raised up on one elbow. "What are you doing?"

He grinned at her, sat down on his bunk, and pulled off his boots. "Just in case you get any ideas, I wanted all the weapons over here by me."

Drat it all! She counted on taking some of those weapons with her when she slipped out of here after he dozed off. There wasn't anything she could do but lie back and pretend to sleep while he blew out the lamp and crawled into his own bed.

For a moment, Silver almost panicked. In all these years, she had always had a lamp by her bed because she was so afraid of the dark. But the fireplace gave out a little light and the lamp might make it to easy for him to see her when she got up and sneaked out. She lay there in the darkness, fighting fear. Would he come crawling into her bunk when he thought she was asleep?

She turned her head and looked at him across the

cabin, curled up in his bunk. He was a mountain of a man and she would be warm and protected in his arms, her face against that big chest. But then he would want to do something to her besides hold her. The thought made her shudder all over. Finally she heard his gentle even breathing that told her he slept.

Silver waited awhile longer to be sure, then sat up and swung her legs off the side of the bed. She was still a little weak but feeling much better, so she didn't think she would have any trouble walking back to town. It couldn't be as bad outside as Cherokee said it was. He was simply trying to discourage her from running away. She stood up slowly and tiptoed around, getting the jacket, her boots, and a little bread. How she'd like to have a weapon, but she didn't dare risk taking one out from under his bed.

Cherokee never moved and she realized he must be exhausted from having been up all night looking after her. Well, who asked him to? He had ulterior motives, he'd admitted it himself. Probably tomorrow at the latest, he'd be forcing himself on her, making her feel obligated for what he'd done for her. Silver didn't want to feel obligated to the 'breed. Except for Al, men always wanted her to repay them with her body.

As she opened the door, Cherokee sighed and turned over. Silver paused in the doorway, scarcely daring to breath, thinking that at any moment, he'd sit up and realize what she was up to. She stood there waiting. After a moment, his steady breathing continued and she cast one last, longing look at the weapons beside him and slipped out the door, closing it behind her.

Not that she was much good with a gun, but it would be

142

reassuring to have one with her. She took a deep breath of the cold air and started down the trail.

The moon came out from behind the clouds, all big and golden, throwing shadows on the dazzling snow as she crunched along the frozen surface. Any other time, Silver would have been struck by the breathtaking beauty of the scene around her, the light catching the glitter of the drifts, the blue spruce trees with their frosting of snow. Now she was too busy concentrating on putting as much distance between her and that big brute asleep back at the cabin.

Her breath hung like smoke on the chill air when she breathed and her face was already cold. She couldn't remember how far it was in to town, but if she set a steady pace and didn't overexert herself, surely she would make it by morning. Better yet, when she got closer to Buckskin Joe, some passerby or some rancher might spot her and offer a horse or even a sleigh.

Somewhere she heard the lonely howl of a wolf echo and reecho through the hills. Silver looked up, saw it silhouetted against the moon, and hesitated. Wolves would be hungry and bold at this time of the year. *Suppose the pack scented her?*

She half turned and looked back toward the cabin. In the moonlight with the smoke curling lazily from the chimney, it looked so snug and warm and safe. Maybe she should go back and wait for Willie and Bill to bring help. Then she chided herself and kept trudging forward. Probably that wolf would never smell her. Anyway, she was in more danger from that animal back at the cabin who made no bones about what he'd like to do to her.

Somewhere, the pack answered its leader's howl and

then she saw the black outline of the animals running along a distant ridge in the moonlight.

She wouldn't even think about the wolves. The possibilities were too scary. Silver kept walking. While the snow behind her had a crust to it, now she had come to an area that had no frozen surface. She took a step and sank in the white, soft powder almost to her knees. It was slower going now and she found herself breathing hard. She hadn't realized she was so weak. Her hands and feet were beginning to feel the cold.

She paused, panting, wondering how far she had come. The wolves howled again and the sound echoed through the hills and bounced back at her. The sound seemed much closer now. *Would they smell the scent of the dried blood on her bandage?*

The snowy scene around her no longer seemed beautiful, it seemed full of terrifying things. The shadows from the blue spruce seemed like fingers reaching out for her, black against the white, white snow.

The drifts were deeper here. Once she floundered into a soft spot and sank almost up to her waist. If her clothes got damp, it would be easy to freeze to death. Already her feet were losing their feeling. Her fingers seemed to be numb.

Whatever had made her think she could walk all the way back to town? She was going to freeze to death out here on the trail. At least people said it was an easy way to die. She'd heard that you just grew numb, closed your eyes, drifted off to sleep, and never woke up.

It would be so easy to do that, she thought, gasping for breath in the chill air. Maybe she would just sit down in the snow and rest a long moment, then she would get up and start walking again. Silver slumped down in the snow and put her face on her knees. She couldn't remember ever being so tired or so cold.

Maybe she ought to go back to the cabin. Maybe she had a better chance against Cherokee than she did the cold. But even as she thought that, she heard the wolf pack howl again and realized with a start that they were on a scent, running along between her and the cabin. In that case, she didn't dare think about going back. Nor could she just sit here. If she did, the wolves might pick up her trail and follow her to this spot. Freezing to death quietly was one thing; being torn to pieces and devoured alive by a pack of wolves was something else again.

She didn't intend to do either. Drat it all, she intended to live! The thought galvanized her to action and she stood up, brushed the snow off her clothes, and searched around in the drift until she found a sturdy tree limb. This would work as a crutch and maybe as a weapon if she had to fight the wolves off. Silver began to walk again, but she tasted fear like a copper penny in her mouth.

There was no point in thinking about anything but getting to town . . . or dying in the attempt. She put one foot in front of the other and walked, even though she was having a hard time feeling her toes move in her boots.

The wind picked up, blowing past her toward the wolves. Would it carry her scent to the hungry predators? The thought made her walk faster, leaning on the club she found. The animals might be more afraid of her than she was of them. If they should get her scent and trail her, maybe shouting at them and a few good blows with her club would scare them off.

For a moment as she struggled through the snow, she

145

almost wished she were back at the cabin. Cherokee wouldn't let a wolf get her. She'd be safe and warm curled up against his big chest.

Like hell she would! He'd have her on that fur rug in front of the fire, naked and defenseless while he rode her small body and put his hands and mouth all over her bare skin. Better to take her chances against the wolves!

Did she hear someone call her name? Silver stopped and listened intently. Maybe Al and a rescue party were just over the next ridge.

"Here I am!" she shouted. "Here I am!"

Here I am . . . here I am . . . am . . . am . . .

The echo was so eerie, it made her feel even more alone and defenseless. Besides, the wolves might hear her voice if they hadn't picked up her scent. Straining to hear, she tensed and listened. Nothing. She had only imagined that someone called her name.

In the distance behind her, a wolf howled again. It sounded nearer this time, but she couldn't be sure if the pack really was closer or her fear only made it sound so.

Stop it, Silver! she admonished herself. *You've got your club. Keep walking!*

Her breathing came labored now but she kept putting one small foot in front of the other, even though she couldn't feel her toes anymore. *If her feet froze, would she be able to dance?*

Almost in a dream, she saw herself on the stage at the Nugget, dancing and laughing for the cheering crowd. The silver-heeled shoes sparkled in the light as she danced.

Silver Heels! the crowd chanted. *Silver Heels!*

With her feet numb, she had difficulty maneuvering

and she tripped and fell. For a long moment, she lay there, the flakes cold on her lips, and she thought of a laughing little girl making angels in the drifts, of the taste of snow ice cream and the only man who had truly loved her, her daddy, pulling her on a sled.

He seemed to be gesturing to her. *Come with me, Silvia. Your life has been as unhappy as mine. Come with me. Give up as I did and I'll take you to a place where there is no cold or terror or pain. . . .*

"No!" She pulled herself up on her knees. She wasn't like Daddy; she wasn't weak. She might not make it, but it wasn't going to be because she gave up and surrendered to death as he had done. If Death was coming for her, he would have a fight on his hands.

All she wanted to do was sit down on the trail and close her eyes for a few minutes, but she realized that if she did, she might never wake up. Silver managed to get to her feet and stumbled forward again.

The wolves howled behind her, nearer now. She had to believe they had finally picked up her scent.

Silver decided she would not think about that. She would sing to block out their howling and also to keep herself awake. Could she remember the words to any songs?

It scared her to think how confused and disoriented she was while she tried to think about singing. She wasn't even sure which way she was supposed to walk anymore. *Away from the sound of the wolves howling*. Yes, that was it, she was supposed to walk in the opposite direction from the wolves.

"It rained all night the day I left, the weather it was dry, the sun so hot, I froze to death, Susanna, don't you cry. . . ."

The whole thing struck her as funny, especially the part about freezing to death, and she couldn't remember the rest of the words anyhow. It took more energy than she possessed to sing, and besides, she had to breathe deeper and the air was so cold. Maybe that hadn't been such a good idea after all.

The wolves sounded excited behind her; no doubt they had picked up her trail at last. Maybe she could climb up into a tree and wait for them to go away. Silver looked around. All the trees looked no taller than a man and her hands were so numb, she wasn't sure she could climb anyway.

Up ahead in the moonlight was a little rise. She stumbled toward it, the wolves baying behind her. From there, she had a slight advantage with her club, but not much. Beyond that were several big spruce trees . . . if she could make it that far. She wasn't even sure she could stumble to the little rise, but she'd give it a try.

The wolves howled and yapped on the trail behind her, excited over the scent of her blood on the bandage.

Silver swore under her breath and struggled toward the rise. "You devils may get me, but I intend to take a couple of you with me first!" She made it to the rise and turned around, ready to face the oncoming pack that yelped closer and closer as they seemed to smell her scent. Silver braced herself and hefted her club in numb fingers. Freezing to death was one thing, but being eaten alive was something she hadn't counted on!

Chapter Eight

Cherokee awakened suddenly and reared up on one elbow, looking around the cabin that was lit only by the firelight. *What had awakened him?* Maybe a burning bit of wood falling into the glowing coals?

He looked at the fire a long moment, yawning. Usually, he slept so lightly, a mouse tiptoing across the boards would wake him up, sending him grabbing for a weapon. But he had been exhausted from staying up all hours the night before by the girl's bedside.

The girl. Being a taciturn and lonely man, he hadn't realized how much he had begun to rely on her presence. She seemed to be sleeping quietly, her form motionless under her blankets. He settled back down, wondering what time it was. And then he reared straight up in bed. That was what had awakened him—the absence of her soft breathing.

My God, suppose she was dead? His heart almost stopped as he leaped up, crossed the floor in four long steps, and threw her covers back. Pillows. That's what

149

was under the covers, pillows placed so they looked like a body. Why, that little . . .

Another thought crossed his mind that was even more horrifying. Where was she? Maybe she had stepped outside to relieve herself. He pictured how embarrassed she would be if he went outside and caught her in the snow. To protect her modesty, he would wait a long minute. The minute stretched into two.

Maybe she had gone out to the shed for some reason. Cherokee opened the back door and looked in at the sleepy burro that wiggled its long ears at him. Cherokee returned to the cabin.

Surely the little wench wouldn't be loco enough to walk away from here, as far as it was back to town and with all this snow. Anxiously he peered out the frosted window and, not seeing her, threw the door open wide. To hell with her modesty!

"Silver? Silver, are you out here? Answer me!"

Somewhere in the distance, a wolf howled and the sound echoed through the desolate hills. *Wayah*. Wolf. Memories of Cherokee tribal tales about the animal came to his mind.

At least *u-no-le*, the wind, had died down. The moon was big and full tonight, illuminating the snowy scene. A set of small footprints led away from the cabin.

By damn! She was either crazier than any woman he had ever met or she was more scared of him than he had realized. For a moment, he cursed himself for admitting to her how much he desired her body. Surely after he had given his word, she didn't believe he would rape her?

The air was so cold, his breath hung like ghostly fog on

the night air. In this snow and weak as she was, Silver couldn't possibly walk into town. But she could freeze to death trying.

Cursing himself for sleeping too soundly and the girl for her foolishness, Cherokee got his heavy coat and gloves, a backpack of supplies including a bottle of whiskey and extra cartridges for his loaded rifle, and started down the trail after her.

Somewhere in the distance, the wolf howled again and the pack answered him, yapping with excitement. They were on the trail of a rabbit or a deer, maybe. When they caught it, they would tear it to pieces and be swallowing it before the creature's heart had even stopped beating. Could they be on Silver's trail? The possibility scared him, as he thought about her shoulder wound. The slight scent of the blood on the bandage was enough to be carried on the breeze to that hungry pack.

"Silver?"

Silver . . . Silver . . . Silver . . . The echo mocked him.

When he caught that ornery chit, he'd half a mind to turn her over his knee and spank that lovely little bottom for dragging him out in the cold. Cherokee tried to concentrate on how angry he was with her as he strode along, the frozen surface crunching beneath his weight. As long as he thought about how mad he was, he wouldn't be able to get frantic and worried.

God, it was cold! The air seemed to bite at his rugged face and he hunched his shoulders against the chill and kept walking. He thought about the whiskey in his pack and how it would warm him if he would only reach back, get the bottle, and drink it as he walked. Once he had liked the taste and he remembered that flavor now. He

151

shook his head. Cherokee had sworn and he would keep that oath. The whiskey was for *U-ne-ga*, Silver, when he found her.

The wolves howled again. They seemed closer now. In fact, when he stopped to listen, it sounded as if they were between him and Silver.

A quarter mile, then a half, and still the little footprints lay ahead of him on the trail. Once he found where she had stumbled and fallen. Another place it looked as if she had simply sat down in the snow for a while.

He had covered at least a mile and he still hadn't found her. He began to have a grudging admiration for her spunk. In her condition, he hadn't thought she could make it a hundred yards, yet she was still moving ahead of him. Silver either had more grit than the average girl . . . or she was too scared to stop.

The wolves howled again, much closer this time.

"Silver? Silver, can you hear me?"

. . . hear me . . . me . . . me . . .

Did he hear a voice in answer or was it only the echo? Cherokee checked to make sure his old rifle was loaded in case he crossed the trail of the wolf pack, and increased his speed. The cold was beginning to get to him. He tried not to think about whether Silver might be cold—or even lying dead and frozen along the trail. He had no way of knowing how long ago she had left the cabin.

The thought scared him so badly that he said a small prayer to the Great Spirit, A-da-nv-do. He had not prayed since his grandmother died and he had dug a hole all by himself in a hidden place in the Smoky Mountains and buried her. Then as a half-grown boy of eighteen, he had found his way across many miles to Tennessee and

Shawn, his father's friend who had taken him in and treated him like a son.

Cherokee thought of Silver lying helpless on the trail, and broke into a trot, carrying the rifle at the ready. Up ahead of him, the wolves had picked up a scent. Their excited yapping as they ran told him that. *Was it the girl they were after?*

At that thought, he broke into a run, moving awkwardly through the snow. Then he topped a rise and looked down. The moon lit up the scene and the big shadows of the circled wolves almost hid the prey they had trapped. Cherokee took one look at the spunky girl swinging her club and then he took off down the slope. "Silver, I'm coming!"

He stopped halfway, aimed, and took the lead wolf down as it sprang at her. The wolves set up a frightened yelp as their leader fell, then they turned and fled into the brush. Cherokee didn't stop all the way to her.

She fell into his arms, sobbing. "I—I—thought I was going to die! They've been trailing me for a long time . . ."

"I know, I know. It's okay now." He held her tightly against him. "You're safe now, nothing will get you."

God, she seemed half-frozen. He pulled off his gloves and felt her face. "You crazy little fool! You couldn't have made it all the way to town! Were you that afraid of me?"

Her big eyes gave him the answer and he cursed himself for having told her how much he desired her. What kind of a saloon girl would rather face death in the snow than bed a man? Surely she did it all the time?

"Here, I've got some whiskey in my pack." He dug

153

it out.

"No, no whiskey," she struggled, but she was too weak to fight him.

He forced the bottle between her teeth. "Drink it, Silver, if I don't get you warm, you may have frost bite and lose the tip of your nose and some of your toes and fingers."

Even though she fought him, he got a good slug of the whiskey in her belly. He pulled off her gloves and felt her fingers. They were freezing cold. "Can you feel them?"

She shook her head.

He jerked open his jacket and shirt, grabbed her hands, forced one of them under each of his armpits, then pressed her face against his big chest.

Silver struggled and protested.

"Shut up," he ordered, and he turned her face so that his warm flesh was against her other cheek. Her small hands under his arms felt frozen and lifeless. "You're lucky I turned up when I did."

She didn't argue, but pressed her face against him. He felt her shivering through both their clothes, and heard her teeth chatter.

"Silver, I've got to get you back to the cabin."

She looked up at him, trembling with cold. "I was going to town."

"The hell you say! Of all the stubborn, stupid women I ever met, you get the prize!"

Still, he secretly admired her spunk as he swung her up in his arms and stepped over the dead wolf. "Keep your hands under my arms and your face against my chest."

She looked up at him as he started back up the trail. "Aren't you cold with your shirt open?"

154

"Damned right! Now snuggle up there and see if I can put some heat into you by the time we get back to the cabin!"

She acted for a moment as if she would protest, but Cherokee refused to argue with her. After all, he was bigger than she was and she was hurt and half-frozen. He carried her back up the trail with long strides, worrying all the time about her feet. "That was a crazy thing to do! If your toes freeze and you lose them, you won't be dancing for me in those silver-heeled slippers anymore!"

She was shaking all over, but he could feel life coming back to her hands against his bare flesh. Once he got her inside before the fireplace, he could rub her body and get her circulation going and put plenty of whiskey in her. She'd be all right. From now on until a rescue team got here, he might have to keep her tied to the bed.

It seemed as if it took forever to get back to the cabin. Cherokee dumped her unceremoniously on the fur rug before the fireplace and added wood to the flames, building up the fire so that it lit up the whole room.

He handed her the whiskey from his pack. "Here, drink up, while I get you out of these damp clothes."

She started to protest, seemed to think better of it, and took a couple of big gulps while he pulled her boots off and massaged her small feet. "Damned little fool! It would serve you right if you could never dance again!"

With Silver protesting, he stripped her naked, gathered her up, and put her in her bed, piling every blanket in the cabin on top of her. She lay there trembling.

* * *

Silver looked up at him. The expression on his face told her how angry he was. She had never been so cold in her life. More than dying, she was afraid of what frost-bite might do to her looks.

"Are you warm yet?"

She shook her head, afraid to lie to him. She had never seen a man so angry and scowling before. It dawned on her that it was because he feared for her.

He reached under the cover, took one of her arms, and began massaging it, while she protested about him touching her.

He didn't even answer, just kept rubbing the circula-tion back into her arm. Then he began on the other one. After that, his hands worked their way down her bare legs and massaged her feet. "I've seen bigger feet on a child," he said, and she didn't know whether she was supposed to comment or not, he looked so angry.

"Turn over," he ordered.

She started to protest, then she saw the look on his face and did as he told her. The whiskey had made her more than a little dizzy.

He reached under the blanket and rubbed her back, his hands gentle in the area of her wounded shoulder. The whiskey was beginning to work its way into her system now, and she decided that if he was going to rape her, she was helpless to stop him anyhow. She relaxed and let his strong, supple hands knead their way down her body.

"That's more like it," he murmured and then his hands were on her hips, rubbing there. Silver stiffened, but by then, his hands were on the back of her thighs. She turned her head sleepily and looked at him. His shirt was open to the waist, the powerful muscles of his dark chest rippling in the firelight.

She was still trembling with cold, even though she tried to keep him from seeing her shiver.

He frowned. "This calls for desperate measures."

She watched in horror as he stood up and began undressing. "No! You aren't going to—"

"Shut up!" he ordered. "I'm going to get you warm if I have to tie you up to do it!"

While she struggled and protested, he peeled off the rest of his clothes, crawled under the blankets, and pulled her up against him.

As drunk as she was, the hard heat of his flesh against her chilled body made her gasp, and then without meaning to, she molded herself against him, shivering.

"That's it," he murmured, holding her in the crook of his arm. "Take some of my heat, sweet darlin', although it's hell to have you in bed with me when I've sworn not to touch you!"

She didn't believe him, of course. She had no doubt that any minute now, he would roll over on top of her and ram that hard tool of his deep within her. But she was too tired and cold and drunk to do anything but lie there and shake.

He pulled her very close and she felt her sensitive nipples brush against his hot flesh and his big hands cupped and covered her small bottom. She struggled, but she couldn't get away. He had her face against his wide chest, radiating heat into her chilled skin. "Don't fight me, Silver, I won't hurt you. Let me warm you."

There was nothing she could do against his strength except let him mold her against him all the way down their bodies. He smelled of tobacco, shaving soap, and wood smoke. His big maleness throbbed against her belly, hot and virile. She tried to pull away from the feel of it surging there, but he held her close.

His hand came up and covered her breast. "By damn! Even these are cold." He began to massage them, cursing softly under his breath. "Why did I ever tell you I wouldn't touch you? I don't suppose you'd let me out of that vow?"

"Who are you kidding? I know you'll rape me when you decide to!" She glared at him, angry with both him and herself. Never had she experienced feelings like this before. She was afraid of him, but his hand stroked and caressed her breasts until she found herself pressing against his fingers, not wanting him to stop. Her nipples seemed to swell and grow hard at his touch and it occurred to her suddenly that his mouth would feel very hot and wet on her chilled skin. She had a sudden vision of his mouth sucking and licking her breasts, working slowly over every inch of her small body.

The feeling scared her. No man had ever made her think along those lines before. It must be the whiskey.

"Here, roll over," he ordered gruffly. "Let me warm your back."

"And if I don't?"

She kept forgetting how powerful the man was. He didn't answer, merely lifted her and turned her gently so that she lay against the curve of his big frame like two spoons fitting into each other.

"I couldn't stand much more of you brushing those soft breasts against me," he complained. "I was about to forget what I promised."

Drunk and resigned to his male strength and whatever

158

he decided to do to her, she lay pressed against him with his breath hot on the back of her neck, one of his arms encircling her belly.

"Are you getting warm now?" he whispered.

She nodded, sighing at the feel of the heat radiating from his big frame. His manhood felt as hard as steel against her back and his hand massaged her belly. "I'm warm, you can go back to your own bunk now."

"Well, I'm not," he grumbled, "and I don't want to take another chance on you doing a damn fool stunt like that again."

"You aren't fooling me," she complained, the fear beginning to build in her again. "You're just wanting to lie with me—"

"Damned right! Now if I could only ease this ache in my groin, I could sleep!"

Silver stiffened and pulled away from him.

Her jerked her up against him. "Don't be afraid of me, Silver." His breath stirred the hair at the base of her skull. "I'll never, never hurt you; nor will anyone else as long as I can stop them."

Don't believe him, she warned herself, but somehow she did. With an exhausted sigh, she snuggled down in the blankets and slept deeply, hardly aware there was no lamp by her bedside to scare the nightmares away.

Silver blinked awake, trying to remember where she was, why her brain ached so. She heard soft breathing and looked up. For a moment, she couldn't believe it. She lay curled in the arms of Cherokee Evans, her face against his naked chest. With a startled cry, she sat bolt

159

upright in bed, pulling the covers protectively around her naked breasts.

He opened his eyes. "What's the matter?"

Her outrage knew no bounds. "You rotten skunk! You know what's the matter! You got me drunk and got into bed with me!"

"And that's *all* I did," he grumbled. "I wish now I'd poured a little more whiskey down you."

She slapped him hard and his hand moved in a flash, catching her wrist. "Don't ever do that again, Silver. I haven't done anything to warrant that. Remember, I could break you in half!"

"Yes, that's it! Go ahead and hit a woman! You big— you big—" She couldn't think of anything bad enough to call him. Still holding her blanket, she climbed over him and out of the bed, then moaned aloud at her throbbing head. She plopped down on a chair and glared at him. "I hate the sight of you!"

"Do you now?" He stood up and walked naked across the bare floor. "As I recall, last night when I arrived just in time to save you from being a wolf's dinner, you were mighty glad to see me. Stop trying my patience, sweet darlin'. Like any man, I can only be pushed so far."

"And then you'll do what?" she sneered.

He grinned at her. "I'm sure I could think of something."

She carefully turned her head away so she wouldn't have to look at him. "You promised," she reminded him primly. "Remember your promise."

"I wish to hell I could forget it!" He grabbed his pants and pulled them on. "I won't touch you—not until you give me the word."

160

"Don't hold your breath," she snapped back.

He didn't answer. She watched him stir up the fire and begin making coffee. "This is probably the last day you'll have to put up with my rotten cooking," he said. "Whether my pards made it into town or not, I imagine your watchdog will come looking this afternoon. Does he have any idea where you are?"

She hadn't thought about Al in a long time. "I think I told him. I imagine he's worried to death about me."

Cherokee looked up from frying bacon. "Just what is he to you?"

"Not my lover," she said, her face flushing hot.

"Well, of course I didn't think that," he said, "but there's some kind of unusual bond between you."

She didn't say anything. How could she tell him she and Al were both wanted back in Chicago on murder and robbery charges? Al was in love with her; she knew that was why he had done it. She would be forever beholden to him, and while she couldn't return his love, it seemed enough for him to stay close to her.

Cherokee finished frying the bacon, made some coffee, and baked some biscuits in a iron skillet covered with coals. "Sorry there's no butter or fancy jam."

"It'll do," she said, accepting a tin plate while holding the blanket tightly around her. The food tasted good and she found herself gobbling it. "I suppose help will get through today."

"Probably." He sounded regretful, and to her surprise, she wasn't sure how she felt.

They finished eating and he took the tin plate, frowning at her. "Your hair is a tangle; I wouldn't want Al to think I hadn't taken good care of his prize."

161

Cherokee sounded a little sarcastic as he reached for a brush.

"I can do that myself." She tried to take the brush from his hand, then realized her shoulder hurt when she moved it.

"Let me," he said.

With a resigned sigh, she let him brush her hair. Although she hated to admit it even to herself, it felt good. "You could hire out anywhere as a lady's personal maid."

"Anytime you need one, just holler. I can't think of anything I'd like better than looking after you."

"I don't need looking after."

"That's debatable."

There was no point in arguing with the hardheaded half-breed. Once she got away from him, she didn't ever have to see him again. Silver decided she'd pay him a nice reward for helping her. It dawned on her suddenly that he was looking down into the loose blanket at her breasts while he brushed her hair.

"Drat it all! Here, give me that!" She jerked the brush out of his hand and began to brush her own hair, even though it made her shoulder ache. "You remind me of a stallion pawing and prancing about a filly."

"Do I? I can't help it, sweet Silver. You affect me that way."

"Men!" she sniffed with disdain, brushing her hair in long strokes. "Any pretty woman, you want to top. When I'm old and ugly, no one will want me." She hadn't meant to tell him that; it was her biggest fear, that when her looks had finally faded, no one would love or even want her.

162

He looked up from rolling a cigarette. "Silver, there's lots of pretty women in this world, but you're special. I started out just wanting to make love to you, I'll admit that. But now . . ."

"But now?" she paused, looked at him.

He finished rolling the cigarette and toyed with it. "I never thought I'd say this to a woman, but I'd like to be around when you're old. To me, I think you will always be beautiful, even when there's lines in your face and that lovely hair has turned gray. If I'm around, you won't need all those mirrors; you can see your reflection in my eyes and they'll tell you that to me, you are lovely still."

His words sounded so sincere that she was shaken, and then she remembered that, like all men, he would say anything that would get her under him with her thighs apart. *Animals.* That's what they all were—*animals.*

She finished brushing her hair and put it up in a French twist. "Can you find me some more of Willie's clothes?"

"Sure." He lit the cigarette with a burning stick from the fire then went over to dig some things from the trunk. "I'll go see about the burro while you dress."

She held the clothes in front of her and looked up at the big man. "You're a strange guy, Cherokee. I never met anyone like you before."

He shrugged, looking embarrassed. "Maybe it comes from being raised up in the hills by an Indian grandmother. We didn't see very many white people; and didn't trust them and with good reason. The soldiers dragged my *e-tsi,* my mother, away and sent her along with the others on the Removal—the Trail of Tears."

"And your father?"

"He ran off with a saloon whore and went chasing the gold at the end of the rainbow," Cherokee blew smoke toward the ceiling. "Never found it. He'd turn up now and then, tell me how he would come for me when he finally hit it big. All he left me when he died was a few rusty tools and this claim."

"You have a low opinion of white women, don't you?"

He hesitated. "I have my reasons."

Somehow, she wanted to know, to understand him. "Want to tell me about it?"

"No." He stood up. "Let's just say I betrayed a friend over one. She had golden hair and was supposed to be an elegant lady."

And now she had the part to the puzzle. "You were drunk, weren't you?"

He stood staring into the distance, and for a long moment, she didn't think he had heard her. "That's no excuse," he said finally.

"You shouldn't judge all women by that one, or the one that ran off with your father."

He looked at her squarely then. "Aren't you judging all men by one . . . or two?"

Now she was the one to turn away from his piercing gaze. "That's different."

"Is it?" He flipped the cigarette into the fireplace, came up behind her, and slipped his arms around her as she stood there wrapped in the blanket. "I think I could give you what you need, Silver." He bent his head and kissed her bare shoulder. The feeling of his lips on her skin sent goose bumps traveling all over her body.

She pulled away and moved over to stand before the fire. "You're mistaken," she said softly, but she didn't

164

look at him. "I have everything I want—a big saloon of my own, money, men applauding me. I don't need anything else."

"Sure," he said. "The mirrored walls and the lamps on at midnight tell me how happy you are."

"My life is none of your damned business!" She whirled on him. "I don't need you! I don't need anyone, especially not some half-breed who is trying to talk his way into my bed!"

He looked as if she'd struck him and she was immediately sorry, but she couldn't take back her words.

His face turned grim and hard. "I should have taken you when I had the chance," he said. "That's what you expect from a savage like me, and darlin', you're so tempting!"

He turned and went out to the shed, slamming the door so hard behind him, it rattled the windows.

At least now he'd keep his hands off her, now that she'd made it clear she didn't want anything he had to offer. She should feel relieved, but strangely, she felt a little regretful and disappointed. She must be loco.

Silver got dressed and waited for the big 'breed to return. Maybe she should apologize. After all, he had saved her life twice.

But when he came back inside, he ignored her, staring out the window and smoking cigarettes. She had never been through such a long day.

It was a relief when, in the afternoon, he went to the window again, turned, and said, "I think I see a sleigh in the distance. Looks like you'll be leaving. I wouldn't want

165

to inconvenience you by making you spend another night in mortal fear of me."

She started to say something, then wasn't sure exactly what to say. She bit her lip, struggling for the right words, but Cherokee was already opening the door. "I'll get your things together," he said, and he sounded relieved to be rid of her. The way he looked at her told her that he never intended to see her again.

Chapter Nine

It appeared to Silver that half the town's male population had come along with the sleigh.

Al looked both frantic and furious as he stomped the snow off his boots. "Are you all right, Silver? Is there anything you want to tell me?" He glared at Cherokee.

Silver feigned wide-eyed innocence. "Why, no. I can't imagine what you're talking about."

Cherokee, drat his ornery hide, only grinned like a big tomcat caught with canary feathers on his mouth.

Willie and Bill had come along and she was as relieved as Cherokee to see them, reassuring them over and over that she held no grudge and was grateful that they had risked their lives to bring help. She noticed Cherokee avoided her gaze while Al and the boys fussed over her. She told the story of how she'd ended up here while out looking for a claim to buy.

Al looked from her to the big 'breed. "Find anything you liked?" he asked pointedly.

"Not a thing!" She glared at Cherokee. "I think I'd do better to invest my time and money in the Nugget from now on."

With the men jubilant, Doc declared her shoulder healing. She let Al help her into the sleigh and they all went off to town, leaving Willie, Bill, and Cherokee behind. Silver couldn't resist craning her head one last time to look back, but the man she searched for had already turned and gone into the cabin.

So what the hell? She didn't owe him anything except a nice reward next time he came to town. Of course, as angry as he looked, he might avoid Buckskin Joe and go for supplies to one of the other little camps in the area. Drat it all! Why should she care?

Life returned to normal for Silver. Most of the men in the Rockies seemed to drop in to make sure she was all right, and business boomed at the Nugget. Every evening she sang and danced and reveled in the adoration of the crowd. Silver shoes. Expensive gems. There was nothing else a girl could want, she told herself. But late at night, she paced in front of her mirrors, slept with the lamp on, and dreamed that a certain big man held her safely in his arms and kissed her. Gentle kisses. Passionate kisses.

Out in Mosquito Gulch, Cherokee worked like a driven man to keep from thinking about her as spring came to the Rockies. But April brought the first wild flowers that reminded him of her perfume. The brooks thawed and sang as they rushed through the mountains, and when he stopped to listen, he thought he heard her singing.

He tried not to think of her at all and lost himself in hard work on the claim. There was no future in wanting the girl who was the toast of the Rockies. All that interested her was the reassurance she got from mirrors and the reflections in men's eyes that she was a great beauty. Whatever drove her to such vanity, he knew lay in her hidden past. He cursed himself for lusting after such a cold, hard treasure. Yes, she deserved to be called Silver.

The trio found more and more rich ore and they dared dream of becoming wealthy. Willie and Bill talked of retiring to some exotic island with native girls bringing tropical drinks while Cherokee hoped for a snug cabin hidden deep in the mountains. The old men continued to hide their pokes in the woodpile, but Cherokee argued that the dust would be safer in town.

One day, Bill winked at Willie and said, "Phash, boy, why don't you go on into town and bank your stash? We could use a few supplies."

Cherokee pretended not to see the wink. "If I do," he said stiffly, "I may go over to Fairplay. I think maybe the store's better there than the one in Buckskin Joe."

"Suit yourself," Bill answered, "but I shorely like the stick candy Haw Tabor carries."

"If you insist, that's where I'll go. You two sure you don't want me to bank your dust? Sooner or later, word may get around and you'll get robbed."

"What's that again?" Bill put his hand behind his ear and Cherokee repeated the comment.

Bill snorted and pointed to his old rifle. "I kin take care of myself and Willie, too."

Cherokee decided not to remind him that he was half-deaf and that neither of them were as young as they used to be. He got the little burro to carry the supplies and headed down the trail to town.

He put the burro in the livery stable and reached into

169

his pocket, brought the little nuggets out, and watched them gleam in the sunlight. Willie and Bill might laugh at his foolishness, so he hadn't told them. Besides, it was his share of the gold they'd found in the last few days. What he did with it was his own business.

After a little thought, he took some of his nuggets into a shop and had a bracelet made from them. When it was ready later that day, he smiled with satisfaction, slipping it in his pocket. What he intended to do was send it to Silver anonymously. After the way she'd treated him, he didn't want her to know he still thought of her.

He told himself that he wouldn't go into the Nugget, he would have his coffee and catch up on the gossip someplace else. But that evening, as he left the hotel café and started back up the street, he heard music and her high, sweet voice drifting on the spring breeze from the Nugget.

Cherokee forgot that he intended to stay away from her and her saloon. Her voice drew him like magic. Despite all his good intentions, he found himself pushing through the doors of the Nugget. She was on the stage wearing a shimmering, tight dress almost the same pale aqua as her eyes and dancing to one of Stephen Foster's lively tunes, silver-heeled shoes and jewels flashing in the lights.

"Oh, Susanna, oh, don't you cry for me, I come from Alabama with my banjo on my knee . . ."

With his gaze on her, he moved slowly to the bar and leaned on it.

Al grunted, "Oh, it's you. I hoped you would stay away. You're bad for her, Cherokee."

Cherokee turned and looked at the ugly man. "She say that?"

170

"I say that!" He slammed a cup of coffee in front of Cherokee so hard, some of it sloshed out on the polished walnut. "All you can think of is gettin' her in bed. She needs a man who'll understand her and keep his hands off!"

"No man could see her and not want her." He sipped the coffee and watched her dance, the noisy crowd clapping to the music. "I know I don't have a chance with Silver; I'm not sure any man does. As long as she's obsessed with her own beauty, she hasn't a place in her life for anything else."

"She's had a hard life," Al said. "Her beauty is all the security she's got."

"Looks don't last forever. What'll she do when she's old and men don't notice her anymore?"

Al scowled. "She'll have security from her money, and she won't have to depend on men anymore when her looks are gone."

Cherokee shrugged, watching her dance. "Sounds like a pretty lonely future."

"At least she won't be sellin' her body just to eat," Al said. "All the men she's known have let her down—except me. I tell her she's smart not to trust them."

"Is it smart for *her* or only *you?*" Cherokee turned and looked at him. "You don't want her to find anyone else, Al; you're afraid of losing her."

"I'm afraid of some sonovabitch like you hurtin' her," he grumbled and began wiping the bar. "Silver's been hurt enough already."

Al knew a lot he wasn't telling, Cherokee realized. There were a million questions he would like to ask, but he didn't think he would get any answers.

Silver finished dancing to thunderous applause and

bowed. "Silver Heels!" the crowd shouted until it became a chant, "Silver Heels! Silver Heels!"

She bowed and smiled at the audience, thinking that here was where she belonged, a star to be adored and applauded. She hadn't been thinking straight when she had been trapped in that cabin. Why, she'd almost started to think she might be happy just dancing and singing for an audience of one.

The piano began one of her favorite numbers and she sang:

"Tis the last rose of summer, left blooming alone. All her lovely companions are faded and gone . . ."

She looked out at the crowd and saw Cherokee Evans leaning on the bar. For just a moment, her voice faltered at the sight of him, and then she steeled herself and kept singing:

"I'll not leave thee, lone one, to pine on the stem, where the lovely are sleeping, go sleep thou with them . . ."

That was right, wasn't it? In only a short time, her own looks would be faded, but like a lovely butterfly, she must think only of today and not worry about what would be her future fate. No man would really want her when she was no longer pretty.

The men in the audience wiped their eyes and blew their noses as she sang of faded beauty and dreams, dead as the last roses of summer with winter's chill coming on. When she finished, there was no sound for a long moment and then the men cheered and stamped and whistled, "Silver Heels! Silver Heels!"

She bowed and came down the steps from the stage. Drat! What should she do; pretend she hadn't seen him?

172

That would be ludicrous since he stood head and shoulders above the others. Maybe the best thing was to treat him in a casual, breezy manner as she did all the others.

Silver sauntered over to the bar. "Well, long time no see."

"I've been busy," Cherokee stammered, looking down at her. She knew he was staring at the swell of her full breasts in the tight, low-cut aquamarine dress. Let him look and lust. He hadn't gotten her body then and he wouldn't get it now.

"I see the shoes have given you a nickname that stuck." He nodded toward her glittering feet.

"It appears so." She sipped the coffee Al put before her. "And how are things up on the claim?"

"All right, I reckon." His hands shook as he rolled a cigarette.

"I wasn't sure I'd ever see you again."

He gave her a hard look, the lit match halfway to his mouth. "I wasn't sure either."

"I want to thank you again," she said and tried to appear cool and distant.

"I thought with that thanks, you promised me a reward."

"Certainly." She gestured to Al, who stood there listening. The bartender immediately handed her the cash box, and before Cherokee could protest, she turned and sailed toward her velvet cubicle.

Once inside, she closed the drapes and put the box on the table. "I did promise you a reward, didn't I?"

He loomed over her. "To be honest about it, if my partner hadn't shot you, you wouldn't have been in that fix. By the way, I never did get a good answer as to what

173

you were doing out there."

She hesitated, not looking at him.

"You came looking for me, didn't you? Why?"

"I did not!" She glared up at him. "I told you I was thinking of buying a claim and got lost."

"I don't believe you."

"I don't give a damn what you believe! Anyway, I promised you a reward for your help." She opened the box.

"You know what I want, and it's not your damn money!"

She looked up at him, watching him breath deeply. Faintly through the drapes, the sound of the piano, laughter, and faro drifted. Cherokee stood close enough to touch, and electricity seemed to almost spark from him like lightning in a storm. There was something dangerous and excitingly forbidden about the man . . . and frightening. "I'm not going to give you that, you know it."

He laughed. "Can't blame me for trying!"

"Don't expect me to feel obligated if you turn down the money." She put a pile of gold coins on the table.

He swept them to the floor with a sneering gesture and they rang and rolled across the floor. Before she realized his next move, he grabbed her and kissed her.

Silver panicked and struggled, beating against his chest, but she couldn't cry out for help because his mouth covered hers and she was helpless against his strength. The heat of his hands burned into her waist and then he moved one of them down to cover her bottom, lifted her off her feet, and pressed her against him so that she felt the heat of him all the way down both their bodies.

She beat him about the face with her small hands and

tried to break away, but he held her easily, his hard maleness throbbing against her belly through their clothing. His tongue was in her mouth, probing and caressing. She tried to bite him, but he seemed to pay that no heed. Helpless against his raw virility, she realized suddenly that fighting him only aroused him and she went limp in his arms, shaking as he kissed her.

He took a deep shuddering breath and stood her slowly on her feet. He looked a little surprised. "Damn you," he whispered, "for making me want you the way I do!"

"Damn you for manhandling me!" she snapped back, more angry with herself than him. His mouth and body had aroused emotions in her she didn't even know existed. She liked her life the way it was and he could only destroy that.

"Silver. Yes, it suits you, all right. Tell me, if I'm willing to give you all the gold I've got, will you let me have one night of your time?"

She slapped him so hard, his head snapped back.

"If you were a man, I'd kill you for that," he snarled.

"And if I were a man, I'd call you out and kill you right out there in the street!" She was livid with rage.

"Why don't you tell your faithful watchdog?" Cherokee said sarcastically. "I'm sure Al would come gunnin' for me if he knew I'd dared to touch you."

"And you'd kill him! I'll bet you're good with a pistol." She was trembling now, eyes filling with tears.

He looked angry, frustrated, and totally confused. "Silver, I shouldn't have done that. I couldn't stop myself—"

"Get out!" She managed to keep her voice low although she was bordering on hysteria. "Get out of my saloon!"

175

"I'll do more than that. When I finish my business tomorrow, I'll get out of town. From now on, I'll go to Fairplay for supplies." He turned and strode away.

She stood there a long moment, composing herself before she knelt, picked up the scattered money from the floor, took her cash box, and went to the bar.

Al stared at her curiously. "Are you okay?"

She didn't look at him. "Fine. I'm tired, though. I'm going upstairs. You'll close up, won't you?"

He nodded and she handed him the cash box and fled to her rooms, locking the door behind her. The kiss had left her more shaken than she cared to admit, even to herself. Along with the fear had come an urge to hold him close, to let him touch her, dominate her, mesh together like two wild, primitive things.

Silver felt both afraid and disgusted with herself. A man like that would change her future if she succumbed to animal desires. He would destroy her by getting her with child and then deserting her.

She closed her drapes and checked her image anxiously in one of the many mirrors. *Was that a tiny new line at the corner of her mouth? Did she only imagine that there were fine wrinkles around her eyes?*

Cherokee lusted after her because she was pretty. If she wasn't beautiful, she was worthless. Long before the sands of time had run through the hourglass, Silver intended to be financially secure. There was no place in that plan for a penniless half-breed who only wanted to slake his lust on her body.

She slipped into a sheer, expensive nightdress;—pale blue silk that felt good on her skin. Silver went to bed and drifted into a restless sleep.

She dreamed that she stood on an auction block on the

176

stage of the Nugget. She wore the silver shoes and the sheer nightdress. Men buyers stared at her hungrily as the bidding began. The auctioneer made her turn around slowly, parade up and down. She wouldn't look at the audience, knowing they could see through her clothing. Her stepfather, Jake Dallinger, and Bart Brett were bidding for her and she stood there, small gold chains tying her wrists and ankles. Suddenly Cherokee was bidding for her.

What's the bid? the auctioneer said, banging his gavel.

One kiss, the big 'breed yelled out, *one kiss!*

Sold! The hammer came down with a resounding bang. *Come and claim your woman!*

Cherokee came to the stage, swung her up in his arms. *You're mine now, Silver; you always knew you would be.*

Neeley, Brett, Jake Dallinger, and a dozen others raised their voices in protest, wanting her, but Cherokee silenced them with a glare that was black as thunderclouds. *She's mine*, he said. *I bought her soul and body with one kiss. I'll kill any man who disputes my ownership!*

They all backed away, apparently afraid of the big 'breed. She was safe at last . . . safe from everyone but him.

He carried her up to a hotel room with a big bed.

Silver held her wrists out to him. *Aren't you going to turn me loose?*

He shook his head and looped the chains over the headboard so that she lay there helpless. As she waited, her heart pounding with apprehension, He began to slowly open her nightdress. *I'm going to return that kiss with interest*, he promised softly. *Don't fight me, Silver, you're my slave and I'm going to enjoy that ripe body!*

She was naked now and he was pulling off his clothes.

Here's that kiss, he whispered and he put his mouth where her legs joined, and she gasped at the sensation. She had never had a man kiss her there, but with the golden chain looped over the headboard, she was helpless. Whatever he did to her with his hands and mouth, she couldn't stop him, nor was she sure she wanted to. What men had done in the past was use her, but Cherokee was teasing her, thrilling her until she begged him not to stop.

Then suddenly Elmer Neely and Bart Brett were there, protesting and pushing Cherokee away. *No one can ever have her but us. In her mind, she can never accept a man because of us . . . us . . . us . . .*

Silver woke and sat bolt upright in bed. She glanced at the door, saw that it was bolted, and sighed as she put her knees up and laid her face against them. A nightmare. The lamp didn't help all that much after all. It must be very late; the saloon downstairs was quiet.

She got up and paced the floor, wondering what to do about the big 'breed. Now he was invading her dreams. Damn him and his kiss. She'd been doing just fine until he came into her life. She was rich and successful and she didn't need him to mess things up.

Cherokee leaned against a door post across the street, stared up at her window, smoked a cigarette. A light burned dimly as always behind the drapes of her window. He had been standing here ever since the Nugget closed for the night, some hours ago. He ought to go to his own room and go to bed, but he knew he couldn't sleep. He shouldn't have kissed her. He had thought that once he finally tasted her mouth, he'd realize she was just a woman after all, only prettier than most. The bawdy house down the street looked as if it might still be open. What he should do is go there, get roaring drunk, and take the prettiest blond whore in the place.

If all white women were whores, why wouldn't Silver let him buy her? He'd tried everything to seduce her, offered to pay all his hard-earned dust, to no avail. Maybe he just hadn't offered enough.

He reached into his pocket, brought the small bracelet out, and watched it gleam in the moonlight. It was nice, but nothing compared to the jewelry she already owned. If he sent it to her, would she laugh at his small gift? When he had been facing her across the table this evening, why hadn't he given it to her? Had he been secretly afraid she would sweep it off on the floor the same way he'd done the coins she tried to give him? Why the hell couldn't he forget about her? There were other women in this town—women who'd offer, not only their bodies, but their passion. And all he hungered for was the shimmering, quicksilver sensation of hers.

Was she really afraid of men, or was she only a tantalizing tease? Was there more to this girl than just her beauty? There were a lot of pretty women; Savannah had been pretty. Silver seemed different. He almost sensed a soft, sensitive vulnerability that called out to the dominant, protective maleness of him.

He dropped the bracelet in his pocket with a sigh, and shifted his weight. He ought to go to his room. Instead he stood and watched her window. As he smoked and looked up, he saw her shadow pass before the drapes and then pass again. What had awakened her and agitated her so?

179

He watched her shadow pace up and down a long time before he tossed the cigarette away. He wasn't quite sure what he was going to do, but he wanted her to know he was out there . . . if she had changed her mind. Although he didn't want to admit it, even to himself, the kiss had changed things, changed the way he felt about her.

A little uncertainly, he crossed the street, climbed one of the roof posts, and swung up onto the little railed balcony that ran along the windows. "Silver? Silver, are you all right?"

Silver froze and listened. "Who's there?"

"Cherokee Evans."

She went to the window, and looked out through the crack in the drapes. "Go away! What are you doing out there?"

With the window closed, she couldn't be sure what he was saying. She unlocked it, raising it just a fraction. "Go away! What the hell are you doing on my balcony?"

He frowned. "Worrying about you. I saw your shadow pacing. Are you all right?"

"Go away! I'm fine. If Al catches you, or if the law sees you as he's making his rounds, they might shoot first and ask questions later."

"If you're worried about that, let me in." He put his fingers under the window.

"Drat it all, no! Go away!" She tried to close the window, but his fingers were in the way.

What should she do? She realized too late that she should never have opened the window. His big form loomed against the moonlight. Silver looked uncertainly toward the door. All she had to do was throw it open, scream loudly, and Al would come running. He'd pull both triggers on that shotgun without asking any questions and no jury would convict him for protecting his employer.

"Silver, I've got a gift for you."

"I don't want anything from you, just go away and leave me alone!" Her voice sounded ragged, even to her.

"You aren't all right. I can tell by your voice. What's wrong? What's happened?"

"Nothing! Go away!" She wrapped her arms around herself protectively, and began to pace again. Even though she swallowed hard, she was afraid he might hear the choking sobs.

"You aren't all right; I'm coming in."

All she had to do was run over, and slam the window down, he'd move his hands right quick! Then she could lock it. Instead, she stood there, watching. He raised it slowly. She backed against the door. Frozen with fear and indecision, she watched him climb through the window, and close it and the drapes behind him.

"Get out of my room!" she snarled at him. "Or I'll scream for help!"

He smiled at her. "If you were going to do that, you would have the moment I threw my leg across that sill." He crossed the carpet, and stood close enough to touch. "I don't know what it is with you Silver, I don't know if you're teasing me, holding out for more money—"

"I don't need your damned money! I've plenty of my own!"

"Then what does it take to get you?" He reached out and put his hand on her bare shoulder. It seemed to radiate animal heat.

"Please don't touch me." She turned away from him.

"Your words say that, but your tone says different."
He put both hands on her shoulders. She couldn't stop
the trembling that overcame her at his touch—the
touch that brought back thoughts of the cabin. But more
powerful, more terrifying memories overcame those.

"Are you cold?" His hands were kneading her bare
shoulders and the lace straps of her nightdress slid down
her arms.

"No—yes—I—I don't know."

He pulled her back up against his big frame and one of
his arms slipped around her waist. "You're like a fever in
my blood, Silver. I keep hoping that once I've had you,
I'll realize you're just another woman after all, just
prettier than most."

"Just a pretty whore!" Her voice came brittle, and
hard.

"If you say so. I've never made any bones about what I
want from you." His other hand slipped across her
breasts and he hugged her to him, pulling her back
against him.

The arm across her breasts seemed to burn like fire,
and without meaning to, she arched her back a little to
press her nipples against the heat of it as the hand on her
waist moved lower. "I—I've been everything you think I
am, Cherokee, a pretty toy for a man's amusement."

"No, that's what's driving me loco—those hard eyes
and that soft mouth say you're soft and defenseless and
vulnerable." He pulled away from her suddenly and took
a deep breath. "I'm a lot of things, Silver, but I'm not
enough of a bastard to take advantage of you. Here, I told
you I had a gift for you. It's not much, compared to the
fine stuff you already own, but maybe, well, I thought
you might like it."

182

She felt him reach in his pocket, and take her hand. When she looked down, he had put a dainty chain bracelet with gold nuggets dangling from it around her wrist. Then he moved away from her. She turned and watched him cross toward the window. "You've spent all this time trying to get me to surrender and now you've changed your mind?"

He paused, his hands on the window frame. "I still want you, Silver." He drew a long, shuddering breath. "God, how I want you! But I think I'm beginning to fall in love with you and that's no good for either of us."

It was because of her beauty, she thought. No one ever wanted the real Silver, the person behind the pretty face. The lump in her throat grew until she had to swallow to hold it back. Tears rose in her eyes and overflowed.

"For God's sake, Silver, don't cry! I feel like the world's worst outlaw now!"

She stood there, shoulders shaking. "I—I don't want you to go."

"Silver, I'm only human," he said. "I've had as much of this as I can stand. If I stay, I won't be able to stop myself from making love to you and you don't want a man to touch you."

"I've got good reason," she whispered.

He gave her a long, searching look. "I've no doubt of that. If I could get my hands on the sonovabitch responsible, I swear I'd kill him for it!"

And then she wasn't quite sure how, but she was in his arms and he held her tightly and kissed the tears off her cheeks. "Don't cry, sweet darlin'. Oh, don't cry!"

He swung her up in his arms, carried her, and sat her gently on the bed. "Good-bye, Silver. I'm going back up to the claim. You won't see me anymore. From now on

183

when we need supplies, I'll send my partners."

He started toward the window.

She raised her hand in protest. "Wait, don't go."

Cherokee paused, one foot on the sill. "Don't stop me, Silver. It's hard enough to leave now. If I stay, I'm not sure I can keep myself from making love to you, and I gave you my word I wouldn't."

"Please . . ." She slid off the bed, moving toward him, afraid of what was about to happen, yet more afraid to let him leave forever. "I—I release you from that promise. Oh, please don't go . . ."

And then he was on his knees before her, his arms clasped around her hips, pulling her against his mouth while he kissed her there.

With a low moan of surrender, she clasped his head against her body, dizzy with response his hot mouth created as he kissed her womanhood.

Chapter Ten

"Cherokee . . ." She didn't know whether to stop him or urge him on as his mouth kissed her there. His hands clasped her bottom and began to work her nightdress up her legs until his mouth was on her flesh, the tip of his tongue caressing and teasing. Her legs gave way under her and she collapsed into his arms and slid onto the thick carpet.

"Tell me to stop and I will," he whispered. "Tell me you don't want me to do this to you." And his mouth caressed up her belly to her navel.

"I— I don't want you to . . ." She tried to repeat it between gasping breaths, but could not seem to finish.

"I'm yours to command," he said more urgently, and she felt the heat of his breath as his tongue flicked her navel. "Tell me not to touch you, and I'll get up and leave."

"Don't . . ." She writhed under his kisses on her bare skin. What was it she was supposed to tell him? *Oh, don't stop. Don't stop.*

He pressed her breasts together with his two big hands

185

and buried his face in the deep cleft between them. Automatically, she reached out to hold his face and guided his mouth to her nipple. He sucked there until she moaned with desire.

She must make him stop and leave her room. Any moment now, he would shove her thighs apart and throw his whole weight on her. While she wept and struggled to escape, he would ram into her, impale her on his hot sword of flesh and it would be agony; it had always been agony.

Very gently, he stood, reached down, and swung her up in his arms. He stood there looking into her face as if searching for answers. "I don't understand you," he said softly, and his eyes were mystified. "It's almost like making love to a virgin."

But of course in her heart, she was a virgin. She had been raped repeatedly, but no man had ever made her desire him so that she surrendered and wanted what he had to give. She thought that, but she didn't say it; he wouldn't understand and he didn't care about her feelings. Like all the others, he only wanted a pretty plaything on which to vent his lust.

"Silver?" He was asking with his eyes and she didn't know the answer. If only he would hold and caress and kiss her, not wanting to do that terrible thing to her, not expecting her to want it, too.

While she struggled within herself for the answer to his question, he carried her over and sat her on the edge of the bed, her nightdress still gathered around her waist.

"Silver, you're trembling again. Are you really afraid of me?"

And then she couldn't hold back the sobs. "Not you, them!"

186

He gathered her into his arms and she wept against his shoulder, her long hair covering both of them. "Who, Silver? Who has hurt you? I swear to God . . .!"

She hadn't meant to tell him; she had never told anyone and Al had only guessed at some of it. She began to tell a little of it, sobs racking her, and he put his hand gently over her mouth. "Don't, sweet darlin' don't put yourself through that, it doesn't matter. None of it matters." He kissed the tears from her eyes. "I'd better leave."

"No, don't leave me! I'm so afraid, so alone . . ." She put her arms around his neck and pulled his face against her breasts.

"I'll stay awhile then," he said gently, "and then I'll go. You're shivering. Are you cold?"

"A little."

"Then let me warm you. I seem to be good at that." He lay down on the bed, still fully dressed, pulled her against his chest, and covered them both. She could feel his hard maleness against her but he only held her close and stroked her hair.

"I shouldn't have told you," she said.

He looked down at her and she saw the confusion in his dark face. "I don't know what you are," he said finally, "and I thought I knew. I thought I knew about all white women."

His manhood felt rock hard against her body. "If you—if you want me, I'll let you."

He sighed and she felt the tension in his big frame. "If that's the way I get it, if you're only going to 'let me,' thanks but no thanks."

"You're saying no?" She was shocked.

"I'm saying I expect a little passion from a woman."

187

She felt embarrassed. "I don't know about that."

"No, I really don't think you do."

Could she fake it? If she let him, would she lose him? Was she only a conquest, and once he had enjoyed her body would he move on to new conquests?

Almost shyly, she reached to kiss his lips and it seemed almost to startle him. "Teach me," she whispered. "Teach me to like it."

"Are you sure you want me to?"

Did she? "I—I know you'll have to hurt me, but if you want me—"

He interrupted her by swearing softly. "What kind of animal do you think I am?" He bent and kissed her sweetly, gently brushing against her lips until she opened them to his caressing tongue. His hand stroked her bare belly and then moved lower to cover her mound. His touch sent electric currents running through her, and when she gasped, he sucked her tongue into his mouth.

His hesitant hand gradually separated her closed thighs and he stroked along her velvet ridge until she shuddered, wanting him to touch deeper and he did, his fingers stroking and prodding. "God, you're built small," he said. "Any man could tear you open if you weren't ready for him."

She reached and took his large rigid maleness in her hand and knew he would hurt her if she let him take her.

He groaned aloud when she put her hand on him. "Silver, I haven't had a woman in months and you've had me ready to go since the first moment I laid eyes on you. You'd better take your hand away."

She didn't. The fact that it gave him pleasure pleased her as well, more than she would have ever guessed.

He bent his head to her breast while his fingers

continued to stroke her insides. His maleness was rigid and wet with his seed and the scent of it excited her even as his mouth sucked and pulled at her nipples. Silver moved her hips restlessly, wanting him to touch her deeper. Her heart began to drum hard against her rib cage and she was sure he could feel it against his lips. His other arm was around her and his hand caressed her bare skin until she was breathing heavily with her mouth open.

"That's it, Silver, come to me, surrender to it. You want it, you know you do."

She wasn't sure what it was she wanted, but she spread her thighs farther apart, tilting her pelvis up for his stroking touch. "Cherokee?" She was suddenly afraid of what seemed to be sweeping over her. "Cherokee?"

"Relax and let it happen," he whispered with the tip of his tongue in her ear. "Let it happen. Surrender to me . . ."

He was whispering to her, encouraging her, urging her, and she didn't know what it was that he wanted. Certainly he could be getting no pleasure from this, and that was what sex was all about, satisfying a man's body.

A tremor began to build deep in her, sweeping over her and she couldn't control it, couldn't stop herself from trying to cry out. When she did, his mouth covered hers, his tongue going deep so that her cry of release went only into his mouth.

She wasn't sure what had happened, she only knew that when the room stopped spinning, he still lay holding her and whispering to her. "That's it, sweet darlin', sweet, sweet Silver."

She felt wet and warm from her belly to her knees, and more than that, she couldn't stop herself from weeping, but she didn't understand why. For the first time that she could remember, she felt she could turn off the lamp and sleep securely—as long as he held her and stroked her like this.

"I'm not through," he said, and before she realized what he was doing, he slid down in the bed. His mouth was on her, his tongue hot and caressing, stabbing deep within her body. It felt like a ribbon of fire inside as his hands stroked her thighs, spreading them for his eager mouth.

She found herself whimpering, tangling her fingers in his tousled hair, holding his face against her body as she used him for her own satisfaction. In moments, he had her writhing again while her hand stroked his throbbing hardness.

Silver lay gasping and spent, still holding him in her hand. She had never experienced desire before, much less ecstasy. It had been like quicksilver, sparkling, changing into something even more beautiful as she rode the crest of an emotional wave. Quicksilver passion.

She looked up into his eyes and saw the hunger there. She ran her hand down the length of his maleness, thinking how big he was, and that when he rammed into her, she would have to bite her lips bloody to keep from screaming aloud.

He must have seen her frightened expression in the dim lamp light. He shook his head. "I won't ever hurt you, Silver. I want to erase those ghosts from your past."

He pulled her close and kissed her tenderly, then rolled over on his back, still holding her in his arms. "If it's going to happen, you'll have to make love to me."

She was embarrassed to admit she had never taken the initiative before and wasn't sure quite what to do. "Are you going to take your clothes off?"

190

"If you want me to." He stood up, and in the lamp light, he began to undo his belt and pull off his boots. He looked twice as big naked. He lay back down on the bed and put his arms under his head.

She hesitated, then bent so that her long locks fell like a pale silken shower over them both and she put her mouth on his nipple and was disconcerted at the way he moaned and caught her head, pressing it hard against his chest, encouraging her to do it again and again until his nipples were as hard and swollen as her own.

She slid down in the bed and kissed his sword, paying homage to his maleness in an almost pagan manner.

"Don't do that, Silver," he warned her. "I'm only a man, after all, and I've almost lost control several times already."

She wanted to please him, even if it hurt her. Very slowly she slid her body down on him. She hadn't realized how wet she was and it surprised her that it didn't hurt. She kept waiting for it to hurt.

His hands were wet with sweat and trembling as he reached out and grabbbed her waist. She was small enough that his hands almost spanned her as he lifted her and brought her down on him again. "Ride me, sweet darlin'," he whispered. "Oh, ride the hell out of me!"

She looked down at her creamy white legs forking this dark-skinned brute who was like a wild mustang stallion. And suddenly she wanted to ride him, wanted to come down on him hard and deep, feel him convulsing and swelling deep inside her body while his hands caught her breasts as they hung over his face and pulled them down to his lips.

Then he was bucking under her, ramming strongly as his virile body came up off the bed and into hers. He caught her hands and brought them to his nipples and then his two big hands caught her waist and held her. It was cool in the room, but they were both shiny with perspiration from the exertion of their straining bodies.

She felt the surging tremble, the straining of his powerful body, and then hers seemed to lock on to his, wanting what he had to give even as he began to pour his seed into her with a ragged gasping of breath. Her body convulsed even as his did, and as darkness enveloped her, she felt him shudder and give up all the hot, virile seed he had been saving for so long.

They slept awhile, locked in each other's arms, entwined in a tangle of her long, pale hair. But toward morning, Cherokee sat up on the edge of the bed and stretched. "I think I'd better go back to my hotel. I'd just soon some early riser didn't see me leaving through the window."

She nodded, not quite sure what the new day would bring now that he had satisfied his body. She was afraid to ask about their future so she only watched him dress.

He came over to her, and took her face between his two big hands. "Sweet Silver," he whispered. "I love you." He took her small hand in his, the bracelet on her wrist sparkling in the faint light. "Here's a treasure to keep in your pocket." Very slowly, he kissed her palm, and closed her fingers over it. Then he went to the window and was gone.

Silver lay on her bed, staring at her closed hand. A kiss. She held a captured kiss to remember him by. That and a bracelet. She opened the hand against her lips, savoring the warm touch of his mouth that seemed to linger there.

192

In that moment, she relived their coupling;—his mouth on hers, dominating, demanding. Had she done the right thing in surrendering to him? Did he really love her, or was she only a conquest to be added to his list and snickered over when men gathered for a drink and talked about women they had known?

Cherokee went back to his room, washed up, changed clothes, and lay down across the bed to sleep. The night had left him exhausted and drained. He wasn't sure what to do about the relationship now. True, when it had all begun, all he wanted was to satisfy his lust with the beautiful blonde's body; he hadn't thought of her as a human being. To him, she had been only a whore, despite her cool demeanor. But now that he had taken her, he had a feeling he couldn't get enough of her. Loco as it seemed, he found himself wanting to marry her and have children by her.

That was impossible, of course. She might have surrendered to passion, but how would she feel about leaving the glamorous limelight to change diapers on a mixed-blood Indian baby up in some cabin in the mountains? Cherokee realized that unless he made a big strike, Silver was more successful than he was and he wouldn't consider living on her money. But to ask a beautiful, wealthy, and successful girl to give up everything to be the wife of a poor, half-breed prospector was ridiculous. She would only say no, and he wasn't sure his pride could stand that. He was still awake when dawn came and outside he heard a horse gallop down the main street and a man shouting. Cherokee ran to the window and pushed it up.

"War!" the rider shouted, dismounting from the lathered sorrel horse. "Pony Express just galloped

193

through Julesburg with the news a few hours ago! We're about to be at war!"

What he feared most had transpired. Cherokee leaned out the window and shouted down to the rider as people ran out to surround him. "Hey! What's happened?"

The wiry cowboy shouted back, "South Carolina soldiers have fired on federal troops at Fort Sumpter! The war has finally started!"

Cherokee groaned aloud. Ever since Lincoln's election last November, Southern states had been slowly seceding, beginning with South Carolina. Still everyone had hoped that when cooler heads prevailed, the South would not take drastic action. But it had come to that. And despite everything, deep in his heart, Cherokee Evans was a Southerner.

He could forget all his plans, all his dreams. Everything he had fantasized with Silver was now ended. When he headed for the Nugget Saloon, excited clusters of people had gathered up and down the street, discussing the news. Shouts of the happening were aimed at newcomers as they came out to see what the ruckus was about.

When Cherokee entered the deserted saloon and Silver met him at the door, she still wore his gold nugget bracelet, but he knew by her face that she had already heard.

"I've got some coffee made," she said and gave him a long, searching look.

He sank slowly into a chair, his heart heavy. "I'm a Southerner, Silver, I'll have to go."

"Why? You don't own any slaves, do you?" She set the coffee down before him and he sipped it, grateful for the strong, bracing taste.

194

"There'll be a lot of men who'll rise up to defend the South who don't own slaves, who hate slavery." He thought of Shawn O'Bannion. "We can't stand by and see the South overrun by Yankee raiders, the women raped, everything destroyed."

"But it was the Southern leaders who stole the Cherokees' land," she argued. "You owe them nothing."

He drank the coffee and looked at her anxious face across from him. "That's probably true, and I reckon there'll be Cherokees fighting on both sides. Both sides will want as many tribes as they can get as allies. Somehow I feel when it's over, no matter who wins, the Indians will lose."

"Then why go?" She hesitated, looking down at her cup. "Is it—is it because of last night?"

How could he ask her to marry him now? He owed allegiance to his beloved South. More than that, he owed more than he could ever repay to Shawn O'Bannion, the good friend he had betrayed. "Yes, last night changed a lot of things, but we can't discuss that now. I've got to go help my friend, Silver. His fine plantation will be one of those that will be overrun, sacked, and burned. Shawn raises some of the finest Tennessee walking horses in the world. The raiders will take them all if they get into Tennessee."

"I see." She spoke so softly that he barely heard her as she toyed with the nuggets on her wrists. "Will you—will you come back anytime soon to see me?"

"Reckon not. Colorado Territory will probably stay with the Union, which means I would be looked on as an enemy soldier." The idea of being parted from her even one night tore his heart out. If he weren't careful, all his resolve would melt in his love for her. He had a duty to the South and to Shawn O'Bannion, whom he'd betrayed. A real man must put his duty before his own selfish desires. He caught her hand, kissed the palm, and folded her fingers over it. "Here's a treasure to remember me by."

She jerked her hand away and stood up. "Well, it really doesn't matter," she said. "I don't want you to go thinking you meant anything special to me. What's one damned Rebel more or less? If you ever get back in the area, you might look me up—if I'm still around and haven't taken up with someone new by then." She started to turn away and he reached out and caught her arm. "Silver, was last night nothing to you?"

She shrugged and gave him a tight-lipped smile. "An enjoyable romp, as it was to you. That's why I'm such a good whore; I can make any man feel he's special. Now go off to your damned, noble war. It'll send the price of gold and silver zooming;—great for business. I wasted enough time; I've got a saloon to run!"

He felt furious and betrayed. So she was only a skilled whore. He had been right after all. "With that act you put on, sweet, you could convince any man of anything. You even had me fooled!" He pulled her to him, hurt that last night had meant nothing to her. "Let me give you something else to remember me by!"

Before she could protest, he dragged her to him and kissed her deeply. For a split second, she melted against him, returning his kiss with heated ardor, and then she pulled away. "Consider last night payment for the bracelet!" she sneered. "But next time, it'll cost more than a poor half-breed like you can pay!"

She flounced away and up the stairs.

He stood staring after her, crushed and humiliated.

What a fool she had made of him. How she would have laughed if he had told her of his love, had asked her to marry him. And to think he had been about to ask her to wait for him until he returned from the war!

Cherokee didn't look back as he turned on his heel and left. He got the needed supplies, loaded them on the burro, and went back to the claim. There he told his partners what had happened and what he felt he had to do. They sympathized with him, told him they would keep working the claim and save his share until he returned. With a heavy heart, Cherokee returned to town, took some of his money from the bank, and bought a good horse.

He thought about trying to see Silver again, but decided he had had as much hurt as he could stand. His grandmother had been right about white women, he thought bitterly as he rode slowly past the Nugget Saloon and on out of town.

Silver watched him ride past from her upstairs window. She struggled with her feelings, wanting to run after him, not wanting it to end like this. Then she remembered that she was nothing but another pretty conquest to him, that he really cared nothing for her. He was like the others after all.

But while she struggled with the decision, he rode on down the street and the moment was lost. She watched his figure grow smaller and smaller in the distance and she kept looking long after he was lost to sight. Then she threw herself down on her bed and wept until she could weep no more.

When she got up and looked in one of her many

mirrors, she was horrified to see her eyes red and swollen. She must not let her grief destroy her beauty; it was really all she could count on. As long as she possessed a flawless face, she had security that no man would offer her. In the meantime, she had a saloon to run. Silver stared at her hand. *A treasure to keep.* Without thinking, she put her palm against her heart, and the bracelet he had given her tinkled as she did so. She changed into a gaudy silver-spangled dress as night came on, splashed cold water on her face, put on the silver shoes, and went downstairs to the only life she knew.

Cherokee made his trip south with a heavy heart. Already the states were gearing up for the coming fight, but he had no stomach for it. He was going because it was his duty and because he owed this to the friend he had betrayed.

He avoided riding out to Shannon Place plantation because he didn't want to face Shawn's beautiful but faithless wife. Instead, he went to the nearby village, asked around, and was sent to a camp where Captain Shawn O'Bannion was helping train raw recruits.

He dismounted and handed his reins over to a big, redheaded private. "Is Shawn here?"

"Yes sir! Right over yonder." The young man pointed toward a tent and Cherokee grinned in spite of himself at the twangy Tennessee accent.

Cherokee went in, and stood for a long moment looking down at the tall, handsome man in a gray uniform who bent over the maps spread before him on an improvised table. The years had been kind to the Irish immigrant, Cherokee thought. Except for a little gray in the black hair, Shawn O'Bannion didn't look like a man who must be close to forty years old.

"Yes?" He looked up, fixing Cherokee with eyes as green as shamrocks. "Cherokee!" He came around the table, and clapped him on both shoulders. "Aye, and it's glad I am to see you, lad! I'd been wondering if I was going to have to fight the Yanks without you by me side!"

They shook hands warmly. "Shawn, you're the best friend I ever had. I had to come. No matter what it cost me, I couldn't live with myself if I let you down."

But he had let him down, Cherokee thought, that one night when Shawn was away from the plantation. He could only pray to God that Shawn never found out that the young beauty he'd married and the boy he had raised to a man had betrayed him. For this reason, his debt to the Irishman must come before anything else; he'd sworn to make it up to the man who had taken him in when his grandmother died.

"Drink?" Shawn reached for a bottle.

"No, I quit. I was afraid I would end up like my father."

"Oh?" Shawn looked at him a long moment, shrugged his broad shoulders, and poured himself one. "Good Irish whiskey! Seems to me we used to have us some lovely evenings over a bottle in the old days. I never did understand why you left so suddenly. Savannah has asked about you."

Cherokee didn't meet the other man's eyes as he flopped down in a chair, and rolled a cigarette. "Didn't you get my note?"

"Aye. Still, lad, it was sudden like."

"How's everyone?" Cherokee asked to change the subject. "Is Shadow with you?" Shadow was Shawn's big mulatto body servant who had been with the Irishman for many years.

Shawn shook his head. "Shadow felt drawn to fight on the other side and I told him to go with my blessings. A man does what he feels in his heart he must; that is, if he's a *real* man."

Cherokee looked up suddenly and realized Shawn was staring at him keenly. At that moment, he had a distinct feeling that Shawn knew he had been betrayed.

"And your son?"

"Fine. Though 'tis a disappointment to me that the boy seems to take more after the St. Clairs than the O'Bannions. But then Savannah coddles and spoils him so."

Cherokee didn't say anything. He knew that the couple disagreed on the rearing of the young blond son.

Shawn sipped his whiskey. "You didn't tell me why you left so sudden or where you went."

"Felt that Evans urge to go looking for the rainbow," Cherokee said. "Maybe I've just got the wanderlust like my father. He had that claim up in Colorado that I'm working with his old partners."

Shawn held up his glass in a toast and beamed at him. "Here's hopin' you strike it rich as I did in California. Then you, too, can own a big plantation and everything that money can buy."

Including a young, elegant, blue-blooded wife like Savannah St. Clair, Cherokee thought. Something about Shawn's expression made Cherokee blurt out without thinking, "And are you happy with all that your money has bought?"

Shawn looked startled; his green eyes stared into Cherokee's a long moment. "I dreamed of being among

200

the landed gentry from the moment I got off the boat," he said softly, as if he were thinking aloud. "There was a high-born lady that a poor, Irish boy couldn't have . . ."

Cherokee waited for him to continue, but the expression on the handsome Irish face told him O'Bannion was thinking of some other time long ago. "Well, Shawn, by damn, you showed them, didn't you? You've got everything that success can buy—even the lady."

"Not *the* lady," Shawn whispered, and then he seemed to realize he had said too much and came to attention briskly. "So now we'll be into a war and I may have to kill men who've done me no harm to hang on to the way of life I love."

Cherokee smoked and shook his head. "I think we'll see an end to this way of life. I'm afraid we're going to come out on the losing end of this fight."

Shawn's handsome face saddened. "We're a pair, aren't we, lad? Both opposed to slavery, yet fighting for the South because we love her. You're right; our side can't possibly win."

"If England or France needs our cotton badly enough to come in on our side—"

"The English?" Shawn shuddered and then laughed. "They do say politics make strange bedfellows. Still, by gorrah, I never thought the son of an old sod like myself might end up fighting on the same side as the hated English."

He looked into his glass. "We'll do the best we can with what we've got, Cherokee, but we're outnumbered and outgunned. And I'll tell you a little secret; I don't think the English want our cotton badly enough to fight on the side of slavery. I don't think her people will stand for it!"

Cherokee smoked and studied the man who meant more to him than a father. "I'd follow you into hell, Shawn, you know that, and so would anyone who knows you."

"Before this is over, I'm afraid that's exactly what you will do," the Irishman said gravely. "But enough of this. I've got to get you into uniform." He stood up, went to the door of the tent, and called out. "Private Dowdy?"

The big redheaded boy came in, and saluted.

Shawn smiled. "Cherokee, this is private William Dowdy, lately of Bedford County, Tennessee. He was a blacksmith there and now he's shoeing horses for the Confederate states when he's not my orderly. Private Dowdy, meet my old friend, Cherokee Evans, and see that he's taken care of. We've got a war to fight!"

Cherokee stood up. Regret it as he might, he had made his choice. His loyalty to the man who had raised and trusted him, and saving his homeland, had to be the uppermost priority in his mind right now. The beautiful blonde whose heart was as hard as the metal of her name would have to remain only a moment in his past—like Savannah. Saloon girl or wealthy plantation wife— there wasn't a nickel's worth of difference, no matter what his heart told him.

For Silver, one day blended into another as spring passed slowly and summer came on. For a while, she thought she could not live with the pain of having given her heart to a man who was no better than the rest after all. To him, she had been only an evening's conquest, a pretty toy to amuse himself with. Why hadn't she remembered that in the West, there were only two kinds

202

of women as far as men were concerned and she was the wrong kind?

Still she didn't take off the bracelet and sometimes she dreamed that he made love to her again, kissed her palm and closed her fingers over it. *A treasure to keep . . .*

The war brought an even bigger boom to the Rockies with the Union needing Colorado's gold and silver to pay for guns and uniforms. Silver's Nugget Saloon did a profitable business. She still danced and sang for her adoring customers and checked her features every night to make sure her face was as flawless as ever.

She intended to throw the silver shoes away because they reminded her too much of the man she had given her heart to, but she couldn't bring herself to do so, any more than she could take off the gold nugget bracelet. She left the lamp burning at night by her bedside because of the nightmares that plagued her again now that he was gone.

No man was invited up to her room and no one, not even Al, knew about the one night Cherokee Evans had spent there. She knew that men whispered that her heart was as hard as her eyes and the metal she was named for, but she didn't care. No one knew that after she sang and danced and laughed with the customers, she went upstairs, locked her door, and alternately cried for Cherokee and cursed his name.

It was a hot summer day when a trio of Mexicans herded the small flock of sheep down the main street to provide meat for the hungry prospectors.

Silver had just come from the Haw Tabor's store and she paused now in front of the Nugget to smile at the trio trying vainly to keep the nervous woolies moving while the animals ran every which way, baaing and bleating.

One of the men paused for a long moment, looked her way uncertainly, then collapsed in the street.

Instantly, Silver ran and knelt by his side. Others came running, too. She managed to get his head in her lap and looked around for help. "Al? Al? Drat it all! Where are you? I need you!"

The bartender looked a little ill himself, she thought as he stuck his head out the saloon doors, then pushed his way through the crowd. "Silver, you'll get dirty."

"I can't help that. This man is sick. Get some men to help and carry him into the Nugget."

Around her, she heard a murmur that the herder was just a Mexican and not worth bothering about.

With a rush of anger, she glared at the people and put her hand on the man's forehead. He was burning with fever. "Al, help me!"

Al grumbled, but he got Hank and Zeke and some of the others to help carry the herder in and lay him on one of the Nugget's tables. Then she sent someone running for Doc, but he was out at a distant ranch delivering a baby and wouldn't be back for a day or so.

In the meantime, Silver decided to do the best she could for the pitiful wretch. She moved him into a spare bed and everyone who worked for her took turns helping with him. Even the customers came in to have a curious look at the feverish and unconscious Mexican whose friends had evidently deserted him now that they had sold their sheep.

Word spread about the Mexican and his mysterious ailment. Silver herself sat by his bedside, only leaving to rest when Al himself offered to take over for her. It seemed to her that half the town came by the room to visit and gossip before Doc finally got back and came to the Nugget to diagnose the case.

But by the time Doc got there, Silver already knew. She looked from Al's horrified face to Doc's, then back down to the Mexican's. His face was broken out in big blisters and pustules. Even if he lived, he would be horribly scarred for life.

She had never been so terrified as she was at that moment because, like everyone else, she'd heard how deadly and contagious the disease was.

She took a deep, trembling breath, looking at the man's disfigured face, then back to Doc. "Is it—is it what I think it is?"

Doc nodded. "My God, Silver, as contagious as this is, you should have left him to die in the street!"

"I couldn't do that, Doc." She took the man's hand. "Even if I had known, I couldn't have ignored his need—not even if I had known he had smallpox!"

Chapter Eleven

It was smallpox all right. Within days, the deadly killer spread like wildfire through Buckskin Joe. Half the town was sick or dying, the other half, including Nellie and many of the saloon girls, fled in panic, spreading the disease still farther.

Silver, Al, and a handful of others toiled without rest to ease the misery of the dying while Doc pleaded vainly for outside help. His messages to Denver fell mostly on deaf ears; doctors and nurses themselves were too afraid to come.

An English doctor named Jenner had come up with a vaccination to protect from smallpox, but there was none in the town, and anyway, it was too late for those already stricken.

No hotel or other saloon would accept the sick, so Silver turned the Nugget into one giant hospital room. That closed down her business, so there was no money coming in. When Doc began to run out of supplies, she sold her jewelry, all but the gold nugget bracelet Cherokee had given her. That she never took off; she even slept in it. Then to buy food and medicine, she spent the rest of her own money while Al complained.

"Silver, think of yourself! Remember, you won't always be pretty. When you're old, you'll need the security your gold will bring."

She merely shrugged and kept working at Zeke's bedside. "I couldn't live with myself if I didn't do everything I could for these poor devils, Al."

He took a swig of bitters. "You know what your biggest problem is, Silver? You got a heart soft as butter; maybe that's what I love the most about you."

It was the first time he had ever said anything like that to her. "Love" made her think of Cherokee and it hurt to think she had been used. At least she wasn't expecting his baby. She had mixed feelings about that. "Al, you don't look so good yourself. How do you feel?"

"All right," he said, but his face told her otherwise. "Look, Silver, get some rest."

"There's too many sick people for that." She straightened up and put her hand on her aching back.

During the night, Zeke died and then Old Hank. She hadn't time to even stop and weep for these special friends. There were too many who needed a cold cloth on a burning forehead, or a spoonful of broth.

By the next day, Al's face was broken out in the horrible splotches. He was too weak to get up off his bed. Silver ached with weariness as she laid her face against his arm and wept.

"Silver," he whispered, "get out of this town before it's too late!"

"I couldn't leave you; not after all you've done for me. If everyone runs, who'll care for the sick?"

"Get out, I tell you!" He was almost savage with her.

"If you get this, most likely you'll die. The few who survive with be horribly scarred."

Her flawless face. Her money was gone and her jewelry. All she had left for security was the Nugget and her beauty. She winced at the image of herself covered with scars. "No, I can't leave, Al; I owe you."

He reached out and put his hand on her head. "It's so ironic, you know that? I'm dying anyway; have been ever since we left Chicago. You were the one good thing that ever happened to me, Silver, I had to save you from Brett."

She cried then, her tears dripping on his homely face. "Oh, Al, I—I didn't know!"

"I didn't want you to," he whispered. "Something else—I was wrong about that big half-breed. Crazy jealous of him. He's the right man for you; I knew it the first time I seen him . . . big, gentle. He'd take care of you . . ."

"I'm afraid you're wrong there," she said and brushed the hair back from his fevered brow. She didn't tell him she had been waiting for a letter all these weeks and Cherokee hadn't written.

Doc came over, and stood looking down at them, his weathered face grim with fatigue.

"Doc," Al said, "try to talk some sense into her. I don't mind dying, the pain was getting too much to bear. But she's so beautiful . . . and so alone now . . ."

"Oh, Al, there's hope still." She looked desperately to Doc, but he gave her just the slightest shake of his head. At that point, she couldn't hold back the grief she had battled through all these sad, weary days, and she sobbed. "Oh, Al, how can I ever make it without you?"

He smiled wanly. "Because you're strong, kid, you're a

survivor. You haven't come all this way to die of smallpox in some spot that will soon be a ghost town . . . promise me one thing, kid."

"Oh, anything, Al!" She held on to his feverish hand, willing him to live.

Al looked up at her, trying to tell her how much he cared for her, but he couldn't put it into words. She had been the only light in his worthless, pointless existence. "When I'm gone, will you come once in a while to the graveyard and put wildflowers on my grave? You know, the ones that remind me of your perfume? Bury me in a high spot so I can hear the breeze singing through the trees and maybe I'll think it's your voice."

She nodded and swallowed hard. "Wildflowers. Of course, if that's what you want."

There were so many things he wanted to say to her and had never had the nerve; he was just an ugly nobody and she was so very beautiful. Last week, when he had realized that his time had about run out, that if the cancer didn't get him, the smallpox might, he had sent a letter up to Julesburg so the eastbound Pony Express would get it to St. Joe, then to Chicago. In it, he had told the authorities he took full blame for Brett's murder and the robbery. He didn't want Silver to be afraid for the rest of her life.

His strength was fading fast. He had to tell her about that letter. "Don't be afraid," he whispered. "Don't be afraid. I did it because I love you, Silver, I wanted to help you . . . I wouldn't trade this past year for a chance to live to be a hundred . . ." He had to tell her what he had done to protect her, but he didn't seem to have the energy to get the words out. He was so very, very tired and the room was growing so dark. "Letter . . . I love you,

Silver, I . . ."

Silver held on to his hand as if, by doing so, she could stop him from going. "Yes, Al?" He was trying hard to tell her something. "Yes, Al?"

Doc sighed and leaned over and put his hand on her shoulder. "Silver, he's gone."

"Gone?" For a long moment, the words didn't register although Al lay very still, an ugly man with wide shoulders who had killed a man to help her. "Oh, no!" She put her face against him and cried until there were no tears left.

That afternoon, she followed the wagon carrying the crude, hastily built coffin out to the little graveyard and watched as some of the prospectors dug a grave next to Hank and Zeke and all the others. She was too weary and felt too bad to even cry anymore.

Doc looked at her, worry etching his face. "Silver, are you all right? You don't look too good."

"I'm fine. I can't get sick, too many people need me." Almost woodenly, she gathered an armful of wild flowers and spread them over the graves. "Oh, Doc, when this town's boom days are over, and everyone's gone away, who will look after the graves?"

"Emma and I will as long as we live," Doc said softly. "We expect to live out our lives here. And maybe people who haven't even been born yet will care enough to come by now and then, say a prayer, and leave flowers."

She didn't hear anything else. Her legs suddenly gave way under her and she lay with her cheek on the raw earth of the grave.

From very far away, she heard Doc's voice. "Oh, my

God, I knew she'd been driving herself too hard! Someone help me and run tell Emma we're bringing Silver to our house, the Nugget's full of sick people already!"

She tried to tell him that she wasn't sick, just very, very tired, and that in a moment she would be all right. In a minute, she would get back up and help with the sick. She only wanted to lie here awhile.

When she closed her eyes, she saw Cherokee's rugged face and he was smiling. *I love you, sweet Silver, you with the quicksilver laughter, you of the dancing feet . . .*

"Silver shoes," she gasped. "Yes, I must dance. . . . Please, the shoes. . . ."

She felt herself being lifted up into the wagon that had carried the coffin, and she struggled to sit up, but someone held her down. "Silver shoes," she begged.

Doc's voice echoed around her. "Someone go back to the Nugget and get those damned shoes! I don't think she'll rest easy until she has them."

The wagon jolted and she knew it was moving, but it didn't matter to her. *Letter.* Al had asked about a letter. No, she hadn't gotten one from Cherokee, but maybe he couldn't get a letter through to her.

In her mind, she danced on the mountainside in the silver shoes and Cherokee swung her up in his arms and carried her away to a cabin to be his wife. *I love you, sweet darlin', I'll always love you so . . .*

She remembered next that she lay on the bed in Doc's house with his plump wife, Emma, hovering above her. Silver liked this room. It had a big mirror, and when she came to visit, she always reassured herself that she was still beautiful by studying her reflection. Someone put the shoes in her hands and she smiled and slept, holding them tightly to her breast.

Cherokee, oh, Cherokee. Why did you go away when I loved you so much? The shoes and the bracelet were all she had left of his memory and she clung to them like a drowning man grabs on to a life preserver.

She was so very hot. Funny, she didn't remember late summer here in the Rockies being so very, very hot. She would only lie here a few minutes more and then she would get up and go help Doc with all those sick people. She knew she needed to get to her feet and go help, but she was so hot and so very tired.

When she awakened, she couldn't remember anything but a blur of words or even if she had imagined them. Her arms were crossed over her breasts. When she looked down, she saw she clasped the silver shoes tightly and the dainty gold bracelet was still on her arm.

How long had she lain here since she'd collapsed in the cemetery? It seemed like longer than a couple of hours. It was dark outside, and yet a strange glow lit the room and flickered on the wall by her bed.

With effort, she swung her legs over the side of the bed and almost toppled to the floor. What was she doing in a nightgown? She'd been in a dress only moments ago when she had fainted in the graveyard. She was barefooted, too. Well, she had the silver slippers, she'd put those on.

She stood up and grabbed the bedpost to keep from falling. She had been more tired than she had thought.

"Emma? Doc?" No answer. She must be alone in the

house. If she wanted to go to the Nugget and help, she needed a dress. It took all her energy to search the room for her clothes, but she couldn't find them. Funny, the big mirror was gone, too.

Maybe she could wear something of Emma's. The doctor's wife was about her height, but heavier so that the plain calico dress hung on Silver, hiding her figure modestly.

The glow on the wall seemed to flicker as bright as day. Curiously, Silver went to the window and looked out.

The Nugget was on fire! A group of people stood watching as it blazed into the dark night sky. Her saloon, her security, was going up in flames while people stood and watched and no one ran with buckets to fight it. What kind of friends were these?

Doc stood with the others, watching the Nugget burn. He looked over at his plump, elderly wife. "It's sad, Emma. We're seeing the end of an era here. I don't think the town will ever recover from all this."

She put a comforting hand on his arm. "You couldn't help it, John. You said the place was a pesthole, since it had been used as a hospital. This had to be done."

Doc sighed, watching the flames. "Most of her employees and half the town have either died or fled to other parts in these weeks she's been at death's door. Silver's had so much bad luck without losing her income, too."

Emma pursed her lips. "Even now, she's prettier than the average woman; it's just that she's not perfect anymore."

"I'm afraid that was the most important thing in her

213

life—her beauty. It went deeper than vanity; it was something from her past. I had hoped that big half-breed would care enough about her to change all that, give her some security . . ."

The Nugget collapsed in on itself with a resounding roar and sparks flew up into the dark night.

One of the grizzled miners standing next to him cleared his throat. "Doc, I know you said we had to burn the place, but how'll Miss Silver live now?"

Doc took a deep breath of the scent of burning wood. More than lumber and paint were going up in smoke. A woman's dreams were being destroyed, too. "There's talk of making up a kitty to help Silver rebuild. She's such a heroine with everything she's done during this epidemic. Senator Walcott himself sent a thousand dollars."

The miner whistled low in awe. "Hear that, fellas?"

The men around him turned.

"I'll donate!"

"And me, too!"

"And me!"

A cry went up through the crowd. "Yes, I'll put in some money!"

Doc smiled. "It's the least we can do. I wish we could do more—you know, some kind of tribute that will last forever."

Emma looked at him, then back at the fire. "You mean a monument, like a statue in the park?"

"Better than that," Doc said. "A statue in a park would soon be forgotten. I'd like to do something so that a hundred years from now; maybe even a thousand years from now, people would see it and remember that once upon a time in the old West, there was a woman who cared enough about other people to sacrifice everything

214

to help them."

The miners around him murmured approval. "What should it be, Doc? What could we do that would last? What's better than a statue or a monument to our Silver Heels?"

The moon came out from behind the clouds. Away in the distance, it lit up the silhouette of a beautiful, snow-capped mountain. A thought came to him, and for a moment, he was so overwhelmed by the idea, that he could not speak.

"Boys," he said finally, staring at the majestic peak. "What's more enduring than a mountain? A hundred, five hundred, a thousand years from now, it will still be there. A woman's beauty is like a wild flower; it blossoms briefly and then fades. But love, the kind of love that Miss Silver demonstrated, lasts forever. Nothing endures eternally like true love and the mountains!"

"Hear! Hear!"

He turned to stare at the beautiful, lonely peak, even as the Nugget's flames rose still higher. "Boys, let's rename that summit for our very own heroine. Our grand-children, our great-grandchildren, will see it and remember Colorado's most beautiful lady!"

"Doc," one of the miners said, "she's not a great beauty anymore."

"Oh, yes, she is!" Doc said with such feeling that his voice shook. "To those of us who knew her, she's more beautiful than ever because of what she did. I say we rename that peak for her. Who agrees to Mt. Silver Heels?"

A roar went up from the miners as they threw their hats in the air. "Yea! Hurrah for our town! Hurrah for Miss Silver! Hurrah for Mt. Silver Heels!"

Doc took out his handkerchief and wiped his eyes. "Emma, let's stay to make sure the fire doesn't spread and not disturb our patient tonight. Tomorrow, we'll tell her about the honor."

Emma looked up at him. "And then you'll give her a mirror and tell her about her face, too?"

He had a sense of dread. "She's still pretty," he argued. "She needs to understand that."

Emma linked her arm through his. "Yes, she is—prettier than most. But I'm afraid it won't be enough, John. She'll be devastated."

Doc sighed and his shoulders slumped. "God, I wish Cherokee Evans was here. Somehow, I think it would make a difference."

Back at Doc's house, Silver stood petrified by the window, watching the orange and yellow flames licking against the black velvet of the night. What kind of friends were these who set fire to her saloon and then stood calmly and watched it burn? All her future income, all her hopes and dreams, were literally going up in smoke. She had to do something!

Grabbing a shawl out of the wardrobe, she staggered out into the darkness toward the fire. And even as she stumbled toward the main street in her silver shoes, the building collapsed in on itself with a roar. She was ruined! How would she ever earn a living with her saloon burned to the ground? Except for the gold nugget bracelet she wore, her jewelry was gone, her money, too. What kind of friends would do this? And they were actually cheering! She could hear their voices on the wind, see the hats tossed in the air. They were glad her saloon was gone!

She was alone, no friends, she thought in confusion.

216

Al was the only one who had cared about her and now he was gone and the others had turned on her. She would go away. Where? Her dazed mind couldn't put anything together. Silver turned and walked down the road that led toward Fairplay. That was supposed to be a big boomtown. Well, she had lost her saloon, but she was still pretty and she could entertain. She'd get a job in one of those big saloons and start all over again. There was no use staying here with Al dead and Cherokee never coming back.

Silver walked a long time. Finally a peddler and his rattling wagon came along the road and she waved him down and climbed on the back.

She didn't want anyone to recognize her or ask questions, so she wrapped the shawl around her head so the peddler wouldn't see the telltale pale hair. She hoped the ungrateful people at Buckskin Joe never found out where she'd gone.

She finally fell asleep in the back. At dawn, the driver awakened her, and gave her a sympathetic look. "Miss, this is where I turn off."

Automatically, she got out of the wagon and looked around. "Where's Fairplay?"

"Just over the next rise. You want a ride there?"

Silver shook her head. She hadn't really decided what to do, but she needed to earn some money. She wanted to get cleaned up first before she went into town. How she wished she had something to eat.

The old driver must have guessed that. "I have sandwiches with me; I'll share with you."

She took a sandwich with a nod of thanks and watched

him drive away. Then she sat down on a rock and gobbled her meal.

Her hand went to her hair and she realized how tangled and mussed it was. And the dress. She looked down at the shapeless brown calico. In the nearby meadow, she saw a pond. She would wash, comb her hair, and fix herself up as best she could. She hadn't brought a costume, but maybe one of the other girls would lend her one. At least she had her dancing shoes.

The sun came up slowly as Silver combed her hair. There was just the slightest chill to the dawn. How could that be when it was summer? She distinctly remembered how hot it had been the day she collapsed. She looked around. *Then why were all the leaves on the aspen trees turning gold?* It was more of a puzzle than she could deal with. She leaned over the still water and it reflected light like a mirror. Drat it all! She wished she had a brush. She combed her hair the best she could with her fingers.

There was no soap, but at least she could splash water on her face. Silver leaned over the still surface of the pond. For a long moment, she stared, wondering who that girl was.

Oh my God! Her hands flew to her face, her flawless face. Beneath her fingers, she felt the tiny scars, the telltale marks of smallpox. Her beauty was gone forever!

For an hour, she gave herself up to hysteria. Her worst nightmare had happened. She was worthless now; she would never find a man who would love her.

But Silver was a survivor. Finally she wiped away the tears and thought about what she would do next. Where would she go? How would she make a living? She looked at her reflection again in the placid water and then examined her body. The scars were small and she was still pretty, but not a great beauty anymore. Maybe she could still get a job as an entertainer. Fairplay was a thriving boomtown; there would be saloons here where she could sing and dance.

But suppose someone from Buckskin Joe should come through town and see her? She flinched, not wanting anyone's pity. No, she wanted to close the door on her past forever. The memories were too painful. Too bad she wasn't in New Orleans. Down there, she had heard, they had a holiday called Mardi Gras where everyone went masked. If she could do that, no one would be the wiser.

Could she still do it? She had no money, but she had Cherokee's gold nugget bracelet she could pawn. Keeping the shawl closely about her, she went into town, pawned the cherished possession, and bought fabric and a gaudy new dress. Hiding in an abandoned storage building, she fashioned a glittering mask.

Silver took a breath for courage, put on the scarlet dress, the silver shoes, and the elegant mask, went to Fairplay's biggest saloon, and asked to see the owner.

He was a shrimp of a man wearing too much rose-scented hair oil and red sleeve garters. "Who the hell are you, girlie?"

She smiled coyly behind her mask. "Let's just say my identity would surprise a lot of people. I can sing and dance; let me audition for you. Think about how the men would be intrigued by a mysterious masked lady."

He grinned and lit a cigar. "I reckon that means you are either running away from a husband or some rich family who don't cotton to the idea of what you're doing."

"Let's just say I'm from east of here, and they're looking for me, all right."

219

He leaned back in his chair and studied her. "You know, it just might work. I never heard of anything like it before. Tell you what, girlie, I'll try you one night, and if the customers like you, you're hired. What's your name?"

She gave him a flirtatious smile, although her spirits were as low as the soles of her shoes. "You can just call me the Mysterious Masked lady."

"Okay." He stood up, taking a deep draw on his cigar. "I'll bet behind that mask, you're a great beauty."

She had to swallow hard at that point. "There's— there's some who used to think so."

"We'll see how you do tonight."

Of course she was a great success that evening. Her flying feet and high, sweet voice were a hit with the men of Fairplay. More than that, they were intrigued by the identity behind the glittering mask.

Every night that month, there were men in the audience who yelled out, offering to pay huge sums for her to take the mask off. But Silver only smiled coyly and took another bow.

A couple of weeks passed. She redeemed her precious bracelet and sewed a few dollars in the hem of her petticoat for an emergency. When she wasn't on stage, she kept to herself and mingled with no one. Silver still slept with the lamp lit, but there were no mirrors. Once the silvery things had been her friends, now they were her enemies. She gave no thought to her future past the night's performance. She slept poorly, dreaming that Cherokee decided to return for her, kissed the palm of her hand, and folded her fingers over it. *Here's a treasure for you.*

Then just as she went into his arms, he looked into her

220

face, frowned, and pushed her away. *The Silver I loved was a great beauty. You're not that girl, and that's all you had to offer . . . offer . . . offer . . .*

She woke up sobbing and found herself alone in her little room above the Fairplay saloon. At least she had a job and she could eat. Silver's biggest worry was that someone from Buckskin Joe would turn up, recognize her, and pity her. She'd rather be dead than pitied.

She didn't stay at the saloon long enough for that to happen. One evening, a drunk climbed on the stage during her performance and tried to pull her mask off. In sheer desperation, Silver fought him off and ran from the stage. To be unmasked in front of a crowd, to display for everyone that she was not the great beauty she had been—the thought horrified her. That night she gathered up her things and fled from Fairplay.

Chapter Twelve

Silver fled into the night, taking the precious shoes and the bracelet with her. The gaudy dress she left behind with a note for one of the dancers at the Fairplay saloon who had been kind to her. She wore the shawl and the plain brown dress with the few dollars sewn into the petticoat.

Now what would she do? Silver paused on the outskirts of town, thinking. There were too many memories back in Buckskin Joe to return there. Besides since they had burned her saloon, they were probably glad to be rid of her.

The starlight reflected on the silver shoes and she remembered the night Cherokee had given them to her and the way she had danced on the stage before the cheering crowd. *Silver Heels! Hurrah for our Silver Heels!*

It seemed so long ago. When she closed her eyes, she almost felt his big arms around her, his mouth hot and gentle on hers as he taught her about love. He was gone, never to return. Her beauty was gone, too, as well as her wealth and fame. All she had left were her memories and the shoes and braclet. No one could take those away from her.

Memories. In the end, maybe they were the sum total of a person's life. When good times and things and people are gone, you have the memories always. Even when she was a very old lady, she would remember how she had danced and sang for him, how the crowds had cheered, how he had gathered her to him and taught her to surrender to love. It had been so very brief, but so very precious.

In some ways the memories hurt. She would never again be a glamorous star with her face scarred, and the mask idea wouldn't work; there would always be some drunk who would try to pull it off. No, better she should close the door on her past and find a new life altogether. She wanted Silver Heels remembered as she had been, not pitied for what she had fallen to.

Denver was the biggest city in the territory, as many as five or six thousand people, and thirty or forty saloons, everyone said. In a teeming place like that, it should be easy enough to blend in and lose oneself. Between walking and catching rides on wagons, she finally made it there.

The town at the junction of the Platte River and Cherry Creek was indeed a bustling boomtown. Denver sprawled on both sides of Cherry Creek, now that the little town of Auroria had become simply West Denver when the stage line chose to put its offices in Denver proper. The two had been rivals for the many prospectors and wagon trains passing thourgh or buying supplies. There were rumors that the South would try to capture

Colorado Territory sooner or later to get gold and silver to finance the purchase of guns and powder. There were even rumors that both sides were recruiting the Indians to fight for them.

Silver kept her shawl bundled around her as she walked down the street. Denver was a wide-open boomtown all right, soldiers everywhere, drunken miners fighting on the sidewalks, wagons and people hurrying about.

Her money wouldn't last forever. She must get a job. Doing what? She rented a cheap room, and bought the local paper, the *Rocky Mountain News*. For several days she read the ads, not sure what to do. There weren't many jobs for women. They were either housewives, saloon whores, or servants. Most of the openings wanted references and Silver didn't have any. While she was a good cook from her days on a farm, she was turned down because she didn't look like what a cook was expected to look like, and she had no references. What to do? As high as expenses were in a boomtown, her little hoard of cash wouldn't last very long.

What kind of job could she get without references that didn't entail working in a saloon? The day she spent her last dollar, she saw an ad that appealed to her:

Wanted: Governess for small girl. Good pay, room and board. Apply in person, the Duchess's Palace.

She hadn't known there was any nobility in Colorado Territory. A long time ago, when she was a schoolgirl, she had once dreamed of being a teacher. And she loved children. Could she possibly qualify for this position?

224

MORE PASSION AND ADVENTURE AWAIT... YOUR TRIP TO A BIG ADVENTUROUS WORLD BEGINS WHEN YOU ACCEPT YOUR FIRST 4 NOVELS ABSOLUTELY *FREE* (AN $18.00 VALUE)

Accept your Free gift and start to experience more of the passion and adventure you like in a historical romance novel. Each Zebra novel is filled with proud men, spirited women and tempestuous love that you'll remember long after you turn the last page.

Zebra Historical Romances are the finest novels of their kind. They are written by authors who really know how to weave tales of romance and adventure in the historical settings you love. You'll feel like you've actually gone back in time with the thrilling stories that each Zebra novel offers.

GET YOUR FREE GIFT WITH THE START OF YOUR HOME SUBSCRIPTION

Our readers tell us that these books sell out very fast in book stores and often they miss the newest titles. So Zebra has made arrangements for you to receive the four newest novels published each month.

You'll be guaranteed that you'll never miss a title, and home delivery is so convenient. And to show you just how easy it is to get Zebra Historical Romances, we'll send you your first 4 books absolutely FREE! Our gift to you just for trying our home subscription service.

BIG SAVINGS AND FREE HOME DELIVERY

Each month, you'll receive the four newest titles as soon as they are published. You'll probably receive them even before the bookstores do. What's more, you may preview these exciting novels free for 10 days. If you like them as much as we think you will, just pay the low preferred subscriber's price of just $3.75 each. *You'll save $3.00 each month off the publisher's price.* AND, your savings are even greater because there are never any shipping, handling or other hidden charges—FREE Home Delivery. Of course you can return any shipment within 10 days for full credit, no questions asked. There is no minimum number of books you must buy.

Silver looked down at herself. Yes, the brown calico dress was perfect, but she needed some plain, no-nonsense shoes and she must do something about this mane of silver hair.

With regret, she pawned the gold bracelet again, bought some shoes, some drab dye for her hair, and had herself fitted for horn-rimmed spectacles. This seemed to puzzle the shop owner, especially when she had them made with plain window glass. As she started to leave, she turned back. "Oh, where would I find the Duchess's Palace?"

The short man looked at her over the top of his own spectacles. "Now what would a prim thing like you be wanting in that hellhole?"

"I beg your pardon?"

"It's a saloon, ma'am, one of the toughest in town. The owner claims she's a Spanish Duchess."

Her hopes fell. "I suppose it's a mistake then. I saw an advertisement about a governess position."

"Oh, that," he said. "I might have known that's what you were—a governess. I think the Duchess has been trying to hire someone for quite a while with no takers. It's not the kind of place a prim school teacher would work."

Silver listened with wide eyes while he told her of the Palace's bad reputation and its location down near McGaa Street, the tough area of saloons and bordellos in Denver. "Take my advice, ma'am, and stay away from the Palace. It's not a place for a respectable girl like yourself."

She nodded and thanked him, went back to her room, and thought about it. What would a child be doing in a

225

saloon? The Palace sounded like the kind of place Silver was trying to avoid. Still, if the Duchess was not having any luck filling the position, she might not be too choosy or insist on references.

Silver was desperate enough to try anything. She dyed her hair a drab brown, did it up in a bun on the back of her head, and put on the prim spectacles and the sensible shoes. When she forced herself to look at her reflection in a passing store window, she decided she looked like people might expect a governess to look.

On the bustling street, men didn't turn and stare at her as they used to in Buckskin Joe, and when one bumped into her, he gave her a respectful bow and stepped out of her path. *Why, I'm respectable-looking,* she thought in awe. There were only two kinds of women in the West. *I look like the other kind of woman now.* She had traded her beauty for respectability. It was almost ironic.

McGaa Street looked like a rough place, all right. She found out it had been named for an early prospector. The area around McGaa and Blake Streets was home to the rougher element of Denver. Silver continued along the street, remembering to walk in the prim manner that a governess might assume.

The Duchess' Palace was several blocks away—an imposing two-story frame building. Was she out of her mind to try this? She'd never get away with it. On the other hand, there was a little girl in this terrible place who needed someone to care about her and it might be a peaceful retreat for Silver to lose herself from all her memories.

The inside was elegant, all red velvet and ornate tables. A carved rosewood bar with a huge mirror ran down the length of one wall. Everywhere she looked were poker table and faro setups. The place smelled of whiskey and cigar smoke and cheap perfume. It was empty this early in the morning, one lone black boy sweeping up.

Silver looked around at the piano, the stage. The Palace was much fancier than the Nugget. A few months ago, Silver could have come here and been the star performer; now she was applying for a drab position behind the scenes.

She asked to see the Duchess, and the boy yawned and pointed up the ornate stairway that began in the center of the huge saloon.

Could she possibly convince anyone she was a respectable governess or would they see through her and realize that she was only a scarred saloon girl looking for a refuge from the world?

With heart beating hard, she hesitated before the door at the top of the stairs with an OFFICE sign on it. She needed this job. If nothing else, she had spunk. She rapped on the door.

"Come in."

Silver said a little prayer and entered. The office was done in an overly ornate Victorian style as if someone with more money than taste had decorated it. The woman in the low-cut yellow dress sitting behind the big desk was dark and pretty in a vulgar, overblown way. Her black hair was done up in an elaborate hairdo and she wore a great deal of expensive jewelry.

Silver wished immediately that she had not come. The woman's dark eyes were as hard as obsidian. She might have been Spanish, or Mexican, or Indian. But she was older than Silver. "I—I've come about the

227

governess position."

The woman laughed and her voice was hard and sarcastic. "Well, I certainly didn't think you were applying for anything else! You look like a governess—all drab and prim. What's your name."

"S—Sylvia Jones."

"Miss Jones, have you asked about this place?"

She wasn't quite sure what to say but she wasn't a good liar. Basically, Silver was an honest person. "Frankly yes, I did."

"But you came anyway?" The other woman looked amused as she leaned back in her chair.

"I need a position," Silver said with as much dignity as she could muster.

"You must! The last two quit before a week was out." The other woman laughed and drummed her nails on the desk. The light reflected off her rings and bracelets. Expensive baubles, Silver thought. If there was anything she knew, it was good jewelry.

Silver looked her in the eye. "Is the child that difficult?"

The woman laughed again. "I like you, Miss Jones, I find you very amusing! You'll find my daughter sweet, I'm sure. It's just that the Palace is not the sort of place prim governessess feel at home in. It's not even the sort of place a Duchess from Seville should feel at home in."

Silver looked around. The office with its gaudy Victorian furnishings and big, black safe behind the desk reminded her of the Velvet Kitten. "I would not be expected to mix with the other employees, would I?"

"Of course not! I'm looking for a person who can teach my daughter all the proper things to do. I never had those

228

opportunities myself. Later I'd like to send Waanibe back east to school. Maybe she'll marry into society and they need never know how her fortune was made."

"It's commendable that you're so ambitious for your child," Silver said. "I hope your husband shares your—"

"I am not married," the Duchess cut her off icily. "Whatever I have, whatever I give my child, I did all alone, with no help from anyone, least of all her father."

Silver wasn't quite sure what to say, although she knew the feeling. Another saloon girl who had succumbed to a man's promises. *Here but for the grace of God* . . .

"Miss Jones, you have an Eastern accent. I assume you aren't from this area originally?"

She wasn't about to tell where she was from. The Duchess must have little experience if she thought an Illinois accent sounded "Eastern." "I suppose you could call my former home 'Eastern.'"

The Duchess looked impressed. "A real Eastern governess for Waanibe. Can you take her in hand, teach her about etiquette and being a lady, all the things she needs to know if she is to move up in the world?"

"I'll do my best," Silver answered truthfully. What she knew of etiquette and proper manners, she had learned while she lived in Elmer Neeley's imposing home. "I can also teach her some of the basics like reading."

"More than anything, she needs a companion. I'm mostly busy with running the Palace and don't have time for her."

"Mothers who care can always take the time," Silver said without thinking.

The Duchess glared at her coldly. "Let's get one thing straight, Miss Jones. I love my daughter because she is all I have to remember of the great love of my life. I'm not the motherly type. Besides, business is very competitive and Big Ed Chase and his saloon, the Arcadia are my biggest competition in every way. He thinks he can run me out because I'm a woman."

"It is hard to survive in a man's world, isn't it?"

"Especially in my case," the Duchess said. "I know what they whisper behind my back, but I assure you I'm of the Spanish nobility. I came here during the first boom days of late fall of '58 with two hundred and fifty dollars, and I opened the Palace."

Silver thought the Duchess had the hardest eyes she had ever seen. Here was a woman who would let nothing stop her from getting what she wanted. "You seem to have been very successful."

The other woman played with her rings. "I've struggled and fought my way to the top, no matter what I had to do to get there. My daughter will be able to move up and do and be what I never could. Someday Waanibe will move in the best circles if she's properly trained and my hard-earned money will see that she gets there!"

"I'll do the very best I can." Silver suddenly felt very sorry for the little girl. She wasn't quite sure how she felt about the hard, ambitious mother. She reminded Silver a little of her own mother, reliving her own dreams through a child.

"I believe you would." The Duchess looked at her a long moment, turning her expensive rings over and over on her brown fingers. "If you would like the job, it's yours. The salary is twice what I'm told I should expect to

230

pay a governess and you have a very nice room down the hall from the nursery."

Silver hesitated. She didn't want to worry about some drunken cowboy or soldier coming along the upstairs hall, mistaking her for one of the whores. "Are the girls on that wing?"

The Duchess glared at her. "Of course not! I don't want my daughter associated with them. That's why as soon as she's old enough, I'm going to send her away to school. But of course, if the war continues for many years, that may be a problem. The girls are on the opposite end of the hall. My daughter thinks they are just dancers and entertainers, which in a sense, they are." She smiled thinly as she stood up. "Now would you like to meet your new charge?"

"Certainly."

The woman motioned for Silver to follow and went through the side door of her office, yellow satin skirts rustling. Silver followed her, carrying her valise. They were in an ornate bedroom full of Victorian furnishings, tassels, and velvet. On the dresser was a jewelry box, the jewelry scattered across the top of the dresser.

The Duchess frowned, stopped to pick the baubles up, put them back in the box, and closed it. "Waanibe loves my jewelry and I just can't keep her from playing in it. Like mother, like daughter, I suppose." She looked up quickly at Silver. "Of course, it's not really fine jewelry."

"Of course," Silver said, wondering why the Duchess lied. Silver knew good jewelry when she saw it, even though she no longer owned any. Perhaps the woman thought if anyone realized it was real, she might be robbed, even by her own girls. Maybe like Silver, the precious ornaments were her security that would finance her for a while if something ever happened to the Palace.

"Well, my daughter's obviously been here, judging from the jewelry. Let's look in the nursery." She led the way through an opposite adjoining door into a large room decorated for a little girl. It looked as if no expense had been spared. As Silver watched, a small dark head popped out of the toy box.

"Waanibe, you little rascal! I've been looking for you!"

The Duchess pulled a sturdy little girl who looked two or three years old out of the pile of toys. "I've got someone who wants to meet you. Say hello to Miss Sylvia, who'll be looking after you from now on."

Silver smiled and held out her hand to the little girl. The child peered at her shyly. She was sturdy, ebony-eyed, and dark-skinned as a half-breed. Her black hair was done up in braids across the top of her head. "'Lo, Silvery."

The Duchess frowned at Silver. "Perhaps you would prefer she call you Miss Jones?"

"No, Silvery is fine with me. Come here, Waanibe." She held out her arms.

The mother handed the child over with what seemed a sigh of relief to Silver. "I really don't have time to be bothered with her. You two will eat together and stay out of the way up here on this wing."

"Yes, ma'am," Silver said. She hugged the little girl to her, noticing she had a birthmark on one of her chubby fingers. "Waanibe and I will be great friends. That's an unusual name. Is it foreign?"

232

The Duchess frowned. "I suppose you could say that. It means Singing Wind. Do the best you can to keep Wannie out of my way, Miss Jones, and turn her into a young lady. I keep thinking that someday her father might return, if not for me, maybe if he ever hears about her."

Silver waited for the woman to go on but the Duchess seemed to be lost in thought. It dawned on her then that the Duchess didn't care much about the child at all and, small as she was, the child sensed it. "Could I see my room now?"

Waanibe smiled. "Go see Silvery's room, too."

Silver put the child down, but the lonely little girl grabbed her hand. The Duchess led Silver, the toddler still clinging to her hand, through the nursery into a spacious bedroom done up in pale aquas and turquoise. It was a cheery room with pretty, dainty furnishings. Someone besides the Duchess must have furnished it— maybe the last governess. "Oh, this is lovely!"

"Not quite fancy enough for my taste," the Duchess said, "but I'm sure a prim thing like you feels right at home here." She played with a bracelet impatiently. It appeared to Silver that the woman had already spent more time on this governess thing than she had wanted to.

"It's fine." Silver smiled down at the child hanging on to her hand. "I think Wannie and I will be great friends. We'll build castles out of blocks and I'll read you stories."

Waanibe's dark eyes were as bright as a chipmunks. "Silvery have rings and bracelets to play with?"

"No, sorry, afraid not." She thought of the gold

233

nugget bracelet. Maybe in a week or so, she'd have enough money to buy it back—if the store owner didn't sell it first.

The Duchess said, "Just keep Wannie out of my things and away from the business. That's the main thing."

She turned and left the pair standing in the bedroom.

The Duchess felt nothing but relief as she returned to her office and settled herself again behind her ledger books. The new governess looked acceptable and might have been pretty—if she didn't dress so mousy and wear her hair like an old maid, along with those serviceable shoes and thick glasses. Somewhere along the way, the girl had had smallpox; the telltale scars were on her face, but they were few and tiny. Actually they were hardly noticeable at all. She couldn't tell anything about the rest of Miss Jones in that frumpy dress; not that such things mattered in a governess. It was just that the Duchess was used to assessing other women for their marketability to cowboys and soldiers.

She sat down behind her big desk, nibbled on the end of her ledger pen, and sighed. Iron Knife. He was never very far from her mind. She had loved him as she had never loved another man, although she had slept with many besides the big Cheyenne half-breed. In fact, within a day or so of the time she had seduced the Cheyenne, she had been raped by a big, ugly white scout. She smiled. She'd gotten even with the scout, though— she'd knocked him unconscious and robbed him. That was back in the fall of '58. The scout's money had financed the opening of the Palace. Ever since then, she had been on her own, scheming in every way she could to be rich and successful. She had not seen either of the two men since. For a while, she had been afraid the scout would search her out, and take revenge. But it had been three years and he had never turned up. She hoped he was dead, and not an easy death either.

But the half-breed Cheyenne was something else. She lived for the day that he would finally hear about his daughter and come to Denver. Maybe he would even leave that white girl he loved. Certainly the white girl didn't love him the way she did. Too bad the child had not been a son. No warrior could look with disfavor on a woman who had given him a son.

Waanibe. Singing Wind. It was the Duchess's own language. She loved the child only because she was Iron Knife's and because someday he might return for the two of them. When he did, Waanibe would be pretty and well mannered, know how to dress and talk the way high-born white girls did. She would dangle his daughter as bait to keep him. In the meantime, the Palace was running up great profits. The Duchess turned and stared at the big black safe on the floor behind her desk. Money was power and she never intended to be without either again. Nothing in the world mattered to her as much as her priceless jewelry and the money in her safe. Except the big Cheyenne half-breed she had seduced.

She looked down at her bracelets and smiled, thinking she deserved to buy herself some new bauble with all the money coming in. The Palace ran the most crooked card games in town. The drinks were watered and the whores were the most beautiful anywhere in Colorado Territory. In short, the Palace catered to any and every weakness of men—if they had enough money to pay for it.

She must keep the new governess away from all that. Miss Jones looked a prim sort and the Duchess didn't want her to quit. She wanted Miss Jones to look after her lover's child and leave the Duchess free to make money. Maybe if when Iron Knife finally came, if he didn't want his child, she would just give Wannie away. There must be some family out there who wanted a child. Maybe the Duchess could bribe Iron Knife with all that money in her safe to stay with her. That hope was what made it all worthwhile.

Silver leaned over the adorable child. "Wannie, we're going to be great friends." She remembered something and smiled at the memory. "Here, let me give you a treasure." She took the chubby little hand, kissed the palm, and solemnly folded Waanibe's fingers over it. "That's for you to put in your pocket 'til you need it."

The child looked at her clenched fist and chortled with delight. "Silvery's treasure. Better than Mama's rings." She put her hand in her dress pocket. "Keep it forever."

"No, dear, just keep it 'til you need it." She hugged the small body close to hers. "Now you show me your toys and I'll read you a story book."

Silver was content, if not blissfully happy, she thought as the toddler grabbed her hand and led her back to the nursery. She was needed here by this lonely little girl; never mind that the Duchess looked as if she'd have no qualms about stealing pennies out of a dead man's pockets. Never mind that the Palace had a terrible reputation. Her responsibility was to Waanibe now and she could close the door on her own past and start life anew.

But late that night, she lay awake, hugging her pillow to her and thinking of Cherokee. Her bedside lamp burned as usual and there was a sturdy lock on her door. All she had of her old life was the silver shoes tucked safely under her bed, but soon she would save enough to redeem the bracelet Cherokee had given her.

What would happen tomorrow or next week or next year didn't seem to matter anymore. For the moment, she was safe and secure and she was needed. There had been no letters from Cherokee, so she had given up hope tht he might still return to Buckskin Joe. And if he did, she wouldn't want his pity. Only one time had he made love to her, but it was imprinted in her memory, so she could relive it over and over again. And as she slept, she dreamed that he returned and things were as they had been before and he loved and wanted her.

He came into her room when it was late and very quiet and there was no need for explanation. It seemed as though she had seen him only that afternoon.

"You don't know how I've waited for this," he gasped as he pulled the lace away from her breasts so he could reach them with his greedy mouth.

"Teach me about love," she whispered. He swung her up in his arms and carried her to the big bed, her lace underwear twisted about her waist.

He crouched above her, looking down at her. "Before I finish with you, sweet darlin', you are going to know all about love, about how much a man can care for a woman." He bent his dark head and kissed the corners of her mouth and then his mouth went to her breasts.

She gasped and then moaned aloud as the tip of his tongue teased her nipples, making them swell with desire. Silver caught his head between her hands and pressed his face into the soft circles, wanting him to suck them into taut peaks.

He took her hand and put it on his nipple and she was surprised at how hard it was and how he gasped when she stroked him there.

She felt wet and trembling between her thighs. His hand stroked her belly until she shook all over from the ache within her and then his hand moved still lower. His body was pressed against hers and she felt the male hardness of him throbbing and wet against her flesh. The scent of him and the scent of tobacco and wood smoke and the hot male seed sent a rush of excitement through her.

Then his fingers were deep within her, stroking and probing even as his hot mouth sucked her breasts until she whimpered and spread her thighs, wanting still more.

"Touch me," he commanded, and very hesitantly, she reached out and took the big dagger of his manhood in her hand and felt his rich seed warm on her fingers.

She had never felt this kind of excitement before and her trembling increased. The size of him in her hand scared her a little, even in her dream. But she wanted to please Cherokee.

"Spread your legs more," he commanded and she did, afraid, yet wanting him to touch her deeper. His mouth came up to cover her own and her arms slipped around his massive shoulders as his hand probed deep within her.

The spasms began deep within her very soul, and when she came, she cried out but his tongue was in her mouth, muffling her cries, and she could only dig her nails into his shoulders and back. She felt the tiny trickles of blood like a lioness in heat clawing the male.

For a long moment, she knew nothing and then she slowly came back to reality. "What—what happened?"

He laughed softly. "Just as I suspected! In some ways, you really are as innocent as a virgin. I'm going to love you again and again, sweet Silver, until your body and heart and soul are in complete surrender."

She felt his manhood still swollen and hard against her body. "This is not the way I'm used to having a man make love to me."

He kissed her eyelids. "I doubt you've ever really had a man make love to you; they've only used you for their own pleasure."

And at that, she collapsed against his powerful chest and began to cry while he kissed her gently. "Oh, Cherokee . . . Cherokee . . ."

"Now you kiss me," he whispered, and she kissed him shyly as he ordered.

"Now let me show you a real kiss, darlin'," he said, and his mouth kissed every inch of her breasts and belly and then moved lower.

"You aren't going to—"

"You're my plaything, remember? You aren't big enough to stop me from doing anything I want with you, so don't fight me."

She realized the logic of his words, and when he commanded her to let her legs fall apart and offer herself

239

up to his lips, there was nothing she could do but submit to the hot blade of his tongue stabbing there until she gasped and pulled him hard against her while both his hands came up to cover her breasts and stroke them into pointed peaks of desire. Again, she could not control her own body as the surging began and she stifled her cries against the dark flesh of his shoulder.

She lay there, breasts heaving, breathing loudly through her mouth as he knelt between her thighs. "Now, Silver?"

"Oh, now! Yes, now!"

He penetrated her very slowly so that she seemed to feel him pulsating as he came into her. It was too slow for her eager body, and she found herself rising up off the bed to meet him, aching for him to fill the void.

"That's it Silver. Wrap your legs around me."

She was his to command and they coupled together like one living being, her thighs locking him into her, his hard maleness throbbing hot and deep within her until she felt him moan and begin to surge. It was almost as if she could feel the hot, rich life fluid of him erupting within her womb. They were both wet with perspiration, writhing and bucking on the bed, his tongue deep in her throat, her nails clawing his back bloody. If he wanted to escape the sucking pull of her body, he could not because she locked him to her with her legs and she was instinctively refusing to release him until his body gave her what she wanted.

When he came deep within her, her own body met the challenge, riding a crescendo of feeling as it tried to squeeze him in her depths, not letting him escape until he'd given up the seed her womb craved.

Then she collapsed in his arms in sobbing surrender while he held her and kissed the tears from her eyes. Now that she had been awakened to love, her body was greedy for it, and he made love to her all night long until they were both exhausted.

Oh, Cherokee . . . Cherokee . . .

She blinked awake and realized that she still hugged her pillow in her lonely room at the Duchess' Palace and he was only a ghost of her memory.

Weeks passed one into another. Winter came with all its snow and holidays. Silver was the one who made sure there was a Christmas tree and gifts for Waanibe. The Christmas tree was a new holiday decoration that was just coming into vogue the last few years in America, thanks to Queen Victoria of England. Her beloved husband, Albert, was German. He had brought Germany's favorite Christmas custom with him when he married her. Americans had a habit of imitating anything English royalty did, so gradually, Silver heard, the decorated tree was spreading across the country, along with the reading of *A Visit from St. Nicholas,* which had been written more than forty years ago.

The Duchess was too busy with the booming business of the Palace and the gold in her safe. Many times when Silver came to her office, the dark beauty sat with the safe open as if simply staring at the piled-up treasure gave her satisfaction.

She also had Silver's cherished gold bracelet. Silver saved her salary to redeem it, but the day before she intended to do so, the Duchess showed up wearing it.

"Isn't it pretty?" She smiled, holding up her arm so the light glinted off it. "Someone never returned for it."

At that point, Silver almost told the Duchess it was hers, then decided against it. She couldn't prove ownership, and the Duchess would ask questions. Besides, why should Silver want to be reminded of a man who had talked his way into her bed one time and then discarded her while he went off to war? Not that the Duchess would give it up anyway; the woman liked it too much.

It was spring now, early April '62. In a few more days, it would have been a year since Cherokee made love to her and then went off to war. Silver was happy enough, she thought as she went about her duties mechanically. Little Waanibe loved and needed her and she loved and needed the child. Certainly Waanibe was too young to be sent off to school, and besides, with the war still raging, that was impossible.

But that night, she dreamed about Cherokee. He was in some kind of trouble and calling her name.

"Cherokee?" She sat bolt upright in bed and then she sighed with relief as she realized what had awakened her was only a dream. It was late at night—so late that even the saloon downstairs was quiet at this hour.

Cherokee. She sighed and lay back down. Of course there was always a chance he'd been killed in the war, but somehow they had seemed so attuned that Silver thought she would know the exact moment he died, even if it were a thousand miles from here.

No, he had simply enjoyed her body and, after the

sample, had deserted her the way men were so wont to do women. He hadn't even written her. She would like to think that maybe the mail wasn't coming through, but after almost a year, she had to face the fact that he probably hadn't bothered to write, would never bother to write.

Maybe he didn't care about her but she still loved him. For a long moment, she thought about the Duchess. In some ways, they were alike—each awaiting a beloved man who didn't care about her. Except the Duchess had a child by hers. Did that make her luckier or unluckier than Silver?

And what had awakened her? Silver lay back down, but she couldn't sleep. Somehow, she thought, wherever Cherokee is, he's in terrible trouble and there's nothing I can do about it!

Chapter Thirteen

Early April 1862,
near Shiloh, Tennessee.

Cherokee flattened himself against the ground and listened to the shells exploding around him in the darkness. *He was going to die here,* he thought. *He and Shawn and Dowdy and the others of this patrol.*

They had been out scouting the terrain and stumbled into a Yankee offensive that was just beginning. All around them, shells exploded and men screamed as they were torn in half. Cherokee hugged the dirt and thought about Silver. He hadn't wanted to die without seeing her again. Loving her had made all this misery and death worth getting through, even if she didn't care about him. He could daydream about what might have been.

He realized then that he had his fist tightly clenched and he opened it slowly, staring at it in the moonlight. *Here's a treasure . . . put it in your pocket and take it out when you need it.*

Oh, sweet darlin', with your quicksilver laughter, I

244

need it now just as I need you so. He held the palm of his hand against his unshaven cheek, almost seeming to feel her lips on his face, the warm passion of her beneath him the one night he had made love to her. He hoped he had given her a baby. Selfish of him maybe, but no man wants to die without leaving some trace of himself in this world.

Shawn shouted from his other side. "I've got to get back and tell the colonel that the Yankees are massing here for a big push!"

Cherokee looked around the shadowy orchard where they lay. Peaches and apples and cherry trees were in bloom; the scent of those blossoms seemed to mock them. Spring. New life budding, but for the men around him, it would undoubtedly be the season of death.

Shawn shouted again. "Did you hear me, Cherokee?"

Cherokee nodded. "Maybe me and a couple of the others can hold out until the rest of the patrol gets away!"

"I can't ask you to do that, lad. The ones who stay behind are sure to get killed or captured!"

"Go on," Cherokee urged. "I'll keep Pettigrew and Wilson."

Shawn paused. "Wilson's a good man, but Petty may turn tail and run if it gets bad enough!"

"I'll manage," Cherokee said. "You'll need the others later. You'll take Dowdy?"

Shawn nodded. "Aye, if anyone can get through, it's the blacksmith." He paused, shells screaming around them like deadly fireworks. The acrid scent of burning powder made him cough. "Cherokee, lad, I've never told you how much your friendship means to me. You're not much older than the son I might have had if my first love . . ."

245

Cherokee waited for him to continue, then realized he wouldn't. "Aw, don't get maudlin on me now," Cherokee said, and made a dismissing gesture, "there's no time. Besides, Shawn, I owe you. That's the reason I came back. We're friends—*tso-ga-li-i.*" He said it in his Indian language without thinking.

Shawn looked at him a long moment and Cherokee wondered suddenly if the older man could possibly know what a tramp his young wife was, that she and Cherokee had betrayed him. It didn't matter. He owed Shawn. He might have to pay the debt of honor with his life.

They shook hands solemnly and then Shawn crept away through the mud toward where the horses were tied on the other side of the hedge.

Cherokee crawled to Wilson, and told the raw-boned farmer what was at stake.

The other nodded. "For Captain O'Bannion, anything! We'll hold them off, Cherokee, at least until the patrol gets away."

He wished he could count on Pettigrew the same way. Cherokee had chosen to keep Petty because he was the one Shawn needed the least, but he was afraid the chunky redneck was liable to be an undependable coward. He found the man in the darkness.

The bursting shells reflected off the big drops of sweat on Pettigrew's face. "Nagnab it! Not me!" he drawled. "I don't care nothin' about bein' no dead hero!"

"Petty, that's an order! I'm the sergeant! Now grab your rifle and come with me! There's a path through the trees that the Yankees will have to take. Right at that point, I think we can hold them off awhile.

"And then what?" Petty demanded.

Cherokee shrugged. "When we run out of ammunition, we do the best we can to get away under cover of darkness. At least the patrol will manage to get back to headquarters with the information we gathered!"

Petty swore. "That may be important to you, but not to me. Nagnab it! I came to kill Yankees, but not at the cost of my own life so some fancy plantation owner like O'Bannion can escape back behind the front!"

"By damn! I got no time to argue with you, come on!" Cherokee crawled away through the brush. Curse Petty anyway! The man was a good shot, but like most backwoods rednecks, he liked moonshine too much, and he was a coward—not the kind of backup any man wanted to depend on.

With the shells bursting and men shouting and screaming, it seemed a million miles back to where he'd left Wilson holding that high spot overlooking the path through the orchard. Funny, he was probably going to die in the next few minutes and all he could think about was a cup of hot coffee, some clean clothes, and Silver.

"Wilson? How's it going?"

No answer. Cherokee crawled through the darkness to the man's side. "Wilson? I brought Petty back with me. I think the three of us can hold this spot long enough . . ."

It dawned on him slowly that the shoulder he touched didn't move. "Wilson?"

No answer. A shell hit the ground a few hundred feet away, exploded with an acrid scent of powder, and set the brush on fire. In the new light, Cherokee suddenly realized that the top half of Wilson's head was gone.

Oh my God. He swallowed hard to keep from getting sick. There was no time to be queasy, he and Petty had to hold off the Yankees until the patrol got away in the darkness. Cherokee pushed the body to one side and took

Wilson's rifle and cartridges. At least with two weapons, he and Petty could still hold this spot a long time. He was glad Shawn had taken Dowdy with him. The big, red-headed blacksmith was dependable and fiercely loyal. He'd get Shawn to headquarters if he had to carry him on his broad back.

Where the hell was Pettigrew? The Yankees were out there, Cherokee could hear them moving up. "Petty, you watch that curve of the path over there and I'll pick them off here." No answer. "Petty?"

If he'd been killed, too . . . Cherokee crawled back along the trail, looking for a body. At least Cherokee could use Petty's rifle if he had to hold the Yankees off all alone. He'd crawled almost all the way back before it dawned on him and he began to curse. That yellow coward had fled, leaving Cherokee to hold the position.

Well, by damn, he wasn't going to die without taking a few Yankees with him! He'd told Shawn he would delay the Yanks and he'd do it if it cost him his life.

He crept back to the bend of the path, checking the ammunition in his pack. A shadowy figure appeared on the trail and Cherokee took careful aim and dropped him.

Immediately, there were shouts and cursing. "Watch out, men, there must be a Johnny Reb ahead somewhere! Let's get the bastard!"

But instead, when the Yankee officer showed himself just a little, light reflecting off his brass buttons, Cherokee got him.

He reloaded as he heard the man fall. Maybe he wouldn't get out of this alive, but at least he was buying time for Shawn and he owed him that for betraying him. *White women.* Maybe they were all whores like his grandmother said, but at this moment when he was about to die, he wouldn't have traded that one night with Silver for the most faithful Indian girl who ever lived.

Cherokee squeezed the trigger and took out another man. He reloaded as fast as he could, but he knew he was outnumbered. There wasn't any way he was going to escape these Yankees. He was going to die here in the mud of some farmer's orchard in the darkness. In his mind, he heard her quicksilver laughter.

"Silver," he whispered. "Oh, Silver, if I had gotten out of this alive, I wanted to come back and marry you. Wherever you are tonight, I hope you're thinking of me."

He fired one more time before he suddenly felt the muzzle of a gun in his back. "Okay, you Rebel bastard, throw the gun down and put your hands in the air!"

Cherokee obeyed slowly, then stood up, and turned around to look at the brawny trooper in the blue uniform. "Okay, Yank, you got me, but my captain got away. That's all that matters."

The other slugged him with the rifle butt, then spat tobacco juice to one side. "They call me Big 'Un, you Southern bastard. You can say good-bye to the war, Reb. The rest of it, you'll be sittin' out in a prison camp!"

August 1864. Silver slipped Wannie's nightgown over her head, getting ready to put her to bed in the nursery, and thought about Cherokee. She had never heard from him. What had she expected? It occurred to her now that she hoped maybe he had been captured and had no way of sending her a letter. It was easier to believe that than the other two possibilities—that he was dead or just didn't want her anymore. But hadn't she known from the first how men felt about saloon girls?

Denver was even bigger and more prosperous than

before the war, with the government needing her gold and silver to buy military supplies. There had been a lot of trouble with the Plains tribes ever since spring and rumor was that the Confederates had stirred them up, hoping to use them against the Union soldiers. At any rate, the Cheyenne and their allies were on the war path and Denver had been blockaded for weeks with food shortages sending the cost of food skyrocketing, and mail and stagecoach service brought to a halt.

Ben Holladay had bought the stage line two years ago and moved its terminal to Fifteenth and McGaa Streets.

There had been other changes, too. Big Ed Chase had built an even grander saloon called Progressive Hall now that the Arcadia had been lost in last year's big fire.

"Silvery, you aren't paying attention to me."

"What? Oh, of course, Wannie." She hugged the little five-year-old girl to her and finished getting her ready for bed. Silver had grown to love the child like her own. She didn't even want to think about the Duchess sending Wannie away to boarding school when the war finally ended.

She put Wannie to bed in the nursery and went out into the hall. The noise from the saloon drifted up to her, and for a moment, old memories of the Nugget and especially of Cherokee, came back to her. Silver shook her head and went to her own room. She was happy enough, she supposed, and she'd be better off not to think about what might have been. Still, he was much on her mind tonight and she lay awake with her lamp on and her door double-bolted, wondering where he was and if he ever gave any thought to her . . . if he were still alive.

*   *   *

In the moonlight, Cherokee looked at the marks carved in the stone of his cell and sighed. More than two years he'd been in this hellhole of a Yankee prison camp on this bleak sandbar at Point Lookout, North Carolina. Almost two and a half, actually. For all the good he had done Shawn O'Bannion or the South, he might as well have stayed in Colorado Territory. He didn't even know if Shawn and the others of that command were still alive.

God, it was hot in here tonight! He lay on the bare bunk and stared out the barred window at the pale moon, silver as his love's long hair. Down the corridor, other prisoners snored and moaned in their sleep. He'd been locked up in solitary a month this time, along with others labeled "troublemakers," just because he'd started a riot when the food was short again.

Cherokee was so lean, he could count his own ribs when he ran his hand over them. He wondered for a long moment if he would survive until the war ended. Men were dying in military prisons from neglect and disease and no one seemed to care.

What was going on in the outside world, he knew very little, except when a new prisoner came in who could report the progress of the war. Almost always it was bad news for the South. He got no mail nor could send any, so he only hoped things were going well for his partners and Silver back in the Rockies.

Otherwise, they got rumors, and half-truths from their Yankee guards.

Shiloh had been the bloodiest battle of the war up to that point for both sides. Almost twenty-five-thousand casualties.

The telegraph had finally been strung completely across the country in the fall of '61, and the Pony

Express had ended its runs. It had lasted only eighteen months and lost money the whole time, bankrupting its owners.

Last year, Southern troops, barefooted and desperate had detoured toward the town of Gettysburg, Pennsylvania, in an attempt to capture a big shoe store there. Instead, they were spotted by Union troops, attacked, and beaten back with heavy loss of life on both sides. Lincoln made a short speech to dedicate the Union graveyard. His Gettysburg Address impressed most newspapers only with its brevity.

There was a new weapon being discussed, the Gatling gun, that could shoot hundreds of cartridges in minutes. It would be the ultimate weapon if it could be gotten into production before the war ended, which was doubtful.

The South seemed to be hanging on by sheer willpower, with heavy losses and devastation everywhere. In the North, contrary to popular sentiment, instead of marching off to war singing "Glory, Glory Hallelujah," there were draft riots with many killed because men objected to being drafted into the army. They said there were a thousand killed in New York City alone. In the South, where people were starving, there were bread riots. Lincoln was running for reelection this coming November, but the war had dragged on too long and his popularity was down.

The South was still in love with the song "Dixie," not seeming to realize it was a minstrel show song written by a Yankee who was furious over its becoming the Confederate anthem.

This past January, songwriter Stephen Foster had died, a hopeless, penniless drunk in New York's Bellevue Hospital.

Out on the Western frontier, the South had been stirring up the Indians to fight the government troops in order to keep the Union stretched thin. There weren't enough Yankee troops to fight the South and keep the Indians under control, too. There had been rumors all this year that the Union was desperate enough to recruit captured Southern prisoners of war to put on Union blue and go west to fight Indians.

Cherokee watched the moon move slowly past his tiny window, throwing the shadow of the iron bars across his face and the grimy wall. *Silver.* Where was she and did she ever think of him? If he lived until the war ended, would she still be in Buckskin Joe? He took a deep breath and seemed to smell the wild flowers of the Colorado high country; or was it her perfume he remembered? A breeze rustled through a distant tree and he thought of her high, sweet voice and how, like quicksilver, her mood could change from gaiety to passion.

It was so hot in the narrow cell. Cherokee would have gone insane ages ago if it hadn't been that he could escape in his mind. He closed his eyes and went back to Colorado. He stood on the narrow balcony outside Silver's window, and in the August heat, her window was open.

He climbed through. In the flickering light of the lamp she always kept by her bed, he saw her lying on top of the covers, her blue silk nightdress unbuttoned all the way down in the heat. A light sheen of perspiration shone on her satiny skin and her pale hair spread over the pillow.

I've finally struck it rich, he said, looking down at her. *I've brought you gold dust from my own mine.*

Her aqua eyes flickered open, and she took a deep breath, her full breasts moving in the light. *Cherokee? Oh,*

I've waited forever for you to make love to me again!

He held out the bag. *I'm not poor anymore. I've got plenty of gold and I want you to have it.*

She started to protest, but he silenced her with a gesture. Opening the bag of gold dust he poured a steady stream in the cleft between her breasts and slowly moved his hand so that he left a trail of gold down her belly that overflowed her navel. Then he moved lower still. It felt erotic to be caressing her with the costly treasure, pouring the little stream down both her naked thighs and then back up again, covering her mound with priceless gold.

He sprinkled the glittering dust back up her belly, around her nipples, and over her breasts. The sheen of perspiration made the gold dust cling to her skin so that when she breathed, it glittered in the moonlight. *A golden idol,* he thought, *and now I'm going to worship at this shrine of love.*

Very slowly, he unbuttoned his shirt, threw it to one side, reached to undo his belt, let his pants slide to the floor, and stepped out of his boots. She lay there, glistening in the moonlight, a fabulous fortune in gold reflecting light from her ripe, naked body.

My grandmother says you're all whores, but I don't care. I've paid a fortune for this privilege, he said. *Now give my my money's worth.*

She held up her hands to him and he lay down on her feeling the priceless gold clinging to his hot, damp skin, too. Then he entered her and began to ride her like a stallion servicing a mare in heat. She locked her glittering legs around his hips. *I'm not a whore, Cherokee. I've waited all this time for your return. No matter how things seem, I'm not a whore.*

254

I don't care what you are. I love you, Silver. I can't help myself.

Her breasts glittered in the moonlight like two costly jewels and he put his hands on them, cupping them, pushing them up for his mouth. He could feel her muscles tightening on him, her supple body rippling under his in the rhythms of love. Even her flawless, beautiful face glittered with gold and it excited him to think he had strewn the costly powder with such abandon. This mating would cost a king's ransom, but he would call it worth it. He dared not hope that she could love him for himself.

He slipped his hands under her small hips, tilting her up for his long, slow thrusts. Tonight, he would put his baby in her belly. When she was big with the fruit of his seed, she would have to turn her back on everything the Nugget represented and go away with him to be his mate in some cabin high in the Rockies. There would be so much gold that he would spread it for her to roll in before he coupled with her. Afterward, she would dance naked for him, clad in nothing but the glittering gold dust, the bracelet he had given her, and the sliver shoes.

Her hands were on his waist even as her long legs locked his body to hers. She arched under him, pulling him down into her, biting his nipples and digging her nails into his back in a frenzy. *Deeper,* she begged, *deeper!*

He had meant to make it last a long, long time, but her body seemed to be pulling the very juice from him, demanding that, like a virile stud, he service her need. They rolled about on the tangled covers in a frenzy of mutual passion and desire, the gold dust sparkling in the moonlight as their bodies moved. He couldn't get any deeper into her, although he tried. His male rod felt big as

255

a gold bar, throbbing and hot as molten metal in her depths.

And then she gasped and pushed her tongue deep in his throat, her nails digging into him even as her glittering legs held him prisoner. *Give it to me,* she whispered, *give it to me. You know what I want!*

Her nipples felt swollen under his chest as he held her very close and rammed into her one more long moment of ecstasy. Then her body began to grip his maleness, forcing it to give up what it was she wanted, squeezing the very life juice from him into her waiting womb. They thrashed wildly for a moment and then, as they reached that crest at the same heartbeat, they froze into stillness—the only sound the creak of the bed, the quivering of muscles, and the whimpers of urgency.

He was pouring himself into her, giving her everything he had to give and it still wasn't enough. Her body locked onto his, demanding still more, and he was filling her with virile seed. Filling her . . . filling her . . .

Cherokee woke trembling and gasping. For a long moment, he was not sure where he was or what had happened to Silver. Then he realized he was still in the sweltering, cramped cell with the moonlight shining full upon him and he turned his face to the wall and banged his fist bloody against the stones in misery and despair.

The next day, he was again thrown in with the general prison population and discovered there were new captives being admitted. And among them was his old friend, the redheaded blacksmith, William Dowdy.

"Bill! By damn! You're a sight for sore eyes! How's Shawn? How's the war going?"

256

The young man's mouth dropped open in amazement. "Cherokee? We thought you was dead!"

"If I have to stay in this hellhole another six months, I very well may be! Tell me the news!"

"Petty made it back, said you and Wilson was both killed."

Cherokee cursed, and ran his hand through his hair. "That damned Petty deserted me! Wilson was killed all right and I've been a prisoner ever since that night. Do you have any tobacco?"

The big blacksmith shook his head. "Yanks took it off me first thing. I reckon they ain't seen any the whole war, just like we ain't seen much real coffee. Will a fella even be able to get a drink here once in a while, Cherokee?"

"I don't know. When I gave it up, I gave it up for good. But I have to admit that once in a while, I think about how Irish whiskey used to taste." He led Dowdy over to a corner of the prison yard and they sat down in the shade of the big broad wall that surrounded the desolate, treeless sandbar. "We don't even know much about what's going on out there."

"Well, we're losing and losing bad; looks like it's only a matter of time," the boy sighed.

"We did hear that. The captain all right?"

"He's Colonel O'Bannion now," Dowdy drawled. "I reckon he's fine. We got separated in the fightin' right after the Fort Pillow thing."

"Fort Pillow?"

"Ain't you heard?"

Cherokee leaned back against the wall and shook his head. "No, tell me."

"Forrester's Tennessee troops captured the Yankee fort. When our boys found out it was manned by former

257

slaves, they went crazy. Petty was one of those who started it, although O'Bannion tried to stop it. Turned into a massacre, it did. Our troops even burned and buried some of those black soldiers alive!"

"Good God! War makes men do crazy things, doesn't it?"

Dowdy nodded and looked around at the handsome arrogant Rand Erikson, who had just crossed the prison yard. "Who's the fella who struts like a rooster?"

Cherokee frowned and looked at the tall blond aristocrat the blacksmith pointed to. "Oh, him? A real Southern gentleman—rich and spoiled. He only joined up so he could wear a pretty gray uniform to all the cotillions and thrill the plantation belles. Then he got captured and even his daddy's money hasn't managed to get him released. He's a pain in the —"

"What's the prison camp itself like?"

"Point Lookout?" Cherokee asked. "compared to what? Hell? Some days I'm not sure I'm not there already. Some die every day from bad food or disease. There's no trees, just sand and wind. It's cold in the winter and sweltering in the summer."

"Can we escape?"

Cherokee shook his head. "But I'm getting desperate enough to do anything to get out of here. We've heard gossip about the Union enlisting prisoners to join up and go west to fight Indians. They call them Galvanized Yankees."

"You gonna join if you get the chance?"

Cherokee scratched the world "Silver" in the sand thoughtfully. "I don't know. My own tribe is fighting on both sides of this war. The South has promised the Indians their own separate nation if the Confederacy wins, so you can see why the Plains tribes are trying to help the South. A man will do a lot of things to live and I'm not sure I can survive another six months in this place."

"Whatever you do, I'm gonna do," young Dowdy said. "At least we will be outa this place and we won't have to fight against our own people!"

And so it was that a few days later, the two, along with a thousand other former Confederates, including Rand Erikson, found themselves in the new First Volunteer Infantry. They boarded the big transport ship, the *Continental,* in a Virginia harbor, and were on their way to New York City. The group was divided there, and Cherokee and Dowdy were among the six hundred loaded onto trains and sent to St. Louis.

The first week of September, Cherokee and William Dowdy, wearing Union blue, were now at the Missouri River boarding a big stern-wheeler named the *Effie Deans* to go up river. Final destination: Fort Rice, Dakota Territory, where the First Volunteer Infantry was needed to fight the Sioux.

The two settled themselves on the deck along with hundreds of others and watched the young colonel bark last-minute orders to the ship captain before the crew cast off and the ship started upstream.

Dowdy shook his head. "He don't look like much, do he?"

Cherokee scowled. "Young and green and scared," was his verdict, "and maybe Dimon's got a right to be."

"What do you mean?"

Cherokee looked at the overloaded deck, a sea of blue

uniforms. "Do you realize that except for the boat crew, a twenty-three-year-old colonel, and a handful of his own men, what we're got here are six hundred former Southern troops? And it's a long, lonely trip up the river."

"That's right, ain't it?" the blacksmith drawled. "It wouldn't be all that hard to overpower him and his officers, take over this boat, and head South to rejoin our own side."

"Watch it!" Cherokee cautioned him. "Keep your voice low! What you're talking is treason and Dimon's bound to have spies mixed in with these troops."

"I don't give a damn," Dowdy said, pulling off his blue cap and running his hand through the bright red hair. "I'd shore do it if I get the chance. Would you, Cherokee?"

Cherokee thought a moment, then shook his head. "I swore an oath and gave my word. I'm not a man to go back on my word."

"But if it was given to a damned Yankee—"

"It's still *my* word," Cherokee said, "and I just can't break it, even to a Yankee. Call it foolish, call it old-fashioned, it doesn't matter. Like I said, Dowdy, be careful. As big as you are and with that shock of red hair, you stand out in a crowd. You don't want to say things that would attract our young colonel's attention. I think he's just itching to make an example of someone."

They found out just how scared the green officer was the next day as the boat inched its way upstream. He called an assembly of the whole six hundred troops and announced that it had been reported that Willian Dowdy

260

was urging treason. There would be a hearing, the officer announced, but he intended to make it clear that he would tolerate no treason or talk of uprisings among the former Confederates.

The hearing as such was a joke. In vain, the big, clumsy boy pleaded his innocence. In vain, Cherokee appeared before the hearing, speaking in the blacksmith's defense and protesting Dowdy's arrest while the boat chugged up the muddy Missouri.

The verdict was a forgone conclusion. Cherokee had already sensed that from the hostile faces of the officers hearing the case. Still he was shocked when Colonel Dimon announced that William Dowdy had been found guilty, and would be taken ashore the next day and executed.

There was a collective gasp from the assembled men when the verdict was announced.

Cherokee asked to see the colonel in his cabin and protested that even in war, no soldier could be executed for any reason without a chance to appeal. Anyway, the President himself had to sign the documents in a case like this and Lincoln was well known for his kind heart, and more likely than not, would commute the sentence.

"Sir, you just can't do it," Cherokee said. "You are overstepping your authority."

The youthful officer stood up and paced the small cabin. "My authority is what's on the line here, Evans. You think I don't know it hasn't crossed everyone's mind how easy it would be to mutiny, take over the *Effie Deans*, and float her back down the river to rejoin Southern guerilla fighters?"

"I tell you Dowdy is innocent!" Cherokee said. "He's not smart enough to plan something like you suggest. It was just loose talk."

"What's loose around here is discipline, Evans," The slightly built officer eyed him coldly. "An example has to be made so these men will know I mean business and will deal with troublemakers like yourself and the private without hesitation."

"Are you threatening me, sir?"

The young officer glared at him and Cherokee saw nervous sweat on the other's almost beardless face. "Let's just say I will command, I will control this bunch of Rebels, no matter what I have to do!"

"It's on your conscience then." Cherokee turned to go.

"Aren't you forgetting something, Evans?"

Very slowly, Cherokee turned around and gave him a deliberately insulting salute.

He went up on deck where Dowdy sat in chains.

The blacksmith raised his head. "Well?"

Cherokee shook his head. "I still think he's bluffing. I think at the last minute tomorrow, he'll commute your sentence. I just can't believe he'd overstep himself to the point that he'd execute a U.S. soldier without going through proper channels, which takes months."

From the other end of the ship, they heard the sound of hammering.

Dowdy looked scared. "Cherokee, you'd better tell the colonel that if he's bluffing, he's wasting a lot of time and good lumber havin' the boys build me a coffin."

"I reckon I got you into this, and I'm sorry. We'd both been better off to have stayed in the Yankee prison."

"Now, Cherokee, you couldn't know this would happen. If I was you, I'd watch my step. I hear rumors you're next on his list because you're my friend and someone the men would follow."

Cherokee spat contemptously. "That wet behind the ears pup wouldn't dare execute two men on this trip. I don't even think he'll execute one."

"Cherokee, he's running scared—afraid of an uprising out here in the wilderness. A scared man'll do just about anything."

"Reckon so," Cherokee said. "Can I get you anything, boy?"

Dowdy's hands trembled. "I'd like to have a glass of cold buttermilk and a hunk of hot cornbread dripping with melted butter from one of my mama's Jersey cows. I been waking up nights dreaming about that ever since I was captured. You ever dream over and over about something you love and know you most likely will never have again?"

Cherokee thought of Silver and nodded. "I'm sorry I can't get you any buttermilk, son. And I don't imagine these Yankees know anything about cornbread. Us Cherokees like to fry it in deep fat along with fresh-caught catfish."

"And a mess of greens," Dowdy said wistfully "Poke, picked early in the spring when it's tender and fresh; with a hunk of salt pork to flavor it. And fried green tomatoes. Law, I'd give anything for a plate of fried green tomatoes."

In the background, the hammering pounded rhythmically and the *Effie Deans* churned her way through the muddy water.

He had to keep the boy's mind off what those carpenters were building. Cherokee put his hand on Dowdy's broad shoulder. "If we had that dinner, would you rather have fried chicken or ham?"

The boy considered seriously. "Nobody cures a ham like my daddy, all slow-smoked and done with brown sugar. For dessert, I'd like either pecan or sweet potato pie, Cherokee, finished off with some of that strong Cajun coffee like the Louisiana boys drink." He sighed. "Finally, I'd like a big slug of corn likker."

"Sounds good. Even the whiskey. But I swore off that and I'm honor bound to keep my word." Cherokee leaned back against the rail and listened to the sawing and hammering from the other end of the deck. "And afterward, maybe we'd entertain some pretty belles out in the porch swing." He thought about Silver. "You got a girl, Bill?"

The other shook his head. "There's a girl I favor; but I was always too shy to press my case. Don't reckon she's still waitin'."

"I'll bet she is," Cherokee said. "When we go back after the war, I'll speak your part to her and see what she says."

Dowdy brightened. "Would you, Cherokee?"

"What are friends for?"

Friends. Tso-ga-li-i. He knew what friends were for, Cherokee thought bitterly. They were to keep you talking and remembering so that time passed; to drown out the sound of the hammering and sawing on your crude wood coffin, and to keep you from dwelling on what was coming on the morrow.

At approximately noon on September 9, 1864, the *Effie Deans* moored up along a riverbank in the desolate area above the settlement of Omaha, Nebraska Territory.

While the other soldiers watched in sullen disbelief, a squad of soldiers marched Private William Dowdy off the boat and formed an open-sided square.

Cherokee watched in amazement and disbelief. "Dimon won't really do this," he grumbled. "He's trying to scare everyone, that's all. At the last minute, he'll call the whole thing off."

"You better keep quiet, Cherokee," one of the men next to him on the rail said. "I hear rumors that you're next for daring to buck him."

As Cherokee watched, another six men carried the wooden coffin ashore, followed by the bewildered blacksmith in chains. They put the crude wooden box on the ground and Dowdy slumped down on it while the soldiers started digging a hole.

The gawky youth turned and looked toward the boat. In the warm September sun, sweat beaded on his red face and ran down his neck into the collar of the blue uniform that he had put on to survive—only to survive.

Cherokee stared back at him helplessly, then looked around for Dimon. But the officer was in his cabin, having turned over the dirty work to a lesser officer who looked miserable as he directed the men who dug the hole.

How ironic. How unjust, Cherokee thought. Surely the rash young officer wasn't going to break all the rules and carry this thing through. Surely at the last minute when the hole was dug and the firing squad lined up, Dimon himself would appear and call the whole thing off. Yes, of course that was it.

He had the wildest impulse to go over the side, attack the squad with his fists, and somehow rescue the scared boy. The two of them would take off running through the tall prairie grass. For miles around, there wasn't a tree—nothing but a gently waving sea of grass.

Dowdy looked at him, gave him just a hint of a smile, and shook his head. *Don't*, he seemed to say with his eyes. *Don't try anything foolish, Cherokee, they'll kill you for it. Don't do it!*

Nothing seemed real. Cherokee stood on the deck with the others. The breeze blew toward him and brought him the slight scent of wild flowers among the prairie grasses.

Almost in a trance, he heard the sound of the shovels, the water slapping against the sides of the boat. A man near him coughed and from somewhere in the grass, a *guque,* a quail, called: *Bob white. Bob, bob white . . .*

The sun beat down on the scene, making his skin itch under the blue wool, reflecting off the rifles and the brass buttons of the men on shore.

The men were through digging the hole. They stepped back and waited.

Cherokee stood almost paralyzed on deck, watching along with the others. A cottontail rabbit hopped out of the grass, reared up on its hind legs, and sniffed curiously at all the men on the shore, the boy slumped on the wooden box, and the pile of fresh black dirt.

The firing squad was lining up, coming to attention. The officer in charge came over, took Dowdy by the shoulder, stood him up, and offered him a blindfold. The young man hesitated, then shook his head. He looked toward Cherokee and his mouth formed the silent words: *Good-bye, friend.*

"Ready!"

The firing squad brought their rifles to their shoulders. The movement made the light catch their brass buttons. Any moment now, Dimon would run out on deck and stop this, Cherokee thought frantically, looking toward the officer's cabin. The door remained closed.

"Aim!"

Bob white. Bob, bob white . . .

"Fire!"

Chapter Fourteen

"No!" Cherokee screamed, but his shout of protest was drowned out by the sudden crack of rifles. Even as he watched, his young friend stumbled backward, paused for what seemed like an eternity, then crumpled and fell.

The frightened quail exploded up out of the grass in a flurry of wings. The rabbit took off in a flash. The echo of the rifles echoed and reechoed for a long moment, and then in the sudden stillness, Cherokee heard the men around him let out a collective sigh as if they had all been holding their breath. He felt so hot in the blue wool that for a long moment standing there smelling the sweating stink of close-packed bodies, Cherokee thought he would be sick. Then he swallowed hard and fell to his knees on the rough, wooden planks.

Through the other's legs, he could see the men on shore lifting the big body, putting it in the wooden box, nailing the lid down.

Ham like my daddy cures it and maybe pecan or sweet potato pie . . .

I'll speak your part for you . . .

Oh, would you, Cherokee, would you do that?

Somewhere in Bedford County, Tennessee, a pair of elderly people might be sitting down to dinner at this very moment, not even knowing that their son lay newly dead on a riverbank, forever far from home.

The squad put the box in the hole and filled it in. Then they marched back on board and the gangplank was raised.

The *Effie Deans* blew her whistle, and with a shout, the lines were cast off and she drifted away from the shore even as the big paddle wheel came to life and began to churn the muddy water.

Cherokee, still almost in a state of shock, walked to the rear of the boat and stared back. The prairie grass still blew and a rabbit peeked at him from the grass. Only a mound of fresh dirt disturbed the vast, empty stretch of desolate prairie.

Good-bye friend. Good-bye . . .

The *Effie Deans* churned her way up the river. Cherokee stood at the stern and stared at the little mound of dirt until it was finally lost from view. And then he collapsed on the deck and shook, full of fury and anger as the night came on.

He wondered if the upstart colonel had plans for Cherokee, too. And if the brash young officer was foolhardy enough to execute the naive blacksmith, Cherokee decided Dimon wouldn't hesitate to kill anyone else he considered a threat.

Cherokee had given his word to fight for the Union. But as far as he was concerned, the Union had broken its word to its soldiers. Everything had changed now. He didn't intend to wait until Dimon had time to plan a fitting end for Cherokee.

He said nothing to anyone as he ate his supper and made his plans. The rifles were stacked up near the cabin. How would he get one? Out here in this desolate prairie, a man without a weapon among wild animals and hostile Indians was a dead man. Somewhere upriver, he would have to steal one of those guns and get ashore when the *Effie Deans* tied up to send a patrol to hunt a little fresh meat. Cherokee would make his plans carefully.

A couple of days passed while he schemed. Then something happened that changed things so that he no longer had time for elaborate plans.

Night had fallen and the men lay in their blankets on the crowded decks and slept as best they could. There was a guard, but he was posted at the far end of the deck.

A man crawled to him in the darkness. "Cherokee?"

He didn't move. "What?"

"You done me a favor once and the boys are riled about Dowdy, so I'm tellin' ye."

"Telling me what?"

He saw only the outline of the soldier in the moonlight, and wondered who it was.

"We heard talk," the man whispered.

"What kind of talk?"

"First thing in the mornin', Dimon is gonna arrest you, too, on some trumped-up charge. He's afraid you'll lead the men in a revolt."

Morning. No time for elaborate plans. "And then?"

"Whata you think, Cherokee? You're to be shot!"

Cherokee's heart seemed to falter and then beat faster, as he remembered all too vividly the shooting of Private Dowdy. "I'm much obliged for the tip, soldier."

270

The man nodded and crawled away.

What to do? He didn't have a weapon and he hadn't finished his plan that would aid his escape. He would have to make his move tonight. Even with a weapon, if he managed to survive the current and make it to shore, he was miles from any white people. He'd be alone among thousands of hostile Indians who had been raiding and burning along the entire Western frontier since spring. But if the plains weren't crawling with Indians on the warpath, the Union wouldn't have been desperate enough to recruit former enemies for frontier duty. Suppose his informer was wrong? He could stay and hope Dimon wasn't plotting against him, or take his chances in this wild country alone.

The moon came out, all silvery pale, and he thought of the girl he'd left back in Colorado Territory. It seemed like such a long time ago. He wondered for a long moment if Shawn O'Bannion was still alive and what had happened to Shawn's little son and his haughty, beautiful wife.

Silver. *U-ne-ga.* He would probably never see her again. He closed his eyes briefly and saw her in his mind—her long, pale hair hanging loose about her shoulders, hiding her full naked breasts. Her eyes were hard but her mouth was soft and her lips opened as he kissed them. Did she still have the shoes he had bought her or even the gold nugget bracelet? By now, she might have married or left Colorado. He made a vow then that he wanted to hold her in his arms again and that if he made it all the way back to the Rockies, this time he would ask her to marry him and beg forgiveness for ever leaving her.

Cautiously, he turned his head and looked at the

sentry. The man appeared to be asleep at his post, his head sunk down on his chest. The stack of rifles was near him. Cherokee glanced up, studying the night sky. A big bank of clouds was moving slowly over the moon's face, darkening the night. He figured fast. With the clouds across the moon, Cherokee would have several minutes to maneuver before the scene was illuminated brightly again. His life might depend on those several precious minutes.

Cherokee got to his knees and watched the guard. The engine groaned rhythmically, the stern wheel churning water. Somewhere among the sleeping forms on deck, a man snored and a frog along the bank croaked loudly.

The clouds drifted across the moon's surface as it hung like a gold piece in the ebony sky. He crawled between the sleeping men toward the stack of weapons, mentally calculating how far it was to the rail. Could he crawl through all those sleeping bodies with a rifle? Would the movement awaken the sentry? He had to be careful and not alarm any of the sleeping troopers as he crept across the deck. If he should trod on a hand or awaken anyone suddenly, he might cry out.

Cherokee's mouth tasted so dry he could hardly swallow and his hand had picked up a splinter from the rough wood planking, but all he concentrated on was reaching those weapons.

He was close—so close and yet so far. Again he measured the distance to the weapons and then to the rail with his eye. If luck was with him, he would steal a rifle, crawl over the side of the boat, lower himself into the water, and swim to shore. With the noise the big paddle wheel was making, the slight splash wouldn't even be heard. It would be morning before he was missed. Even then, they weren't likely to come back down river searching for Cherokee, because they wouldn't be sure where they had lost him. They might even think he had fallen overboard and drowned.

Luck wasn't with him. He was only another couple of yards from the weapons when a man cried out in his sleep near him. The guard jerked awake and whirled toward the sound even as the moon came out from behind the clouds, lighting up the deck almost as bright as day.

"Halt! Halt or I'll shoot!"

For an agonizing heartbeat, Cherokee paused, making his choice. The weapons were too far away and the guard shouted again and swung toward him with his rifle. Men came up off the deck and soldiers scrambled for weapons. He didn't stand a chance. Without even thinking, he dived for the rail even as he heard the crack of the rifle behind him.

A pain burned into the base of his skull as he went over the side, and for an eternity, he was in the air. Then he felt the muddy waters of the Missouri close over his head.

Sergeant Baker fired wildly at the dark shape diving across the railing. "Halt! Halt, I say!"

Christ! The bastard was escaping! He fired at the man as he went over the side. Immediately, men were jumping up from the deck, shouting and gesturing. Lamps flickered on all over the *Effie Deans* as men struck matches to coal oil lamps. Colonel Dimon himself came running with a lantern. "What's going on here, Sergeant?"

Baker stopped picking at his bad complexion and saluted. "One of the men went over the side, sir! I shot at him, don't know if I hit him or not."

The young colonel turned to those gathering around him. "Stop the engines! Get some light out here!"

In the confusion of running, shouting men, the colonel glared at him. "Baker! I'll see this goes on your record. I understand you used to be a captain. Now with this, you may end up a private! Let's go look at where that man went over."

Christ! That uppity bastard would mention his record, Baker thought as he picked at his pimples and followed the colonel to the rail. It wasn't fair that he himself always got such rotten duty—assigned to raw frontier. Before the war started, he'd been stuck in Ft. Smith, Arkansas. Now just because he'd made a little mistake in judgment a few months ago and had gotten half a platoon wiped out, he was being shipped to a new hellhole. What he really wanted was to return to New York. He should have deserted while the *Continental* was docked there, but he was too much of a coward.

The *Effie Deans* shuddered to a halt midstream with men shouting and hanging over the rails, looking into the river. The moon shone big as a gold dollar, the stars glittering overhead, reflecting off the dark water. In the dim light of the lantern, Baker squatted and studied the deck. He put his finger in the scarlet smear and grunted with satisfaction. "Christ! I told you I hit him, sir!"

Colonel Dimon bent and looked, then stared out at the brown water. The stern wheeler had come to a complete halt in the middle of the river. "You men shine those lights over the side! Anyone see anything?"

Baker looked out at the fast-moving current. There were no ripples at all and it was a long way to shore. "Sir, I imagine the stupid bastard's at the bottom of the

274

Missouri now. No wounded man is strong enough to swim that distance." He gestured toward the distant shore.

Dimon looked at the spot of blood on the deck. "I suppose that's true," he mused aloud. "Besides, even if he managed to get to shore, with no weapon and wounded, he won't last very long. Anyone know for sure who it was?"

The men around them grumbled under their breaths, but no one answered.

"Very well," Dimon snapped, "we'll know when we do roll call in the morning."

"Sir," Baker said, "shall we put out search parties in boats or along the shore?"

The colonel shook his head. "We're behind schedule now what with having to take time to shoot that fellow. As I said, even if he managed to make it to land, which I doubt, he won't last long wounded with no weapon and no food. He'll be lucky if a war party doesn't find him and torture him to death."

Baker looked out over the muddy surface of the water again. The glimmer of the lanterns didn't carry very far, but the reflection of the full moon on the surface showed the water smooth as far as the eye could see. The dumb Johnny Reb was dead, all right, but not before he'd finished ruining Baker's career.

Dimon turned to the ship's captain. "You may get underway again, captain. We've got a long way to go to fight the Sioux."

The captain's face in the lamplight looked shocked. "You ain't gonna make any attempt to find that poor devil?"

Dimon shook his head. "No, I'm quite satisfied we've

275

seen the last of him. I hope it was one of our major troublemakers." He looked around at the sullen men on deck. "Let this be a lesson to you all. I am in command here and there's no point in deserting. Now let's go north and fight Indians like you signed up to do! Captain, get underway!"

Cherokee had felt the dull pain explode at the base of his skull as he went over the side, diving headfirst over the rail. It seemed like an eternity he hung in midair and then he hit the water, went deep into its cold depths, and felt the current tugging at him, dragging him down.

Dazed as he was, he couldn't seem to move for a long moment, and he knew he was wounded and probably drowning. Why not give up and let go? It seemed such an easy way to die—just close his eyes and take a deep gulp of water. Soon it would all be over, no more pain, no more sorrow, no more struggle.

Then he saw Silver's dear face in his mind. *I need you, Cherokee, my love . . . come back to me . . . come back. I've saved a treasure for you . . .* In his mind, she kissed his palm and closed his fingers over it. *Put that in your pocket and remember me . . . remember . . .*

He had to live. He had to go back to Colorado Territory and ask that girl to marry him. Cherokee began to fight his way to the surface. His water-logged clothes pulled at him, trying to drag him under. He wasn't going to make it, he thought, struggling to rid himself of the heavy uniform jacket. Even as he fought to get to the life-giving air of the surface, he felt the current sweeping him along downstream. Just as he knew he would die, he slipped out of the coat and broke the surface of the river, gasping and gulping in the air.

Somewhere upstream, he heard the *Effie Deans* shuddering to a stop, the shouting and confusion. But he couldn't see anything. He treaded water and tried to see how far away the stern-wheeler was. She must be up around a curve of the river, because although he heard the noise drifting on the wind, he didn't see anything.

By damn! The night was as dark as the devil's heart!

What happened to that full moon and the stars? But wasn't he lucky that it was suddenly so foggy and overcast? The darkness of the night would hide him.

Cherokee's head ached so badly, he couldn't get his bearings or see any landmarks along the riverbank. The colonel might put out search parties in boats or walking along the shore. If Cherokee was found, no doubt he would be shot. That alone kept him from yelling for help. Better to drown or perish alone on the shore than be recaptured and executed. At least this way he had a chance. The other way he had none at all.

The current pulled at him, washing him farther downstream. Choking on a mouthful of the muddy Missouri, he tried to get his boots off as he tread water, but failed. He felt exhausted and his head ached. If he could only make it to land, he'd worry about all his other problems at daylight.

It took almost superhuman strength on his part, but he began to swim, listening for frogs along the bank to guide him to shore. Far away, he heard the *Effie Deans*'s engines start again and smelled the smoke from her machine room as she got underway. He kept swimming without looking back.

The wind carried the sounds of the boat's big stern wheel churning water as she once again moved upstream.

Good! They were moving on; maybe convinced he was drowned; or at least deciding not to waste their time looking for him. He couldn't make it much farther. Just when he'd decided he couldn't take another stroke, his feet touched bottom and he waded ashore and collapsed in the mud.

Cherokee lay there, saying a little prayer of thanksgiving and in too much pain and too tired to move. He had joined the Union army in good faith, although he had no personal vendetta against Plains Indians. Like poor Dowdy, he had only been trying to survive until the war ended. When the sun came up, he'd figure out what to do next. Wounded, without any supplies or even a weapon, he was in dire straits out here miles from civilization, but maybe he could fashion himself a boat from bits of driftwood or hollow reeds and float down the river to civilization. From there, somehow he would get back to Colorado and the woman he loved.

But that was tomorrow's problem. Right now, he needed some rest. He stretched out with a grateful sigh and dropped off to sleep. In his mind, Silver ran toward him and into his waiting arms.

He awakened suddenly and sat up. By damn, his head ached! It was not yet dawn although he felt as if he'd slept for hours. The night was still black as the inside of a cave. Cherokee lay back down, staring up in the darkness. He couldn't do anything until morning. Then he would decide where he was and make his plans accordingly, maybe catch some fish in the shallows for breakfast. Thank God he had a few matches tucked away in a little metal box in his pants. But his tobacco was all wet. Well, no cigarette, but he couldn't have everything.

He thought about building a small fire from buffalo chips or driftwood, then shook his head. Because it was so dark, he couldn't see to gather fuel, and the fire might be spotted by a war party or army patrol if there were any in the area. No, he couldn't do anything until morning. He'd just have to put up with wet pants although his bare upper body was cold. He dozed off.

When he awakened, it was still dark. It seemed like the longest night Cherokee had ever spent. He felt the back of his skull, decided the wound wasn't as bad as he'd thought. The rail must have caught most of the force of the bullet. His head still ached a little, but funny, he wasn't cold anymore and his pants were almost dry. How could that be?

Bob white. Bob, bob white.

Strange, he yawned, *since when did quail move about and call in the darkness?* When he listened, he heard other birds, even the call of a hawk circling overhead. Hawks didn't fly at night any more than quail. *What the hell kind of strange birds were these?* The moon must be out finally, he could feel its heat on his face. *Since when did the moon put out heat?*

Bob white. Bob, bob white.

Was this strange night ever going to end? Cherokee put his hand up before his face, and wiggled his fingers. He didn't remember ever experiencing a night so dark he literally couldn't see his hand before his face.

Overhead, he heard the hawk wheel and call again. He turned his face upward, trying to see the bird, and felt the heat on his face.

A thought came to him;—a thought so terrifying, he didn't even want to consider it. It was tough enough to be

279

wounded and alone out here on this vast prarie without supplies or weapons, but that other possibility was just too horrible even to think about.

Bob white. Bob, bob white.

Again he put his fingers up before his face, feeling his hand shake at the suspicion. His fingers were against his nose and still he couldn't see them.

Cherokee turned his face upward and felt the relentless heat on his face, knowing suddenly that it was the sun. Now he lost control and screamed out in frustration and anguish. It wasn't dark. He was blind! Stone blind!

September. The days and weeks and months hung so heavy on her with the war dragging on and on. Silver helped little Wannie pick up toys from the nursery floor, and thought about the latest headlines in the *Rocky Mountain News.* The Cheyennes were talking peace. It couldn't come too soon for jittery Denver. With thirty-two recorded Indian attacks since last spring, ninety-six whites killed, including the Hungate family almost on the outskirts of town, twenty-one whites wounded, and eight captured by the hostiles, the people of the Territory were in an ugly mood. Many muttered that the Cheyenne and their allies couldn't be trusted, no matter what their chiefs said, and no peace should be discussed until the Indians paid in blood.

Waanibe ran to the window and looked out at the street. "Oh, come look, Silvery, Indians!"

"Indians?" Silver came to the window and stared at the scene below. Trees were already turning gold and russet in the late September air. Lots of soldiers, mounted Indians, and several horse-drawn wagons carrying forlorn-looking white women and children. "Yes, the *Rocky Mountain News* said Black Kettle and the chiefs were bringing in some white captives and asking for peace."

She wondered suddenly if this meant the Southerners had given up trying to take Colorado for its gold, or maybe that the Indians were just weary and sensed the war against the encroaching whites was hopeless. She felt sorry for everyone concerned. In her heart, she hoped that the Civil War would soon end, even though, when it did, the Duchess would no doubt be sending little Wannie off to boarding school. Silver didn't have any idea what she would do then. "Get your dolls, Wannie, we'll play awhile."

"I'd rather look at the Indians." The little girl had her face pressed against the glass. "They look sad and tired, Silvery. So do the white people."

"That's the way war is, Wannie. Now get your dolls."

The half-breed Cheyenne warrior, Iron Knife, rode his bay Appaloosa stallion at the front of his braves across the prairie. Over the next rise lay the river.

Sometimes he knew the bluecoats used the stream to float their boats as they journeyed upriver to their forts. For that reason, he paused on the rise and searched along the water for any signs of danger.

He was a big man, a warrior who had counted many coups, a honored owner of the *hotamstit*, the Dog Rope awarded to only the four bravest of the brave among the Dog Soldiers.

The sun felt hot to his whip-scarred, muscular back,

for he wore little besides a breechcloth and moccasins. On his sinewy brown chest were scars from the sun dance. His hair, black as a crow's wing, was pulled in a braid over his left ear, and a single earring, formerly a brass button from a cavalry officer's uniform, gleamed in his right ear. The others rode up beside him, looking toward the water.

He signaled his cousin. "Lance Bearer, we camp at the water for the night."

The other Dog Soldier nodded. "You think we have found all the war parties then?"

Iron Knife nodded. "I am satisfied that we have carried out Chief Black Kettle's orders. All our people will be gathering in now to await instructions while he and the other chiefs are in the white man's city, Denver, to return the white hostages and ask for a peace parlay."

His other cousin, Two Arrows, frowned. "Iron Knife, you have lived among the whites. Do you think they are sincere? Will the bluecoats keep their word?"

Iron Knife, son of the great chief, War Bonnet, and the beautiful white captive, Texanna, furrowed his handsome face and considered. "Any more than the graycoats who promise us our own country if we help them in their war?" He shrugged. "We can only hope so. This fight the tribes have waged since last spring has taken a terrible toll on whites and our own people. When we gather at our camp on the Big Sandy, we will know more."

Two Arrows laughed. "We are both eager to get home to our families. We have been gone too many suns."

Iron Knife nodded, thinking of his love, the Boston debutante, Summer Van Schuyler, who had run away with him in the spring of '59. Now she was known as Summer Sky, his woman. He was never happy when she and their three little ones were not close by his side. But as an honored warrior, he was bound to carry out the Cheyenne chiefs' orders.

The young boy, Bear Cub, rode up beside him. "I am glad you brought me along. The bigger boys will envy me when I tell them of our advantures."

"We brought you because your brother is one of my warriors and you begged so hard." Iron Knife grinned. "Besides, Bear Cub, your drawings interest me. And too, you turned out to be handy at gathering fuel and hobbling horses. Speaking of that—I'm hungry. Let us ride on down to the river and camp."

His sharp eyes missed nothing as they topped the rise and looked around. The treeless prairie stretched like a sea of grass around them and beyond that lay the muddy river the whites called the Missouri. He and his men had been sent out to call the stragglers in, urging the war parties to stop attacking wagon trains and passing army patrols. They could not win against the whites, he knew. The few years he had spent among his mother's people in that faraway place called *Tejas*—Texas—had taught him that.

Besides he could not bring himself to spill the blood of beautiful Summer Sky's people anymore. A truce and peace were the only answers, but it was difficult to convince the Cheyenne warriors, greatest fighters of the plains. There was only one white man that he hated enough to kill—Jake Dallinger,—and that man was safely in the white soldiers' prison.

But now his keen eyes spotted something by the river and he reined in, raising his hand in warning. "Hold on! What is this we see?"

For a minute more they looked. It was a man, a big

man, clad only in bluecoat pants and sprawled in the mud, his face partly in the water.

Lance Bearer said, "I see only one. Why would one soldier be out here on patrol? Where are the rest? Can it be a trick?"

Iron Knife looked up and down the river. From here, they could see for miles. "It is strange," he admitted. "Maybe he is dead and fell from a passing boat."

The others grunted and nodded. That was the likeliest explanation.

Cautiously, Iron Knife led his men down the rise. "Be careful, our experience with whites tells me it may be a trick. He may have a weapon."

They rode toward the man slowly. He was a big man, Iron Knife noted, big as he himself and dark as a half-breed in the sun. The man lay on the riverbank, his muscles rippling in the sun. As they rode up, the man leaped to his feet, brandishing a stick, and Iron Knife realized he had been trying to kill the tiny frogs that splashed in the water as the horses approached.

Cherokee tensed, his stick at the ready. For several days, he had been able to see nothing at all, and now all he saw was the barest blur of approaching horses. "Who's there? Stay back, I'm armed!"

"So we see," said a deep voice in stilted English as if the owner didn't use the language often, "although your little stick doesn't strike fear in any of us."

Another rider translated the words into an unfamiliar language and a bunch of men laughed and hooted.

Indians? Soldiers? Renegade robbers?

"A man fights with what he has, even though he may die," Cherokee said with as much dignity as he could muster, although he knew he hadn't a chance against armed men. "Who are you?"

"Well spoken like a brave man," said the leader again. "We are Cheyenne, on our way back to our camp in the Shining Mountains that you call the Rockies."

Colorado. They were going to Colorado. Cherokee felt his heart leap at the thought of his love, but of course this war party would torture him. At least maybe that was better than slowly starving to death as he had been doing for the last few days since he had jumped from the deck of the *Effie Deans*

"White man, what do you do with the stick?"

He was only the dim outline of a big man on a horse. "I—I'm trying to catch a frog."

The other's saddle creaked as he dismounted. "You are hungry?"

Cherokee hesitated. He had too much pride to admit it. "Don't come any closer or you will find out how strong I can swing this stick!"

"You are brave indeed to try to hold us at bay with no weapons." The other's voice sounded gentle, sympathetic. "You don't act as if you can see us."

"I can see well enough to knock your head from your shoulders if you come one step closer." Cherokee retreated a little.

"Are you Indian?"

"Half-breed. Cherokee. Why do you care if you plan to kill me anyhow?"

The other grunted. "Soldier, I am Iron Knife of the Cheyenne. My chiefs will be meeting soon with the

285

whites. We try to call a truce to this fighting."

Cherokee held on to his stick. "Why should I believe you?"

The big form shrugged. "Why should you not? If I meant you harm, I would have already killed you. Do you think a silly stick would protect you against warriors who have counted many coups?"

It made sense, and anyway, he couldn't fight them all. He lowered his stick.

The big form turned to the mounted men and spoke in their language, then turned back around. "We will camp here tonight and move on tomorrow. If you wish, you may ride with us."

Cherokee's heart began to beat with hope. "You ride to the Shining Mountains? That's where I would like to go."

"Good! That is settled. We will sit and smoke a pipe until there is food ready, Can you walk?"

"I—I don't know. I've had no food for several days since I was wounded." And at that point, he fainted.

When he came to, he lay next to a warm fire and the Indians had cooked some rabbits and gave him one. Ravenous as he was, Cherokee almost burned his fingers on the crusty, delicious meat. He gobbled, trying hard to see the brave who had befriended him. "I'm much obliged. I'll always remember that a Cheyenne called Iron Knife helped me when I needed it."

The other grunted and ate his meat. "I would like to live at peace with all men so that my children can grow up and live as I have lived. But times are changing, and I see that I am powerless to stop it. Only one white man do I hate, and him I should have killed rather than merely gelding him. His name was Jake Dallinger."

"Jake Dallinger." Cherokee paused in eating and said the name again to himself. "If he is Iron Knife's enemy, he will be mine, too."

The brave must have lit a pipe. Cherokee could smell the tobacco burning.

The Cheyenne said, "Dallinger is an evil man. I hope the spirits smile on you and you never cross his path. Here, share my tobacco."

Gratefully, Cherokee took it. Already his spirits rose. "If you are going to Colorado anyway, would it be asking too much if I ride along with you? I have partners in Buckskin Joe. They will look after me."

"You have no woman to do this?"

Cherokee sighed. "There was a woman. But I can't seek her out if I can never see again. I don't want her pity."

Iron Knife made a disapproving sound. "If she were the right kind of woman, she would want you anyway, but I understand your reasons. Our medicine man examined your wound when you were asleep. I think luck smiles on you or you would already be dead. The bullet seems to have struck you a glancing blow, or maybe only a fragment hit you."

Cherokee savored the tobacco and listened to the men moving about the camp, the neighing of horses. "At first, I couldn't see at all. Now I can at least see daylight and dark and blurred shapes. Maybe my vision will improve."

"Perhaps. Men live by hope, do they not? I still have hope that whites and Indians can finally live peacefully together. We are both half-breeds. I'm sure you have suffered as I have from hatred on both sides."

Cherokee agreed, his heart warm toward the other man. "Together, we will do what we can toward peace."

They rested for several days, then the Cheyenne gave Cherokee a spare horse and they rode toward the camp at Big Sandy Creek. The days blended into a blur of weeks. From the chill in the air, he knew it must be the middle or late *Du-ni-nv-di*, October. Cherokee's eyesight improved a little by the time they reached the main camp.

Iron Knife said, "You can rest here a day or so, then I will take you on to this town called Buckskin Joe."

In a few days, Cherokee thought with mounting excitement, *I might be with my beloved Silver.* Then he thought about his handicap. If his sight didn't improve, he wouldn't seek her out. He couldn't burden her with a blind man. If he stayed in Mosquito Gulch, she need never know he'd returned.

Silver opened the nursery door. "Waanibe?" Drat! Where was the child? She'd better check the Duchess's room. If the little girl was playing in the jewelry box again, her mother would be upset. Silver wished the woman would put her baubles in the safe instead of leaving them on her bureau. Of course probably no one but herself realized the jewelry had any real value and Silver had never told anyone.

She pushed the spectacles back up her nose and smoothed the drab dress as she walked through the nursery, opened the door to the Duchess's room. The little girl stood in Silver's glittering slippers and wore dozens of the Duchess's bracelets, rings, and broaches. "Ah ha! There you are, you little rascal! Your mama will scold you and me both if she catches you!"

288

"I'm playing dress-up." She smiled at Silver, maddeningly sweet with her black hair and dark eyes, all wrapped in one of the Duchess's finest lace shawls.

"I know what you're doing and your mama won't like it. You can wear my shoes, but leave your mama's jewelry alone. Let's go to my room and read a story book."

"Okay, Silvery." Obediently, Waanibe took off the jewelry and laid it in the velvet box. "Mama says the war will be over in a year or so and then I'll go off to school. You're going with me, aren't you?"

"We'll talk about that later." Silver brushed her dyed hair back into her severe bun while reaching for the child's hand. She had known from the first that eventually Wannie would be sent off to boarding school. After all, how long could an innocent girl stay in a rough bordello like the Duchess's Palace? What would Silver do then? She loved the child like her own—like the dark-skinned child she wished she had had by Cherokee.

They went back to the nursery, where Silver took the glittering shoes off the little girl's feet, snuggled her up, and opened a story book. She read it automatically and finally closed the book and looked down at the little girl. "Now, Wannie, wasn't that a good story?"

The chubby five-year-old nodded. "Good story, Silvery. I like it when the prince came for her and they got on the horses and rode away to live happily ever after."

Happily ever after. Wasn't it too bad that life wasn't like a fairy tale? Silver smiled and nodded absently, thinking of Cherokee. It had been three and a half years since he had ridden off to fight. She had no idea whether he was alive or dead. In the meantime, she had made a life for herself as governess to the Duchess's child and she

289

was happy, she supposed. At least a lonely little girl loved her.

The child said, "Let me give you a treasure, Silvery." She kissed Silver's palm and closed her fingers over it. "A treasure to put in your pocket."

Silver laughed. "Let *me* give *you* a treasure." She put a dime in the child's hand and closed her fingers over it. "Now that treasure will buy lots of things—candy for both of us."

"I love you, Silvery, I wish you were my mama." She hugged her governess.

"I love you, too, sweet darlin'." Without thinking, she had used his words. His rugged face came to her mind. Why did she keep thinking of him? If he weren't dead, she would have heard from him somehow—if he wanted to keep in touch. Of course he might have returned to Buckskin Joe.

Silver herself had gone back on the anniversary of the smallpox epidemic each year to lay flowers on the graves of Al and the others who had died from the disease. Some of the blooms had scattered seeds and now there were wild flowers throughout the graveyard. She didn't let anyone see her when she went, not that there was anyone much left in the little settlement. In a few more years, it would be a ghost town. Prospectors now were going on to bigger strikes, and places like Fairplay were booming. Besides Silver didn't want anyone who remembered her beauty to see her and pity her.

Cherokee. The memory hurt. "Let's wash up for dinner," she said, holding Wannie so the little girl couldn't see the tears that came to her eyes and threatened to overflow. She had to swallow hard before she could speak. "Later, I'll read you another story."

"If the prince ever comes for you, can I go along?" Waanibe's dark eyes danced with enthusiasm. "I'd like to be your little girl. When I do see other children on the street, they're mean to me. They call me 'half-breed.'"

Half-breed. She almost felt Cherokee's lips on hers. "I don't think a prince is coming for either of us anytime soon," she said gently.

"Let's play dress-up now," Waanibe pouted.

"No you don't!" Silver caught her by the sash of her dress. "What we're going to do is wash up. Then we'll have dinner and go out and get that candy."

Waanibe nodded with enthusiasm. "A treasure to put in my pocket?"

"A treasure to put in your pocket!" she promised and tried not to think about Cherokee. She didn't know whether he was alive or dead. One thing was certain; if her half-breed prince ever did return, he wouldn't want Silver with her scarred face.

Chapter Fifteen

Late October 1864. Jake Dallinger glared at the prison warden and ran his fingers through his gray-streaked beard. "Now that I'm gettin' out, do I get my whip back?"

The grim officer hesitated, reached behind his desk, and handed over the silver-handled bull whip. "We even saved that smelly fur vest and the old Western hat of yours with the feathers in the band. What you don't get back is your weapons."

"Gawd Almighty!" Jake drawled in protest, grabbing the whip and rolling its lash up. He hung it on his belt. "A man kin get hisself kilt out there in the West without weapons."

"Then don't go west. There's Indian trouble there anyhow. You'd be smart to head east."

"Cheyenne most likely and their allies." Jake spat to one side and stared at the port wine birthmark on his hand. "I'd like to kill me a few of them. If it weren't for one of their warriors, I wouldn't have ended up in your damned prison."

"I had hoped being here for five years would have

taught you something," the officer said coldly, "but I suppose that's too much to hope for. Just stay out of trouble, Jake. I don't want to see you back here."

"I'd die before I end up back in prison," Jake muttered. He took the whip and the other things the warden handed him, turned, and walked out the iron gates. He didn't have a horse or a gun. Never mind, it wouldn't be much trouble to steal one and some weapons, too. Stay out of the Rockies? Hell no! There were Cheyenne to kill in Colorado Territory and there was no one Jake hated as much and with good reason.

The only woman Jake had ever really loved, Texanna, had spurned him many years ago to run away with War Bonnet, and had produced the half-breed son, Iron Knife. Back in the spring of '59, that now grown son, Iron Knife, had gelded Jake in a bloody knife fight and handed him over to the army for trial. If Jake had been smart enough to leave Iron Knife's woman, Summer Sky, alone, he wouldn't have ended up in prison.

In between Texanna and Summer, there had been another girl with almost milk white hair he had lusted after and sold into a whorehouse in Chicago Silver. He wondered for a moment if Bart Brett still had her.

Women. They had been his downfall. There was also an Injun gal Jake wanted revenge against—a little Arapaho named Gray Dove who had robbed him and knocked him in the head. He had a feeling he knew where she might be, too. Yes sir, he would get even with all of them. He'd been brooding over it for more than five years now. But first, he had to have some weapons and a horse.

It was all so easy for the big Georgia cracker. First he

293

picked a lonely prospector who told him there was still a few strikes in the South Park region of Buckskin Joe and Fairplay if a man wanted to work hard. He invited Jake to share his fire and what little food he had. In the middle of the night, Jake garroted the man with the lash of the big bullwhip. Then Jake stole the prospector's bowie knife, his little stash of gold, an old Sharps rifle, and the man's horse. Jake didn't want to work hard to get gold; he'd rather rob lonely old prospectors who might be hiding a stash. Fairplay or Buckskin Joe. Jake headed up into the Rockies.

The town of Buckskin Joe wasn't much, he decided as he rode down the main street. He'd seen better towns. A pile of blackened rubble showed where some building had once stood that hadn't been rebuilt when it had burned. He reined in, looking around.

Down the street came a rattletrap buggy driven by an older man with a mustache and rumpled suit. He looked like a respectable citizen who probably knew everyone in these parts. Jake hailed him and the buggy reined in. "Howdy, stranger, I'm lookin' for an old friend and I plain forgot directions to his claim."

"I'm Doc Johnson," the other said. "Who's your friend?"

Jake took off his hat and scratched the red scar where he'd been partly scalped by Indians many years ago. He thought fast. "Bob Smith." It was the first name that came to him. "Of course, he might be using a fresh handle now." He laughed. "Minor scrap with the law a few years back."

The doctor nodded. "Common enough in these parts. I don't recollect anyone by that name. We haven't had too many new people since the smallpox epidemic near wiped out this town, even though it is the county seat. I suspect they'll take that away from us when they see we aren't growing."

"On the other hand," Jake drawled, and grinned agreeably, "he might be calling hisself Bill or Tom."

Doc pulled at his mustache. "Did your friend have a partner or maybe two?"

Jake pretended to puzzle over it. "Wal, he might have. It's been a long time."

"I wonder if that might be old Bill and Willie up in Mosquite Gulch?"

"Might be. Describe him to me."

The gullible doctor described both old men in detail.

"Why, that's him, the old rascal!" Jake beamed. "You say he and Willie are alone up there?"

Doc nodded. "There's a third partner, a big half-breed who went off to the war and never came back. Reckon he was killed."

"Course I wouldn't want to make Bill feel beholden to an old friend if there ain't enough dust up on that claim to go around . . ."

"Oh, I think they're doing fine," Doc hastened to assure him. "Been trying to get them to put their pokes in the bank, but they don't get in too often." He pointed vaguely in the distance. "It's not too far from Mt. Silver Heels."

Jake turned and looked at the snow-capped peak. "Funny name for a mountain."

Doc told him the story.

"I knew a purty gal named Silver once. Don't suppose it could be the same one."

Doc shrugged. "Likely not, although this one was a beauty a man wouldn't soon forget—until the epidemic and she got the smallpox. She went away, but a couple of folks think they've seen her all dressed in mourning and a veil, putting wild flowers on the graves along about dusk."

"Ghost story, huh? Sounds like someone's had a wee bit too much of the hair of the dog that bit him!" Jake guffawed and lit one of the cheap, strong cigars he favored.

Doc shrugged. "She's a legend, and that's a fact. No one knows what ever became of her. Dead most likely."

Jake nodded absently, his mind already on two old prospectors up in the Mosquito Gulch. He exchanged a few more pleasantries and rode out.

It was even easier than Jake had thought it would be. He saw the smoke from the little cabin from a long way off. Dismounting, he hid his horse and sneaked up to the claim. He caught unawares one who limped and garroted him with the handle of his big whip. It was something he had learned from his bitter enemies, the Comanches. That tribe feared to die by hanging or choking because they thought a man's spirit escaped out of his mouth as he died—unless he died by hanging or choking. Then his spirit was trapped in the dead body forever. Jake shuddered a little at the thought. He was superstitious enough to believe it himself. Gawd almighty! He sure didn't want to go that way!

Now he went up to the cabin. A small burro munched hay in the corral and a man sang in a cracked, off-key voice from inside. Jake opened the door and sneaked in. Years of living around Indians had taught him to step lightly as a scorpion. The old man had his back to Jake, cooking something in the fireplace. A board creaked under Jake's boot and the old man paused. "Willie, is that you?"

Jake moved between the old codger and the rifle leaning against the door. "Nope, it's me, you deaf bastard." He leveled his Sharps on the old man. "Now you tell me where you hide your stash and maybe I won't have to torture you before I kill you."

The old man was stubborn. Jake had to use his whip on him. But in the end, old Bill told about the stash in the woodpile. Jake didn't have to even bother about killing him. The old man died of the beating just before Jake was planning to enjoy killing him. Too bad.

Jake wiped the blood from his lash, recoiled it, and hung it on his belt. Then he put the gold poke in his fur vest and went back to his horse. Now he wanted some whiskey and some gambling and good times. Most of all, he wanted revenge. From the last conversation he had had with the little Arapaho gal before he raped her and she hit him over the head and fled, he thought she might have gone to Denver City. That's where he would look. After that he'd figure out a way to even the score against the Cheyenne.

Jake rode into Denver. The size of the town at the joining of Cherry Creek and the Platte River surprised him. He left his horse at the Elephant Corral, the big stockyard on McGaa Street.

"Why do they call it the Elephant Corral?" he grumbled to the Indian stable boy. "I don't see no elephants, just the most horses and oxen and wagons I ever seen in one spot."

The boy laughed. "It's the biggest, mister, covers most of a city block. Folks that come through here are on their way to see the elephant you know, share the adventure of goin' West."

He realized the boy was waiting for a tip, but he cuffed him instead. "Redskin bastard. I got no use for Injuns, kids or not."

Hitting the boy made Jake feel better. He turned and walked slowly down the street, looking around. Yep, this must be the street with all the action, he thought, noticing the stage pulling in. Saloons and bawdy houses lined the street. Loud music drifted from open windows in the late October air and there was a bustle of horses and people up and down the avenue.

He paused before the Progressive Saloon, decided he wanted a drink, and went in and leaned on the bar.

The brawny bartender looked up. "What'll you have?"

"I'd like some Georgia moonshine, but reckon I'll settle for whatever you got."

The man poured, frowning at him. "That accent. You a Johnny Reb?"

Jake savored the whiskey with a sigh. It had been a long time since he'd had whiskey. "Stranger, would you believe I don't give a damn who wins this war? Who owns this place, anyhow?"

"Big Ed Chase, but Brett's the new manager."

Jake came alert. "Bart Brett?"

"No, Lon Brett."

"Lon got a brother named Bart?"

"How the hell should I know?" The bartender shrugged. "Here he comes, ask him yourself."

Jake turned as the bartender moved on down the bar.

A handsome, gray-haired man in a silk vest and string tie looked him over. "Did I hear you asking about Bart?"

"Might have been." Jake looked him over shrewdly. "I used to do a little business with him in Chicago. How is he, the old rascal!"

The other hesitated, took a deep breath, and frowned. "Don't you ever take a bath? Let's talk a little."

He led Jake to a secluded table in the almost empty saloon. "My brother is dead, killed by his most trusted man, who emptied his safe and ran off with one of the girls."

"Al? Aw, mister, you must be mistaken. If ever there was a man loyal to Bart Brett, Al Trovato—"

"From what I heard later of the woman, she would have turned any man's head. They say she was a real looker with almost white-blond hair."

Jake laughed and lit a stogie. "That can't be anyone but Silver. Yep, she was special, all right. If there was a woman who could cause a man to commit murder and robbery, Silver would be the one."

"You could recognize this girl?" Brett hunched toward him. "I never saw her myself."

Jake nodded, beginning to sense a chance to make a little money. He could understand a need for revenge; wasn't that his own driving force? He thought about it a minute, decided there was no point in telling Lon Brett that Jake had been the one to bring the girl to the Velvet

Kitten. "I wonder if she's still with Al. The two of them together would be easy to spot, and he might be working as a bartender somewhere."

The gambler drummed his fingers on the table. "The bastard's dead by now. He sent the Chicago police a confession about the time the war started, taking full blame for everything and saying he was dying."

Jake smoked his cigar. "So why are you looking for the girl?"

The other snorted in derision. "She must be partly to blame. A man doesn't break a friend's neck and clean out his safe without some help or encouragement from the lady. Obviously he was in love with this Silver; that's why he was trying to shield her."

"If you'd ever seen her, you'd know she had the tits and body to make a man forget everything but gettin' between those long, slim legs. Even old trustworthy Al. What makes you think they came out West?"

"The Pony Express postmark on that letter he sent the police."

Jake threw back his head and guffawed. "I got news for you, Brett—the Pony ran all the way from St. Joe to San Francisco. That's a lot of lookin'."

"I know it," the other said grimly. "I've checked all up and down the line. Someone in Julesburg who used to work for the Pony thought he remembered hearing of a couple that fit the description."

"Colorado Territory is a big place to look."

"The way I figure it, they might have headed to some boomtown and used my brother's money to open a saloon. If she's in the saloon business, sooner or later, she's bound to end up in Denver, so I came here a couple

300

of weeks ago. When I finally find her, I'll extract my own justice for her part in Bart's death."

"If a man was to find her, what's in it for him?"

"A lot. The Bretts are a rich, respectable family. My brother and I were always the black sheep, but my family still don't want anyone to get away with killing one of us. I've got nothing but time; figure I owe Bart this."

Jake combed his beard with his fingers, staring at the birthmark on them. "I'll be on the lookout. Matter of fact, I'm looking for a woman, too, Injun girl, maybe working in a saloon herabouts—dark, purty, ambitious."

Brett shook his head. "Doesn't sound familiar. Only woman that comes to mind is some high-born Spanish Duchess who owns the Palace, our biggest competitor."

"The Palace, huh? Wal, I might just have a looksee. How do I find it?" He drained his whiskey and stood up.

"Can't miss it; straight down the street, around the corner, only two-story building left that's frame."

"Oh?"

"Yeah, there was a bad fire April a year ago; whole downtown went up in flames but the Palace. We all rebuilt in brick. Big Ed says he thinks the Duchess paid someone to do it, trying to get rid of the competition, but who knows?" He stood up. "You looking for a job?"

Jake put his hand on the handle of the big whip. "Maybe. Depends on what kind of offers I get."

The other named a figure.

Jake grinned. "Not bad. But maybe someone else will offer more. I'm for sale to the highest bidder."

Lon Brett nodded and held out his hand. "My kind of man. Remember about that Silver girl."

301

" I never forget when there's money involved." Jake tipped his hat back and left. Gawd Almighty! He never would have thought that about Al. But then that little gal had been a beauty. He wondered suddenly if she knew she wasn't wanted by the Chicago police. Blackmail could be a powerful weapon. Of course his chance of running across her was slim. Now he had his hands full tracking down Gray Dove, and any clue was better than none.

Lon Brett was right—Jake had no trouble finding the Palace. Not only was it the only frame building left along the street, it was a grand place of polished wood and brass spittoons, with a fancy stairway coming down in the center of the main saloon. It looked like a place that catered to rich, elegant gentlemen who wanted a little entertainment. Jake had only a slim hunch, but if it didn't pan out, he wasn't any worse off than before.

A black boy stopped mopping and looked at him. "Suh, we ain't open in the mornings. Come back later."

"Shut up, nigger. Where do I find the Duchess?"

The boy leaned on his mop and pointed up the stairs. "First door."

The scarlet carpet on the fancy stairs was thick and high class, Jake thought with approval as he went up and looked down the halls. The whores would be up here, too, most of them still asleep if they'd worked late last night. This was just the kind of place Jake had planned to open with the money the little Arapaho bitch has stolen from him. He opened the door marked OFFICE, went in, and closed it softly behind him.

A sultry, black-haired beauty sat behind the desk, chewing a pencil and studying the open ledgers before her. She wore an orange dress that set off her dark skin,

302

and the bodice strained across generous breasts. Fine jewelry gleamed on her hands, wrists, and neck.

Jake stood there looking at her.

She raised her head slowly. For an instant, her eyes widened and her mouth dropped open.

Jake grinned. "Hello, Gray Dove. It's been a long time."

She jumped to her feet and tried to run past him to the door, but he caught her arm. "Now is that any way to greet an old friend?"

"Friend! Why you dirty bastard, the last time I saw you, you raped me!"

"And you knocked me in the head and robbed me, so I reckon we're even."

She tried to pull away from him. "Let go of me or I'll scream and the law'll come running!"

"Go ahead and scream then," he said softly. "What do you think they'll say when I tell them this fancy place was started on money you stole from me back in the fall of '58?"

"You can't prove that!"

"We'll see. One thing I kin prove, I'll bet, is that you ain't no Spanish Duchess. The way Denver feels about Injuns right now, what do you think it would do to your business if the gentlemen who come here found out you was just a little Arapaho squaw?" He held on to her arm so tightly, she winced.

She blinked. "Jake, you wouldn't to that, would you? I've put a lot of work into the Palace—"

"And my money."

"I—I'll pay you back."

"I want more than that, Gray Dove . . . or should I call

you Duchess? As far as I'm concerned, we're equal partners—share and share alike. You'll just tell everyone I've been a silent partner and have finally come to help you run it."

She pulled out of his grasp and frowned at the marks on her arm where he had bruised her. "Where the hell have you been all this time?"

He went over and sat on the corner of her desk, noting the big safe behind it. "In prison, thanks to that half-breed you was so crazy about."

"Iron Knife?" She whirled around and her face told him she still loved the Injun bastard.

"Yeah, Iron Knife. The sonovabitch cut me like a steer! Last time I seen him, he was riding away with that white gal that he was so loco over, Summer."

Her pretty face turned ugly with jealousy. "Summer returned from Boston to him?"

"Yep. If they're both still alive, I reckon they're together out there somewhere, him kissin' her all over, his lips all over her—"

"Stop it!" the Indian woman snarled at him. "Stop it!" Her rage was uncontrollable as she paced and cursed, "Well, Summer may have him, but I've got the last laugh! I made love to him just a couple of days before I saw you last Jake! I've got his . . ." A look of sudden fear came over her face.

"You got his what?"

"Nothing. I didn't mean nothing." She looked scared. "Okay, Jake—I suppose we might as well be partners. I could use a man's help around here."

He laughed. "And I want all the privileges that go with a partnership besides the money—any of the girls I

304

want, whiskey. I've got some ideas that I think will increase your business."

She whirled on him. "I don't need your ideas! I already got most of the business in town."

"I heard that." He took the pokes of gold out of his vest. "You may have bit off more than you can chew by crossing Big Ed and the others. I think they're beginnin' to think of playin' rough. Besides, with my ideas, we kin end up with most *all* the business."

He saw the greed in her eyes. "How?"

"Missy, if you don't beat all!" He tossed the gold sacks out on the desk. "Maybe that's why we sure make a good pair, we are both unscrupulous and ruthless about getting what we want. Here, to show you I trust you and that there's no hard feelings, here's my gold to hold in your safe—partner."

She came over and looked down at it a long moment. "You're too lazy to try prospecting. Where'd you get that?"

"What do you care as long as I share it with you? Ain't those funny little gold sacks though?"

The girl was too greedy to be cautious, he thought with satisfaction. She went over and bent to whirl the combination. Jake watched carefully, remembering the moves of the dial. If he needed to clean out the safe, he'd know the combination. She swung the big safe's door open.

There was a sudden rap at the door. Gray Dove looked at Jake.

He whispered, "Find out who it is."

"Who's there?"

"Miss Jones and Waanibe."

Jake gave Gray Dove a questioning look.

"It's the governess and my little girl."

"You got a kid?"

Gray Dove hesitated. "I—I don't even know who fathered her, Jake. You know how I was about men."

She was hiding something. He saw fear in her eyes. "I remember how you was about men, all right. I always said if you had as many stickin' out of you as had been stuck in you, you'd look like a west Texas cactus. I'll bet you got callouses on your back from lying with a man on top of you."

"Duchess?" the voice called again.

Jake gestured. "Tell 'em to come in. You're gettin' mighty uppity with a governess for a bastard kid."

"Come in," Gray Dove said.

A woman came into the room leading a small girl by the hand. The kid look as Injun as her mother, Jake thought boredly. There was no telling who fathered her, the way Gray Dove used to get around.

"Miss Jones, this is my—my partner."

Jake looked at the girl and yawned as he scratched himself. She looked like a governess all right, plain and prim, peering at him through thick spectacles, drab hair pulled back in a no-nonsense bun. But there was something that tugged at his mind, Maybe it was the way she was staring at him, all wide-eyed. "Gal, ain't we met some place before?"

She looked a little faint. "I—I don't think so, Mister—?"

"Dallinger," he said, grinning, "Jake Dallinger. Funny, I have a thing about faces. I'd swear you look familiar."

306

The girl had recovered her poise. "I don't think so, but then I remind everyone of their school teacher or old maid sister."

The little girl came over and stared up at him. "Have you known my mama a long time?"

Jake didn't like kids but he smiled at her anyway. If he got on the good side of the kid, she'd most likely tell him all the secrets of this place. "A very long time."

"Waanibe," Miss Jones stammered, "that's not polite. You must remember your manners so you will do well when you go back East to school."

The child immediately curtsied. "If you're a friend of my mama's, maybe I should give you a treasure."

Jake blinked. "A treasure?"

The child kissed her chubby palm, folded her fingers over it, and held it out. "For you," she said conspiratorially, "for your pocket."

Intrigued, Jake held out his hand and Waanibe put her hand in his big one and opened it slowly. He stared at her chubby fingers and began to laugh.

Gray Dove looked surprised, then baffled. "It's just a silly game those two have going."

Waanibe leaned close. "Do you like to play dress-up? We can get Mama's jewelry and Silvery's shoes—"

Jake looked up. "Who's she talking about?"

Miss Jones looked flustered. "My—my name is Sylvia and she never could pronounce it." She turned to the mother. "Duchess, if we may go outside now . . ."

"Of course, run along. Mr. Dallinger and I have a lot of catching up to do."

Jake watched the two close the door and waited for a long moment as their steps faded down the hall. "I'd

307

swear I've seen your plain little governess someplace. If she was fixed up some, she wouldn't be half bad."

"Don't be charitable, Jake, it ain't like you. She's plain as a mouse and prim as a church deacon. Sometimes I think Waanibe cares more for her than she does for me."

Jake got up and shut the safe's door. "I never thought of you as the motherly type, Gray Dove—unless you cared something about the father."

"I don't know what the hell you're talking about. I told you I didn't know who fathered her."

"But if you thought she was Iron Knife's, you'd be afraid I'd hurt her, wouldn't you?"

"Jake, that's nonsense! She's dark because she's mine!"

He studied her keenly. Yep, Gray Dove might have slept with a lot of men, but she was sure the kid was Iron Knife's. That alone gave him all the power he needed. If she only knew how ironic the whole thing was. "You want to hear a good joke?" he said, and then reconsidered. "Never mind. I'll tell you some other time. By the way, partner, I intend to enjoy everything about this place, including the whores."

"I thought you said Iron Knife—"

"There's other ways to enjoy a woman besides that," Jake said, and stood up slowly. "I bet I could even pleasure you. I remember you enjoy being treated like a bitch dog in heat. You liked to be humiliated and hurt before you got what was coming to you."

Before she realized what he was up to, he grabbed her arm and pulled her to him.

"Let go of me, Jake." She tried to twist away from him, but he held her and ran his dirty, hairy hand down the low-cut neck of her dress.

"No, partner, I'm gonna enjoy the prettiest of your whores but I'm gonna start with you. I recollect I wasn't quite through when you hit me over the head."

He grinned as he ripped open the front of her dress with such force that tiny buttons went flying. "You still got nice tits, Gray Dove, and I like that in a woman." He jerked down the lace straps of her chemise and ran his hands over her big, dark nipples.

She submitted grimly, her mouth a hard line.

"You got a bed somewhere?"

"I didn't think a man who'd been—"

"The bed!" he snarled. "I'm about to pleasure you with something big and hard that will make you think a stallion's been at you."

She looked as if she might protest, then led him into the room next door.

Jake whistled low, looked around, and locked the door behind him. The room was lavish, the kind of ornate room a man dreams of taking a fancy whore to—red velvet drapes and satin sheets, jewelry scattered across her bureau. He looked over at it.

"It's just fake," she said. "The kid likes to play with it, It ain't the real thing."

"In that case, you ought to be satisfied with what I got to offer then. I'm gonna enjoy this, bitch, and you are, too. I promise you that. Now get your clothes off. I want to see you buck naked when I climb all over you."

He sat down on the edge of the bed and watched her strip, her dark body ripe and beautiful as he remembered it. "Let your hair down, missy. I like a woman's hair hanging loose where I can tangle my hands in it; then pull and twist it until she begs me to stop. And you better make me happy, you hear? I ain't had a woman in all those years I been in prison, so from now on, when I get in your bed, which is often, you make me like it. You got a lot of talent, Gray Dove, use it!"

She stood there naked before him. "And if I don't?"

"Oh, you will, all right, because you're afraid of what I'll do about that brat if I decide to. Now get in this bed."

He began to take his own clothes off and flopped down beside her. He was hairy as a bear and her satin skin felt good when he lay on her and squeezed her breasts up to two points for his greedy mouth.

She gasped. "You gelding! You useless steer! You ain't half a man!"

"Shut up, bitch, I got what it takes to satisfy you!" He reached for the big, silver-handled whip.

Chapter Sixteen

November 1864. Silver pulled her cloak around her as she sat on a bench and watched Wannie skip stones into Cherry Creek. The creek flowed placidly now when only this past summer, it had flooded so badly that the *Rocky Mountain News* had moved its offices from the creek into Denver.

In the brisk cold, around the pair swirled the hustle bustle of a booming town, but Silver was too upset to notice much. Drat it all! What was she going to do? Jake Dallinger had turned up unexpectedly after all these years and acted as if he intended to stay at the Palace.

At least he didn't seem to recognize her in her prim disguise, but he was evidently searching his memory. She had been avoiding him as much as possible, but sooner or later, he might put the pieces of the puzzle together. Her inclination was to gather up her things and leave town before that happened.

"Look, Silvery, look!"

She nodded absently and smiled at the little girl. Drat! How could Silver leave Denver? She loved this child as her own. The Duchess was an indifferent mother. In fact, Silver had a distinct feeling that the dark beauty kept the child only because she had loved the father. No, until Waanibe went off to boarding school, Silver felt she must stay to look after her little charge. And yet to do so increased the danger that Jake would recognize Silver and contact the Chicago police.

"Silvery, look, I have a treasure for you."

Her mind busy, Silver held out her hand for the kiss, but instead, Waanibe put a jeweled broach in it. "Oh, Wannie, have you been in your mama's jewelry again? You're going to get us both in trouble! Now empty your pockets."

She held out her hand and the child sulked a moment, then emptied her pinafore pockets and slipped a gaudy ring off her finger. "I was just playing dress-up."

How could she be upset with such an adorable imp? Silver gathered up the jewlery and hugged the little girl. "If you want to play dress-up lady, wear my silver shoes, but leave your mama's things alone. I wish she wouldn't be so careless with this stuff."

Silver stood up and took Waanibe's hand. She knew that although the Duchess denied it, the jewelry was worth a fortune. No one else seemed to realize it but Silver. Secretly she worried that some of the things might be lost or stolen and that the Duchess might accuse Silver of taking them. In that case, Silver might be fired, thus separating her from the small girl she loved as her own. The only piece that tempted her was the gold nugget bracelet that Cherokee had given her and the Duchess had redeemed and now owned. Silver would like to have that back, but when she timidly asked the Duchess if she could buy it from her and pay it off a little at a time, the sultry beauty told her coldly that it wasn't for sale.

Cherokee. She saw him in her mind's eye, felt his kiss
and the warm strength of his muscular arms. If only he
would come for her and they would take Wannie and run
away. Then she remembered her scarred face and shook
her head. He wouldn't want her now, but that didn't keep
her from wanting him.

She watched the little girl play while she sat and
worried about how to deal with Jake Dallinger. She felt as
if she was running out of time. With cold weather moving
in, the snows would start any day now. She and Waanibe
would have to spend a lot of time indoors at the Palace,
which would throw them into more contact with the big,
bearded scout. What on earth was Silver going to do?

Cherokee's vision improved slightly during the time he
and the Cheyenne rode all those long miles to the
Rockies. Iron Knife had supplied him with deer skin
clothes and moccasins to replace the ragged blue pants
and ruined boots, along with a pistol. He and the
Cheyenne had become good friends and talked long
hours of their hopes and dreams, the possibility that the
Indians might finally live in peace side by side with the
whites. He even told him a little of his friendship with
Shaw O'Bannion and the big Shannon Place plantation
on the Mississippi.

Cherokee listened wistfully as Iron Knife told him of
his white love, Summer Sky, and their three little
children. How he wished he could find that kind of
happiness with Silver, but he couldn't ask her to marry
an almost blind half-breed who might never completely
regain his sight.

313

Iron Knife reined in. "We are on the edge of the town you described. I'll leave you here, my friend."

His big form was only a blur to Cherokee, but he held out his hand and the other took it. "Iron Knife, I'm much obliged for saving my life. If I can ever do the Cheyenne a favor, I'll do it."

They shook hands solemnly.

Iron Knife said, "Will you be all right, Cherokee, if I leave you here? You are welcome to return to my people."

Cherokee shook his head. "I have partners here and there's a doctor who might be able to help me. And if my sight ever returns, there's Silver."

Iron Knife said. "I understand. Good-bye, Cherokee. Maybe we will meet again sometime." He turned and rode away.

Cherokee saw only the blur, and listened a long time to the sounds of the Appaloosa stallion's hooves. He was more scared than he was willing to admit, afraid that he would be a burden to Willie and Bill. And suppose Silver saw him on the street before he could find Doc and ride out of town?

He took a deep breath, straightened his shoulders, and rode slowly into Buckskin Joe. The buildings were only a blur to him and there were few people on the quiet street. What had happened to the noisy boomtown? Cherokee had to pass the Nugget and he was dreading it. When he rode past, he realized suddenly there was nothing there but a pile of blackened rubble. He reined in, worried and confused.

"Cherokee?" A familiar male voice. "Cherokee Evans, is that you?"

He turned his head at the sound of a heavy man

314

climbing down from a creaking buggy. "Doc? Doc Johnson?"

"Why, if you aren't a sight for sore eyes! We thought you might be dead in the War!"

Cherokee dismounted carefully, turned toward the voice, and held out his hand. The other took it warmly. "Doc, what's happened? Where's everyone? Where's Silver?"

Doc peered into the man's face. *What was wrong here?* Cherokee's eyes looked blank, as if he weren't really seeing him. "Cherokee, is there something wrong?"

"I—I've got a problem, Doc." He looked as if he was reluctant to talk. "Let's get off the street; I wouldn't want Silver to see me."

How much should he tell the big man? "Sure, we'll go up to the house and Emma will—"

"No, let's go to your office. I need your help. And on the way, I want to know what's happened to the Nugget and this town."

It dawned on Doc suddenly as Cherokee stood there that the man was at least partially blind. "Here, I'll tie up the horses, then you take my arm and we'll go to my office. Silver's not here anymore, Cherokee. She left town."

"What happened?" There was both anguish and relief in his voice.

How much should Doc tell? The man was evidently almost blind from the war wound, why break his heart, too? "There was an epidemic, Cherokee; your Silver was quite a heroine. In fact, the boys named a mountain for her, Mt. Silver Heels."

Cherokee smiled and repeated the words softly. "Has a nice ring to it."

Doc grunted in agreement. "Most of the town, including her bartender, died and the rest of them fled. We had to burn the Nugget after we used it for a hospital. Buckskin Joe's slowly turning into a ghost town."

"Al's dead and Silver's gone? Where?"

Doc led him into his office and the other man sat down. "No one knows, Cherokee. She was from someplace back East, maybe she went back there. Some folks say they've seen her about dark out here in our cemetary putting flowers on the graves, but who knows?"

Cherokee leaned back in the chair and sighed. "As pretty as she was, she's probably a big star somewhere or she's married some wealthy man."

"Maybe." Doc had already decided he wasn't going to tell Cherokee about Silver's scarred face. Since he was blind and would probably never cross her trail again, let him keep his memory of the great beauty she had been.

Doc examined him, then shook his head. "Cherokee, I wish I could tell you something, but I'm just a country doctor. That wound at the base of your skull affected some nerves that have something to do with your eyes."

Cherokee cursed under his breath. "I can barely see forms, tell daylight from dark. Whenever I look around, I see misty rainbows around everything."

"You may get better and you may not. I wish I could tell you something else; but only time will tell. Maybe one of those fancy doctors in a big place like Denver could give you more hope."

"I have a hard time even doing something simple like rolling a cigarette." Cherokee put his face in his hands. "I'm no good to anyone this way."

Doc thought about Silver. It seemed ironic somehow—she had fled because she didn't want anyone to see her ruined beauty and the man she loved was almost blind. If Doc had any idea where she was, he would try to get them together again.

Doc rolled a cigarette and handed it to Cherokee, then lit it for him. "Stop feeling sorry for yourself. You can still handle a shovel, can't you, if someone tells you where to dig? Those old partners of yours are getting pretty feeble. I imagine they'll be glad to get you back."

Cherokee took a puff of the cigarette and grinned. "Yes, of course. How are the old rascals anyhow?"

"Haven't seem them for a while, but then they only get into town when they run out of supplies. Come to think of it, an old friend of theirs was in town a couple of weeks ago or so, and asked directions out to their claim."

"Oh?" Cherokee stood up. "I think I'll go on out there myself, Doc." He hesitated. "Would you mind . . ."

"Of course not." Doc jumped to his feet. "I'll get a saddle horse and tell Emma where I'm going, then I'll ride out there with you."

They rode out to Mosquito Gulch.

"Careful, Doc," Cherokee cautioned when Doc said they were almost to the gully. "Old Bill has always been so afraid of claim jumpers, he's liable to shoot first and ask questions later."

"I remember!" Doc said, thinking of the time Silver had been shot. "Hallo! Hallo! It's Doc and Cherokee!"

No answer. They waited a long moment, then shouted again. Still no answering shout.

Doc pulled at his mustache. "I've come out to see them once or twice in the past, they always come running when they hear my shout. Let's ride on in."

Doc had a strange feeling that something was wrong because he saw no curl of smoke drifting in the direction of the cabin. Up ahead on the trail, he saw what looked like a bundle of old clothes. "I see something, Cherokee."

He dismounted and walked toward it, dread rising up in his heart. *Oh my God.*

"Doc, what is it?" Cherokee dismounted.

"It's Willie, or what's left of him." Doc knelt and looked at the old man. "He—he's been dead awhile, I'd say."

"Dead? What the hell—?"

"The cold up here in the hills has preserved the body. Looks like he's got marks on his throat." Doc took a deep breath. "I'd say he's been garroted."

"Dead? I can't believe it. Who would hurt a harmless old man?" Cherokee's rugged face was a mask of grief.

"I don't know. Maybe we'd better get up to the cabin and see about Bill."

Cherokee remounted. "Who would do something like this? Doc, describe the man who was in town looking around."

As they rode up to the cabin, Doc described the big, bearded man. "Maybe it's just a coincidence, Cherokee, maybe it happened after he came and left."

"Maybe. I hope Bill's all right."

Doc didn't say anything. The cabin looked deserted, no smoke drifting from the chimney and the door stood open. He dismounted cautiously and went around back. The little burro appeared to be out of hay and water.

"Doc?" Cherokee yelled behind him, "Doc?"

"Get down, Cherokee," Doc sighed and pulled at his mustache. "I'm afraid of what we're gonna find inside."

It was worse than he'd expected, old bloodstains everywhere. Evidently, old Bill had put up quite a fight before he died. The scent of death hung over the place even though the November air was cold.

Cherokee stumbled through the door. The smell told him what his eyes saw only dimly. "By damn! Not Bill, too!'

Doc knelt by the pitiful, scrawny body and looked at the marks on it. "I reckon that stranger was to blame, Cherokee. I'd almost swear Bill's been whipped to death and that man wore a silver-handled whip on his belt."

Cherokee swore and banged his fists against the wall. "And I'm blind and can't do a damned thing about tracking the bastard down!" He felt his way to a chair and flopped down on it, his shoulders shaking.

Doc looked around at the few things of any value in the crude cabin. "Why would anyone want to kill that harmless pair?"

Cherokee roused himself. "Doc, look and see if the woodpile's been disturbed. That's where the boys keep their gold. Never could get them to use a bank. It was in a couple of little Indian beaded bags they'd traded for."

Doc went out to look. "You're right, Cherokee. The woodpile's a mess. I reckon that's what the dirty bastard was after. And to think I gave him directions to get up here! If I had only known . . ."

"You mustn't blame yourself, Doc," Cherokee said gently. "I just wish I knew where he'd gone and had my eyesight back, good and clear, for a few minutes. Now we'd better bury them. I can still see well enough to help bury my old pards."

*   *   *

They finished up the task and rode back into town, taking the little burro with them.

"Cherokee, what'll you do now? With Christmas coming, I hate for you to be alone. You're welcome to stay with me and Emma."

"No, I've got a little money in the bank here, enough to get me by awhile. There's no reason to stay in Buckskin Joe. Too many sad memories around here now. You give the burro to some kid. I've got to find out if there's any hope for my eyes."

"You'll be going to Denver then?"

Cherokee nodded. "If you'll help get me to the bank and to Haw Tabor's to buy some clothes, then put me on a stage."

Doc stood looking after the stage as it pulled away. Yep, Cherokee Evans had enough grief and problems to deal with. He knew he'd done the right thing—not telling him about Silver. After all, he would never cross her path again. Let him live with his memory of her flawless beauty.

Cherokee stepped off the stage in Denver. All around him was a blur of passing people and horses. It was frightening not to be able to see clearly although it did seem to him that his eyesight was improving daily.

"Shine, mister?" a small boy's voice inquired and a small hand pulled at his coat insistently.

"No." Cherokee shook his head impatiently at the small blur by his side. With such impaired vision, how could he find a doctor or even a hotel room?

"Please, mister. I haven't shined a pair of boots all day."

Cherokee paused. "You got folks?"

"No, I look after myself. Shine?"

"I tell you what I'll do. I don't see very well, so I'll pay you to help me get around. You know this town?"

"Do I? Anyone'll tell you Keso knows everyone, can tell you anything you want to know."

"Keso, huh?" Cherokee smiled. "Is that Indian?"

He could sense the hesitation. "You got something against Indians, mister?"

"Nope, I'm a half-breed myself. Cherokee, they call me."

"I'm Cheyenne. My name's really *Poh'Keso*. It means Fox."

Cherokee didn't say anything. The boy must be just a stray, claimed by no one. His mother might even have been one of the many Indian girls who hung around forts and settlements like Denver to work as whores for the soldiers. "I tell you what, Keso, I was just about to have some dinner and I'd buy yours if you'll take me to a good café."

"You mean *inside* at a *table*?"

Cherokee winced. Obviously the kid was used to eating scraps from the back of the restaurants. "Inside. Let's go."

The child took his sleeve. "I know everything about this town, boss, you just tell me what you need."

"First we eat, and then you find me a doctor, okay? One that you know is the most successful."

And off they went.

But that doctor told him about the same thing that Doc had. The wound was healed but there must be some nerve damage. His sight might improve, but there was no guarantee Cherokee would ever regain his sight completely.

Sunk in gloom, Cherokee let Keso lead him to a cheap hotel on McGaa Street and then he paid the boy and told him to come back early in the morning.

"But it'll be Sunday. There won't be much going on."

"That's okay. We'll eat and you can take me around town."

"Are you gonna stay in Denver, boss?"

"Keso, I don't know what I'm going to do. I just don't know." He collapsed across the bed and heard the boy leave quietly. *What was he going to do?* His money wouldn't last forever and he couldn't just sit here, hoping his eyesight would improve. If he could see, he'd go looking for that big, bearded man with the whip Doc had described. He was helpless! Helpless without his sight!

In sheer frustration, Cherokee rolled over and pounded his pillow with his fist until he was exhausted and dropped off into a troubled sleep. He dreamed of beautiful Silver. She ran from him, laughing and looking back over her shoulder, teasing him to follow her. And when he tried, he stumbled over something and fell. Come back . . . come back, sweet darlin' . . .

When he sat up in bed suddenly, there was enough light streaming into the room to know it was morning.

True to his word, the little street urchin came back to take him to breakfast. Later on the street, Cherokee asked him, "Do you really know everything that goes on around here?"

"In this section of town I do." He sounded confident,

almost cocky.

"I want to know if you've seen a new man in town, big, bearded, maybe looks like a buffalo hunter."

"There's lots fit that description."

"This one has been partially scalped and carries a silver filigreed-handled bull whip."

There was a long moment of silence.

"Keso, didn't you hear me?"

"Is this hombre a friend of yours?" The child's voice sounded hesitant.

"Hardly! You seen him?"

"Sure, he gave me a good kick when I first held his horse down at the Elephant Corral. I even know his name—Jake Dallinger. When a real mean 'un shows up, everyone remembers him."

"Jake Dallinger," Cherokee said thoughtfully, "now why does that sound familiar? Do you know where I can find this man?"

"Sure. I've seen him coming and going a lot the last couple of days from the Duchess's Palace."

"What's that?"

"A tough place, boss, you don't want to go there. They cheat at cards and there ain't anything you can't buy if the money's right."

Cherokee cursed his blurred vision. It was a little better, but not much. What would he do if he came face to face with the man who had murdered his partners? In the shape he was in, Cherokee couldn't challenge him to a showdown. "At least walk me down there, Keso, so I'll know about where the place is."

"It ain't open this early, boss."

"I don't care. I just want to know about where it is."

He put his hand on the boy's thin shoulder and they

walked along the busy street. Cherokee hoped that to a casual observer, it wouldn't be noticeable that he couldn't see.

Wagons creaked past in the muddy street. A dog barked somewhere.

"Boss, we're almost there."

Very faintly, a high, sweet voice drifted on the crisp autumn air. In fact, it might have been the breeze singing through the mountains. Cherokee paused, transfixed, listening.

"Boss, not yet, we still got a little way to go."

Cherokee started walking again, but his whole attention was on the voice that grew louder as they approached.

"'Tis the last rose of summer left blooming alone, all her lovely companions are faded and gone . . ."

Silver's favorite song and Shawn O'Bannion's, too. In fact, it had been one of the most popular songs of the War.

Keso guided him and stopped him, announcing they were across the street from the Duchess's Palace. "Are you all right, boss?"

Cherokee couldn't answer, he felt so overcome as the singing continued.

"I'll not leave you, lone one, to pine on the stem. Where the lovely are sleeping, go sleep thou with them . . ."

Silver. It couldn't be anyone but Silver. Of all the people he hadn't expected to find in Denver was the girl he loved. Buy why not? A beautiful star like her would naturally gravitate toward a rich, boomtown to open a new saloon.

He managed to get control of himself. "Keso, is the saloon named for a woman?"

324

"Sure."

"What's she like?"

"The Duchess? A real looker! Men always turn when she goes by."

It had to be Silver, all right.

"Boss, she ain't for you."

"Keso, did I say she was? I was just curious, that's all."

"She's got plenty of money, I reckon, and this big saloon. Something else, boss. She's got a kid who looks part Indian."

Cherokee thought his heart would stop. "How—how old is this child?"

"I donno. A little girl. I've seen them on the street sometimes, but more likely the kid's with her governess."

Cherokee did a quick mental calculation. "Could the little girl be about three years old, you think?"

Keso made a noise as if he was considering. "If she's no older than that, she's a little big for her age."

Big like me, Cherokee thought, *and part Indian.* He'd had a feeling in Buckskin Joe that Doc was holding something back, something he wasn't telling Cherokee. And now he knew what it was.

He stood listening, so torn with emotions, he didn't know what to do. The piano and her high, sweet voice drifted on the still air. His heart told him to run into the Palace, and sweep them both up in his arms. On the other hand, Silver was evidently as rich and successful as ever if she could afford a governess for their child. What could he—a blind man with little money—offer her, unless he managed to get back what the big cracker had stolen? No, he couldn't burden Silver. He almost wished he had not found her. To be so close and not be able to take her in his arms, carry her off, and make love to her was more than he could stand.

"Come on, Keso, let's get away from here."

"Wait, boss, that man you were askin' about—he just came out of the Palace."

"Jake Dallinger?"

"Yep, he's walking off down the street now."

And suddenly Cherokee remembered where he had heard that name before; Iron Knife had mentioned him. Surely Silver wouldn't be mixed up with a bad hombre like that. A thought occured to him. "Keso, do you suppose he was just having a drink?"

"Don't think so. The Palace ain't open in the mornings."

Silver was singing again, a Stephen Foster song, the haunting, sad words drifting on the air.

I dream of Jeannie with the light brown hair . . ."

He had to be close to her if only for a moment. "Keso let's go over there."

"You sure, boss?"

He nodded and they crossed the street slowly. Cherokee stood in front of the bat-wing doors, listening to the piano, the high sweet voice with a little girl's joining in. Oh God, if he could only see them!

"Keso, you stay right here. I'm going just inside the door." He had to see her. He had to!

Cherokee went in. With his blurred vision, he was aware of shapes like a stairway and poker tables. He could smell the usual saloon smells of whiskey and stale cigar smoke.

And then he saw the outline of the two at a piano in the shadows. If only they would move out into the light. If only he could see better.

". . . *many were the sweet notes her merry voice would pour, many were the blithe birds that warbled them o'er . . .*"

Her voice drew him like a moth to a flame. He must not let her see him, pity him. He was too proud to accept her charity. And besides, Silver must have changed since he had know her. The Silver he knew had a reputation for running a clean card game. No one was ever cheated or mugged when she ran the Nugget. Had she gotten mixed up with Jake Dallinger?

Everything in him wanted to go to her, and take her in his arms. But he loved her too much to be a burden to her. He turned and hurried toward the daylight of the door. And in his haste, he stumbled over a chair.

By damn! He ran outside. "Keso, get me out of here quick!"

"You steal something, boss?"

"Keso, let's go!"

The tone of his voice must have startled the boy because Keso grabbed his hand and led him at a trot down the wooden sidewalk.

"Hey, boss." He felt Keso turn and look over his shoulder. "That little girl came outside and is watching us leave."

"Just don't look back!" Cherokee said. He was so completely undone, he had Keso lead him back to his hotel, and then the little boy went off to shine shoes for the afternoon, promising to return later.

Cherokee flopped on the bed and shook. Now what in the hell was he going to do? The man he was after must be connected to Silver somehow, yet Cherokee couldn't deal with Jake because of his eyesight. Maybe if he stayed and waited, his eyes would improve enough to get Dallinger. But the longer he stayed, the bigger risk he ran that Silver would see him somewhere. Cherokee would rather be dead then accept her pity.

Silver turned as Waanibe jumped from the piano bench and ran through the bat-wing doors. "Wannie? Come back here!"

She got up from the piano and hurried out on the sidewalk, grabbing the child by the hand. "You aren't suppose to go out alone."

"I was looking at the man."

Silver glanced around but didn't see anything. "What man?"

"The man who came in the saloon and stood at the back watching us."

That was unusual. Why would anyone do that? "What did the man look like?"

"Big man," Waanibe said, and grinned adorably. "Part Indian. Could he be my daddy?"

Silver shook her head absently, her mind busy. "Tell me more about him."

Waanibe described him and told how he had hurried away with an Indian boy.

Could it be? She made Waanibe describe the man again. Silver fought an urge to run after him, screaming his name. Instead she collspsed on the steps. For more than three years now, she had turned and stared at every big-framed man who passed, looked at any man who was dark and rugged, expecting that when he drew close, it would be the one she loved. And now perhaps she had found him, or rather, he had found her. Waanibe's description left no doubt in Silver's heart.

How had he tracked her here? Doc? Had someone passing through Denver told Cherokee where to find her? She had thought her drab governess disguise was so good because it had fooled Jake Dallinger.

There was no question in her mind about what had just happened. Cherokee had come looking for her, had seen her, and fled. He didn't want her now that he had seen she was no longer beautiful. Somehow deep in her heart, she had nourished the tiniest flicker of hope that it might not make a difference—he had said something like that to her once. But in the end, he was just like all the other men. Beauty was everything to them, and what a woman was like—*really* like deep inside—didn't matter if she didn't have a pretty face.

Tears came to her eyes and she closed them, remembering that one night, the way he had made love to her and kissed her palm. *Here's a treasure to save for when you need it.* He was just like the others after all. Damn him! Damn him for it!

"Silvery, are you crying?" Two little arms around her neck.

"No—no, of course not! I—I just got something in my eye, drat it all!"

"You look awfully sad. Let me give you a treasure."

Silver automatically put out her hand, and this time, the child put a shiny penny in it.

"Silvery, you can buy some candy with this treasure."

Silver laughed and hugged the child to her. "You rascal, I think we'd better go upstairs and work on our alphabet. Candy later!"

Silver could hardly keep her mind on anything the rest of the day. When she and her small charge went out for candy, Silver found herself searching every street and building for Cherokee, half hoping, half dreading that she would run into him. After all, he'd already had one look at her and rejected her. She wouldn't be able to stand the humiliation of seeing him someplace and having him turn away.

Waanibe pulled her sleeve. "There's the boy the man was with."

"Where?" She looked where Waanibe pointed. A handsome Indian boy about ten or twelve years old was polishing boots on the street corner. He looked like a typical tough streetwise kid. What was his connection to Cherokee? *Could he possibly be Cherokee's son?* Did that make any sense? This child looked like a full-blood. But maybe Cherokee had an Indian wife. If so, he had sired this child before he met Silver—the boy's age told her that.

"Stay here, Wannie." She left the little girl in the candy shop, and ran across the street. "Hey you, I want to talk to you."

For a minute, she thought the boy would grab his shoeshine box and run. She saw doubt and fear in his face. "Whatever it is, miss, I didn't do it."

Her heart went out to him. Although he was older than Waanibe, he was certainly as neglected. If he was Cherokee's son, how could he allow the boy to live this way?

"You're not in any trouble," Silver assured him. "You know me?"

"Sure, I seen you around. You're the governess for that cute kid that belongs to the Duchess."

"What's your name, son? Where's your mother?"

He shook his dark head. "She's dead. They call me Keso, it's Cheyenne for Fox."

Did he look at all like Cherokee? She fished around in her pocket, and handed him a dime.

"You want your shoes shined, miss? I don't often do ladies—"

"No, Keso, I want some information about that man who was with you this morning."

Immediately a guarded, suspicious expression crossed the handsome brown face. He held the dime out solemnly. "If I got to get Cherokee into trouble to earn this . . ."

So it was him. She hadn't been mistaken. "He's not in any trouble," she assured him. "Keep the dime. I want to know about that man. He—he may be an old friend."

The boy scuffed his ragged moccasins in the dust of the sidewalk. "His name is Cherokee, and he's not from here. He's been asking about the Duchess and the little girl."

"Why would he do that?"

The boy shook his head. "I don't know, miss."

Silver stared down at him, her mind busy. Why would Cherokee be curious about the woman and her child? A memory came back to her. The Duchess had said her daughter was fathered by a half-breed lover. Oh, God, could she have meant Cherokee? Had he come to see an old mistress and his daughter, then fled in confusion because he suddenly recognized Silver and didn't want her to see him? She wanted some answers. "Keso, what hotel is the man in?"

"You sure he ain't in any trouble?"

"No, I just want to talk to him."

"The Essex, miss. But maybe there's something you

331

should know . . ."

"What?"

He hesitated, biting his lip. "Never mind."

She was too upset to do more than nod at him, whirl, and flee back across the street to Wannie in the candy shop. Tonight when it was too dark for Cherokee to see her face plainly, Silver intended to get to the bottom of this!

Chapter Seventeen

Silver waited until after dark when Wannie was in bed and business at the Palace was in full swing. Then she put on her cloak, slipped down the back stairs, and out into the night. Silver was still afraid of the dark, but there was a harvest moon on this crisp night, and in her prim disguise, no man looked twice at her, much less tried to bother her.

It took all the nerve she had to mount those stairs at the Essex and stop before his door. Silver took a deep breath. *How could she bear to have him see her face?* Then she noted how softly the light glowed from under the door, almost as if he were sitting before the fireplace in the dark. If only he wouldn't light the lamps, he need never know.

Then she lost her nerve. She couldn't do it, couldn't have him see her this way. Let him live with the memory of her as she had been—if she had ever meant anything to him at all. A board creaked under her foot as she turned and walked away.

*   *   *

Like most people with sight problems, Cherokee's hearing had become acute. He had been sitting staring into the glow of the fireplace when he heard a board squeak outside his door. Someone passing by? A thief checking to see if he was in?

Throwing caution to the wind, he went to the door and threw it open. *Nothing*. And then the faintest scent of wild flowers came to his nose. He ran out into the hall, forgetting that he didn't want her to know of his handicap. "Silver? Silver, is that you? Come back!"

He could barely make out a slim form at the end of the hall. If he didn't have to light the lamp, she need never know he was all but blind.

Silver stopped, trying to decide what to do. The hallway was barely lit by a coal oil fixture at each end. He wouldn't be able to see her face. She would turn and say a few words to him, pretend she cared nothing for him. Then maybe he wouldn't come back to the Palace and she wouldn't have to risk having him see her ruined beauty. In the seconds before she hesitated and turned around, a million possibilities ran through her mind. Tomorrow she would flee Denver so he would never see her. Tomorrow . . .

But oh dear God, there was tonight—only tonight.

"Cherokee?" She stood in the shadows of the dim hall as did he. For an electrifying second, they stared at each other and then she forgot everything, everything but him. With a glad cry, she ran down the hall and into his outstretched arms.

"Silver! Silver, is it really you?" He crushed her

334

against his wide chest as he lifted her off the floor and his mouth claimed hers, dominating, consuming with inner fire. "I've waited so long for this . . . dreamed only of this!"

She didn't want to think, she wanted only to feel, to experience the joy of love, of being loved. She let him crush her against him as if he were trying to pull her inside his very soul, and she kissed him again and again, dizzy with the scent of his tobacco and shaving soap and the salty, masculine taste of him. His shirt was rough against her face and his big hands burned into the small of her back. "Oh Cherokee, if you only knew how many times I've dreamed of this moment back in Buckskin Joe, dreamed of you riding in and me running out to meet you!"

A salesman came down the hall, stared at them curiously, and went on.

Cherokee said, "I think we need to get out of the hall."

He swung her up in his arms and carried her inside his room, kicking the door shut. "Sweet darlin', I won't light the lamps, I want it to be as it was that long ago night, the moon full as a gold piece and you in my arms."

She felt only relief as he sat her on the bed. At least they had tonight before he discovered her secret, and tomorrow seemed like a century away. He knelt on the floor before her, taking her small face between his two big hands. "I've tried to forget you, Silver, but I can't. Whenever I closed my eyes, your face slipped into my dreams like the scent of your perfume."

There was so much she wanted to ask, so many things to be said, and yet it was enough to say nothing at all— just to *be* and stay here in his strong arms, held protectively against his chest.

With the dawn she must leave forever, so he would never see her. But tonight he saw her only with his hands, his lips, his heart, and he must never know the truth. Tomorrow she would pack her things and run away. There was nothing else to be done. She didn't want his pity. "Oh, Cherokee, my dearest, may I stay with you, be with you all night?"

He kissed her eyelids gently. "Will they miss you at the Palace? Are you needed there?"

She thought of her little charge, tucked safely asleep in her bed. "No, they'll manage without me. They'll never know I'm gone."

She melted into his arms, opening her lips so that he might caress her mouth with his tongue. This was their moment in time—the last time she would ever have with him—and it was more than she had expected. The memory would have to last forever. She didn't know if he really loved her or if he had ever loved anyone else, but it didn't matter. Tonight, as his hand reached to undo the small buttons at her throat, he was hers and hers alone.

For a long moment, his hand caressed her throat. He laughed softly. "What did you do to your hair?"

She reached self-consciously to pull the hairpins from the tight bun, and shook it loose to fall about her shoulders. In the glowing darkness, she thought the shadows would keep him from realizing the drab, dyed color.

He undid her bodice, pushed the sleeves off her shoulders, bent his head to kiss the pulse of her throat, and brushed along her shoulders with his warm lips until every nerve in her body seemed alive—no, on fire—with

336

the wanting of him. She found herself trembling.

"No, you quicksilver nymph, I won't be hurried with the taking. I've waited and dreamed of this moment for more than three long years and I intend that for both of us, it will last and last." His fingers caught the lace of her chemise and slipped it off her shoulders so that her breasts filled his hands like full ripe fruit. He leaned toward her slightly so that she lay back on her elbows and threw back her head, offering her bare breasts up to him in sweet surrender.

He pushed them together with his palms and bent his head to the deep crevice. "You always have the scent of flowers," he whispered as he put his face against the cleft and took a deep breath. The heat of his breathing seemed almost to burn her skin and then his tongue flicked along the valley and caressed her breasts. Silver gasped and felt her nipples swell with desire and she arched up, offering them like a sacrifice to his greedy, sucking mouth.

He lay her down on the bed and she pulled his body against her mouth, nibbling at his nipples while he groaned and her hand went to stroke his throbbing hardness.

"Oh God, Silver!" he gasped, and then he reached to undo his pants, took her hand in his, and covered his hot manhood with her hand. He felt big and hard and throbbing in her fingers and the aroused scent of him drove her wild.

Then his hand stroked her thigh to her lace underthings. She almost tried to stop him, but he whispered, "You're mine, Silver, surrender to me, sweet darlin', submit and let me thrill you!"

All she could do was let her thighs fall apart while he

caressed and stroked her. She felt it coming on and began to tremble.

"Not yet!" he commanded. "Not yet, sweet . . . hold off until you can't stop it any more than you can stop a prairie fire from blazing out of control."

She tried to hold off as he stroked her but then she couldn't control her body, couldn't stop its convulsions, and the heat rose up her body until it roared out of control and nothing could stop it.

She lay there, breathing heavily through her mouth, watching him in the dim light while he unclothed her a little at a time, almost as if it were a ritual, prolonging but heightening his own desire while her own quicksilver passion rose and deepened. He pulled her shoes off, and worked her silk stockings down her thighs and slim legs with excruciating slowness, his fingers caressing her skin. He held one of her little feet between his hands and kissed the instep. "Such tiny feet—no bigger than a child's." He kissed along the arch of her foot, nibbled on her toes, and then kissed his way back up her legs with deliberate slowness. "Do you still have the silver slippers?"

"Yes, nothing could make me part with them." She hoped he wouldn't ask about the bracelet. How could she tell him the Duchess now owned the gold nugget bracelet he had given her so long ago?

"I dream of you dancing naked for me," he whispered, "clad in nothing but your silver shoes and your long blond hair."

She would not tell him that her hair was dyed drab brown now; there was no reason for him to ever know. She would not think of tomorrow when the sun was

338

bright; she would think only of these few hours they would have of darkness, before she fled Denver forever.

Then as she watched him, he took off his own clothes and came to her, kissing her face and holding her tenderly as if he would never let her go. She was wet with wanting him and she spread her thighs and pulled him to her.

"Slowly," he whispered. "Slowly, Silver . . . I've waited too long not to enjoy this as long as I can make it last, like a child with sweet candy."

He came into her so slowly that she found herself pulling at him, digging her nails into his flesh, wanting him now and deeper still. And then he lay on her a long moment, and she felt him big and surging and hot inside her like a virile stallion.

"Give it to me," she whispered. "Oh, dearest, please . . ."

He put his hands under her small hips, tilting her up for deepest penetration. Then he began to ride her, slowly, rhythmically, thrusting deep within her as he moved faster and faster. In seconds, he moaned aloud and rammed into her one more time. They meshed and strained and blended together into one living, breathing form.

She remembered only the moment she felt him begin to give up his seed into her waiting, velvet vessel and then she was floating in a darkness that felt like a wondrous death.

They lay locked together, hearts pounding against each other, flesh dewy with the heat of love.

He lifted her chin with his fingers and kissed her, oh, so very gently. "And now that I'm sated, I love you still,"

339

he whispered. "Oh, Silver, if this could only last forever! If I could only tell you . . ."

She waited for him to finish, but he only kissed her again. "Kiss me," he said, "as if it had to last me forever!"

How did he know that? Was he only talking or had he guessed that she never planned to see him again after dawn broke?

And he made love to her again and again, fiercely, then again tenderly until her lips and breasts were swollen with his kisses and her skin was smeared with his seed. Finally, with his body still locked into hers, they both slept.

It was almost dawn when Silver awoke with a start. She realized with horror that when he opened his eyes, he would know her terrible secret and would turn away from her with pity. Gently, she rolled him over and lay looking at him, brushing the black hair back from his forehead.

I must leave you now, my dearest, she thought with a sigh of regret. Then she remembered how he had taught her to part. She took his hand and kissed the palm, tenderly closing his fingers over it. *Here's a treasure to keep. Sometime when you are lonely, think of me.*

Quickly she rose and dressed. Putting on her spectacles and pulling her hair back into its severe bun, she opened the door. He still lay asleep as she stood looking back at him. She loved him more than anything on this earth, but she couldn't live with his pity, and more than that, she wouldn't obligate him. Nor could she leave town because of Waanibe. At this point, she didn't know what to do. Maybe she could simply refuse to see him if he came to the Palace, send a message that she'd

340

changed her mind or found another man. Eventually he would go away, heartbroken. But wounded hearts sometimes heal and he would someday find another love—one whose face wasn't scarred. She must leave him now. Steeling herself, she closed the door and fled back to the Palace.

Cherokee came awake, realizing Silver was up and moving around the room. *Good God, it must be almost dawn.* He panicked. What would he do when she realized he was almost blind? By damn, he didn't want her pity. Last night, the consequences of the coming morning were the last things on his mind. He feigned sleep, keeping his eyes closed. For a long moment, he didn't realize that the sound he heard was the quiet closing of the door.

"Silver?" He opened his eyes and sat up. His vision was much better today, but still he would need assistance to do simple things, and it wasn't near good enough to be able to handle a gun when he went after Jake Dallinger. There were still a thousand unanswered questions about everything, including the child, and maybe he would never have the answers. He sat up on the edge of the bed and buried his face in his hands. Time, that was what he needed—time to find out if his eyes would finally see well enough to seek justice against Jake Dallinger. More time to earn enough money so that he wouldn't be a burden to Silver—if she would have him at all. Maybe she would laugh if he suggested she sell the saloon and go off and live a simple life high in the hills someplace.

Today he would scout out the town with Keso and

341

become familiar with it, so he could get around more easily and see if he could learn anything more about Jake Dallinger.

What his heart longed to do was go find Silver, laugh with her, talk with her. There was no way he could do that without her finding out about his sight. Last night was all he might ever have of her. He knew he would probably never again hold her in his arms.

Silver hurried along the deserted streets and through the front door of the Palace, just in time to bump into Jake Dallinger, who was coming down the stairs.

"I—I've been out for an early morning walk," she gasped.

"Have you now, missy?" He grinned as he reached out and grabbed her wrist. "In that wrinkled dress and your hair all mussed? You surprise me, gal, I thought you was a dull little gray sparrow and now I find out you may have blood pumping under that drab outfit after all."

She tried to pull out of his grasp, but he held on to her, his ugly face wrinkled in thought. "I don't forget folks I've met, and I swear I know you from someplace, missy. Sooner or later, it'll come to me."

She drew herself up primly. "I'm sure you're confusing me with someone else."

"Maybe." He let go of her wrist and leered at her, making a game of her discomfort. "I swear to Gawd Almighty, gal, if you'd do something about that drab hair and ugly clothes, a man might tend to overlook that scarred face."

She forgot caution. The spunk of the old Silver came

back and she slapped him so hard, his head snapped back.

The look he gave her caused her to tremble. He rubbed his cheek. "You sassy little bitch! I ought to take you to bed! When I got through paying you back for that slap, you'd be begging me to stop." He put his hand on the big silver handle of the whip on his belt.

"I—I'll tell the Duchess if you don't leave me alone," she said.

"You just do that, missy," he drawled and ran his fingers through his gray-streaked beard. "I'm her partner now, and I plan to have a say in how things are done."

She hadn't run a gambling hall without learning to bluff at poker. "You give me a hard time and I'll quit. You know how hard it is to get a governess for a little girl? How would you like Waanibe running amok through the Palace at all hours?"

He smiled slowly and looked down at his hand with the port wine stain between his fingers. "Feisty brat, huh? Wal, maybe that's to be expected."

"May I go to my room now?" She said it stiffly and he moved and let her pass. She didn't look back but she could almost feel his gaze like hot hands on her body as she marched upstairs.

Inside her room, she locked the door and leaned against it, trembling. She no longer felt safe behind her old maidish costume. All the old terrors of the things men had done to her came back with a rush. She knew from the gossip that Jake was sleeping with both the Duchess and any of the whores he chose. There had been whispering about what went on when he went into a girl's room and closed the door. No one, especially the girls he chose, wanted to talk about what he did to them.

Worse yet, in the few days he'd been here, the climate at the Palace had changed. It had always been a tough place, but Jake was adding all sorts of erotic and perverted ideas. Not that they didn't bring in money. The Palace had customers they had never had before and there was whispering about what went on in some of the rooms upstairs . . . for a price. It was being whispered about around town, too; Silver had heard the shocked words, the anger. Back in '62, an angry mob had burned down the River House Saloon because its excesses had finally pushed even a tough boomtown like Denver to righteous indignation. Although if the truth be known, Silver wasn't sure that the Duchess hadn't had a hand in encouraging the mob to destroy her competition.

Could something like that happen at the Palace? It was the only frame building left on the street after the blaze had almost wiped out downtown Denver a year ago last spring. It was the sort of thing either the Duchess or Big Ed Chase would do to a competitor if they got the chance and they had been rivals a long time.

Still unsure what to do next, Silver went to the washbasin to clean up and get ready to face another day with the little girl she could neither steal nor desert. Wannie was holding her when, deep in her heart, Silver knew that for her own safety and her own happiness, she should leave.

His vision was definitely improving, Cherokee thought with relief as the Indian boy came to take him to breakfast. If this kept up, in a few days, he might not need Keso anymore.

They had breakfast and then went outside into the cold November morning. Anytime now, the blizzards would blow through the Rockies. Keso said there was already snow in the high country; it shone on the mountaintops.

Cherokee imagined cold winter days with himself at the head of the dinner table in a cozy log cabin. There would be a wild turkey, quail, or venison he had shot. Silver and the little girl would be making biscuits or maybe pies from berries and tart sand plums.

Keso took his hand and Cherokee smiled at a sudden thought. They might make room for Keso, too, but probably the boy would think a settler's life out in the woods dull after living in Denver.

Keso said, "Boss, there's a crowd gathered on the street corner, and some man is speaking. It looks like Jake Dallinger."

They walked closer.

"Is it?" Cherokee whispered.

"Yes."

Cherokee hesitated. *What was Jake up to?*

The big man cleared his throat and continued haranguing the crowd. "Gawd Almighty, folks, like I was telling you, the army is protecting those red devils out there at Fort Lyon! We good folks of Denver need to help Colonel Chivington."

Some of the crowd murmured agreement. A prospector yelled, "What do you think we should do?"

Jake cursed. "Those damned Cheyenne have about starved us out, cut off our mail and supplies. What would you *like* to do about it?"

A roar went up from the crowd. "He's right," someone shouted. "All able-bodied men ought to go out and join

345

up with the colonel on his campaign. We've had enough of these Indian attacks, of our women raped and children carried off!"

More cheering.

"Recollect," Jake drawled in his unmistakable Georgia accent, "the colonel was a real hero two years ago when the South tried to capture the West for our gold and silver. He done a mighty good job of stoppin' them in their tracks and whippin' them!"

Keso pulled Cherokee's sleeve and whispered, "He's trying to get them to attack the Cheyenne. I thought my people just asked for peace."

"Jake's got a personal reason to hate the Cheyenne," Cherokee whispered. If only he could see well enough to do something about Jake, he thought, maybe in a few more days . . .

Someone in the crowd shouted, "Hey, redneck! You sound like a Johnny Reb your own self!"

Jake guffawed. "Gawd Almighty, folks! The reason I'm in Colorado right now is I ain't a Southern sympathizer. Tell you what, I know this country like I know my own belly button. Used to be an army scout. I'm thinkin' of offerin' to scout for him!"

There was a roar of approval from the crowd.

"Wait a minute!" A new man with a distinct Boston accent pushed through the crowd. "Wait a minute, men. I'm Todd Shaw from the *Rocky Mountain News*. It's my understanding that Black Kettle's people have turned over their captives and are now under the army's protection because they've asked for peace."

"Listen to that Boston accent," Jake drawled. "You can tell Shaw don't have no experience with Plains

Injuns! You speakin' for your paper?"

"Well, no, it's my own opinion. As I suppose most of you know, the *News* thinks more along your lines. An Indian scare cuts back on new immigration and town growth and newspapers are usually in favor of growth so they can sell more papers."

"Then, greenhorn," Jake drawled, his voice full of contempt, "listen to us who know about Injuns! Any frontiersman can tell you that the tribes have a habit of being peaceful in the wintertime when their ponies are lean and the snow is too deep to travel, then in the spring, they go back on the war path."

"Ain't that the God's truth!" someone in the crowd shouted. "And don't forget the murders of that poor Hungate family right outside town!"

"I have powerful friends in the East, Dallinger," Shaw said, "and Colonel Chivington has powerful enemies right here in Colorado who may see this campaign as something to further his political ambitions."

"Shaw, you overstep yourself," Jake said. "Like all these other good folks, I want to protect women and kids, and see this Territory finally become a state. That won't happen as long as the mail gets stopped by murderin' savages for six weeks at a time and new settlers are scart to move here!"

"I'm more afraid of self-righteous citizens and government telling me the end justifies the means!" Shaw shouted with spirit.

There was an angry ripple of words through the crowd and Cherokee began to admire the Yankee from Boston for his bold comments.

"Men," Jake said, "don't pay no attention to the likes

347

of that one. Get your gear together and go on. I'll join up with you out on the trail onct I get some business attended to. We'll leave the likes of Mr. Shaw to sit warm and safe by his fireside, armed with nothing more than his writin' pen."

"The pen can be a powerful weapon," Shaw said, "if it's accompanied by public opinion. Take care, all of you, that you don't go too far."

"Too far?" Jake said. "Shaw, it's you Injun lovers and the Plains tribes who have gone too far!"

The crowd roared approval.

"Now, men," Jake shouted, "let's break this meetin' up. We've wasted enough time. Tell the colonel that I'll be joinin' him later, 'cause he probably could use a good scout who really knows the country and Injuns."

Cherokee stood with little Keso, waiting for the crowd to disperse. He watched the vague outline of Jake Dallinger's form move down the street and realized Todd Shaw still stood there. He walked over to him slowly. "Shaw, I'm Cherokee Evans." He held out his hand. "You may have more guts than brains, but I admire you for it."

The other shook his warmly and laughed. "I have to say what I think, although it's not a popular opinion to have right now. I see you have Indian blood. Are you by any chance Cheyenne or Arapaho?"

"No, but a Cheyenne Dog Soldier saved my life, so I feel indebted to them." Keso pulled at his hand. "Oh, and this is my friend, Keso, who is helping me since I can't see."

"I think I've seen you on the streets, Keso," Todd said in a friendly tone. "Can I do anything to help you, Evans?"

"What can you tell me about the Duchess's Palace?"

Shaw grunted. "Not much. It's a regular den of iniquity and getting worse since Dallinger came to town a few days ago. He's been a silent partner all these years, or so the gossip says. Can't imagine why the Duchess would be involved with white trash like him. If Denver gets enough of it, they're liable to mob together and burn the place down. It's happened before."

Cherokee suddenly didn't want to hear anymore. "If you aren't doing anything right now, I'd be much obliged if you'd tell me about Denver, show me around."

"Be glad to."

And the three of them started off together, Cherokee holding on to Keso's arm.

They spent an enjoyable day and Cherokee was careful not to mention the Palace or its owner again. If there was any scandal attached to Silver, if she had changed her personality and the way she worked, he didn't want to know about it. He loved her too much to care about anything else. His sight seemed to improve more that day; but he still wouldn't want to have to go up against anyone in a gun fight. At this rate, he'd be able to do without Keso in a few days, and yet, he'd grown fond of the kid. *What to do?*

Keso left the big half-breed at the Essex and went out into the night. He didn't really have anyplace to go in this chill air, but he was too proud to admit it to his Cherokee friend. Keso didn't want him to feel obligated and he would if he found out Keso was sleeping in the hay at the stable. That's where he was headed now. But as he walked along the street, the governess came down the block.

"Hello, there." She actually smiled at him. "You're the one I've seen with Cherokee, aren't you?"

Street-wise, he went on his guard. "What's that to you?"

"I just wondered." She chewed her lip as if she was trying to decide how much to tell him.

Keso stared at her in the moonlight. Her face wasn't badly scarred. If she'd take off those glasses, do something about her hair and clothes, she might even be pretty. He turned to go but she caught his arm.

"Keso, about Mr. Evans. I—I used to love him a long time ago."

He felt both curiosity and scorn. "If you care about him, why don't you let him know? I feel sorry for him. He needs someone so much and there's no one but me to guide him around—"

"Guide him around?"

"You know what I mean. Is that the reason you don't go to him? You don't want to be burdened by him?"

"I don't know what you mean."

"Of course you do, lady! He's a good hombre and he can't help it if he can't see—"

"What?"

He looked into her shocked face in the moonlight, realizing he had blurted out too much. "Never mind."

Tears came to her eyes and her mouth opened, then she swallowed hard. "Keso, tell me!"

He had betrayed the trust of a man who had befriended him. "I—I can't. If he wanted you to know, I guess he would have already told you himself. Maybe he's like me—proud. He don't want your pity, miss."

She took a deep breath, seemed to pull herself together. "Never mind, Keso, you've told me what I needed to know." Her expression betrayed that she cared as much about the big, rugged half-breed as he did. "I'm going to him." She turned to leave, then turned back around. "If I need you, where can I find you?"

"At the Elephant Corral—you know, where the Duchess keeps her horses and fancy carriage."

"Don't you have any folks, anyone who cares about you?"

"Just Cherokee," he said, "but that's enough. The two of us are managin' just fine without you." He was sullen and resentful. If she and the man got together, Keso would be alone and not needed anymore.

"I know you're friends"—she patted his shoulder gently—"but you needn't be jealous of me, Keso. I think he may need more help than either of us realizes. I'll look after Cherokee Evans from now on."

As Keso watched, she turned and hurried away down the street toward the Essex Hotel.

Chapter Eighteen

Silver almost flew through the streets. Breathlessly, she paused before his hotel room and rapped.

"Who is it?"

"Silver."

There was a long pause, and for a moment, she thought he would not come to the door. Finally, he opened it slowly. "I—I wasn't expecting you . . . come in."

She came into the room, which was still lit only by the fireplace, and realized now why he'd had no lamps burning the other night. To a blind man, it made no difference if it was light or dark, it was all the same. "Cherokee, I came because I love you. I always loved you. Somehow, we'll work this thing out together."

He closed the door and turned toward her. "I—I don't know what you mean."

"Dearest, don't lie to me. I love you anyway. If your handicap is all that's keeping us apart . . ."

"Oh my God," he groaned. "I never meant for you to find that out until—"

She put her fingers against his lips to hush him and

went into his arms. He drew her to him, kissing her hair. "Silver, there's so many other things involved here, things that are so important—"

"Don't talk; just hold me. Is there anything more important than the fact that we love each other?"

He held her so tightly she could scarcely breathe. She lay her scarred face against his big chest, listening to his heart beat. He stroked her hair and she was content to stand, her arms wrapped around him. How they would manage financially, she didn't know at the moment, nor what she would do about little Waanibe.

"Sweet darlin'," he whispered. "I've waited so long and so many things have happened."

"None of it matters," she said. "It's enough that you love me."

His fingers moved over her face in the darkness, touching each feature. "You will always be so very beautiful to me, even when you're old. And the only mirrors you will ever need again is your reflection in my eyes."

"It's so ironic," she wept. "All I ever thought of was my vanity and now you will never see me age, never see my beauty fade like the rose in the song."

He was silent a long moment. "What you never understood, sweet Silver, is that I wasn't in love with your looks, I would have loved you no matter what. I'm in love with the *you* that's deep inside."

"I love you, too." She didn't believe him; no one could really love her for herself. He loved her because, in his mind, she would always be the flawless beauty he rode away and left so many, many lifetimes ago.

He turned and felt his way to a chair, sat down. "If you don't mind, I'd just like to hold you awhile, feel your heart beating, your pulse against my lips."

And she snuggled up in his lap, stifling an urge to weep because he was blind, because she was scarred. "Life can be so unfair!"

"That's why we should take each moment as it comes," he whispered and kissed her cheek, cuddling her in his strong arms. "No one ever promised that life would be fair or even that we would have a tomorrow."

"Then make this a night to remember," she breathed against his lips. He undid her hair and let it fall in a cascade of silken locks over them both. Then he kissed the hollow of her throat.

They sat a long time before the fire. It was enough somehow that they were finally together. They had both waited so very long.

Then gradually, his hands stroked her skin into fire so that his touch sent goosebumps rising along its surface. This time, eager for him, she unbuttoned her own bodice and his shirt, and pressed her naked breasts against his brawny chest, her nipples against his until the tips swelled with the desire.

"Kiss me," he demanded. "Kiss me like you want me!"

She had never been the aggressor before but she was eager for him and she reached up to cover his mouth, pushing her tongue inside, probing the hot wetness, nibbling at his lips. Beneath her, she felt his manhood hard and throbbing. Her own ardor increased as she bent her head to suck and tease his nipples until he gasped and held her mouth against him. He trembled now, his hands pulling at her skirt and now under her lace pantalets, stroking her.

She slid off the chair, onto her knees, and bent her head to kiss his manhood. She kissed it gently, lovingly,

354

and then she stood up, slipped out of her lace pantalets, and slowly straddled him. For a moment, she thought of heathen idols in temples, great stone male gods where women offered themselves up to sacrifice. She came down on him slowly, taking him within her so deep, it seemed he actually pushed against her womb. His head fell back and he reached out and caught her breasts in his two hands and began to move her up and down on him.

Never had she felt so aroused. His calloused palms brushed against her nipples as he held her breasts. She increased her own desire, rising up, then grinding down on his pulsating manhood. Stroking his nipples as she straddled him, she turned her face up to his. His mouth came down on hers, forcing her lips apart, sucking her tongue deep into his mouth.

They clung together as she rode him—harder, faster, deeper. She felt him strain inside her and came down one more time hard and grinding on his body so that he seemed to explode within her, filling her womb with his virile seed. She had never wanted anything as much as she wanted to erase the hurt he had suffered. Then her own body began its spasms of pleasure, and together they came hard and deep, making her weep in his arms.

He held her close, and kissed her face. "Why do you cry? Did I do something wrong?"

"No, dearest, women cry when they make love and it's good. And this was good, so good . . ."

"I love you, sweet," he whispered and picked her up as he stood, carrying her to the bed a few feet away. "You know what I'd like to see, Silver? You dancing naked just for me, clad only in your long blond hair and silver shoes."

He would never again actually see her with his eyes,

she thought. He would have to see her with his hands, his body, his lips. At that moment, she would have accepted twice as many scars if she could have worked out a deal with God to give Cherokee back his sight.

Cherokee held her close, wondering how much to tell her. He had almost told her of the doctor's predictions that his sight might return. Then she had put her finger against his lips and he grew cautious. Suppose he raised her hopes that he might be able to see again someday and then it never happened? Suppose it never improved enough so that he could hunt, or chop wood, or do anything that a man needed to be able to do around a homestead? Better he should wait.

But there was one thing they must discuss. "Silver," he whispered, "sweet darlin', there's something I want to ask about Jake Dallinger."

He felt her stiffen in his arms. "What about him?"

"Is he a partner in the Palace?"

"Maybe. He had all that gold in the little beaded bags." She sounded nervous.

"By damn! That money came from old Willie and Bill. Someone killed them with a whip and took their stash."

She made a choking noise in her throat. "Oh Cherokee, it's in the safe at the Palace! I had no idea—"

"I didn't think you did," he whispered and a tremendous relief swept over him. "That's the final proof then that he killed them. First I owe them justice. And that gold is now rightfully mine. We'll need it when we marry."

"Marry? Are you asking me to marry you?" He heard both the relief and disbelief in her voice.

"Of course! You think I don't want to give my child my name? She deserves at least that much."

"Child? Let me get this straight." She sat up in bed. "You're only asking me to marry you to give Waanibe a name?"

"No, that's not the only reason," he said. "I love you."

"No, I don't think you do—not really." She began to laugh, a strange kind of laugh. "You're just trying to do the 'decent' thing by me. Wannie's not yours—or mine either. Is that what you thought?"

"But someone said she was the owner's daughter—"

"So she is, by a Cheyenne brave, or so the Duchess says."

"The Duchess?" There was another long pause. "Silver, don't you own the Palace?"

She lay on her back and he leaned over her. "Is that what you thought? Cherokee, I only work there."

He heaved a sigh of relief, but said nothing. The woman he loved wasn't mixed up with Jake, and wasn't wealthy anymore. He did feel a hint of sadness that the child was not theirs. He had already been picturing them as a family.

"I shouldn't have mentioned marriage," he said, thinking that if his sight didn't return, he didn't intend to burden Silver with a blind man; it wasn't fair. And he still had the problem of Jake Dallinger. He couldn't pull Silver into that; the man was too ruthless.

"I understand," she said slowly. "You thought I was mixed up with Dallinger?"

"No, I knew you could never be." He kissed her face. "I just jumped to conclusions when I heard he was somehow involved with the Palace."

"Why don't you bring the law in on this?"

"I'm not sure anyone would believe me. I have to think about a plan."

"Of course." Her voice sounded cool and distant. No, he couldn't make personal commitments now. He shouldn't have blurted that out about marriage. She might feel pity enough to marry him, but he wouldn't be a burden to the beauty. There had always been men aplenty who wanted her. He wouldn't saddle her with the responsibility of a blind man, or at least one who could barely tell daylight from darkness.

"I love you," he whispered and snugled her down in his arms. Finally they both dropped off to sleep.

When he awakened, he knew immediately it was past dawn, and then he almost shouted, for the reason he knew this was because he could see the morning shadows that the sun threw against his wall.

He could see! Not perfectly yet, but much better than yesterday. Maybe the doctor had been right. Hope rose in Cherokee's heart. Maybe there was a chance for happiness between Silver and himself. Maybe . . .

He felt her asleep in his arms and looked down to kiss her. He stared at the drab hair, wondering what she had done to it, and then his gaze went to her face.

For a moment, he stared, unbelieving. She was still pretty, but her flawless face had a few small scars. When he pulled the sheet down, he saw that scars marked her ripe body, too. He knew now what it was that Doc had been trying to tell him and had hesitated about. Smallpox. Of course his brave love had tried to help and had come down with the dread disease herself.

He wanted to gather her into his arms, kiss her awake, tell her it didn't matter, that he would always love her. Then he recalled her remarks about his not being able to see her fade like an aging rose. She had only come into his life again because she thought he would never see her destroyed beauty. If she knew his sight was returning, that he could see her scars, would she run away from him forever, unwilling to believe that he loved her still? He might lose her.

He would rather lose his sight than the woman he loved. For a long moment, he held her close and almost wished he were truly and forever blind. *What to do now?*

Silver stirred and sat up. Quickly, Cherokee closed his eyes.

"Dearest," she whispered and kissed him. "It's morning."

"Is it?" He didn't look at her.

"I'll be your eyes from now on," she whispered, and hugged him to her. "But right now, I have to go."

He needed time to think. Cherokee forced himself to stare blankly past her shoulder. "If you have to, run along. Keso will come after a while to help me."

She got up, dressed, and put her hair in a bun while he watched her, pretending that he saw nothing at all.

Silver said, "Your stolen gold is in the Duchess's safe. I'll try to think of a way to get it for you." She paused as she put on her cloak and reached in the pocket for her spectacles. "As for Jake himself, give up the idea of justice. In your condition, there's nothing you can really do."

Not without letting you find out I'm not blind, he thought. "I reckon not," he said, torn with indecision.

Silver kissed him again and went out. After he heard

359

her footsteps fading down the hall, he got up and dressed. His sight was still a long way from perfect, but it was much improved. He began to hope the doctor had been right and that, finally, it might get back to normal.

Which meant he could deal with Jake. But not without Silver realizing he could see. His honor demanded he mete out justice to his old partners' killer. But if he did so, he would certainly lose the woman he loved because of her vain fears. Honor versus love. By damn! What was the right choice?

Cherokee poured some water in the wash bowl and stared at himself in the little cracked mirror hanging on the faded wall. He decided then he would do anything to keep Silver—anything. Even if it meant that Jake got off scot-free and Cherokee had to pretend to be blind for the rest of his life. That didn't sound too practical, and besides, what would he and Silver live on? He wanted to get her out of the Palace, no matter what she was doing there.

A rap at the door. He hesitated a long moment. Everyone in town thought he was blind. There might be an advantage in keeping the masquerade up—besides his fear that Silver would find out. "Come in."

Keso entered. "Boss, it's me." Even though his sight was far from perfect, Cherokee was struck at how thin and ragged the Indian boy looked. Evidently he needed the money Cherokee had been giving him more than Cherokee realized. That aided him in making his decision to keep his secret, at least temporarily.

"Keso, tell me about some of the other people around the Palace."

The boy shrugged. "You mean the whores and card sharps?"

Surely Silver wasn't working as a whore. "Is there anyone else there?"

"Sure, there's a governess."

"A governess?"

"Sure, boss. She looks after the Duchess's kid. Wouldn't be bad lookin' if she did something about her hair and clothes. She's got a few little scars on her face."

So that was what Silver was doing at the Palace.

The boy leaned against the door. "Anything else, boss?"

"Yes, Keso, today I only want you to take me to one place." He paused and realized how thin the boy was. "I mean, after I buy the two of us breakfast."

He watched the boy's face light up. "Sure! You suppose this could become a permanent job?"

He didn't know what to say. "I don't know how long I can afford to pay you, Keso. I'm running low on money."

He tried to keep his expression frozen, pretending he did not see the disappointment in the handsome brown face. "I understand."

If I had a home, some money, and a wife, I'd adopt you, Cherokee thought. Keso Evans. And then he knew that in his present predicament, nothing could work out happily for anyone. The game of life wasn't always fair. You took the hand you were dealt and played it, with no whining that someone else got better cards.

He managed to dress himself and let Keso lead him to the café. "Keso," he said, "if you're Cheyenne, why don't you go back to them?"

The boy shrugged. "I don't know how to find them. I recollect that it was because of me my mother fled them." He frowned. "Don't remember much, but somehow I don't think the Cheyenne want me."

Why wouldn't they want one of their own? Cherokee thought about it as they ate. It was indeed a puzzle. If he ever saw Iron Knife again, he'd have to ask him. "And now," he said as he pushed his plate back, "I want you to take me to visit Todd Shaw at the newspaper."

The boy grinned, showing even, white teeth. "Sure, Cherokee. And then if you don't need me, I'll try shining a few shoes today. Sounds like we both need the money."

Cherokee flinched. "If you think I'm going to live off you . . ."

"I like you, boss," Keso said softly. "You're about the only person besides my mama who's ever treated me decent. When you run out of money, maybe I can help you."

What could he say without revealing his secret to the boy? "Thanks, Keso, I'm much obliged that you'd do that for me."

They went to Shaw's office and there Keso left him, promising to return in an hour.

Cherokee sat across from Todd Shaw and looked him over. He was a handsome brown-haired man in his middle or late twenties with honest, hazel eyes and an open, friendly manner. Everything about him told Cherokee here was a man born to wealth and privilege. "I wanted to talk to you about a few things, Shaw. I liked the way you stood up to that mob out on the street."

Todd shrugged. "I like to think of myself as the conscience of this town. My boss may sometimes be swept away by popular sentiment, but I try to keep us on an even course between that and what I perceive as what's morally right."

Cherokee stared blankly past a point above Todd's broad shoulder. "Your accent speaks of education from

362

back East. What's a man like you doing here?"

Todd laughed and leaned back in his chair. "Escaping from a staid Boston background and an overprotective mother, mostly. She had my whole future laid out for me and suddenly I couldn't stand Harvard anymore. I decided it would be a grand gesture to run off to 'Bloody Kansas' when that territory was debating whether they would come in as a free or slave state, found the place dull, and came here."

"Do you know anything at all about the Duchess' Palace and the red-neck cracker who challenged you in that mob?"

"The Palace has a bad reputation and even the public's getting fed up. The other saloons and bawdy houses don't like the Duchess, especially Big Ed Chase. If he can ever figure out a way to get rid of her, he will. Today's Saturday, that means the whole street will have one long, drunken brawl going on late tonight."

"And Dallinger?"

Todd seemed to be searching his memory. "The name rings a bell somehow. I'd swear it's the name my brother mentioned to me. Something to do with Jake ending up in jail for attempted robbery, kidnapping, and rape, but that's all I can tell you. Guess they finally paroled him."

That didn't help much. "Todd, I've got a friend among the Cheyenne. Do you really think Chivington's forces will finally attack them?"

Todd shrugged. "If he does, he may need an old army scout like Dallinger to lead him to the Indians. I don't know whether the colonel has a good scout or not. What's your interest in the man?"

He wondered if he could trust Todd Shaw. "I'm sure beyond a reasonable doubt that Jake murdered and

363

robbed my partners. Do you think it would do me any good to go to the law?"

"Probably not. Frankly, Evans, I don't know what to say. I'm not much on taking the law into your own hands, but in this case, if you weren't blind, I'd almost suggest it. Dallinger's a ruthless man, as I recall my brother's comments, and the world would be a better place without him."

Cherokee reassessed the man, trying to decide just how far he could trust Todd Shaw. He had always considered himself a good judge of men, and he had a feeling that before this was over, he was going to need an ally. "If I tell you something, can I know you'll keep my secret?"

Todd nodded. "I like you, Evans. You have my word that whatever you tell me will be held in confidence."

Cherokee took a deep breath, thinking. *There comes a time when we all have to trust someone,* he thought. *No one can get through this world alone.* "All right, here it is. I'm not as blind as I appear. My sight's gradually return-ing—"

"Then why—?"

"Let me finish. I won't bore you with all the details, but I expect that within a few weeks, maybe less, I'll be able to see as well as anyone. That is, if my eyes keep improving as they have been these last couple of days."

Todd stared at him. "Then why are you pretending to be completely blind?"

"I may keep up the ruse forever," Cherokee admitted with a sigh.

"That's crazy. It's impossible to keep up a masquerade like that for any length of time."

"I know that, but I'm desperate. What would you do? I'm in love with a woman whose beauty was once the toast of the Rockies, but she's been scarred. She thinks I don't realize it because of my blindness."

Todd looked mystified. Evidently, he had no idea who the woman was. "You mean, if she thinks you can see she's no longer beautiful, she'll leave you?"

"I believe she's so insecure, she'll assume I offer pity instead of love and she'll flee forever. But if I go after Dallinger and bring him to justice, she's bound to find out I can see."

"A hell of a position," Shaw sympathized. "I don't envy you. What are you going to do?"

"By damn! I wish I knew!" Cherokee slumped in his chair, shaking his head.

"You must love her very much."

"Enough to throw aside everything if I can only keep her," Cherokee admitted.

"I wish you luck then," Shaw said, "but suppose Dallinger gets away and she still finds out and leaves you?"

"I suppose that's the chance I'm going to have to take. Nothing means as much to me as this girl."

Shaw didn't say anything. Cherokee saw the disapproval on his face. The clock on the wall behind him ticked loudly. "Cherokee," he said finally, "I think you're wrong, but it's not my decision to make. I hope to God you don't end up regretting it."

Cherokee said nothing. Todd Shaw had never spent a night in Silver's arms. It was easy to talk about right and wrong when Todd wasn't the one who risked losing a girl like Silver.

Todd craned his neck and looked out the window. "Here comes that Indian boy. He doesn't know either?"

Cherokee shook his head. "No. No one knows but you

and a couple of doctors. I trust you to keep my secret. I only told you because I thought I might end up needing some help."

"I don't know what I can do. I'm no good with a gun, but I do know a lot about this town. If I hear anything I think can help, I'll let you know immediately."

"Hey, boss, I came back."

"Keso? Fine, you can take me back to the hotel now." Cherokee stood up and held out his hand, staring past the child's shoulder.

He let the boy take him back to the Essex and leave. Cherokee lay on his bed, staring up at the ceiling and struggling with the decision about what to do next.

It was dusk when there was a rap at his door. "Silver?"

"No, Iron Knife."

"Iron Knife! Good God!" Quickly he opened the door and let him in. They hugged each other and Cherokee led him over to the fireplace. "What are you doing in Denver? The way folks feel about your people right now, this isn't a very safe place to be."

"One of the half-breed Bent boys came out to the Big Sandy camp, and told me that Jake Dallinger is in town."

Cherokee rolled a cigarette, offered one to Iron Knife, and lit them both. "What is Jake Dallinger to you?"

"I intend to kill him," the other said softly. "He was in jail, but I hear he's out. Dallinger's an evil man. He tried to carry off my woman and kill Todd Shaw's brother. That's what put him in jail back in the spring of '59."

Cherokee sat down and considered. "Is that how you found me? Through Todd Shaw?"

Iron Knife nodded. "He's a friend. Todd tells me he's

afraid there's going to be more trouble. He says Colonel Chivington is out in eastern Colorado now, looking for Indians to attack."

"If that's the case, you're needed by your people. You ought to go back."

Iron Knife smoked and shook his head. "I won't sleep easy until Dallinger's dead. If he gets a chance to do anything to hurt the Cheyenne, he will. That white man carries a grudge that goes all the way back to my father."

Cherokee looked at him for a long moment. Iron Knife was as big as he himself, but he was dressed as a Dog Soldier. "You can't get to Jake Dallinger's, someone would spot you, whereas I've been seen around here for several days and everyone accepts the fact that I'm blind."

"Are you, my friend?"

Cherokee shook his head. "My sight has gradually returned. And I won't let you risk your life to get Jake when I intend to kill him myself."

Quickly he told Iron Knife about finding his partners' bodies and how it appeared one of them had been throttled and the other had been whipped to death.

Iron Knife frowned. "That sounds like Dallinger, all right. Do you think you can take him? I hate to give up that pleasure myself."

Cherokee stood up. "I owe him this, my friend. Don't do me out of the justice I owe him."

"Since you put it that way . . ." The warrior stood up and tossed the cigarette into the fireplace. "I'll go back to camp now and warn my people that we may be attacked." He looked uncertain.

"What's the matter?"

"I'm not sure my people will believe me," Iron Knife

said. "We've been promised protection by the officer at Fort Lyon. I'm afraid Black Kettle and the others will think I'm fearful and suspicious for no good reason."

Cherokee walked him to the door. "Believe me, I think it's wise to be cautious. I heard Dallinger in a mob the other day. He said something about helping the colonel find the Indian camp."

Iron Knife turned with his hand on the door handle. "That would be bad news. Dallinger is a skilled scout who knows the country well. The troops would be at a disadvantage without him."

"Then maybe I can keep him from joining up with Chivington's forces, if he's a mind to. I owe your people that." He paused. "Iron Knife, there is something I've wondered about—I found a stray Cheyenne boy here in town. Why isn't he with your people?"

The big half-breed looked blank. "Who?"

"His name is Keso. Just a kid, maybe ten or twelve. I'm not sure what he's doing here."

Iron Knife scowled. "He's not Cheyenne. He's the pup of one of our most hated enemy, the Ute. I feel for the boy, but he would be killed if he returned to the Cheyenne and I wouldn't be able to stop it."

"But why?"

Iron Knife shook his head. "It's a long story that many of my people know. Just take my word for it, he's a Ute, although he may not even know that himself."

That left the kid no one at all, Cherokee thought. Keso would live on the streets the rest of his life, maybe. There were so many things he wanted to ask, but Iron Knife seemed impatient to leave.

The big Cheyenne held out his hand. "Good-bye, my friend. Someday maybe we will meet again. I will ride out and tell my people what you and Todd Shaw have said. Maybe I can convince them that they are not safe and that we should move our camp. But it would be a lot of trouble to move right now and my people feel safe with the fort close by."

They shook hands solemnly and then Iron Knife slipped out the door and was gone, swift and quiet as a shadow into the dusk.

Cherokee was left staring at the door. He had promised that he would take vengeance on Jake Dallinger. Now just how did he go about doing that without losing Silver when she found out he could see?

Chapter Nineteen

Silver played with Waanibe in the nursery while the afternoon passed, but her thoughts were on Cherokee. *There were only two kinds of women in the West and she was the wrong kind. Hadn't she known that from the beginning?* She had hoped he wasn't like the others, but his hesitancy about the subject of marriage told her he was.

They played Wannie's favorite game, dress-up. Silver let her wear the silver shoes and showed her how to dance, but she made sure the child didn't bother the Duchess's jewelry.

Later they ate supper together. The noise from downstairs was growing louder, but then it always did on Saturday night. With Thanksgiving just past, some of the prospectors were still celebrating the holiday. In fact, Silver was sure some of them hadn't drawn a sober breath since the beginning of cold weather.

She heard arguing coming from the Duchess's office and wondered about it as she got Waanibe ready for bed in her favorite flannel nightgown with the pockets on it.

As she tucked her in, the dark child smiled up at her.

"Give me a treasure and I'll go to sleep."

"You rascal!" Silver smiled and kissed the chubby palm, then closed Waanibe's fingers over it. "Now put that in your pocket until you need it."

Waanibe nodded.

"And go to sleep." Silver closed the door and went down the hall, paused only a moment at the Duchess's door, and realized the owner was talking to Jake. Could it be about Silver? She paused to listen. Sooner or later, Jake was going to figure out where he knew Silver from and then she would be arrested for murder and robbery. What should she do? Even if Cherokee didn't love her enough to marry her, would he care enough to at least try to help her a little? She would wait until it was dark out and then would go to Cherokee's room.

Jake laughed and watched the Duchess pace the floor. "What do you mean, 'this can't go on'? Appears to me it's worked out just fine."

The Indian girl frowned. "I'm almost to the point of throwing you out, you redneck bastard, and taking a chance on what happens if you tell the world everything you know about me. At least you might pack your things and get the hell out of my saloon!"

Should he play his secret card now? "That ain't a nice way to talk, lady. Besides I might decide to take my kid with me."

He could tell she was only half listening. "What kid?"

He grinned. "Waanibe."

"Don't be a fool! She's not yours, she's—"

"Iron Knife's?" He saw the fear in her face. "You don't think I didn't know that you thought the brat was

371

his? If she was, I'd have already killed her. She ain't his'n, but I'll bet even you didn't realize that."

She looked at him for a long moment, the fear slowly replaced by confusion. "I don't know what you're talking about."

He laughed. "Gawd Almight, woman, are you blind? You may have laid both of us within a day or so, but that pup's mine. Ain't that a hoot? You been treasuring that brat because you thought she was Iron Knife's, when all the time, Wannie's mine. I knew it the moment I saw her."

"You don't know what the hell you're talking about!" Rage spread across her sultry face. "If she was yours, I wouldn't care if she died!"

"But she's also half yours, Gray Dove. Don't that mean nothing to ya?"

The Arapaho girl shook her head. "Waanibe cares more about her governess than she does me. You're just trying to cause trouble. She's not yours, I tell you!"

He might as well play his hole card now. Very slowly he came over and held his hand up in front of her face. "See that port wine stain birthmark on those fingers? It's passed down through every generation of the Dallingers, as far back as I can remember—the mark of Cain, my Daddy called it. Now take a good look and tell me your kid don't carry the mark of her pa?"

She stared at his hand and shook her head slowly as if to deny it herself. "She's—she can't be yours. She's dark like her Cheyenne father."

"Nope." Dallinger shook his head, enjoying the pain on her face. "She's dark 'cause she's got an Arapaho mama. It's a big joke, ain't it? You been keeping that kid because you thought she was sired by that big half-breed

372

when I knew from the first day I seen her that she was mine. You hear? Mine!"

For a long moment, she stared from his face to his hand with the telltale birthmark. Then horror and bitterness etched her face and she swore and buried her face in her hands. "You bastard! You rotten bastard!"

"Now is that any way to talk to the father of your child? It appears to me you should be grateful I'm willing to claim her."

"You don't care about her! You don't care about me either."

"Oh but I do. The brat may come in handy someday. In about ten years, she could be working right here at the Palace, turning tricks and making money for us both."

"You low-down sonofabitch! You'd do that to your own daughter?" She slapped him across the face.

He struck her back. Her head snapped to one side and blood ran from a corner of her mouth. "Don't play so righteous with me, Gray Dove. You don't care any more about the kid than I do. You only hoped to use her someday to get that big Injun for yourself."

She wiped the blood from her mouth and glared at him. "The only one who really cares about the kid is Jones."

He thought about the governess a long moment. "She ain't all that bad-looking and I figure she's got a nice body under those prim clothes. I might just try her some myself. You know what they say, 'Still water runs deep.'"

"Leave her alone! Suppose she quits? There's whores a-plenty here at the Palace, but a good governess is hard to come by."

"Gal, I give the orders around here," Jake said, "and you still haven't learned who's boss, have you?" He caught her arm, pulled her to him, and ripped her bodice down the front. "Maybe I just haven't humbled you enough, you brown bitch! Maybe you need more lessons on submission." He reached out, cupped one of her big breasts with his hand, and squeezed hard.

"Don't, Jake, you're hurting me!"

"I like to hurt women," he drawled. "You oughta remember that—it's exciting." He pulled her to him, forced her bloody mouth open with his, and shoved his tongue into her throat while he squeezed and stroked her breasts. "I'm gonna take you from behind, bitch, just like a stallion rearing up on a mare."

"Jake, no!" She managed to pull her mouth away. "There's a Saturday night crowd gathering downstairs, I need to go down."

"They'll keep awhile longer," he said thickly. "The card sharps and the girls will keep them entertained. For the next few minutes, you are going to entertain me. And if you behave yourself and make me enjoy it, I won't tell your brat I'm her old man yet."

"Jake, no!"

"Don't ever tell me no, you Injun whore. You'll do exactly what I tell you to." He slapped her, knocking her backward, then grabbed her arm and half dragged her through the office door into her bedroom. "Come on, bitch, show me your talent and maybe I won't hurt you too bad!" He reached out and ripped the whole front of her dress away.

"I won't submit to you anymore. I'm rich and successful—"

"You're an Injun whore and that's your major talent. Don't you ever forget it." He reached for his whip. "I want to watch you twist and squirm under me, watch

374

your hot body get all excited when I do things to you."

She backed away from him, shaking her head. "Take one of the whores. Take the governess if you want, but just leave me alone!"

He grinned, and ran his fingers through his tangled, dirty beard. "I intend to do all three, Gray Dove. As your partner, I kin do just about what I like."

Silver had listened outside the door for the first few minutes of the conversation. So Jake Dallinger was Waanibe's father! It didn't make any difference to Silver; she had never know or even cared who might have fathered the child. In fact, she had almost been afraid it was Cherokee from a previous time. All she could think of now was that the Duchess or Gray Dove, or whoever she was, didn't want the child. That meant Silver could have her . . . or did it?

The Saturday night crowd downstairs sounded louder and drunker than usual, possibly because of the holiday season, and anything was an excuse for these hard-living, hard-drinking men to down a few more. Then, too, the Palace attracted a rougher crowd than some of the others places. If Denver ever decided it wanted to change its image and become a "law and order" town, the Palace would be one of the first saloons the city fathers would want to close.

She checked on little Waanibe again, made sure the child was fast asleep, then went to her room. *What to do?* Silver longed for the strength and comfort of Cherokee's arms. She wasn't proud where he was concerned. He didn't have to really love her; she'd settle for whatever he was willing to give. Maybe he could tell her what she should do about Waanibe. If Silver didn't do something, the child might end up as homeless and unwanted as that street boy, Keso.

She waited a few more minutes, listening to the laughter and noise from downstairs. What had she done with the silver shoes? And the she smiled, remembering. They were on the floor of the nursery. There was no point in waking the little girl up by going in there to get them. She'd put them away tomorrow. Right now, she longed for Cherokee's arms.

Silver got her cloak and went out into the hall. She'd go down the back stairs where no one would see her. But as she started in that direction, she ran into Jake Dallinger, who was just coming down the hall from the Duchess's room. He grinned as he rolled up the big whip and hung it on his belt.

"Why, howdy, missy, I was just leaving myself. Where in the hell you think you're going?" He caught her arm, and when she tried to jerk away, her spectacles came off.

"Let go of me!"

He stared at her a long moment as if really seeing her for the first time. Then he reached out slowly and began to pull the hairpins out so that the drab locks fell around her face. "Wal, I'll be damned! I must have been blind not to recognize you!"

"I don't know what you're talking about." She tried to twist out of his hands.

"Ya don't, huh? Now ain't that a purdee shame because I sure as hell recognize you, little gal! What are you gonna do to keep me from telling?"

She was so afraid, she shook as she tried to get away from him. "You don't know anything!"

"I know about a purty gal named Silver who went missing along with a man named Al and a bunch of money, leaving the owner dead. I think you're gonna be willing to let me do anything I want to you, Silver, just to keep you from being hanged."

"I'd rather be dead!" She struggled, but he held her and grinned.

"That's easy to say, gal, but I have a feeling you'll be in my bed every night once you think it over. You don't want to get hanged for murdering Bart Brett, now do you?"

"I don't know any Bart Brett!"

"You're lucky tonight, Silver, I already enjoyed the Duchess, but there's always all day tomorrow and tomorrow night and every day afterward. I'm already looking forward to it!"

"You bastard!" Silver managed to pull away from him and ran down the back stairs and out into the cold November night. Oh God, what was she going to do? She couldn't pull Cherokee into this; he had enough problems with his blindness. She couldn't tell him about Bart Brett and the Velvet Kitten. Cherokee already thought of her as a saloon whore, even though he denied it. What would he think if he knew she was wanted for robbery and murder? Or if there was the slightest chance that he cared for her, this would only add fuel to his vengeance against Jake Dallinger.

Cherokee didn't stand a chance against the brawny scout without his eyesight. Maybe she could convince him to leave this town and forget justice. Whatever she had to submit to from Dallinger, it was better than getting Cherokee killed.

She fled to the Essex Hotel.

"Cherokee, let me in! It's Silver!"

Cherokee answered the door, still puzzled over what he was going to do about maintaining his masquerade if and when his sight gradually returned to normal. Whatever it would take to keep Silver, whether it meant lying, cheating, or whatever, he wanted her badly enough to try.

"Silver? I wasn't sure you'd come again."

She came into his arms and her cheek felt cold against his. "I had to."

She was scared; he could sense that. Cherokee held her very close and stroked her hair, which hung in wild disarray as he ran his hand over her face. "Your hair is down and your glasses are gone. Has something happened?"

"I—I just came to tell you I've changed my mind about you."

In the dim light of the lamp, he could see her face and knew she wasn't a good liar.

"I don't understand."

She tried to pull out of his arms. "I've decided I should stay at the Palace. That's where a big-time saloon star like me belongs anyway. If you did want to marry me, you'd stick me in some crummy place with brats crawling around my feet while I hung over a washtub all day."

He tried to mold her against him, but she felt wooden and unresponsive in his arms. "Silver, if I hadn't been blind, I'll level with you, I would have kidnapped you if I had to and carried you off to a cabin where all we did was lie on a fur rug naked in front of the fire and make love."

"No, I—I've changed my mind. You can't expect me to give up everything for a—a blind man."

He winced, looking down at her. He saw fear in her dear, scarred face and wondered what had happened. Had she guessed about his returning sight? No, in that case, she wouldn't want him to see her; she wouldn't have come.

No, that was actual fear in her face. He wondered suddenly if she feared for herself or someone else. If any man had laid a hand on her, Cherokee would kill him. Could it be that his blindness really made a difference to her? That wasn't the Silver he had known. "I suppose that's the reason I kept trying to keep you from finding out."

She turned away from him. "Well, that's all I have to say." She drew in a deep, shuddering breath. "I-I'll go now."

"At least let me love you one more time—something for both of us to remember all those lonely nights in the future."

"Drat it all! Who told you I would be lonely?" She looked up at him and laughed, the old hardness back in her pale eyes. But her soft mouth trembled, making a liar of her. "There's another man, of course. You know me, Cherokee, I'm a saloon girl, a singing, dancing star. I could never get used to having only one man in my bed."

He didn't want to live if he lost her. No, he *couldn't* live if he lost her. "Silver, what is it? What's wrong? All those years in that Yankee prison, all that kept me alive and gave me the guts to go on was the knowledge that someday you would be in my arms again!"

He pulled her to him, kissed her while she struggled, but he didn't let her go. Whatever it was, she wasn't being truthful with him and he would do anything to keep her. If only she were carrying his child, she wouldn't have the option of leaving him. She'd be his. "At least let me make love to you one more time before we part."

"No." She tried to pull away but he was stronger than she was and he held her with one arm while he began to unbutton the front of her dress. "I told you no!"

"Love me one more time," he whispered, "and then I'll let you go without a fuss and won't ask anything else."

He could feel her trembling in his arms. She shook her head in denial as he managed to get the front of her dress open and covered one of her breasts with his big hand. He felt her nipple respond to his touch and heard her sharp intake of breath. "Just once more," he murmured, "and after that, if you still want to go back to this other man, I'll let you leave."

"Please let me go."

He felt the tears drip down on his hand, but he didn't take it from her breast. He had not gone through so much to lose her now.

Cherokee kneaded her breast with his hand, feeling the warm satin of her skin, the nipple swelling with desire against his flesh even as his own maleness began to pulsate with need. If he made love to her every day for the rest of his life, he would never get enough of her.

She pushed at him. "Let me go, or I'll—"

His mouth came down over hers. She fought him, but she was powerless against his strength. He carried her to the bed and laid her down. Cherokee didn't take his mouth away as he lay down on her, both his hands kneading and fondling her bare breasts. Finally she stopped struggling, gasped, and moaned deep in her

380

throat. He sucked her tongue into his mouth and one of his hands went down to pull at her skirt and stroke her thigh.

Her hands came up as if to push him away and, instead, dug into his shoulders, pulling his face down to her breasts. "Oh, Cherokee . . . you make me forget everything except that I'm a woman."

"And you make me feel like a stallion of a man!" He laved her breasts into sensitive peaks with his tongue. She whimpered as his hand went to invade her velvet place. He stroked her there, reaching deep to tease and thrill every nerve of her being with his skillful fingers.

He moved to kiss her there and pull her thighs apart where he could taste the very essence of her body while she arched and gasped beneath him. He unbuttoned his pants, his manhood so hard, it was throbbing.

She lay there, thighs apart, her breasts bare, her hair a silken tangle. And he was suddenly ashamed.

"Silver, I won't force myself on you. If you don't want me—"

He never finished because she reached for him, pulling him to her, and he felt her hand on his manhood as she guided him into her body, tilting up so that she could take the full length of his penetration.

He lay on top of her, feeling himself throb deep in her belly. "Put your legs around me, Silver, those long, beautiful legs." He felt her lock his hips against her so he couldn't escape. His mouth came down on hers, his two hands covering her breasts, his thumbs stroking back and forth across the nipples, and she gasped and shuddered each time he did it. "Now work with me, sweet darlin'," he urged fiercely. "You know what you want from me, what you won't be satisfied until you get from my body.

381

Make me want to give it to you, squeeze it out of me, make me put it deep inside you!"

Her body seemed to be convulsing under him, and he could feel the hot velvet of her sheath squeezing and forcing him to give up his seed. He began hard, deep thrusts. She was really too small to take all of him, he was thrusting against her very womb, but he couldn't stop himself from riding her hard, holding on to her breasts. He kept his tongue deep in her throat while her legs locked his hips against her and her nails dug into his shoulders. They meshed and strained together like two savage, wild things rutting in the darkness.

She began to come under him and he couldn't hold back any longer. He thrust hard and deep one final time, then he felt his pent-up seed gush deep into her womb and she climaxed under him, accepting, no, *demanding* his gift. In her mating frenzy, she bit his tongue while they coupled for an eternity.

When he returned to consciousness, her body was still locked onto his, refusing to let him go. He lay on her, rubbing against her velvet petals until she whimpered and pulled at him so that he rubbed against her until her body convulsed under him again.

They lay still a long time while he kissed her face and then he rolled her over on top of him again. "Sweet Silver, make me want you again," he whispered, "but you'll have to work for it this time."

She began to ride him and he felt himself harden as she moved on him. Her full breasts hung close to his mouth and he clasped her back and brought her breasts down to brush against his face, teasing them with his mouth while she moved on top of him. By damn, maybe she wouldn't have to work so very hard after all, he thought with wonder, as she slid down on him again and again. His hands went down her back to her slim waist. He used his strength to grind her down on his hard tool, using her for his pleasure. But she was in the dominant position, and she was dictating the rhythm to satisfy her own needs. finally he had no more to give and she lay on him, weeping and spent. He held her close and kissed the tears from her face.

"Silver, I don't want to let you go. I love you too much."

"Suppose I wasn't pretty anymore? Suppose—"

"You will always be beautiful to me, sweet darlin'," he whispered as he kissed her, "no matter what time and fate and age do to you. Physical beauty is fleeting, Silver, but I see you with my heart. I'll always love you, and fate and time and age can never, ever change you for me."

She wept then and he held her close and kissed her, wishing he could tell her that he knew her secret already and didn't care, but he was too afraid she would think it pity instead of love and run away, never to return.

Finally they dropped off to sleep.

Jake Dallinger had stood staring after the governess as she went down the back stairs.

Gawd Almighty! He must have been purdee blind not to recognize her! Of course she was wearing glasses and had her hair dyed and done up in a bun, but she was still purty as a speckled pup except for a few small scars on that face. He pushed his hat back and scratched the bald place on his scalp.

Her scared expression had told him she didn't know she wasn't wanted for murder and robbery in Chicago. Now what should he do about that? With a grin of pleasure, he lit one of the cheap, strong stogies he favored and sauntered down the steps and out into the back alley.

A rider galloped up. "Hey, Jake! I been looking for you!"

"You found me. Whata you want?"

"Colonel Chivington sent me to fetch you. The weather's going to be turning cold and our old guide, Beckworth, has the rheumatiz so bad, he's useless."

"So?"

"So the colonel's decided to march out to that Injun camp and wipe them out. It'll take a few days to get there, but they won't be expecting us in bad weather. We don't know the shortcuts. Will you come?"

"Tell the Colonel I sure as hell will!" He named the meeting place on the Plains. "I'll come as quick as I kin get a good horse under me!" Jake stood smoking his cigar and staring after the rider as he galloped away. It was gonna be a plumb pleasure to ride out there and lead the Colorado Third Volunteers to that Injun camp on Sand Creek. They might find it eventually without him, but Jake knew the buffalo plains of eastern Colorado Territory well. He could lead them to that camp so quick, the Injuns might be caught asleep in their blankets. Killing Cheyenne would be more fun than rape—of course, they'd probably do some of that, too. He owed them redskins revenge for what Iron Knife and his father before him had done to Jake. But first he needed to see Lon Brett.

He walked briskly to the Progressive Hall Saloon,

384

found Lon sitting at a back table playing poker, and signaled him that they needed to talk.

"What is it?" Lon joined him at a small table against the wall. "You got something to tell me?"

"I'm going off to help Colonel Chivington," Jake drawled. "May not be back for a few weeks. There's lots of folks out, some of them pretty drunk and rowdy, so you can move around easy without anyone paying you much mind."

Lon's handsome face frowned. "Get to the point."

"The point is, I found that girl you been searching for, and she don't seem to know she ain't wanted by the sheriff."

Lon jerked up, interested. "Where is she?"

"What's it worth to you?"

"Whatever you say it is."

Jake laughed. "She's been right under your nose ever since you hit town. And by the way, that place called the Duchess' Palace that's been givin' you such competition, the Duchess ain't Spanish and she ain't no Duchess. She's just a little Arapaho Injun whore I've known from a long time back. Now how's Denver gonna feel about that?"

"The girl!" Lon demanded, pounding his fist on the table. "What about the girl who helped kill my brother?"

"I'm getting to that." Jake put his hand on the handle of the big whip. "What I want is for you to get rid of the Duchess, and hand the Palace over to me. And I hope you won't kill that Silver girl. When I get back, I intend to enjoy the hell out of her."

Lon grinned. "Handing her over to you might be more enjoyable than killing her."

"I can think of lots of ways to enjoy a woman."

Lon chewed his cigar and nodded. "I'll bet you could!"

Jake stood up. "When I take control of the Palace, I'd like to have the girl awhile for my own private use." He winked. "In the dark, those big tits of hers and those long, slim legs make up for whatever welts you put on her and those few scars on her face."

Lon Brett stared at him. "What the hell are you telling me?"

"You damned fool! The girl has been under your nose the whole time with her hair dyed and hiding behind spectacles and drab clothes so's no one in the world would recognize her.' He pushed his Western hat back. "Now remember what you promised me." He turned to go. "The bitch you're looking for is the governess to the Duchess's kid!"

Chapter Twenty

Cherokee came awake with a start in the darkness, wondering what had awakened him. Silver still lay curled asleep next to him.

The slight rap at the door echoed again. He got up, went to the door, and opened it. Keso stood there.

"Boss, that man, that Jake Dallinger—"

"Shh!" Cherokee held up a warning finger, then looked toward where Silver lay asleep. He tiptoed across the room, got his boots, coat, and pistol, went out into the hall, and closed the door behind him. "Talk soft and tell me what you know."

"That Dallinger fella came to the barn a while ago, saddled his horse, and took off like the devil was nippin' at his heels."

"Headed where?"

"East. Said something about going out the Cherry Creek Road. He's goin' to meet the Third soldiers. Colonel's sent for him to scout the way to the Cheyenne camp on Sand Creek."

Cherokee swore softly under his breath. "The volunteers might not even find that camp if he doesn't get there. At least without a good scout, they'll be slowed down. Iron Knife's gone ahead to warn his people, but who knows if they'll listen to him?"

He stood there a long moment. If he tried to do anything to stop Dallinger, Silver would realize he wasn't blind after all and he might lose her.

"Boss, it ain't your problem. Don't get involved."

"That's just what I was thinking myself, Keso," he said uncertainly, "and yet, if everyone thought only of himself, there would be no justice in this world."

The boy looked at him, puzzlement in his face. "So does that mean you are going to try to stop him? How can you when—?"

"It's a long story, Keso, but I'm gradually getting my sight back. I owe the Cheyenne; they saved my life when I was desperate." He paused, weighing the consequences of his actions. He could ride out to try to intercept Dallinger and help the Cheyenne, but in doing so, he would lose Silver. Honor against love. What a choice!

"Boss?"

He sighed, knowing he had no alternative. "I'm a man, Keso, and a man's gotta do what a man's gotta do, no matter what it costs him personally. This is a debt of honor, and I'm sworn to repay Iron Knife for what he's done for me!"

He started walking at a brisk clip, the boy almost running to keep up with him. "But, boss, the army may find the Cheyenne anyway."

"They may, but I can lessen the chances by putting Dallinger out of action—or at least slow them down.

388

Besides, I owe him justice because he killed my partners."

They went to the barn and he saddled quickly. Although it was late Saturday night, there was a more boisterous crowd than usual on the streets and most of them looked drunk.

"Keso, I may not be back." He strapped on his pistol. "He may get me first, and by morning, she'll know about my sight when she realizes I'm gone, so that's over."

"Won't she be glad you can see?"

"Oh sure, but even if I beat Jake and come back for her, I think she'll run away and hide herself. I won't be able to convince her I love her. She'll call it pity." He swung up on the horse, the saddle leather creaking.

The boy looked up at him hopefully. "You're not coming back?"

"There's a little matter of gold in the Palace safe that rightly belongs to me, but I don't know how I could reclaim it. If I get killed, Keso, you tell the governess what happened and tell her I loved her more than she knew."

"Why don't you come back and tell her yourself?"

Cherokee shook his head. "I hate to say it, but I think she may be too vain to understand, but maybe that's not her fault. Her looks meant more to her than I ever did, I reckon."

He hesitated, wanting to take the lonely boy with him, but he wouldn't expose Keso to danger. He nodded good-bye and put his spurs to his horse. If he could overtake Dallinger and kill him, he might save the Cheyenne, or at least give them a little more time to escape the cavalry. Cherokee didn't look back as he rode through the rowdy crowds in the streets.

Keso stared after the big man riding off to the east. Somehow he had dared hope the half-breed might want a stray kid. Keso would manage alone; he had for a long time. But he would like to be part of a family. With a sigh, he curled back up in the hay and went to sleep.

Lon Brett was more than a little drunk. He knew it because he couldn't focus well on his watch when he pulled it out and looked at it. The Saturday night crowd around him at the Progressive was as drunk as he was.

He leaned back in his chair and tried to keep his thoughts on the poker game at his table and all the laughing people, but his mind was on the girl at the Palace. Damn her to hell, she had had some part in the murder of his brother. He was sure of it, even though the police had that confession from Al Trovato. The Italian was trying to shield her, that was all. There was no legal way Lon could bring her to justice. Hell, he didn't want justice, he wanted revenge!

Lon had a sudden idea and went looking for Big Ed. "You still wanting an excuse to get rid of the Duchess and her saloon?"

Big Ed looked up from his drink. "That's a fool question. You know I do!"

Lon glanced around. "It's a big crowd and rowdy tonight with the holidays going on. Wouldn't take but a few free drinks and a hot speech to get them out in the streets and ready to burn the Palace down. I'm told that's how the Duchess got a mob to destroy the River House Saloon back in '62, when it burned."

Big Ed paused and studied him. "What's going on and what's in it for you?"

"Just say I'm trying to help a friend—you." Lon grinned.

Big Ed said something obscene. "Don't give me that! What's in this for you?"

Lon played with the ends of his string tie. "Well, if your business gets better, I do better because I'm an employee."

"Tell me what you're really after!"

"All right." Lon leaned closer. "I want the governess to do with as I please."

"You mean that drab little thing that looks after the Duchess's kid? I seen her on the street, Lon, are you drunk? She ain't so special—"

"I want revenge for an old wrong," Lon said softly through gritted teeth. "I want to rape her until she begs for mercy and then I want to kill her slow."

Big Ed stared up at him. "I reckon the less I know about that, the better. It would be great not to have to compete with the Palace anymore."

Lon nodded.

"You get rid of the Duchess for me, I sure don't care what happens to the drab mouse. What do you know that might turn this crowd into a mob?"

"A fella just told me something. I'm not sure he meant to. Might have been a little drunk. The Duchess is Injun, Ed, a dog-eatin' Injun—Arapaho."

Ed stared at him through the drifting cigar smoke, thunder-struck. "Ain't that one of the two tribes that's been causing all the trouble around here?"

"Yep." Lon fiddled with his string tie. "When you stop and think of it, don't she look Injun?"

Big Ed stood up and looked at Lon a long moment. Then he pushed his way through the crowd to the bar, and banged on it with one of the big mallets used to knock the plug out of a barrel of whiskey. "Listen, everyone!" he shouted. "Listen!"

The noise and piano music hardly slowed at all. He nodded at Lon and banged the mallet against the bar again. "Free drinks on the house!" he shouted. "Free drinks for everyone!"

Almost miraculously, the crowd heard that. The men raised a cheer, then pushed their way to the bar for their reward.

Big Ed looked around as everyone drank. "And now another free round of drinks on the house!"

More cheering as the bartenders poured cheap whiskey into dozens of outstretched glasses.

Big Ed jumped up on the bar. "A toast!" he shouted. "I want to make a toast!"

Men paused, glasses in hand, listening.

Lon leaned against the table and watched. Big Ed held his glass high and looked around at the crowd. "A toast! A toast to this town that won't let that damned bunch of redskins get by with what they been doing to decent folks!"

A cheer went up, but Big Ed held up his hand for silence. "It only grieves me we got to put up with a damned Injun running a place wide open and calling herself a fancy Duchess! We all know she's nothing but an Injun! Who does she think she's fooling anyhow?"

A murmur went through the crowd.

Big Ed shouted. "Are we gonna stand for this? Are we gonna put up with that damned Injun whore right here in the middle of Denver while her in-laws kill white folks?"

He looked toward Lon and Lon shouted, "Hell, no! We won't stand for it! Will we, men?"

An angry murmur went through the saloon.

Lon shouted louder. "Who's going to help me bring her to justice?"

A cry went up from the drunken crowd.

Lon waved his fist. "Free drinks for every decent man who'll help me clean that redskin and her cheating card sharps and diseased whores out of this town!"

"He's right!" men shouted. "Let's burn her out! She's the only frame building left! Let's burn her out!"

Lon watched as the drunken crowd shouted and surged forward toward the doors, even as Big Ed smiled and retreated back into a corner. It amazed Lon that, like sheep, a mob would do anything suggested to them in the name of "doing what's right." For only a moment, he was dumbfounded, and then he ran to lead the men who pushed through the doors and surged out into the cold November night.

From somewhere, torches appeared, were set ablaze, and handed around. When it was what the democratic majority wanted, shouldn't the people be able to prevail?

Someone thrust a torch into Lon's hands and he paused before the crowd, waving it like a banner. "All right, men, think of the money you've lost in the Palace! Think of that red-skinned bitch spreading the pox around with her diseased whores! Let's do what's right!"

The roar of the crowd drowned his out now and he turned and was swept along the street by the mob, everyone shouting and waving torches. Men along the sidewalks paused and ran to join in, not seeming to know or care where the crowd was bound for, just eager to get in on the excitement.

And it was exciting! Lon took a deep breath of the scent of burning pitch as the bright orange flares lit up the night and the crowd roared and surged around him. His heart beat hard with vengeance. He had waited for this moment a long, long time.

By the time they reached the Palace, the mob had grown to several hundred men, all shouting and waving torches. Where the law was tonight, Lon didn't know or care. If they were smart, they'd stay out of the crowd's way until justice was done.

Customers inside the Palace seemed to rush outside when they saw the crowd coming down the stret. All he had to do now was hold them back for a moment while he went in and got the governess.

"Men!" Brett shouted as they surged around him in front of the Palace. "Men, hold up a moment!"

Only a few even heard him as they pushed forward. "What's he want? I think he's changed his mind and is trying to stop us! Stop us, hell! We're going to do what's right!"

Lon Brett threw up his hand and shouted for silence, but no one seemed to listen. This wouldn't do! He wanted to get his hands on that girl first. "Men! Stop!"

The crowd would not be done out of its fun. As they surged forward, Lon Brett realized too late that a mob was like a wild animal on the loose and looking for prey.

"No!" they shouted. "No, we won't be stopped! Let's burn the Palace! Death to the red-skinned whore!"

Lon tried to hold them back as they pressed forward with their torches. Someone hit him, knocking him against the hitching post. He dropped his torch and wiped the blood from his mouth, still shouting for the mob to stop long enough for him to go in and get the governess. No one paid any attention as they pushed ahead, setting the tinder-dry wood on fire. He managed to run up on the steps before the door. "No, men! Stop! Listen to me!"

All around him, men were torching the dry wooden building and shouting drunkenly. He ran right up in front of the doors and tried to pull a torch from someone's hands. The man knocked him down. Then the dozens of people came at him, walking on him as they hurried to set the Palace ablaze.

Lon Brett screamed in pain, trying to fight his way to his feet and escape from the hundreds of boots that were trampling him as the mob pushed forward. Lon shrieked and struggled but no one seemed to hear him. The crowd moved like some big uncontrolled animal and crushed him beneath their feet. The last thing he saw was the fire catching the paint on fire and men running inside to set fire to the tables and velvet drapes.

At the Essex, Silver came awake with a start, wondering what had awakened her. She sat up in bed, looking around. "Cherokee?"

No answer. Where could he be? The room was dark and she was suddenly afraid of the dark without him by her side. What was that noise outside? She went to the window and looked out. In the black night, a faint orange glow lit the sky. *Fire.*

The thought sent a shiver of fear through her after what they'd all experienced in the April fire of last year. Almost the whole downtown had burned and been rebuilt out of bricks.

The Palace was the only frame building in the area. Silver jerked on her clothes, grabbed her cloak, and ran for the street. *Waanibe*. She had left Waanibe alone and asleep. Silver fairly flew down the steps and out into the street. For a long moment, she looked, trying to pinpoint the source of the blaze. *The Palace*. It had to be the Palace. In that split second, memories came back to her of the Nugget burning with all her hopes and dreams.

Waanibe. Surely the Duchess would get the child out. Silver took off at a dead run toward the Palace.

The Duchess had looked up from her table in the far corner as a bartender came running and shouted over the loud piano, "Ma'am, there's a mob coming down the street!"

"So what? It's the holiday season and Saturday night besides. Some of the boys have had a little too much to drink, that's all!"

He shook his head. "You better come look. Somehow I think there's more to it than that."

She frowned as she went to the window. A crowd marched down the street carrying torches. The orange and yellow flames threw a strange glow over the faces of the mob. A handsome man led the bunch and she tried to remember who he was and where he might be leading the men.

Around her, customers and dancing girls had heard the noise and looked at each other uneasily. A few went to the windows and door for a look.

The piano stopped playing and Gray Dove swore under her breath. With all this excitement, first thing she knew, her customers would be out there in the street, tagging along wherever the crowd was headed and she'd lose money.

"Duchess!" the bartender shouted. "I think they're coming here!"

"Oh hell, no! Why would they?"

But the people around her were already pushing through the doors front and back to get outside. She stood transfixed, staring out at the handsome man raising his arm for silence, trying to tell the crowd something, but the crowd was drunk and angry, not listening to him.

Suddenly, she remembered where she had seen the handsome man before—he worked for Big Ed Chase at the Progressive. For a split second, she remembered how she had encouraged a similar mob only two years ago. Then she realized that the torches were moving toward the Palace doors, the mob surging right over the man who had tried to hold them back. *What in the hell was going on?*

"Stop them!" she shouted at her bartenders and card dealers. "Get out there and do something! Stop them!" But no one seemed to hear her or pay any attention, they were all scrambling for the exits.

Gray Dove stood transfixed for a moment as angry men ran through the front door with their flaming sticks.

They were going to destroy everything she had worked for—everything that meant anything to her! She had worked too hard and too long to stand by idly and let that happen. With a curse, she ran behind the bar and grabbed a shotgun even as someone torched the velvet stage curtains and some of the chairs.

In the smoke that billowed and drifted around her, she hardly saw what she was aiming for, but she fired and the man fell. His torch rolled across the floor and against the ornate bar.

"Stop it! Stop it, I say!" She ran out from behind the bar, swearing and swinging the shotgun, but no one paid any attention to her at all.

Two men grabbed up whiskey behind the bar, took big gulps, then poured the remainder on the flames. The red fire roared even brighter. All the faces around her glowed with a strange light, the flames reflected in the wild, wide eyes. She might as well be dealing with wolves!

Water! What she needed was water! There was always a bucket behind the bar for just such emergencies. Gray Dove ran behind the bar, grabbed it, and splashed it on the flames that had now reached the bottles of whiskey. The bottles began to explode as they got hot, the alcohol feeding the flames. She had to get away from here! Lifting her skirts, she ran from behind the bar and looked around for help. All her employees and the customers had deserted her, running helter-skelter for the doors. Even the whores ran screaming down the fancy stairway, half-dressed, followed by men in their underwear, carrying their boots. Within minutes, only she and a dozen crazy men with flaming torches were left inside.

This was her saloon, and she wouldn't let them burn it! She ran up to one man and fought him to jerk the torch from his hands. When she did so, she swung it as a weapon and caught him across the face with it. His scream was so high, it hurt her ears, and then it broke off in the middle.

"Stop it! God damn it! Stop it!" All around her, tables and chairs and velvet cushions blazed. Men were raiding her liquor stock, drinking, and pouring some on the floor so the flames leapt along it. The acrid scent of burning

398

was all around her, the smoke swirling. The saloon lit up in an eerie glow. Then the heat reached the mirror behind the bar and it exploded like a cannon shot, sending a shower of glass tinkling in every direction.

The Palace was fully ablaze. She wouldn't be able to stop it. The whole fire would be out of control in a few minutes. She could only save what she could carry out in her arms. *What was of the most value in the world to her?*

She paused, looking up the ornate stairway. Already the lush scarlet carpet on the stairs smoldered. She had only a couple of minutes to get up there and get out before she was trapped. Coughing and choking on the smoke, Gray Dove ran up the stairs and stopped uncertainly in the hall. She hadn't seen the governess or Waanibe run out. No doubt they were still asleep in their rooms.

What did she care most about? Once it would have been the child, when she thought Wannie was Iron Knife's. As Jake's whelp, the little girl meant less than nothing. *Money. The gold dust Jake had put in her big safe. The fabulous jewels in the box on her bureau.* Yes, those she could carry out in her arms. With that much wealth, she could start over someplace else.

She ran into her office. First she would get the gold out of the safe and as much money as she could carry, then she would save her jewels.

Faintly, she heard Wannie crying and afraid. *Jake Dallinger's child.* Gray Dove didn't want her; she never had. She realized that now as she ignored the cries and ran to her safe. All the child had meant to her was that someday Gray Dove might use her to get her true love back. Besides, the brat liked the governess best. Well, let them both find their way out the best way they could!

Gray Dove knelt by the safe and began to work the combination. She would sweep all the gold and silver into her skirt and carry it that way, then go save her jewels. There wasn't a moment to lose—the building burned fiercely, the flames lighting up the dark office. She felt the heat around her and hesitated, tempted to get up and run for the back stairs. *Her money.* She couldn't leave it behind. She still had a couple of minutes to save her treasure if she hurried.

The child sobbed faintly but Gray Dove didn't even look up as she swung the heavy door open. The flames behind her reflected off the gold and silver coins stacked in neat piles inside, the beaded bags behind that. Gold and silver—a lot of it! Enough to give her a fresh start someplace. Maybe San Francisco.

Gray Dove raked some of the treasure off into her skirt. Beneath her, the floor trembled and she realized the hungry flames were gradually devouring the frame-work that held up the second story. The safe shook slightly.

Cautiously, she looked around. She had a skirt full of money; she ought to make a run for it. But there was still so much more in the safe. *Her* treasure. *Hers!* She had worked and cheated and schemed to get it; she wasn't going to leave any of it behind! The fire seemed all around her now, the heat unbearable on her dark skin.

A spark fell on her sleeve and she slapped it out with a shudder. When she was just a girl, she and her mother had been captured by a Pawnee war party. Gray Dove had bought her own life by helping the braves torture her mother to death by fire. Then she charmed the warriors with her body until she managed to kill one and escape as he raped her.

Fire. The old memories came back and with it, the horror of burning flesh. No, she didn't want to burn to death, there couldn't be a worse way to die. The building shuddered a little as the floor slumped. She saw the black safe tremble uncertainly and she tried to jump backward, out of its way, but the skirt full of glittering treasure slowed her, and she stumbled as she tried to jump clear.

Almost in slow motion, she fell back as the big safe toppled forward and gold and silver coins went everywhere, ringing as they hit the floor and rolled. The heavy safe crashed forward even as she tripped in trying to get out of the way. Gray Dove screamed with pain as the iron safe crushed down on her ankle.

For a moment, she was in such pain, she thought she would pass out. *Her leg!* She was caught like a rabbit in a trap. Even though it was agony to pull at her leg, she did it, knowing she had to escape or die. There wasn't a moment to lose. Any minute now, the second floor would crash down through the ceiling, taking her and the safe straight down into a fiery hell.

She would not die the way her mother had died! Gray Dove was a survivor. She would crawl out from under this thing and make it down the back stairs. Frantically, she struggled. Forgotten now, gold coins rolled away from her skirt and clattered as they spun on the floor. With desperate hands, she beat and pushed at the great iron safe, struggling to lift it from her leg.

She felt the heat of the flames moving closer. She would not die by inches like some primitive Indian torture. She would not die like her mother! A knife! If she could reach a knife or a piece of broken glass or anything sharp, she would cut her leg off and crawl down the back stairs. Gray Dove twisted and pulled to reach anything

401

she might be able to use, but the only thing within reach was money—lots and lots of gold dust and piles of coins.

Useless. So useless. She would trade them all right now for a ragged piece of metal or a man brave enough to come into the office and lift the safe from her leg. But as she had been that long-ago day among the Pawnees, everyone was intent on saving his own life. No one came down the hall to answer her shout for help.

She began to scream in sheer terror, but the roar of the flames drowned out her voice. She saw her mother's agonized face before her now, resigned, calm. Gray Dove was going to die as her mother had died after all—except she would be surrounded by her treasure, trapped by that she valued most. She threw back her head and laughed, feeling the scarlet flames already singeing her hair.

Chapter Twenty-One

Silver ran through the cold November night toward the faint glow of the fire ahead. *Could it be the Palace?* As the only frame building left in the area, it had to be!

She rounded the corner and sighed as she saw the raging flames. The Palace! It was the Palace! An unruly crowd stood out front, watching the building burn.

Gasping for air, Silver pushed her way through the mob to the front. "The Duchess! Has anyone seen the Duchess? Did she get the child out?"

The men looked at her, shame and drunken bewilderment on their unshaven faces. Obviously no one had thought about the little girl. Silver paused uncertainly, the heat from the inferno hot against her face. There were hundreds of people in the street watching the fire, dance hall girls mixed with loafers and prospectors. The Duchess could be somewhere in the crowd, but Silver didn't see the child anywhere. "I'm going in!"

One of the men caught her arm. "You can't go in there, lady, that place is a tinderbox! Anytime now, the whole thing will collapse!"

That was true. Even as Silver stared up at the roaring flames, she knew that in only a few more minutes, the structure would be totally consumed. But Wannie might still be in her little bed asleep and no one else appeared ready to save her.

Silver pulled out of his grasp and ran toward the front entrance.

"Stop her! Stop that crazy girl! She'll burn to death!" But Silver was too quick for them. Skillfully, she eluded hands reaching out to stop her and dashed through the doors of the Palace.

So this was what hell was like, she thought as the heat seemed to reach out for her, with all its bright orange and red and yellow. The smoke grew so thick it choked her and brought tears to her eyes. She couldn't see—how could she find her way?

The stairs. She could make out the fancy stairway in the glow of the flames. Silver ran up the stairs, although most of them were already on fire, the steps hot under her small feet. "Wannie? Wannie? Are you up here?"

For a moment as she paused in the hallway and looked below, she thought only of herself and what a terrifying way it would be to die, the second story collapsing down into that roaring inferno. She almost turned and ran back down the stairs, wanting to save herself. Then she heard the Duchess scream for help. Silver stumbled into the office and saw the woman pinned beneath the safe.

"Save me! Save me! I'll give you anything! Anything you want!"

Silver ran to her, choking and coughing on the sooty smoke. One look told her the story—the money and the gold were scattered around. The Duchess had tried to save her wealth and the safe had fallen, trapping her.

"Hold on! I'll move it!" Silver put her shoulder against the safe and tried. She would only have to lift it a few inches to free the Duchess's foot. She strained and pushed while the woman screamed. No use. In her zeal to protect her fortune, the Duchess had bought only the very heaviest safe. The thing must weight a half a ton or more.

Silver looked around for a board or anything she might use as a level. If she could just move it a couple of inches . . .

She found a board and put it under the edge. "I'll move it!" she puffed. "I'll move it now!"

The weight of the safe made a liar of her. She strained with everything in her to move the safe those precious, life-giving inches. Perspiration beaded on her face and her arms ached as she struggled. Nothing happened. Around her, the flames leaped higher. "I've got to get help!" she shouted. "I'll get men to come up and lift it!"

"Anything! I'll pay anything!" the woman screamed.

"Wannie!" Silver shouted at her. "Where's Wannie?"

"Forget her! Save me!"

The little girl must be still up here somewhere. The Duchess had elected to try to save her money first.

Then Silver heard the weeping of the frightened little girl over the roar of the flames. "Silvery! Silvery! Where are you! I'm afraid!"

Silver stumbled toward the sound, through the office door into the Duchess's bedroom. She would carry the child out and get some big men to come back in and lift the safe off the Duchess's leg. "Wannie, where are you? I'm coming for you!"

She found her in the Duchess's bedroom, huddled down by a chair. *What was she doing in here?* "Oh, baby, I was so worried about you!"

"Silvery! I knew you'd come!" Wannie threw her arms around Silver's neck and Silver hugged her.

"There, there, honey, we'll get down the back stairs. It's going to be all right, you'll see!"

The flames lit up the jewelry box on the bureau, the light sparkling on the gems scattered in the open box. *A fortune in gold and jewels,* Silver thought. Her own gold nugget bracelet was in that box. But she couldn't carry both the jewels and the child, and the child mattered most of all to her.

"Here, honey, hang on to me, we've got to get out of here!" She struggled to lift the little girl, still clad in her long nightgown. Silver didn't remember her being so heavy. Carrying Waanibe was slowing her down and the flames seemed to be all around them now. She could save herself if she dropped the child and ran for the back stairs.

The thought crossed her mind as she stumbled down the dark hall. Silver didn't want to die, but she wouldn't abandon the child who wrapped chubby arms around her neck and hid her tearstained face against Silver's neck. "I'm scared, Silvery! I'm scared!"

"It's okay, baby," Silver soothed her. "We'll do just fine! Pretend it's a game like dress-up or princess—" She couldn't say anymore; she was gasping for air in the smoky heat that seemed to singe her hair and clothes as she stumbled down the hall toward the back stairs. It seemed like a million miles, and she began to wonder if there was any chance she would make it. Both of them were choking on the smoke now. It seemed far . . . too far . . .

Silver was so very, very tired. It would be easier just to give up and sit down in the hall and close her eyes. If she could just rest a moment or two, then she could go on. But to stop was to die, she knew that. Clutching the little girl to her, Silver forced herself to put one foot ahead of the other as she felt her way blindly down the hall. She had to save this child and get some help for the Duchess. That alone kept her staggering blindly through the thick smoke toward the back stairs.

Finally, she stood at the top of the stairs, the child trembling in her arms. "Wannie, baby, we're almost there. We'll make it now."

She wasn't at all sure about that, but she had to keep saying it over and over to force her legs to work. The very steps were on fire as she started down them, the heat on the soles of her shoes almost unbearable.

Shoes. She had left behind her beloved silver shoes that Cherokee had given her. No matter. What were things like shoes and jewelry worth compared to lives?

The trip along those stairs seemed almost like a descent into hell, the flames of the walls licking out at her as she staggered down them. Finally, she was out into the night. She and Waanibe took deep gulps of the crisp, life-giving air as she half carried, half dragged the little girl away from the building.

Silver turned to look back. The whole saloon was ablaze now. *The Duchess.* She had to get help for

407

the Duchess.

She saw the man she recognized as a reporter for the *Rocky Mountain News*, Todd Shaw. "What's happened? I just got here!"

Silver pointed without turning loose of Waanibe. "The Duchess is still in there. Up in her office! Get some men! She's trapped!"

"I'll go!"

But she caught his arm. "No, you can't move the safe alone. It's too heavy! Get some men!"

He ran off into the crowd to find help. Silver held the child close, realizing Waanibe hadn't asked about her mother once. She would take Wannie back to the hotel and Cherokee. It occurred to her that he wasn't there. Where was Cherokee now when she needed him so badly?

Keso. Keso would know where he was. Uncertainly, Silver turned toward the roaring blaze. Maybe she should try to go back in and see what she could do to help the Duchess although Silver was powerless to move the giant safe. Todd Shaw would get volunteers. But it would take a dozen powerful men to move it enough to get it off the woman's ankle. Then even as she watched, the second story collapsed with a roar and a shower of sparks flew up into the blackness of the night.

"Oh my God!" Silver gasped, hugging the child close and staring with horror at the pile of blazing rubble. *Too late.* It was too late. What to do now?

Cherokee. She had never needed him more than she needed the warm comfort of his arms right now.

Waanibe twisted her little face around to smile at Silver. "I got a treasure for you."

"Not now, baby, we'll play later." Silver never put her down as she started toward the stable. She wouldn't tell Waanibe about her mother yet. Silver wasn't quite sure what to do, but she didn't want to lose the child. Probably some of the do-gooders of the town would try to separate them, and put Waanibe in an orphanage. Cherokee would know what to do.

It seemed like a long way to the stable, carrying the child through the crowds who were all running to see the fire. Even Keso had come out of the stable and stood in the middle of the street, his dark eyes wide. "Miss, what's happened? Is the Palace on fire?"

"The Palace is gone," she sighed wearily, standing the little girl on her feet beside her. "Never mind all that now. Where's Cherokee? He's not in his room."

Keso looked at her along moment. "He's gone."

Silver blinked in surprise. "Gone? How could he be gone? What—"

"He's gone to stop Jake Dallinger from reaching the soldiers. I don't think he's coming back."

A thousand questions came to her mind, but she grabbed the boy's thin shoulder. "How can he be gone? Who led him? If he can't see, how could—"

"But he can see," Keso said. "I wasn't supposed to tell you, but what difference does it make now?"

Her hands flew to her scarred face. She didn't understand any of it. Cherokee could see? She was glad for him—so glad! But that meant he would know she was ugly. She yearned for his love, but she couldn't abide his pity. She turned away. What would she do now?

Behind her, the boy said, "You ain't going after him?"

She shrugged. "I'm glad for him, but he won't need me

anymore if he can see. He'll find another girl some-where—a pretty girl."

"Then it's just like he said! I'm glad you're leaving!" the boy shouted. "You ain't worth it, you know that? You don't deserve to have him! You know why he ain't coming back? He said you would leave him when you knew. That was why he's been pretending to be blind the last couple of days. He didn't want to lose you, but you ain't worthy of him and I hope you never get him back!"

Whirling, she faced the furious child and realized suddenly how much he was suffering because Cherokee had gone. She knelt and grabbed the boy's thin shoulders. "Tell me again where he's gone, Keso. Tell me or I'll shake your teeth out!"

"He's gone to stop that Dallinger fella! If that one don't scout for the soldiers, they might not find the Cheyenne camp, or at least, not for a couple of extra days. He's gone to stop the scout and then he's riding on out. You know what he said?" The boy was screaming at her now. "He said you were too vain and self-pitying to know love when you saw it. He loves you, miss, and all you can think about is your face!"

She stood up slowly. Always, her mother had told her she was worthless without her beauty and yet tonight she knew she wasn't. She had saved a child's life and a man loved her, no matter how scarred she was. Silver turned and looked toward the east. Somewhere out there, Cherokee and the man she feared might already be in a life-and-death battle.

Suppose Cherokee lost? She shuddered at the thought. In that case, Silver might be riding right into Dallinger's clutches and she was so afraid of him. That didn't matter.

410

All that mattered was that she be at Cherokee's side, whatever happened—if he still wanted her.

"Keso, saddle me the Duchess's horse and be quick about it!"

His dark eyes lit up with a grin. "Yes ma'am!"

She took Waanibe's hand and went into the barn as the Indian boy ran to do her bidding. Silver wasn't quite sure what she was going to do, but one thing was certain: if she could overtake Cherokee, she would make sure that he knew she did love him and the rest was up to him.

Waanibe clung to her hand in the darkness of the barn. "I got a treasure to put in your pocket, Silvery."

"Sure, dear, sure." She patted the dark head with her free hand absently. Later she would tell Waanibe about her mother and play games with her, but now she had no time for all that.

Keso led the saddled horse out. "Here you are, miss. If you find him, are you coming back?"

"Whatever he wants to do, I'll do." She paused, trying to decide what to do about Waanibe. What if she left her here and someone took charge of her and turned her over to an orphanage? She might leave her with Keso, but he was just a boy himself. He couldn't stop grown-ups if they decided to take custody of the Duchess's child.

She grabbed Waanibe's waist and lifted her up on the horse, thinking how tall and heavy the child was becoming. Then she swung up on the horse herself, awkward in the billowing skirt. "Which way did he go?"

Keso pointed. "Out the Cherry Creek Road. This is a thoroughbred, miss, faster than any horse in town. If you ride like the wind, you might catch him. And when you do . . ."

411

"Yes?" She looked down on him, feeling Wannie's two little arms about her waist.

He looked up at her wistfully a long moment. "Tell him I wish him luck."

Silver nodded and put her heels to the startled thoroughbred. Its long legs spread out and it took off at a ground-eating gallop.

Cherokee had taken off after Jake Dallinger in a rush, but then slowed his horse as he checked the scout's tracks in the moonlight and realized Dallinger was riding east at a more leisurely pace. Perhaps he knew a short-cut somewhere up ahead or, thinking he had plenty of time, didn't want to tire his horse.

At the Four Mile House, the stage stop four miles east of Denver, Cherokee stopped and inquired. Yes, a big, bearded man had stopped for whiskey and food less than an hour ago. Cherokee felt chilled and the whiskey looked so good, he could almost taste it. But he turned his back with determination and mounted his horse.

After that, Cherokee proceeded along the trail with caution. It was one thing to have Jake Dallinger in broad daylight on a flat plain up ahead of him, it was quite another to be riding through brush along the creek in the dark, with a shrewd, trail-wise scout ahead of him. Jake was smart enough to ambush him if the scout should realize he was being trailed.

For reassurance, Cherokee felt the butt of his pistol and wished he had a saddle gun. A man armed with a pistol was at a distinct disadvantage if he came up against an hombre armed with a rifle, and one of the things Doc

412

had said was that Jake was carrying a Sharps rifle.

The moonlight threw grotesque shadows along the trail. Cherokee listened intently to the noises of the cold night, the Indian ways of his grandmother coming back to him with a rush. Somewhere in the stunted trees along the river, an *u-gu-gu*, an owl, hooted and the hair rose up on the back of Cherokee's neck. In almost all the tribes, an owl hooting at night foretold death. *The question was: whose?*

It didn't matter; he couldn't turn back. He had sworn vengeance for the murder of his two old partners, and given Iron Knife his word that he would do whatever he could to help the Cheyenne should he ever have the chance. This was the chance and Cherokee always kept his word.

Silver. She would have found out sooner or later that he was no longer blind, but if it had been later, maybe by then he would have convinced her that what he felt was love, not pity. When he had met her, he had thought her only a pretty white whore, but now she was a lady to him—a great lady. And he had come to know that all white women were not whores any more than all Indians were "red devils." His grandmother's bitterness at his father had poisoned her thinking, and in turn, she had poisoned her grandson's.

He kept alert as he rode, expecting that Jake was a cunning coyote who might figure on being followed and be lying in wait. Well, Cherokee knew a little about ambush. Not for nothing had his grandmother called him *Tsu-no-yv-gi*, Rattler. How many times had he seen a big diamondback strike with deadly speed and accuracy?

Cherokee thought he heard a sound behind him, and

413

glanced over his shoulder. Somewhere on the other side of the horizon, a giant fire roared. He could see its faint orange glow in the distance. What could be burning? Could that be Denver? For a long moment, he was tempted to turn around and go back, remembering that when a blaze began, without much fire protection, sometimes whole streets burned. But if Silver was in any danger, Todd Shaw would look out for her, and little Keso was a tough street kid who had been looking after himself long before Cherokee ever came on the scene.

The sound must have been only *u-no-le*, the wind, stirring dead leaves behind him. Up ahead was a bend in the trail that passed through a little grove of cottonwood and willow—the perfect place for a trap. Cherokee reined in and considered a long moment. The blood of warriors ran in his veins and the Indian lore of a hundred generations of hunters and trappers now stood him in good stead. As a boy, he and his grandmother had hidden out and evaded the white soldiers many times when the bluecoats had come to drag them away to far-off Indian Territory where they did not want to go. If he was going to ambush a man who trailed him, that shadowy grove was the spot he would choose.

Jake Dallinger crouched in the shadows of the willows, listening. He heard the horse rein in and stamp its feet. It wasn't an Indian—no, that mount had iron shoes. He heard the clink of a horseshoe against a pebble.

So he was being followed. Somehow he had known it. Jake reached up and touched the bald scar in his hair. Many years ago when he had been a wagon train scout in

414

Texas, a Comanche war party had tried to scalp him alive. But Jake had survived that time and he had learned well. No Indian knew any more tricks than he did about living off the land and surviving in rough, hostile country.

Could it be some hombre who wanted to join him to ride out and kill Injuns? Jake shook his head, and spat. This bastard was being too cautious—he'd galloped when Jake galloped, walked his horse when Jake walked his to keep from being heard. Gawd Almighty! *Who the hell could it be?*

Whoever it was, Jake would be waiting for him when he came riding through this grove. It would be a purdee pleasure to gun the bastard down.

Jake laid the barrel of the old Sharps across a log, aiming at that open spot on the trail. He wanted a cigar, but he didn't dare light one. If his opponent was trail-smart, he'd smell the smoke scent and know there was a man waiting in the shadows. Instead Jake stuck a cheap stogie between his yellow teeth and chewed on it.

He heard the horse just around the bend snort at the scent of his own gelding tied back behind him in the trees. But Jake had been cautious enough to tie a rag around his mount's muzzle so it couldn't whinny and alert the other rider.

Whoever was out there was a suspicious sonovabitch. He must be reined in just out of sight around the bend. If he proceeded ahead, there was a clear spot in the brush right in Jake's line of fire. If and when the rider came through there, Jake could knock him right out of his saddle. He wished the moon would come out from behind the clouds again so he could see better.

And then the approaching horse began walking again,

his hooves hitting an occasional rock in the trail. Suspicious sonovabitch, but not suspicious and careful enough, Jake thought with a grin and cocked his rifle. Gawd Almighty! It was as dark as the inside of a cow, Jake thought with annoyance. He really liked to get a man silhouetted against the starlight; made it a hellova lot easier. It was an old Injun trick. That was why Indian war parties stayed off hills and rises after dark; they knew they made good targets against the faint light.

Jake chewed his cigar, watched the open patch in the undergrowth, and listened to the horse's hooves moving toward him at a walk. The man in the saddle probably had his hand on his pistol, but it weren't gonna do him not one dad-blamed bit of good, he'd never get a chance to draw down on Jake 'cause Jake didn't aim to give him a chance at a fair draw. Fair play didn't make for a long life in this country. You took a man out any way you could.

Behind him, a twig snapped. Jake looked around and a cottontail scampered past. If he weren't waiting to ambush a man, he'd have enjoyed blowing that rabbit apart just to watch it die, but he didn't have time for that now. Jake had bigger game in mind.

He refocused his attention on the sound of the horse walking around the bend of the trail. This was gonna be easier than taking a sugar tit away from a baby. The rider would never know what hit him when that big fifty-caliber shell blew a hole in him big enough to put a fist through.

The red, shadowy clouds began to drift away from the moon as the horse rounded the bend and the light threw the horse's shadow across the trail. *Blood on the moon.* Jake remembered the old superstition as he squinted one

416

eye and reached to squeeze the trigger. *Blood on the moon. Someone's gonna die tonight.*

That was shore as hell right! The horse rounded the bend and crossed the clear space in the brush, walking past him on the trail. For a split second, he stared in stunned disbelief at the riderless horse, its reins tied to the saddle horn as it continued on past him. Too late he remembered the snapped twig, the disturbed rabbit hopping out of the undergrowth. He'd been outsmarted! Jake tried to whirl around, but now he felt the cold steel of a pistol against the back of his head.

"Hold it right there, you murdering bastard, or I'll forget I don't shoot men in the back!"

Cherokee cocked his pistol and then took a couple of steps back. "All right, you dumb bastard, lift those hands slow and lift them high! I thought you had more savvy than that, Jake. That's an old Indian trick. Figured you knew that one."

Jake cursed as he turned around, his hands high. "Gawd Almighty! I didn't know I was up against an Injun!" He paused, his eyes wide as he stared. "Who the hell are you and what do you want? If it's money, you've picked the wrong man—"

"Oh, I got the right man." Cherokee looked at the big whip on Jake's belt, the silver handle gleaming in the moonlight. "Remember two old men you killed for a little gold up in Mosquito Gulch?"

Jake's mouth fell open and the cigar he'd had clenched between his teeth fell to the ground. "I seen you somewhere before. Ain't you that blind man an Injun kid was—"

"You think I'm blind, you just try anything. I'd welcome a chance to shoot you down like a dog right here and now." Cherokee hesitated. All this time he had planned to do just that. But now that he had the killer in his gun sights, he couldn't do it. He'd thought he would take pleasure in it, but he knew now he'd only feel shame. Whatever the law did about it, if Cherokee took justice into his own hands, he wasn't any better than the big man who stood before him with his hands in the air.

"They'll be looking for me," Jake said. "If I don't show up in the next five minutes, I've got partners out there on the trail who'll come back to deal with you."

"You damned liar! I know you're alone and heading out to scout for the Third Volunteers!"

Jake frowned. "What's that to you? They're Cheyenne and I can tell by lookin' you're not."

Cherokee laughed. "I owe a man a debt and I gave him my word. A real man always keeps his word, Jake. I got friends in that camp, so if you don't get there, there may be enough of a delay for Iron Knife's clan to escape."

"Iron Knife? Is that damned 'breed there? If I'd knowed that from the first—"

"It doesn't matter, you aren't going out there to scout for the army."

"So what are you gonna do with me? If you think they'll take a 'breed's word against a white man's back in Denver, you're mistook."

"I ought to kill you right here myself and save the cost of a judge and jury."

Jake laughed. "I've shot men down like dogs before, but I'll bet you haven't. You don't have the guts for it."

418

"Shut up or I'll spill yours all over this ground!"

Very faintly in the darkness, Cherokee heard a horse coming down the trail he had just traveled. Who could that be? Friend or foe?

Jake turned his head. "Someone's coming."

"I heard it already."

"I forgot you was a 'breed," Jake sneered. "Got ears could hear a mouse step, I reckon."

"You cry out, you're a dead man."

"I ain't movin' none," the other assured him.

The hoofbeats grew louder, a long-legged horse moving at a fast gallop. *Suppose it was another scout or some outlaw?* Cherokee would be at a disadvantage, already holding one man at gunpoint. Cherokee considered knocking Jake across the head with the butt of his pistol so he could give full attention to the intruder. With Jake's old Sharps rifle, Cherokee could take a man out of the saddle as he rounded the bend.

He turned his head slightly, his attention diverted by the approaching hoofbeats. He could—

Jake moved fast as a striking scorpion, his movement a blur as he grabbed up the rifle off the log and swung it hard. The butt caught Cherokee across the arm in a flash of stunning pain and his numb fingers dropped the pistol.

His arm felt on fire, but with his other hand, Cherokee grabbed the rifle by the barrel as Jake drew it back to swing again. His injured arm was too numb to use; it might even be broken. For a split second as they fought over the gun, he wondered why Jake didn't pull the trigger, then realized Jake didn't want to alert the oncoming rider either. Neither knew whether it was friend or foe.

419

His fingers didn't seem to work, but still Cherokee braved the agony to try to use them, fighting to wrestle the rifle away from the big scout. In the struggle, the Sharps fired, the loud bloom so close to Cherokee's ear that he heard nothing but ringing for a moment as they fought. Whoever was on the trail had been alerted now.

They were of equal strength, but Cherokee's arm was at least badly sprained if not broken. They fought for the gun, crashing through the brush in the darkness like two great stags in a life-and-death battle.

Cherokee felt the sweat breaking out on his forehead as they struggled over the gun. "You bastard! I should have killed you when I had the chance!"

Jake laughed, seeming to realize he was gradually wearing the injured man down. "You was too much of a gentleman, 'breed! Never give the other fella an even break!"

They crashed backward through the brush, the dry branches of fallen trees cracking under their boots, the dead leaves whirling up around their legs. Then Cherokee tripped over a dead stump as they moved backward and he felt himself falling.

Jake jerked the rifle clear, and stood there looking down at him, grinning. His yellow teeth gleamed like a wolf's in the moonlight. "'Breed, I'd really like to make this last, geld you maybe, or at least whip you blood raw, but I'll have to finish you quick so's I can deal with whoever that is on the trail."

He put his hand on a Bowie knife in his belt, its blade bleaming in the moonlight. "I don't know whether to cut your throat, crush your skull with the rifle butt, or garrote you with my whip."

420

"Like you did my partners?" *Keep him talking,* Cherokee thought. *He might get some feeling back in his arm if he only had enough time.*

"Like I did your partners." The scout tossed the empty rifle into the brush. "That's the easiest way." He pulled the whip out of his belt. "Injuns hate to die like this. They don't want their souls trapped in their dead bodies. Wal, I think that's the way you're gonna get it!"

Cherokee lay looking up at him, his right hand still numb and almost useless. If the arm weren't broken, it didn't make much difference now. By the time he could get enough feeling back into it to fight, he'd be dead.

He lay there, the taste of fear in his mouth, listening to the horse moving nearer.

Jake looked over his shoulder and grinned. "I'm gonna take care of that bastard. Then I'm riding out to help wipe out those damned Cheyenne. After that, I'm going back to town. I got me a plan to get rid of the Duchess, and then I'll have it all. There's gal there, a gal who used to be a beaut. I'll bet she still is under those ugly clothes!"

"Don't you touch Silver!" He blurted it out without thinking.

"Wal, now. So you know the little gal from the best whorehouse in Chicago? I put her there myself. Gal had quite a past, bet you didn't know that!"

"She's a lady. No one could ever make her a whore, no matter what they did to her!" If he could just keep Jake talking, the feeling was gradually coming back into his arm. In the darkness, Cherokee moved his fingers, urging the blood to flow faster.

"That right? Suppose I told you that she and Al killed

421

and robbed a man?"

"Reckon she had good reason."

Jake paused, spreading the long lash out behind him.
"Enough of this jawin'! Get ready to die the same way
your partners did, 'breed!"

Silver had ridden hard out from Denver and past the
Four Mile House, Waanibe hanging on to her waist for
dear life. Doubts assailed her as she rode through the
night. Had she taken the wrong trail? Would she find
Cherokee?

It was crisp and cool riding in the darkness and she
shivered and wished she had a coat. At least Waanibe, in
her many-pocketed flannel gown, seemed warm enough.

Somewhere up ahead, she heard a rifle shot echo and
reecho in the darkness. Alarmed, she reined in.

Waanibe said, "Silvery, I'm tired. Where are we
going?"

"Hush, honey," she whispered, and put her finger to
her lips. Her heart pounded like a war drum, so loud she
thought whoever must be up there in that shadowy grove
of trees must surely hear it. She walked the horse nearer,
listening.

It sounded like two big animals fighting and crashing
around through the underbrush. The moon came out
again and she saw a riderless horse standing on the trail
on the far side of the grove. Suddenly there was no sound
at all; the silence seemed deafening.

And then she thought of nothing except the fact that it
might be Cherokee, and if so, her love was in trouble. She
slid off the horse and turned to the little girl. "Wannie,"
she whispered tersely, "you stay here! If I'm not back in a

couple of minutes, you turn this horse and ride back to that inn we passed, do you remember?"

The little girl nodded, looking tired and grumpy. "I've been trying to give you a treasure, Silvery—"

"Not now, honey. Stay here!" Her heart in her throat, Silver sneaked through the brush in the darkness, expecting that at any moment, she would die.

Chapter Twenty-Two

Silver slipped through the darkness. She heard a whip crack like a pistol shot and a cry of pain through gritted teeth. Cherokee! Throwing caution aside, she raced headlong through the underbrush. She saw him in the moonlight, and thinking of nothing else, she ran into his arms.

"Silver! What in God's name—"

"Wal, Gawd Almighty, look who's here!"

Only then did she realize Cherokee had a whip mark across his face. Turning slowly at the drawling voice, she saw the huge, grinning man with the whip. She had unwittingly run into a trap.

Cherokee put his arm around her protectively. "Let her go, Dallinger. She's got no part in this!"

"Now why should I want to do that?" Jake leered at her, the moonlight gleaming on the handle of the big whip in his hand. "Don't know why I didn't recognize you before, missy, just because you've disguised yourself a little. I'll bet your body is just as nice as it was when I sold you to the Velvet Kitten."

He drew back his arm, playing with the long lash.

What could she do to save Cherokee? "Look, Jake," she pleaded, "you let him go and I'll leave with you."

"By damn, no!" Cherokee swore, and tried to push her behind him. "He'll have to kill me first!"

Jake grinned. "That can be arranged easy enough. What I can't figure, gal, is how you escaped Lon Brett. He was determined to get revenge for his brother's death after I told him where you were."

"So you're the one responsible for that mob and the fire!"

"Brett promised to give me the Palace for telling—"

"You can forget that," Silver said. "The mob burned the Palace down. The Duchess is dead."

Jake laughed. "Brett was a little loco, I knew it all along, when he was set on getting you, even though the law wasn't looking for you no more."

She stared at him in surprise.

"You didn't know?" he asked. "Al wrote to the Chicago law and confessed." He looked at her a long moment. "What about the gold in the safe at the Palace?"

Silver laughed. "The joke's on you. Everything at the Palace was destroyed in the fire. There's nothing left for anyone."

Jake brought his arm back. "Then all I get out of this deal is you, missy, plus the purdee pleasure of killing the 'breed here and then helpin' the colonel kill the Cheyenne."

She and Cherokee exchanged looks. Cherokee was obviously hurt—blood from the whip cut dripped across his rugged face, his right arm hung as if useless. She could only hope Waanibe had turned and ridden away. If so, at least the child would be safe. Surely this madman wouldn't harm his own child.

"Jake," she said, "let him go. I'll leave with you."

"You'll do that anyways, gal." He gestured. "Now you come over here by me so's I won't scar you up with this whip any more than you already are."

"No!" She clung to Cherokee as he tried to push her away.

"Dallinger, let her go." And to her, Cherokee said, "Don't be a fool, Silver. He's giving you a chance to live—take it!"

She shuddered all over. "I'd rather die than let him touch me!"

Jake frowned. "I ain't messin' with you any longer, gal. Get over here before I use this bull whip on both of you!"

And about that time, little Waanibe stumbled through the brush in her nightgown and came out into the clearing right by Jake's side.

"Wal, what've we got here?" Jake reached out, grabbed the little girl, and pulled her against his leg. Waanibe began to cry.

"Wannie!" Silver screamed. "I told you to stay back!"

"Silvery! Silvery!" She tried to run to Silver, but Jake had her pinned against his leg.

"Stay here, brat!" He looked at Silver and Cherokee. "All right, gal, come over here by me or I'll hurt the kid!"

Cherokee swore. "You dirty—"

She couldn't let him hurt the child. Almost woodenly, Silver walked over to him and the little girl grabbed Silver around the legs, burying her face against Silver's skirt.

"Jake," Silver said, "you can't hurt this child. Don't you know who her father is?"

426

"Hell yes, I know!" He held his hand out, showing the birthmark, just like Wannie's, on his fingers, then looked down at the little girl burying her face in Silver's skirt. "You think it would bother me to kill her? I got no use for a kid!"

Waanibe looked up at Silver and sobbed. "I been tryin' to give you a treasure, Silvery."

"Hush, dear, hush."

But Waanibe reached in her pocket and came up with a diamond broach. Silver took a good look at the child for the first time all evening. Only then in the reflected moonlight did Silver realize the child's hands and arms sparkled with rings and bracelets. And on her feet were Silver's shoes.

"Wal now, what has the brat got?" Jake said, looking down.

"Not for you, man!" The little girl backed against Silver and defied him. "I was playin' dress-up in Mama's room and I got some treasures for Silvery!"

"Oh my God, she's wearing a fortune in jewelry!" Silver gasped. "Jake, take the stuff, let us go! There's enough here to keep you the rest of your life!"

Jake grinned. "Gawd Almighty! Ain't this a piece of luck!" He glanced around behind him. "When I find his pistol in this brush, I'll take care of the brat at the same time I finish the 'breed. Then, Silver, you and me is leavin' with all these jewels!"

"You animal!" Cherokee swore, but when he moved as if to charge Jake, the scout jerked Silver against him and put the tip of the shiny blade of his big Bowie knife up under her breast.

"Come on, gal!"

The little girl stumbled along with them as Jake

stepped backward, Bowie knife in one hand, bull whip in the other.

Jake glared at Cherokee. "'Breed, don't make no sudden moves." He glanced backward as he dragged her through the brush, looking for the pistol.

Silver felt his hot, dirty hand on her body, the tip of the knife under her breast. It was up to her to do something. Cherokee feared to make a move, afraid that Jake would make good his threat. It was now or never! She put her left fist in the palm of her right hand. Putting all her strength behind that hand, she rammed her sharp elbow up under Jake's ribs with all the strength she could muster.

Jake cried out and swore as he stumbled backward, the Bowie knife flying from his hand into the underbrush. That few seconds was all they needed. Silver grabbed up the little girl and ran even as Cherokee dived for him and the two men meshed and struggled, fighting for possession of the big whip.

Gasping for breath, Silver stopped at the edge of the clearing, uncertain what to do.

"Run, Silver!" Cherokee screamed. "Get out of here while you still can!"

He was disabled and clearly losing to Jake's brute strength. She could not run away and leave him. Besides, even if she did manage to get to her horse, if Jake won this fight, he might ride her down and recapture her, encumbered as she was with Wannie.

The pistol and the knife! If only she could find them in the darkness while the two men fought! Confident of his advantage, Jake tossed the whip to one side as the two went down, the injured man on the bottom.

Jake swore. "Now, 'breed, I'm gonna strangle you with

my bare hands!''

She had to do something quick! Silver sat the sobbing child on a log and got down on her hands and knees, searching frantically in the moonlight. Behind her, she heard Cherokee gasping for air and struggling as the giant scout laughed and slowly throttled him.

Surely the knife or gun might reflect the moonlight! Silver dug through the dead leaves, looking for a weapon. Metal gleamed its reflection. With a glad cry, Silver grabbed it up, then realized she held the big whip, its silver handle catching the moonlight. What could she do? If she swung it at Jake, he'd only chase her down and take it away from her.

She had to save Cherokee. He was still struggling, but weaker now, gasping for air in the silence while Jake laughed and choked him with powerful hands.

She did the only thing she could do. Running up behind the crouching scout, she looped the lash over his head and twisted it around the big handle. She didn't have much strength, but she had her old skills as a dancer, and like quicksilver, she turned and turned, twisting the lash around his thick neck.

Jake shouted in sudden surprise, trying to get his fingers under the deadly lash that cut off his air. Cherokee seemed forgotten now as he tried to stumble to his feet and get to Silver. But she stayed behind him where he couldn't reach her as she twisted the noose tighter. Jake gasped and struggled, his breath coming in strained gasps, as he fought to get his hands under the whip lash.

If he killed her, she wouldn't let go. Like a small snapping turtle, she hung on while her giant prey crashed about, literally yanking her off the ground. Both her hands ached from hanging on to the whip handle, but she was determined not to let go.

Vaguely she was aware that Cherokee had staggered to his feet and was searching through the leaves for his pistol. It wasn't needed. Even as he found it with a glad cry, Jake took one last, agonized breath, pulling at the thin leather cutting into his thick neck, then stumbled and crashed to the ground like a falling tree. As he fell, the whip pulled from Silver's aching hands, but it was too late for the villain. Jake Dallinger's spirit was forever trapped in his dead body.

Cherokee ran over and knelt by the still form. For a long moment, only the sounds of Cherokee's labored breathing and Waanibe's sobs broke the stillness. As Cherokee stumbled to his feet, Silver ran into his arms and clung to him, dissolving finally into tears.

He patted her hair. "It's all right, sweet darlin'. Everything's all right now. You saved my life."

She looked up at him and saw her face mirrored in his eyes. And the love she saw mirrored there, not the scars of the reflection, were all that mattered. "Oh, Cherokee, I've been such a vain fool!"

"I love you, sweet, and you're here. That's all that matters now."

The little girl came over slowly and looked up at them. "Bad man's dead?"

"Yes, honey." Silver patted her dark hair.

Waanibe looked up at Cherokee with curiosity in her dark eyes. "My mama said my daddy was a half-breed. Are you my daddy?"

Silver winced. She couldn't expect Cherokee to take this orphaned child, yet she couldn't desert her. What would she do?

430

But Cherokee knelt and put his arms around the little girl. "Do you want me to be your daddy? If you do, I'd like to be."

Waanibe grinned and looked at Silver. "Can Silvery go with us?"

Cherokee smiled gently. "Oh, we can't go without her! I'm going to marry her, you know."

"Then I've got a treasure for you," the child said solemnly, and she took Cherokee's big hand and kissed the palm, folding his fingers over it. "Put that in your pocket to save for when you need it."

Cherokee winked at Silver. "Now I wonder where she learned that."

Then all three of them were in each other's arms, hugging and wiping away tears. After a long moment, Silver looked at all the jewels Wannie wore and kept pulling from her nightgown pockets. "Oh, Cherokee, what should we do with this? The stuff is worth a fortune!"

"As much as my gold that's gone with the Duchess?" he asked. "Maybe we've got a right to keep the jewelry."

"This is for Silvery," Waanibe said importantly, and taking off the gold nugget bracelet, she handed it to Silver, who smiled as she put it on. "Silvery, are you mad about me playing dress-up with your shoes?"

Silver hugged her and shook her head.

"A family," Cherokee sighed, looking toward the horses. "Well, almost a family. First I've got a man to bury."

They buried Jake in the clearing, but they left the silver-handled whip twisted around his neck. Silver couldn't bear to touch it, and Cherokee said since it had killed men, it was cursed.

As he said, "I don't always believe in Indian superstitions, but I think his spirit deserves to be trapped. He was such an evil hombre, we wouldn't want it haunting the wilderness."

But Silver paused to say a proper word for Jake. Even an evil man needed the hope of God's mercy.

She examined Cherokee's arm and the cut across his face. Neither were as bad as they had seemed at first. The arm was only badly sprained.

Silver said, "What about the Cheyenne?"

"It's out of our hands now," Cherokee sighed. "Nothing else we can do. We can only hope they listen to Iron Knife when he tells them the soldiers are coming, or that the troops decide not to go when Jake doesn't arrive to scout for them." he paused thoughtfully. "We've got one more stop to make in Denver."

Waanibe looked at him in alarm. "I don't have to go back to my mama, do I?"

Silver held her close. "No, honey, you don't." Later, she would tell Wannie about her mother's death, but she had a feeling the little girl wouldn't grieve much. Silver had been more of a mother to her than the Duchess. She thought about another child who needed parents back in Denver. Would Cherokee want another orphaned child? No, maybe she dare not ask. It was a lot to expect from a man.

Finally, they mounted up, Waanibe once again sitting behind Silver, hanging on for dear life. Cherokee took the reins of Jake's horse. "I've got a use for him."

They rode back to Denver, leading the spare horse. The town was quiet at this late hour, the Palace only a distant pile of glowing rubble. The gold was still there, mixed in the ashes, but it was cursed treasure. They wouldn't want to sift through the embers for it. And they had most of the jewels.

So why had they returned? Mystified, Silver kept her horse alongside Cherokee's as he rode down the street. He reined in before the stable, and called out, "Keso! Keso, are you in there?"

Silver looked over at her love and her heart was full to bursting. "Oh, Cherokee, I had thought about suggesting it, but I was afraid you wouldn't want another—"

"What is it?" The Indian boy stumbled out of the barn, rubbing sleep from his eyes. "Who's there?"

Cherokee grinned. "Keso, I've come by this extra horse and I thought you might like to have it."

The dark eyes grew round. "For me? A horse for me?"

"Sure!" And he tossed the reins to the boy.

The smiled faded. "Boss, I—I can't afford to feed no horse."

"You could on a big ranch that grew its own hay."

The boy looked from one face to another. "I don't know what you mean."

"Well, Keso"—Cherokee pushed his hat back—"I'm making me up a ready-made family here and I don't have a son. What's a family without a son? You know a ranch has to have hands to work it."

Tears came to the boy's eyes. He tried to speak but couldn't. Waanibe had already slid to the ground before Silver could stop her. "Does that mean he's going to be my brother?"

Cherokee nodded. "Reckon so, if he doesn't mind having you for a little sister."

Little Waanibe caught Keso's hand. "Then here's a

treasure for you to put in your pocket and keep." She kissed his palm and folded his fingers over it.

Keso made a face and wiped his hand on his ragged shirt. "Ugh! Am I gonna have to put up with this kid wanting to kiss on me like that?"

Cherokee winked at Silver. "Son, believe it or not, there'll come a day when she'll be something besides a kid and you might like a woman kissing on you."

"Well, if she goes with the deal, I reckon I can put up with her. Here, kid!" Keso gestured to her, grabbed her up, and put her on the back of his horse. Then he swung into the saddle. When he looked over at Silver, his eyes shone. "You know I always dreamed of having a real family, and especially a pretty mother like you!"

For only an instant, Silver winced, and then she realized that, like Cherokee, the boy was looking at her with eyes of love.

"Come on, family," Cherokee said, turning his horse around. "It'll be dawn soon, and it looks like it might decide to snow. We're gonna have the best Christmas anyone ever had this year."

"Christmas?" Keso asked. "You mean, with one of them trees, and gifts and all?"

Silver's heart sang. "And pies and food. I can cook, believe it or not!"

Cherokee smiled. "Somewhere in this territory, there's got to be a preacher who doesn't mind performing a morning wedding."

"Good!" Waanibe piped up. "And I get to dress up!"

Keso looked over his shoulder at her. "Hush, kid! Clothes ain't what's important to a wedding."

Silver laughed and shrugged at Cherokee. "I think we've got our work cut out for us with this pair!"

"We can handle it," Cherokee said. He reached across and took her hand, squeezing it. "We can handle anything as long as we have each other, Silver. I love you."

"I love you, too, my dearest."

In the pale pink of the coming dawn, the little family turned their horses and rode out of town together.

Epilogue

No one ever knew what really happened to Silver Heels, so in Colorado today, they still tell the tale with a sad ending. According to the legend, after catching smallpox, Silver Heels ran away to hide because of her scarred face, only returning now and then to put flowers on the graves at Buckskin Joe. They say her weeping ghost, clad in mourning and wearing a heavy veil, sometimes appears in the Buckskin Joe cemetery. Unlike you, they don't know she and her lover were finally reunited.

Perhaps the half-breed miner and his sweetheart do live eternally in the wilderness of the Rockies. Sometimes late at night, locals say you can see the reflection of her silver shoes as she dances on the peak that bears her name. Only cynics insist it must be a star or the moonlight shining on abandoned ore piled by a played-out mine.

But those same cynics hear the tinkle of rushing creeks and never recognize it as her laughter, or smell the scent of her perfume and mistake it for wildflowers.

Maybe Silver Heels and Cherokee live forever because, while beauty fades, true love like theirs can never really die. If you believe that, too, I invite you to walk the streets of the deserted Colorado ghost towns late at night as I have done. When the moon is full, you might see the sparkle of her shoes and hear the tap of her dancing feet.

And the other sound? Perhaps you will think at first it's the breeze sighing through the abandoned buildings, but listen—listen with your heart. Very faintly, the wind will carry the echo of that old saloon piano and Silver's high, sweet voice singing to her love.

To My Readers

Yes, there really is a Mt. Silver Heels in the state of Colorado. The mountain was originally called Mt. Morton, and is located approximately eight miles northwest of the town of Fairplay. That's near the ski towns of Vail and Breckenridge. The tale of the dance hall girl by that name is also told in other gold and silver mining states, but only Colorado boasts the named mountain, so it is likely the legend began there.

There is nothing left of the gold camp of Buckskin Joe except its cemetery. Although it is still in use, many old markings have been lost, and big trees have grown up through some graves. Local tales say that Silver Heels' ghost walks that graveyard at night, dressed in mourning gray, weeping for those who died in the smallpox epidemic. I got an eerie feeling standing in that cemetery just before sundown and decided I did not want to stay to see if it was true.

Smallpox was a terrible scourge that the Spanish brought with them to the New World. It wiped out more than half the Indians in Central and South America, enabling the invaders to conquer the people. Later it was one of the first diseases used in "germ warfare" by the British who gave infected blankets to northern Indians. It gets its name because it was feared second only to the "great pox," syphilis. The last death in the United States from smallpox occured in 1949. The last smallpox deaths anywhere in the world occurred in 1977. Today the disease has been wiped off the face of the earth—except for samples contained in two test tubes: one in Moscow, and the other in the Centers for Disease Control in Atlanta, Georgia.

By the way, I talked to a neurosurgeon about Cherokee's sight while I was reasearching this book. He told me a person could suffer an injury to the base of the skull and have nerve damage that would only temporarily blind the victim if the wound wasn't too severe. In this case, Cherokee would gradually regain his sight.

Is there still gold to be found in Colorado? Yes, it's still mined commercially in Mosquito Gulch, and now and then, someone pans a little from the streams. If you'd like to try it, you can buy equipment in many shops and get instructions. Just remember not to trespass on private land. A word of caution: don't try the road up Mosquito Pass unless you own a good four-wheel-drive vehicle.

The biggest gold nugget ever found in America was found at Carson Hill, California, in 1854 and weight 195 troy ounces (162 pounds). The biggest ever discovered in the world was the "Welcome Stranger" nugget, found in Australia in 1869, weighing 2,248 troy ounces. You figure out how many pounds that is!

While Buckskin Joe is gone, the town of Fairplay still exists, but as only a shadow of its rowdy, boomtown days. Fairplay may be the only town in the world with a burro buried under an elaborate gravestone on its main street. Prunes, a little pack burro who worked the mines of the area, lived to be sixty-three years old. Buried with him are the ashes of his last owner.

Fairplay has also moved Haw Tabor's old original store into town as part of a tourist attraction. Some of you may recognize Haw Tabor as the man who became one of the richest men in Colorado, then a U.S. Senator. He finally left his wife, Augusta, for a young beauty known as Baby Doe. But that story is too long and tragic to tell here. Even the President of the United States attended the wedding. Baby Doe's wedding dress cost $7,000 when the average working man didn't earn half that in a year. The dress is on display at the Historical Museum in downtown Denver, the same museum that displays the Cheyenne sketch book mentioned in my Zebra hologram that came out in January 1990, *Cheyenne Caress*, #2864-4. This book is still available from Zebra.

If you get to Denver, be sure and see the state capitol building, the only one with a 24-carat-gold-covered dome. The gold came from Colorado's own mines.

Gold and other metals are not the only things of value to be found in that state's mountains. The biggest block of marble ever quarried in the world weighed 100 tons and came from west central Colorado. Today that piece of marble marks the Tomb of the Unknown Soldier in Arlington Cemetery.

Colorado is a fascinating place to visit and I highly recommend it to you. Its nickname is the Centennial State because it came into the Union during 1876, the year our country turned one hundred years old. It holds the honor of being the second state to give women the right to vote in 1873. As I told you in an earlier book,

Wyoming was the first.

The U.S. government did indeed recruit Southern volunteers from Yankee prison camps during the Civil War to go West and fight Indians. The execution of William Dowdy, the red-haired blacksmith from Tennessee who was aboard the *Effie Deans*, actually occurred on September 9, 1864. A twenty-three-year-old Yankee colonel, Charles Dimon, determined in advance that he would execute a Galvanized Yankee on the trip to maintain discipline and show his authority. Illegal in the manner in which it was done, the poor unfortunate Dowdy was given a hasty trial, found guilty, taken off the boat just above Omaha, shot, and buried on the bank of the Missouri River.

If you have any interest in Native Americans, you are surely familiar with the Cherokees' tragedy. The first gold strike in American was in Georgia in the 1830s, making whites clamor for possession of the land. The party that discovered gold in Colorado was made up of Cherokees. In Georgia, with Cherokee land and most possessions confiscated, the government started them on a long death march in the autumn of 1838. Some hid out in the hills, refusing to go, and their descendants are in the South yet. Almost one-fourth of the Cherokees in the march died before they reached Arkansas and Indian Territory. At the moment of this writing, they are discussing adding a new emblem to their tribal flag to represent this Indian holocaust. A memorial was recently dedicated in Faulkner County, Arkansas.

Approximately 43,000 Cherokees still live around Tahlequah, their tribal headquartes in northeastern Oklahoma. They put on a wonderful outdoor pageant, Tsa-La-Gi, every summer.

A nearby museum that might interest you is the Five Civilized Tribes Museum in Muskogee, Oklahoma. If you time your visit in the early spring, the flowering azaleas of nearby Honor Heights park are magnificent.

The Cherokees are the largest tribe in Oklahoma and, according to the U.S. Census Bureau, the largest in the country. However, the Cherokees themselves say their own more accurate tribal records list less than half the number the census claims and that the Navajos are still the biggest tribe.

I've had a surprising number of letters from readers who have reason to believe they are part Cherokee and wonder how to investigate. The chances of attaining official tribal membership now are slim. To do so, you'll have to produce birth and death certificates, etc., proving your ancestor was one of those listed when the Dawes Commission made up the roll of all the members of the tribe back at the turn of the century.

As far as the Sand Creek Massacre, it has been written about so much, that I won't go into great detail here. Of course, I have already been up there to walk the site and interview the present owner. There's not much to see, but if you want to go there, please remember that it is on private land and respect that rancher's rights. The site is in southeastern Colorado, not far from the Kansas border. Look for the nearby town of Chivington on the map. One of the best books on the subject has been written by a friend of mine, another Edmond resident, Dr. Stan Hoig.

Before some of you write and ask about the safety of Iron Knife's family, I'll tell you that they escaped at Sand Creek. Many of the others weren't so lucky. The little boy, Bear Cub, was wounded but lived to play a major

442

part in *Cheyenne Caress.*

If you read my second Zebra Heartfire, *Cheyenne Princess,* about Iron Knife's missing sister, you already know about the Great Outbreak of 1864. The Plains tribes realized that many of the white men had gone off to fight each other during the Civil War. They saw this as a golden opportunity to try to take back their land. Through the whole spring and summer of that year, the Cheyenne and their allies were on the war path.

Whether the Confederates actually caused much of this trouble or only took advantage of it to further their own aims has been a subject for speculation and debate. Denver itself was cut off and placed under martial law. Its people suffered severe shortages of food and supplies. Because of the Civil War, there weren't enough troops to protect the settlers. That was why the Union was desperate enough to use former Confederate soldiers along the frontier. But the attack at Sand Creek only caused more Indian trouble.

If some of the characters in the book you just read seem familiar to you, it's because they came originally from earlier books. Big 'Un and Pettigrew came from *Bandit's Embrace,* but Iron Knife, Summer Sky, Gray Dove, Jake Dallinger, and even Sergeant Baker were characters in my first novel, *Cheyenne Captive,* the Zebra Heartfire that launched both that line and my career in 1987. *Captive* made the Waldenbooks Best Seller List, placed in the *Affaire de Coeur* Reader's Poll of the Ten Best Historical Romances of 1987, and won the *Romantic Times* Award that same year as Best Indian Romance by a new Author.

The novel you hold in your hands is number seven. Besides the books previously mentioned, there have been three other Zebra Holograms. I wrote about Chief Quanah Parker and half-breen Maverick Durango in September 1988, *Comanche Cowboy. Comanche* placed in the *Affaire de Coeur* Reader's Poll of the Ten Best Historical Romances of 1988, and sold out.

In March 1989 came *Bandit's Embrace,* ISBN #2596-3, about Colonel MacKinzie's covert raid against the Kickapoo and Mescalero Apache down in Mexico. *Bandit* was named to the *Affaire de Coeur* Best American Historical Romance list of 1989. It is still available from Zebra.

Then in July 1989, I told you about the Pony Express and the Paiute Indian wars in *Nevada Nights,* ISBN #2701-X. *Nevada* was a finalist for the 1988-1989 *Romantic Times* Reviewer's Choice for Best Western Romance award. It is still available from Zebra.

No, I don't have any extra copies of any of my seven books, but you can order the ones still available at this moment, *Bandit's Embrace, Nevada Nights, Cheyenne Caress,* and *Quicksilver Passion,* from your favorite bookstore or directly from Zebra. See details about mail orders on the advertising pages of this book. Send the cover price plus 50¢ each postage. My early Holograms are $3.95. Beginning with the January 1990 titles, the rising costs of paper pushed the price up to $4.50. You'll need title, author, and ISBN# to order by mail. If the romance editor gets enough letters asking about my first three books, I think they will finally be reprinted for those who want a complete set of this long series which I call: "Panorama of the Old West."

I don't do a newsletter, but if you'd like to write me, include a stamped, self-addressed long envelope and I'll be happy to answer and send you a bookmark. Sometimes letters are lost in the forwarding process. I always answer my mail, so if you haven't heard from me, I didn't get your letter. In the future, write me directly at: Box 162, Edmond, OK 73083-0162.

Zebra is forwarding some mail out here to Oklahoma and my readers ask questions. Did I see the television show *Unsolved Mysteries* in October 1989, about the "ghost lights" near Marfa, Texas? Yes, I did. But remember I told you about those lights myself way back in 1987 in *Cheyenne Princess?*

For those of you who wrote, worried about the government killing the wild mustangs that I mentioned in *Nevada Nights*, you will be delighted to know there's a happy ending. There are now two refuges for the wild mustangs besides the Nevada ranges, one in South Dakota, one right here in Oklahoma. While the government is still trying to adopt out many of the wild horses, those that are too old or too ugly to be adopted have been turned loose to live peacefully on 18,000 acres the government has leased for them up in Osage and Washington counties in northeastern Oklahoma. The Prairie National Wild Horse Refuge is near the town of Bartlesville. It seems fitting somehow that these wild horses now run free on the vast prairies of Indian country, right here in my home state.

Some of you are complaining I don't write the books fast enough. Sorry, but I spend as much time researching as I do writing. The only way I could do more books is cut out all the research. Would you really like that?

For those who want to know what happened to little Waanibe, the half-breed Arapaho girl, and Keso, the Ute boy who thinks he's Cheyenne, those are stories I will finish later, as well as the tale of Shawn O'Bannion and his elegant wife, Savannah. Arrogant and handsome Southern aristocrat, Rand Erikson, who was in the Yankee prison with Cherokee, will turn up again in a future book, as will the historic ship, the *Continental.* Yes, even Lulu, the whore who stole Cherokee's father, and Elmer Neeley will appear again and get what's coming to them in another book. No, I haven't forgotten about other stories I didn't finish telling. Iron Knife will finally meet his lost sister in a future book. Be patient.

For those who are keeping up with my career, I am most grateful for the 1988 *Romantic Times Magazine* Lifetime Achievement in Indian Romance trophy I was awarded and the two Silver Pen Favorite Author awards that *Affaire de Coeur Magazine* gave me in 1989 and 1990. You readers have helped build my career by telling your friends about me and I'm much obliged, as we say here in Oklahoma.

Yes, that is my photo on the cover of the *Romance Reader's Handbook,* and again, yes, I do have an article in the book, *How to Write a Romance and Get It Published,* which came out in a revised edition in 1990. Besides loyal readers, those in the publishing industry itself have been kind to me. I am happy to tell you I am signing a new contract with Zebra Books that assures you the series will go on for at least four more books through 1993. However, I will have only one book out in 1991, probably in early autumn. Alert your bookstore to watch for it.

What's it about? In my research, I have uncovered an incredible true story about an Apache brave who scouted for the U.S. Cavalry in Arizona. In 1886, Geronimo and his warriors were at last defeated. The army decided to send these ringleaders by train far away to prison in Florida. In an unbelievable twist of injustice, someone

446

also ordered that the loyal Apache scouts be chained and sent as prisoners, too.

On the outskirts of St. Louis, Missouri, one of those Apaches managed to overpower a guard and escape from the train. He was all alone, half-naked, injured, in chains, and without weapons. Worse yet, he was thousands of miles away from home with armed citizens and the U.S. Cavalry searching for him with orders to shoot to kill.

Determined to return to his own land, he decided to take a hostage, and chose a beautiful woman alone on a farm near the railroad tracks. How could he know he had selected a girl who hated his people with a terrible vengeance? She was the widow of a Cavalry officer who had been recently killed in action against the Apache.

I invite you to return to the West that existed more than a hundred years ago. Together, we'll experience this desperate and romantic adventure crossing the continent with the Apache savage and his voluptuous captive.

Come slip back in time with me . . .

Georgina Gentry

Here are a few of the dozens of research books I used that you might find at your public library:

Brown, Dee, *The Galvanized Yankees,* University of Illinois Press, 1963; University of Nebraska Press, 1986.

Butler, Anne, M., *Daughters of Joy, Sisters of Misery: Prostitutes in the American West,* University of Illinois Press, 1985.

Ehle, John, *Trail of Tears: The Rise & Fall of the Cherokee Nation,* Anchor Doubleday, 1988.

Hoig, Stan, *The Sand Creek Massacre,* University of Oklahoma Press, 1961.

Noel, Thomas J., *The City and the Saloon, Denver 1858-1916,* University of Nebraska Press, 1982.

Ware, Captain Eugene F. *The Indian War of 1864,* Crane & Co., 1911. Reprints: St. Martin's press, 1960; University of Nebraska Press, 1963.